Falling to Pieces

Falling to Pieces

A Harvest Valley Romance

by Annette Lyon

BLUE GINGER BOOKS

Chapter 1

Carter reached for one of the paint brushes held between his teeth. He dabbed a little burnt umber on the bristles then used the color to add highlights to the hair of the dancer on the canvas. She sat on a wooden floor, one knee up, the other tucked under her. Her head tilted to one side as she untied the ribbon of a battered pointe shoe. Her chestnut hair was pulled into a bun, but wisps had escaped it during her practice time.

He bit the end of the brush again—he had three in his mouth now—and sat back to study the painting. Not bad, but not quite right, either. The lines of the figure were good, and he liked how the play of light and shadow had turned out, but he could never quite get that face to look how he pictured it.

His back had grown stiff from two straight hours of working at the easel. He stretched as he removed the earphones he always wore while working. Sometimes he listened to white noise, but today he'd put on an instrumental play list. With the headphones off, he heard his phone ringing on his desk on the other side of the room—a clip from "The Dance of the Sugarplum Fairy."

Toni's ring tone. No sooner had he taken two steps toward his desk than the phone went still. Aw, well. She'd probably leave a message. Might as well tidy up and then call her back. He grabbed the brushes and headed over to the paint thinner on the counter. Maybe Toni wanted to hang out tonight. Get a video and eat popcorn. As he cleaned the paint from the tip of a brush, he pictured having Toni in his arms, smelling her faint perfume, resting his head on hers.

Too bad that even if he put his arm around her—as he often did—and even if she snuggled close—which she also often did—it wouldn't mean anything beyond "friend" to her.

As he scrubbed the paint off the brush, the handle snapped between his fingers. He found his heart speeding up at the thought of her, of how long he'd waited for her to look at him as a man, not a buddy. He'd given up hope more times than he could count since he first noticed her in junior high when her locker was only two away from his. She didn't remember him at all until their high school algebra class sophomore year.

He'd always hated math, and that year, algebra almost did him in. "I don't care what X equals," he'd said under his breath one day when the marks on the board seemed nothing but a foreign code.

Toni, sitting in front of him, had smiled widely and turned her head just enough to whisper back, "I don't care about X either. If it's that important, I'll have to marry someone who cares."

Toni's comment took Carter by surprise; a laugh escaped him before he realized it. Mr. Kerr turned around and peered at the class. Carter gazed studiously at the teacher, but he could feel his face heating up and more laughter building up inside him.

That was the first time she'd ever talked to him. She'd mentioned several times how that was her first memory of him. He still remembered how she'd lowered her chin as her shoulder shook; she was trying to hold back a chuckle.

He'd made her laugh. It was a triumph.

When Mr. Kerr turned back to the board, Carter leaned forward again and whispered, "Don't you dare. I'd be bored stiff with anyone who actually cared about X."

From that day, they were friends. Within a few months, Toni Harper called Carter Mackenzie her best friend. Eight years after high school graduation, they were still at each other's sides, having weathered the ups and downs of both high school and college. Their friendship remained as strong as ever.

He'd dated other women—had gotten serious several times. But he'd always broken it off. As great as Lauren and Angie and Sarah had all been, they'd never be Toni.

Grunting with frustration, he tossed the pieces of the useless paintbrush into the garbage can under the counter and left the other two by the sink. He grabbed a rag and wiped remaining paint thinner off his hands as he strode over to his phone, where there was indeed a message waiting for him. Then with trepidation, he sat at his desk to listen to the message. He tossed the rag aside and picked up his phone.

"Hey, it's me. I'm in a bind and hope you can help me out. It's the dance studio's annual Valentine's Day party, and my date bailed on me. Thing is, if I don't bring a date, Allen will never let me hear the end of it. Party starts at eight thirty. I'd really appreciate it if you'd be my plus one. Call me back as soon as you get this, 'kay? Love ya." With a click, the message ended.

Love ya. He heard that often. What he wanted to hear was *I love you, Carter. I'm in love with you.* Or something remotely in the ballpark.

His phone was silent, but he kept it against his ear, eyes closed, as he pressed the fingers of his other hand against his eyes.

He should tell her no, because at this rate, she'd start thinking that he was always the easy fallback. She needed to realize that he had a life outside of her. That . . .

Who was he kidding? He'd known the second he heard her ring that he'd do whatever she needed. He pulled the phone away from his ear and stared at it, willing it to send a text with the right words. Something. Anything.

He'd go tonight. And he'd pretend to enjoy himself, for her sake, and to get Allen, the studio owner, to back off from bugging her about being single.

But first, he'd clean up his pseudo studio—the corner of his office at the high school where he taught art. He spent a lot of evenings and weekends here, when he wasn't home doing graphic design on the side for money to supplement his pathetic teacher's salary.

First get this place cleaned up and locked, and then he'd

return her call after he'd gotten himself to stop thinking about her as the woman he loved. He needed to switch the gears in his brain back to best friend mode.

The clock on the wall read 7:30. He could get out of here, call her, take a quick shower, and pick her up in time to make it to the party. Barely.

Chapter 2

As Toni waited to hear back from Carter, she headed to the bathroom to fix her hair and makeup for the party. She tossed her cell on the bed on her way past so she'd hear it when he called.

And Carter had better call soon. If he agreed to come, Allen, the studio manger, would stop asking about her nonexistent love life. He'd see she had prospects.

Not that you could call her best friend a "prospect." The thought make her smile as she plugged in her curling wand. As it heated, she dug around her makeup bag, looking for concealer for the new zit on her chin. She dabbed on the coverup, a little more under her eyes, and started blending it in.

She must have read her would-have-been date wrong. Not that he was serious dating material either, but he'd seemed eager to go out. He'd moved into her apartment complex about a month ago and seemed to find excuses to run into her. He was cute enough, wore nice clothes, and he flirted well—a great combination in front of the studio.

Not to mention in front of *Clint*, the new ballroom instructor and head of the studio's youth ballroom company. He was a bit shorter than most men she'd dated, but she didn't mind. Plus, he had a classic Latin ballroom dancer build as well as the dark hair. And *those eyes*. Whenever he and his competition partner practiced at the studio, Toni had envied the woman, wondering what it would be like to feel those smoldering eyes on her. Every time she saw Clint, her heart beat a little faster. She had yet to manage a coherent sentence around him.

The coverup taken care of, Toni applied foundation and then blush. Putting on makeup always felt good; Toni loved seeing her drab self come to life with color. Too bad she couldn't apply some kind of equivalent "makeup" so her hips wouldn't look so wide, her thighs so fat. At the thought, her eyeshadow applying hand paused mid-swipe, and she glanced at her reflection in the mirror. She stepped back to take in more of herself, unable to stop a grimace from staring back at her when she eyed her body.

Disgusting.

Maybe it was the reason she hadn't found love yet; her body disgusted men.

Toni blew out a breath and stepped forward again, hiding her lower half with the counter and trying not to think too much about her thighs as she returned to applying brown eyeshadow and eye liner. Good thing Carter hadn't found his soul mate yet either; she wouldn't know what she'd do without her best friend. She didn't kid herself that a wife would take kindly to Carter calling or hanging out with another woman.

Last spring when he'd gotten serious with Lauren the yoga instructor, Toni had been so lonely that she'd curled up every night with a bowl of corn chips and a mug of nacho cheese sauce. She'd gained five pounds by the end of April—not a minor problem for someone who wore a leotard for a living.

Good thing I know how to get rid of those pounds, Toni thought with satisfaction. After Carter and Lauren broke up, Toni lost all five pounds in ten days—plus two more the following week.

At the memory, Toni realized she hadn't eaten anything since an apple and four ounces of light yogurt for lunch. Good. She had more self-control than most people she knew, and the few times she did break down and eat like a whale, she had ways to make sure the food wouldn't turn into pounds. She'd figured out that last bit out after the nacho debacle. In her busy, harried life, at least there was something she had control over. To an extent. Her body was still ugly.

But the party would provide plenty of caloric temptation tonight; good thing she hadn't eaten much today. Toni glanced at the clock. Seven thirty. She'd have to leave in forty-five minutes at the latest; Allen didn't believe in starting anything "fashionably late."

Call soon, Carter, she thought as she finished up her mascara. After a thin layer of lipstick, she turned to her curling wand. Her fellow dancers were used to see her with a bun; tonight she'd wear her long hair down in big, gentle curls.

She'd finished the curls and had grabbed the hair spray when her phone went off with her favorites ring—the sound of a quacking duck. Carter had picked the ring tone as a joke once, and she'd never changed it. She dropped the hair spray bottle and nearly flew to her bed to answer the call.

"Hello?" she nearly croaked into the receiver.

"Hi, dear."

"Oh hi, Mom." Only then did she remember that her family members were also on her favorites list, and therefore also had the duck ring. She hoped she'd managed to mask the disappointment in her voice.

Time to give Mom her own ring. Or Carter a different one. Or both.

"Antonia. Sweetheart."

Normally Toni would have rolled her eyes at hearing her full name—she'd avoided any and all Willa Cather books once she realized her mother had named her after one. But this time, her mother's tone stopped her. "Mom? Is something wrong?"

"Can you come to the hospital?"

Toni felt as if a crowbar had knocked the wind out of her. She put her hand on her stomach as if to cover the blow. "Who's in the hospital? Are you hurt? Sick?"

"No, I'm fine. It's Dad."

Toni's heart clenched. "What happened?" She pictured the crushed glass and twisted metal from a car accident.

"He collapsed on his evening run. A neighbor found him and called 911. The doctors aren't telling me much, and I was so upset, I only heard half of what they said—but it's got something to with his heart. He's in surgery now." She paused and sniffed. When she spoke again, her voice trembled. "Can you come?"

"Of course," Toni said, her own voice unstable now. "I'll be right there." Her mother needed someone, and until one of her four siblings could come home from out of state, she would be that person.

Toni hung up and raced around her apartment, trying to find her car keys and then her other shoe. Somehow her memory had started to go lately; she was constantly losing one thing or another. With one shoe successfully in hand and the other on her foot, she raced for the door. One step out, a gust of snow hit her in the face. She'd forgotten a coat. And her cell phone.

As she turned back in frustration, her phone quacked again.

I really need to change the quacks to different rings. No telling if this was her mother or Carter. She grabbed the phone from the back of the couch to answer as she hurried to the closet for her coat. A glance at the screen showed that it was Carter.

"Hey," Toni said as her coat slid off a hanger. She shut the closet with her hip and headed for the door for the second time.

"Got your message," Carter said. "And yes, I'll go with you to the party. I can be there in twenty, assuming I'll look presentable enough for Gary if I comb my hair and throw on a sweater."

"Carter . . ." Toni's voice cracked, and she dropped onto the back of the couch. It was that or risk her knees failing her altogether.

"You okay? I didn't think your date had that kind of power over you. He's an idiot to bail."

Toni laughed, almost a bark as she started crying. Carter knew all there was to know about Toni, from every thought she'd ever had about any guy, to her innermost dreams and fears. Except girl stuff, like her period and how she hated her body. She didn't tell him that kind of stuff; she wasn't a sadist. But Carter did know as well as she did that Derek had no chance of anything with her beyond a date or two.

"It's not about Derek. My mom just called," she said, and explained what had happened and where she was going.

"Can I do anything to help?" Carter asked. "I'll meet you at the hospital."

"No, you don't have to do that," she said, grateful that she knew Carter really would drop everything for her at a moment's notice. She could call on him no matter what. "I'd better go alone at first, see how things are going."

"Okay, but call when you can to let me know how he's doing. And how *you're* doing. I'll be here all night. See, my date for a party just stood me up."

Toni smiled at that and wiped at her eyes. "I'll call. Promise. You're the best."

"Yeah, I know. Don't forget. I'll be waiting for you to call."

After she hung up, she took a deep breath before heading for the door. Snow hit her in the face again. She groaned with frustration as she returned to the couch where she had dropped her coat.

She drove to the hospital in a mental blur, thinking of her father—what she'd do if she lost him—and fighting off tears. As she made her way along icy roads, her thoughts kept turning to her father. How at Christmas last month, just like every year, he loved to belt out carols in a voice reminiscent of Kermit. How he always added extra layers of candy to his gingerbread house just so he could have more to eat later; design could go hang.

Aside from Christmas, Dad had always been the family health-food joke—at nearly sixty-seven, he still exercised six days a week and ran an annual marathon. His favorite meal consisted of a huge salad, light Italian dressing on the side. Her younger brother, Sam, always joked that he'd outlive all his kids.

Yet now he lay in the hospital, possibly with his chest cracked open and surgeons' gloved hands poking around.

For the first time in years, she recalled hearing about an uncle who had died young from a heart problem. Toni had never met Uncle Al. Was he why her father had seemed almost obsessed with health—to avoid his older brother's fate?

And would her father meet the same fate after all? She couldn't picture life without him in it. Every major decision in her life went back to her father. He'd always been there for her, pushing her to succeed.

You can't go, Dad. I love you.

But that love was tempered by a fear she'd had as long as she could remember—that she'd disappoint him.

I'm a success, she reminded herself as she parked. She'd worked hard to be where she was—a professional dancer. She'd choreographed for celebrities, taught at big conventions, and performed at some of the biggest venues in the west. She loved what she did, and she was good at it.

Dad had wanted an Olympic gymnast. She crushed that dream when she dropped the team and refused to move away to live closer to an Olympic coach.

She got out and locked the car but stood there, staring at the hospital entrance, even though the air was frigid.

She loved her father.

And she feared him.

In almost equal parts. She took a deep breath and forced herself to go inside.

Chapter 3

First things first: Toni needed to find her mother. Second, find out her father's status. Then she'd figure the rest out from there. Her brain was muddled enough from emotion and adrenaline that she couldn't think past that—she'd come up with a to-do list soon. No point in calling siblings if Mom already had. No point in doing much else until she talked to her mother.

She found a receptionist and asked about her father, who was still in surgery. Toni was directed to a waiting area. She thanked the receptionist and walked with hurried strides, hoping to find her mother there.

As she walked, thoughts of an uncertain future bombarded her. Would Dad live to see her get married? Would he be there to meet her children—his grandchildren? Assuming she ever got married or had kids. With every birthday she had, the likelihood increased that she'd never find the right guy.

Toni shook her head and pulled out her phone, tempted to call her mother instead of waiting to see her in person—anything to occupy her mind. When she saw the surgical waiting area ahead, she braced herself, knowing she'd get the brunt of her mother's roller coaster of emotions. Patricia Harper wasn't known for handling stress well. Toni would have to deal with anything from hysterics to withdrawal. With another deep breath, she walked on and found her mother pacing back and forth along a row of padded chairs, toward a mounted television and away from it, her black leather purse clutched tightly in her hands.

"There you are," she said, and nearly pounced on her daughter with a huge hug. Toni held her mother close as if she needed to be held up.

Toni pulled back. "Any news?"

Her mother nodded. "They had to do a double bypass. The doctor said . . ." Her lower lip trembled. "He said that I may have saved his life by giving him an aspirin after I called for the ambulance."

"So he'll be all right?" A wave of relief wanted to wash over her, but Toni held it at bay until she heard confirmation.

Her mother teared up. "It's still touch and go, but they seem optimistic. He'll be here for a while." She nodded behind Toni, down a corridor where the doctors surely came from to talk to family. "The surgery's over, and I'm losing my mind waiting to see him, but they won't let me yet." She looked at Toni and placed a gentle hand to the side of her face, eyes watering. "I'm so glad you're here. I've been beside myself. Haven't even been able to eat anything." Her lips trembled again. "But now that you're here . . ."

"It'll be all right, Mom." Toni reached up and cupped her mother's hand in her own. It felt as if they had switched roles, and her mother suddenly needed the mothering. "Come on. Let's get you something to eat. Maybe by the time we get back, we'll be able to see Dad." Toni had no desire to eat anything, but food always calmed her mother, and getting some food would definitely be the best way to comfort her while they waited.

Her mother's extra forty pounds were a testament to the power of food in curbing her stress. As they headed toward the cafeteria, Toni swore yet again that she'd never let herself go like that. Not like Allen's wife, a ballerina in her former life but who could now stand to lose at least eighty pounds. Toni couldn't imagine what she'd looked like in her prime, doing turns and lifts in pointe shoes, looking weightless as a true professional did.

Toni ordered shakes and fries—her mother's definition of comfort food. Her mom talked and talked, telling the whole story of her husband's collapse with every tiny detail as she shoveled fries and spoonfuls of liquified ice cream into her mouth. She didn't notice that Toni pretended to eat the same fry the entire time and never touched her shake, preferring instead to sip on the water bottle she carried with her everywhere.

As her mother finished the last spoonfuls of her shake, Toni's phone beeped with an incoming text. Only then did she remember that she hadn't contacted Allen about her father. Sure enough, when she opened the message, it was Allen being his typical obnoxious self.

Still coming? Or did your date stand you up? I could round up my nephew to be your +1.

It was all Toni could do not to roll her eyes, but she just managed to, which kept her mother from asking about the text or Toni's job or her love life. Or lack thereof. She kept nodding in reply as her mother continued talking. She'd shifted from the topic of the heart attack and ambulance ride to a piece she'd seen on TV while waiting in the ER waiting room.

Toni tapped out a quick reply to Allen.

My dad had a heart attack. I'm at the hospital; I won't be coming.

She almost added "Sorry" but stopped herself and just hit send. Let him stew in his sarcastic juices and apologize to *her.* At least she'd replied to Allen, and he wouldn't be on her case anymore tonight.

Her mother got up to dispose of their trash and put the tray away as Toni moved to put her phone back into her purse. Another text dinged, so she pulled it out, hoping it wasn't Allen after all. Carter.

Checking in. Any news?

This time she smiled. Her mother noticed as she returned, because she piped up. "What's the smile for? Did a boy text you?"

Toni shook her head, still smiling, although now it was part thanks to Carter, and part because her mother still talked to her as if she were a teenager. *Sure. A "boy" texted me.*

"Just Carter," Toni said, showing her mother the screen. "I promised to call later."

She typed out a reply. *No news yet. I'll let you know.*

They headed back to the waiting area. Toni's mother still chattered on—the food had clearly calmed her if she was talking this much—but she'd changed subjects again. Now the topic was Carter.

"Such a nice boy," she cooed. "Has he found his special someone yet? He's so good looking, I would have thought he'd have been snatched up years ago. Why aren't the two of you together, anyway?"

Only when she stopped talking did Toni realize her mother expected an answer—but to which question? "He's still single."

Fortunately, before she had to dodge any other comments, someone behind them called, "Are you Peter Harper's family?" A nurse in Sponge Bob scrubs hurried to catch up. A glance at the waiting area a few yards ahead showed it to be empty.

"We are," Toni's mother said. "I'm his wife. This is our daughter. How is he? Any news?" Her last words tumbled out one after the other, and she held her hands clasped under her chin.

"The surgeon will be out in a few minutes to update you on your husband's progress. He's been moved up to ICU on the fourth floor."

"ICU?" her mother said, voice going up a notch as she gripped her purse handle.

The nurse smiled her reassurance. "Standard procedure after this kind of surgery. No worries."

As the nurse walked off, Toni couldn't help but wonder what it would be like to go to work wearing scrubs covered in cartoon characters instead of a form-fitting leotard.

It would be tempting to binge because no one can see your shape, that's what.

Only a few minutes later, the surgeon arrived. He looked to be in good spirits, which Toni took as a good sign.

"The surgery went as well as can be expected," he told them. "I'll go over the timetable and some other things like his medications you'll need to know about. But I'm sure you're eager to see him. You can go up to ICU now."

"Thank you so much," Toni's mother said. Her body visibly relaxed, and after the doctor left, Toni and her mother headed to the elevators that went to the ICU floor. They found the unit easily enough, checked in with the nurse at the desk, and then went through the double doors and down a corridor to the third room on the right.

The two of them stepped across the threshold. Now it was Toni's turn to hold her breath; what would her father look like? He'd always been almost like Superman to her in his strength. She didn't know if she could handle seeing him frail. The bed seemed too big for him, making his six feet seem smaller.

She and her mother each took a side of the hospital bed. Her mother held his hand. "Peter? It's me, Patricia. I'm here now."

He opened his eyes slowly then blinked a couple of times as if trying to get the world into focus before rotating his head to the left. Every movement was slow. He managed a weak smile and a tiny squeeze of his wife's hand before closing his eyes again. Apparently he still had a lot of the anesthesia in his system.

Toni watched her mother hold one of his big hands in both of hers and stroke his fingers. "You aren't looking so good, Mr. Harper," she said, reaching up and rubbing her thumb against her husband's cheek. "You need a shave."

Peter Harper cracked a smile, but his eyes remained closed. "You look fabulous as ever," he croaked.

She put a finger to his lips. "Don't talk. You need your rest." She looked to the other side of the bed, where Toni stood. "Toni came."

Her father gave her a grateful smile and reached out for her hand. Toni hesitated, unsure how to approach or touch him, half afraid she'd disturb out his IV and monitors or hurt his chest. She gave him her hand, and he squeezed it limply. "Thanks," he whispered. "I can count on you. You've never let me down."

He didn't seem to notice how Toni flinched at his words. How they grated, made her want to yell. *I know you'll never let me down* was the ghost Toni had lived with her whole life, fighting to keep her father happy.

Why did that matter so much? She was an adult now, with a grownup life and grownup concerns. She hadn't heard that sentiment in years. Yet it still managed to make her feel six.

The effort of those few words seemed to drain her father completely. His eyes closed again, and he slipped into unconsciousness. Toni turned her head and blinked to keep from crying.

Her mother noticed, smiling. "Your dad will be all right, sweetheart. I'm sure of it."

That wasn't why she was crying. *It should be.*

Her mother brushed his hair to the side, away from his forehead then leaned in close and kissed his cheek. Feeling as if she was invading a private moment, Toni released his hand and took a step toward the door so her parents could be together.

She lowered her eyes to the hospital bed, not wanting to see her father so weak and still. He didn't seem like her father. Yet she found her eyes moving toward him in spite of herself, taking in how different he looked from the image clinging to in her mind, in which he still had dark-brown hair. In reality, it was almost entirely gray. The wrinkles on his forehead and around his mouth seemed deeper, more pronounced. And when had he gotten those age spots his hands?

This wasn't the same person who used to hoist her onto his shoulders when she was four years old. Those arms could hardly lift themselves now. That would change, she knew, as he regained his strength. But the eerie feeling as if she'd lost something lingered. The heaviness of it all pressed on her chest; Toni felt as if she couldn't get enough air.

"I'll leave you two alone," she said in a loud whispered. Her mother nodded and waved.

Toni headed back through the double doors to the ICU waiting room, where she collapsed on a couch and tried not to cry. Carter. She could let him know the latest. Texting could help her avoid tears too. She pulled out her phone.

Dad's out of surgery. ICU for now. It went well. Waiting to hear more.

After clicking send, she realized how low her phone battery was—only at eight percent, well into the red zone. On a normal night, she'd be going to bed about now, which meant she'd also be charging it up overnight. It would likely be dead by the time she got home.

Battery's dying, she typed into a second text. *I'll still call when*

I get home.

With that text sent, she decided to turn her phone off to conserve what little power remained—but not quite yet. Carter might reply. He didn't let her down. Not a minute passed before the phone dinged with his incoming text.

Glad the surgery is over. Hang in there. Call when you can. Love ya.

She replied with a smiley face then turned off her phone. She looked at the doors leading into the ICU area, feeling somehow guilty for not staying with her mother. Toni glanced at the clock beside the nurse's desk. She'd stay out here for another thirty minutes, and then she'd bite the bullet and go back in. She'd spell her mother by sitting with her dad, and then take another break.

They wouldn't be able to stay in her dad's room all night, but Toni knew her mother wouldn't leave the hospital while things were still so iffy.

Whatever happened, it would be a long night.

Chapter 4

Carter tried not to think too much about the Valentine's party. Would he have had a fantastic time, or a miserable one? He sighed, sitting alone in his condo. He clicked around the TV in hopes of finding a movie to stream, and otherwise whiled away the hours, waiting for Toni to call with an update.

Over the course of the evening, he left a couple of voice messages and several texts, reminding her to call. She probably wouldn't get any of it until she turned her phone on again, and that wouldn't be until she plugged it in to charge on her way home.

He abandoned the TV in favor of working off his pent-up energy with a workout in his spare-room-turned-home-gym. If it hadn't been a freezing winter night with inches of slick ice, he'd have gone for a run outside. Five miles on the treadmill didn't do it, so he spent the next forty-five minutes doing weights—first his regular routine, and then, because Toni still hadn't called, he went for some personal bests.

Even pumping iron wasn't enough to keep him from glancing at his phone every few minutes to make sure Toni hadn't called or texted. He finally gave up and took a shower—a cold one, then collapsed onto his couch and grabbed his iPad.

Halfway through a game of Spider, he reached for his cell on the arm rest of the couch and clicked it to check the time. Ten thirty. He sighed and went back to arranging the cards on the screen. Toni would surely stay with her mother for a long time. His eyes felt heavy, making him yawn. He refused to fall asleep, risking the chance that Toni would call, and he'd be jolted awake, answering with a frog voice. No, she needed to know he cared enough to stay up.

He tossed the iPad to the couch and went to grab a Diet Coke from the fridge, making a point to grab the three empty cans already on the side table, to throw away them, too. He hoped he wouldn't run out before the night was over; he'd never been a coffee drinker, but now he wondered if he should have kept some on hand for emergencies like this when he needed to stay awake.

I'm not a college kid anymore, he thought as he opened the fridge and pulled out a can. There had been a time when going to bed before midnight was early, when he could pull all-nighters and function fine the next day.

After popping the top, he downed half of the can. On second thought, he snagged another can from the fridge before heading back to the couch. He had only three more in the 12-pack. If he ran out of Diet Coke, maybe Excedrin would work.

Carter finished the first can as he reached the couch. He set both cans on the side table and glanced at his iPad. Watching YouTube videos and playing solitaire wasn't keeping him distracted and awake. Something else would do a better job—his *other* tablet. The drawing tablet he'd saved for and plopped down a thousand dollars on. That's what he used for most of his freelance work. Tonight he'd sketch with it to unwind and pass the time.

He went to his computer desk in the other room and brought the tablet to the couch. This tablet did everything a sketch pad could do, with all the benefits of a computer. Even the pressure he used while drawing carried over—the tablet had over a thousand pressure levels, so he could create pencil-like drawings as good as the real thing. An hour of sketching would focus and calm him, like Toni said that dancing and stretching did for her.

Toni. Everything always circled back to her. Always had, ever since junior high, when he couldn't get the pretty girl to notice him. During some patches in his life, other women had come into the picture, of course, and he'd thought some could become Mrs. Carter Mackenzie. But he'd never managed to picture his life without confiding in his best friend, of getting his girlfriend and his best friend to connect—really connect—and accept each other. His girlfriends had never been able to get past jealousy—or suspicion—of Toni.

He rolled the tablet's pen between his fingers, thinking of the first reason his past girlfriends hadn't dealt with Toni: jealousy. He'd always tried to assure them that she was just his—platonic—best friend.

But in quiet moments like these, with no students calling his name and no assignments to grade, his heart admitted the truth. Toni would never be *just* his best friend. His heart had always belonged to her, and it always would.

The idea of lifetime of waiting, alone, for her to return the same feelings wasn't exactly his idea of a great life. He'd have to get over her, somehow, someday.

But that time was *not* when her father was in ICU.

His eyes drifted to the iPad beside him. He had a freelance job due next week for a dance-wear company's logo; thanks to Toni and his practice sketching her over the years, he'd developed a steady stream of dance-related clients.

He reached for his iPad and flipped again looked at the images the company had sent as examples of what the feel they were going for. A dancer, yes, but a dancer in motion. He'd taken some photographs of Toni after her studio's Christmas recital last month. He often did that for this very reason—she made a great model for his freelance gigs. One of the recital pictures would probably work.

He tapped his way through several images to find it. There it was—Toni on pointe, wearing a white ballet costume with a tutu, posing on stage for her students' parents in what he'd learned was an arabesque, with her arms in fourth position. She looked like a fairy ready to take flight. A silhouette of Toni in that pose would be perfect.

He began sketching, referring to the photograph as he roughed in the basic lines and gradually added detail, until her eyes shone, her arms reached, her hair seemed ready to move with the slightest breeze.

Sometime later, he pulled himself out of his art and checked the clock. He'd gotten lost in his work again—actually, lost in drawing Toni. It was a good piece, he thought, as he sat back and looked at it. But it was too complex for a logo. He'd have to do a different piece for the job. But he'd keep this sketch; it was too good to scrap.

Having decided not to use this image for his client, Carter returned to the drawing to make it look more like Toni. It was an activity as good as any to pass the time as he waited to hear from her. Line by line, her face came to life, showing the personality he knew deep down, several layers below what she usually showed the outside world, and a woman more confident than Toni tended to be. He still couldn't quite get her eyes right and never had. But she was beautiful and powerful and gorgeous.

And not his.

Enough torturing yourself. He sighed, clicked the drawing tablet off, and set it aside. He took his glasses off and rubbed his weary eyes. Drawing usually made him feel better. Even when it was work. But tonight, drawing had only made him feel worse.

Would he ever touch Toni, not in a friendly hug, but in an embrace? Would he ever kiss more than her cheek in a hello or goodbye, but to kiss her—really *kiss* her, using his lips on hers to let her know the depths of his feelings?

Carter stood. Time for another cold shower. That would keep him awake.

As if that's why I need one. He needed something to distract him from Toni, even though she was the reason he was up this late. Maybe he could pull out a favorite old comedy like *Some Like It Hot.* And he'd try to laugh.

He headed to the bathroom with a determined stride. Cold. Ice cold.

Then Jack Lemmon and Tony Curtis. Better than thinking about how he'd never have Toni.

Chapter 5

"Honey? Sweetheart?"

Toni woke with a start when her mother touched her arm. Her back had a knot in it thanks to the funky position she'd been in when falling asleep on the hard couch. Her brain slowly cleared as understanding came into focus about where she was. She sat up and squinted at the bright overhead lights. "Is everything okay with Dad?"

Her mother nodded then looked over her shoulder at a fifty-something man standing behind her in scrubs and a lab coat with blue script embroidered on the pocket. The name was too far away to make out. Toni had to wonder if the surgeon kept a coat like that nearby to throw on after surgeries so he'd look more official than an orderly. Or more formal or something.

"Dr. Scofield here came to talk to me about Dad's prognosis and things," Toni's mother said. "Could you go in and be with him while I'm gone? It shouldn't take long." Her voice was calm and soothing, but her hands were clasped so tightly around the handle of her purse that her fingers were white—belying her calm exterior.

"Sure. I mean, of course." Toni still had a few mental cobwebs to get rid of.

"I want someone with him all the time, just in case," her mother said. A hint of stress entered her voice. "Don't leave his side. Promise me."

"I promise," Toni said, smiling. "I'll stay by Dad's side until you're back." She raised one hand like a Boy Scout making the scout oath. Her mom chuckled a bit at that, recognizing it from when Toni's brothers were young.

"Thank you, my Antonia," she said, and kissed Toni's cheek.

Under the circumstances, Toni didn't even have the urge to correct her mother. If using her full—if somewhat dated—name made her mother feel better, so be it. The doctor moved down the hall, her mother following close behind. Toni grabbed her purse and strode through the double doors, only vaguely registering middle-aged woman in scrubs monitoring the nurse's table.

Next thing she knew, Toni had gone down the hallway and entered the third room on the right. Crossing the threshold felt like entering another world—beeps and hums, the smell of antiseptic . . . the still form of her normally larger-than-life father, who was normally always talking and moving.

Seeing him like this felt surreal.

She took a seat beside her father's bed. He had a tube sending oxygen into his nose, something she'd seen on only one other person—her grandfather, days before he died. She shuddered at the thought and cleared her throat, hoping that breaking the near silence would also clear her mind. No dice. All she could think about was her father, her grandfather, illness, death.

She sat there, wondering whether she should talk to him—was he remotely conscious right now? She forced herself to look at him, to not turn away. After swallowing deliberately, she turned face on and studied him and the bed, determined to prove to herself—to him?—that she wasn't a coward.

Dad had an IV dripping some kind of clear fluid into his arm. Something else connected to the IV—maybe one of those painkiller pumps she'd heard about. He'd certainly need that soon. She kept looking. An oxygen monitor was clipped to his left index finger, and a readout on one of many digital devices showed his oxygen saturation level. She knew from her grandfather's death that anything below 90 wasn't good, and that an alarm went off if the patient's oxygen went that low.

She remembered the annoying sound—not loud, but grating—something she'd always associate with her grandfather's death. Eventually the nurse had taken the monitor off, because he was dying, so of course his oxygen would keep dropping until it was at zero.

Her eyes moved on. A blood pressure cuff around her father's left bicep. There was the oxygen tube looped around his ears, feeding air to his nose. Plus a few other plastic tubes and random wires she couldn't identify. His hair was matted down and sweaty. Maybe he'd been given one of those disposable hair coverings that look like shower caps.

Her eyes were drawn to his chest, which was covered with his hospital gown, so she couldn't see the damage from the surgery. Underneath that thin layer of fabric was where the doctors had probably sawed into his chest and pried it open. She swallowed again and turned away instinctively. Instead of forcing herself to look, she let herself stare out the window at the head of the bed.

A nurse walked past the door on her way to another room. Toni made out sounds, which she now recognized at the nurse taking a patient's vitals—the blood pressure cuff inflating, the beep of the temporal thermometer. The nurse had to be close; she'd probably come in next to take Dad's vitals.

The antiseptic hospital smells started turning Toni's stomach. They were exactly like the ones from when her grandfather had died in the hospital. She'd been only ten or eleven, but it might as well have been that morning, so clearly had the memory returned with the odors.

More muffled sounds from the corridor—hums and beeps, and occasionally someone—likely family members of other ICU patients—walked past. Many had red-rimmed eyes and carried tissues, followed by the nurse doing her rounds. What a depressing place to work.

Toni wished her phone had enough battery power for her to spend time with mindless games of solitaire. Or she could have a texting conversation with Carter. Not tonight. If she'd be spending a lot of time in the hospital, she'd have to bring a charger in her purse. She dug through it now in hopes of finding her e-reader, only to remember that she'd left it on her night stand. Maybe she could sneak out to the waiting room for two seconds, just long enough to snag a magazine to read.

But no, she'd promised her mother that she wouldn't leave her dad, even for a minute. Mom had to be back soon. How long did it take to get an update from the surgeon—unless the update was complicated and had bad news. Toni's stomach twisted; she took a deep breath in hopes of loosening it.

The silence started driving her crazy, so to maintain some semblance of sanity, she decided to speak, to talk about her and her father—memories she had of him. Maybe Dad would hear her, maybe not. Either way, at least she wouldn't feel quite so alone as she had.

"So, Dad, this whole thing has got me thinking about the past—stuff I'd forgotten altogether. Remember how you taught me how to fish? That summer at the reservoir, I was what, six? I think you spent more time untangling my line from logs and plants than I spent fishing. I don't think you caught any fish either—you spent the whole time fixing my line and putting more Power Bait on it."

She glanced over at the bed. No reaction. Pale face, shallow breaths. She eyed the oxygen stats from the clip on his finger—91. Which was fine, so long as it didn't dip further; she didn't think she could handle hearing that alarm anymore.

She cleared her throat and began again. "Then there was the time I wanted to play Risk with the boys, but they all said I was too young and wouldn't get it. So you let me be on your team, and we totally wiped them out." She laughed at that one, knowing full well that she hadn't done anything strategic that night. Smearing her brothers—taking over all of Asia and then the rest of the world—had been thanks entirely her father's skill. "It was so late that I think I fell asleep for part of the game, but when we won, you never mentioned it."

Toni found herself smiling as she thought back to her childhood. She talked about going on long summer walks in the foothills, playing basketball out front with her dad and brothers, making root beer with dry ice.

But the more she took a walk down memory lane, the farther

apart the happy images became. Soon she had to pause and think hard to find something happy to talk about. Her happiest memories were up to about age nine. After that, they grew sparse.

Her brow furrowed at the realization. What had happened about that age? It wasn't as if her father had left the picture. On the contrary, he seemed to be at her side—or in her ear—as often as ever, but the circumstances hadn't left pleasant memories.

All she could picture was Dad shaking his head in disappointment, his tense voice. Sometimes he yelled, and something it was just a tone, one she'd come to feel sick to her stomach at hearing. But for the life of her, she didn't remember much of what he'd said, only a few specific things he tended to repeat and repeat.

She did remember the tone, though, and the angry eyes.

You'll never let me down.

That she remembered. She still heard it on a regular basis. She could almost hear her father's voice saying those words for the thousandth time. She grunted in frustration; the sound was so loud in the otherwise near-silent room that it startled her. Toni quickly turned to her father, hoping he hadn't heard. But a look at her dad confirmed that he hadn't been disturbed by the noise.

She leaned against the chair, disturbed by the memories and feelings coming up tonight. Just the thought of her old gymnastics competitions—and Dad's "constructive criticism" after each event—made her nauseated all over again. Hugging herself, she stood and paced the room—so small she could take only four steps toward the door and four steps back. She felt like a trapped mouse, unable to escape.

Soon, she told herself. *Mom will be back soon, and then I can leave. And get in the car. And charge my phone. And call Carter.*

But Mom hadn't come back. Toni lifted her wrist to check the time, only to realize that she hadn't worn a watch, and her usual "watch," her phone, was still turned off in her jeans pocket. She ran one hand through her hair and pulled. The tension on her scalp felt good in an odd way, like a pressure-release valve.

She leaned against the doorway, her back to Dad, looking toward the ICU entrance to watch for her mother's return.

In spite of herself, Toni worried what her father would see if he woke up and saw her standing there. He'd have a great view of her imperfect body. The thought was enough to make her want to pull on a big parka—or wear a set of baggy Sponge Bob scrubs—to hide her shape from him.

In seventh grade, she'd had a dress she loved that was loose-fitting and hid her changing shape well. The beginning of puberty had been difficult—oilier hair, acne, and, the worst part, weight gain. To her mother's credit, she assured Toni that some kids just got a little chubby when they hit puberty.

"It's normal," Mom had said. "It's like your body is storing up fuel for a big growth spurt. Then the growth spurt hits, and you shoot right up and get skinny as a twig. You did that two or three times as a toddler, too."

But her mother's words didn't help, because of Dad's comments.

"Keep putting that much peanut butter on your toast, and you'll end up looking like beached whale."

"Would you like some pie with your whipped cream?"

"Do you really need a second helping?" That one was always with this sad little look on his face, as if he were pleading with her to please not be a fat pig.

His words created a beast that constantly hovered over Toni's shoulder, saying she wouldn't be good enough for anyone—including a man—if she didn't look just so.

Dad and his health-crazed mentality. His phobia of having a fat child. Yet he was the one who'd had the heart attack. So much for health food.

When she was thirteen, he'd bought her an exercise DVD—his way of being passive-aggressively "helpful." And then as she worked out to the DVD, he commented on her form or mentioned what her heart rate should be for a proper fat burn.

"You want to be in the right zone for that," he always said. "Too high, and you're getting a good cardio workout, but you aren't burning the fat, and that's what we want right now. Isn't it, princess?"

Every memory from puberty on was about her body and her failure at gymnastics. He'd had plenty of other expectations his princess was supposed to live up to. She refused to think of them right now. Not when they sent anger pulsing through her body like liquid venom. She wanted to yell and scream in his face. Yet when she looked over his shoulder, he looked fragile and helpless.

Against her will, tears tumbled over her cheeks. *Find a happy memory. There has to be at least one. Maybe from when I was older.*

But try as she might, all she could come up with were moments when she'd disappointed him and when he tried to "encourage" her to improve.

Along with the never-ending mantra of "You'll never let me down."

Deciding to face her fears, she deliberately turned around to face her father's sleeping form. She studied him, trying to comprehend that this weak body had been the one who inflicted the fear of failure into her. She could hardly believe that *that* man had caused her so much heartache.

Granted, he'd changed over the years. His hair was not only graying, but it had receded and thinned at the top. But overall, he still looked as Toni remembered him during her childhood. She wiped at her cheeks and dried her hands on her jeans as her mother pushed through the double doors and walked toward the room.

When she saw Toni's tears, she pulled her daughter into a tight hug. "Oh, honey, I know it's hard. He'll be all right."

Toni hugged back, wishing her mother had been a strength for Toni when she was young instead of a weak thing standing back, letting her husband take control of trying to raise his only daughter to perfection. Toni pulled back and wiped at her cheeks with both hands.

She sniffed and took a deep breath. "So what did the doctor say?"

Mom looked over at Dad, who was still sleeping heavily. "He should be okay," she said with the ghost of a smile. "He'll be in the hospital for about a week—but he'll be out of ICU in a day or so. When he's home, he'll have a long recovery—and a handful of pills to take every day. But yes, they think he'll be okay."

"I'm so relieved," Toni said, stress draining from her body. Her father may have had his problems, but she didn't wish him dead.

"Why don't you go home now?" her mother said. "You're exhausted, and I'm okay here now that we know your dad's doing all right."

"Not yet," Toni said, shaking her head. "You need some rest. Go take a nap, and I'll stay with Dad until you're back. *Then* I'll go home."

"I'll be fine. I'm glad we got a bite to eat earlier. That'll hold me over until morning. I'll get home for a shower and a change of clothes in the morning."

Toni raised her eyebrows, giving her mother the same look she herself had received countless times as a kid. Her mother laughed and put a hand on Toni's cheek.

"What would I do without my Antonia?" She smiled then leaned in and kissed Toni's cheek. "You're right; I'll go rest a bit, but then you're going home."

"Deal." Toni nodded toward the waiting room. "But first, I'm going to grab something to read."

"How about this?" Mom whipped out her tablet and handed it over. "I don't know if you'll find any novels to your liking on there, but you're welcome to anything in my library—and feel free to download something else if you want to; I'm happy to pay for a book or two. Oh, and there are lots of fun games on there, especially word games. Do you need me to show you how to work it?"

"Thanks," Toni said, taking the tablet. "I think I can figure it out."

Her mom nodded, saying nothing as she gazed into the hospital room again. "I don't want to leave him tonight. He may need me." She turned back to Toni. "I won't be long. I can tell you're ready to fall asleep on your feet."

Chapter 6

Her mother managed to doze for two hours before coming back to spell Toni. Her normally perfectly styled hair was lopsided, and she had the imprint of fabric, probably her sleeve, on her cheek.

"I'm so sorry I slept that long," she said, groggily patting her hair into place.

"You needed your rest." Toni handed over the tablet, which had been just what she'd needed to keep herself distracted—lots of mindless games, plus a romance novel she'd found in her mother's library and had read a few chapters of. She wouldn't mention that one, not to her mother, who tended to be prudish. Based on the little Toni had read of the book, Mom had a secret spicy side to her.

"Time for you to go home, sweetheart," her mother said. "I can tell you're ready to fall over."

No argument there. "You sure you'll be okay without me?"

"I'll be fine." Mom tapped a finger on Toni's shoulder as she added, "Now drive carefully on the roads. They're bound to be a skating rink."

"I'll be careful. Promise." Toni slung her purse over her shoulder and headed for the door. She turned back. "Call me in the morning to let me know how he's doing, okay?"

Her mother nodded. "Of course."

"Is there anything else I can do for you tonight? I could run to the house and get some of your things for you."

"Just call your brothers. They'll want an update. Or maybe you can send one big email to everyone. Whatever you think is best. I won't be near my computer for a while, and I don't think I'd hold it together on the phone anyway."

"Sure thing," Toni said.

Her mother came over and leaned in for one more hug. "Thank you so much for coming. I needed you." She gave Toni a light kiss on her cheek, pulled back, and brushed her hair aside. "I know I can count on you."

Of course Toni was glad she could help her parents. Of course she'd always be there in a crisis. But the words felt sour. The words were too close to her father's lifetime mantra. *The family can always count on Toni to never let us down.*

Growing up, that had been her job description. She swallowed back emotion from the memory and said, "Love you, Mom. Goodnight."

Toni headed to the elevators. She leaned against the wall on the ride to the main floor and nearly fell asleep. But a few minutes later, when she exited the hospital, the ice-cold January air shocked her awake. Her breath came in thick white puffs, and she found herself hunched up as she trudged through falling snow to reach her car—and wishing she'd worn boots or parked in the covered garage. Her feet would be sopping wet by the time she got home.

She got in the car and, teeth chattering, put the key into the ignition and turned on the engine. As it idled—and, she hoped, warmed up so the heater would blow warm air—she plugged her phone into the charger and turned it on.

It was only then that she realized it was nearly two thirty. No wonder she was tired. She'd assumed the emotional stress had been the only thing taking its toll. By the time her phone finished booting up, she was buckled in and ready to head out, but something on the screen caught her eye.

The phone icon had the number 13 next to it, meaning that many missed calls and messages, and she had 19 text messages. She was willing to bet nearly all of them were from Carter, but she tapped the text icon to be sure. Yep. All from Carter. She scrolled through them to be sure he didn't have an emergency of his own. He didn't; every text was a reminder to let him know how things were, even if she got home in the middle of the night.

The thought made her feel warm inside despite the freezing interior of the car. Good old Carter. He knew she'd hesitate to call this late and made sure she'd do it anyway because she'd need the chance to vent. How did a girl get so lucky to have such a great best friend?

She pulled out of her parking space and headed for her apartment, driving at about half the speed limit because, as her mother had predicted, the roads were ice, with more snow coming down. At least the roads were also nearly empty, and she hit mostly green lights, which meant little need to brake on the slippery streets.

By the time she found a parking spot in the covered garage and trudged up the metal stairs to her apartment on the fourth floor, it was quarter to three. As she locked the door, she felt drained and ready to fall over, but her emotions were too tightly wound to attempt sleep.

She fumbled for the hall light switch, clicking her phone on to use as a flashlight. She remembered the messages on it and smiled again. With the living room light on, Toni went to her bedroom, changed into her most comfortable yoga pants and sweatshirt, and went back to the living room with her phone. She dropped onto the cushions to check her messages.

She had four voice mails. Two were from Carter. The first one came up. "I know you won't be home yet, but just thought I'd remind you to call when you get back. I'll be up."

As she listened to the next message, Toni eyed the time on her phone, wondering if she dared call him this late in spite of all the texts and voice messages telling her to. Even if he'd intended on staying up, he must have fallen asleep by now. The second message, no surprise, was from Allen.

"Hey, um . . . Sorry to hear about your dad," he said. "Too bad you missed out on some great games. We still have a cupcake here with your name on it. Unless this was all a lame excuse to get out of socializing with your coworkers. I hope your dad really is in the hospital . . . Wait. That didn't sound right. You know what I meant. I hope. Anyway, check in when you can."

After that awkward message, she couldn't be offended. Her boss meant well, even if his methods were misguided. Toni sat on the couch, put a throw pillow behind her neck, and remembered that she hadn't made her food assignment for the party—a green salad. Oops.

The third message was from Josh, the second oldest in the family, asking for an update on their dad, and the last message was Carter reminding her that he was still awake.

He knows me well. After she deleted that message, Toni's thumb hovered over his number. She desperately wanted to talk out her feelings with someone who would listen, but Carter could be asleep and would definitely be tired.

But Josh's message reminded her of their mother's one request for the evening. Toni went to her room, grabbed her laptop from the floor by her bed, and opened it to write a quick email to her brothers. She kept it short but sweet, included Dad's room number, and promised to send more information when she had it.

Just as she clicked send, her the phone went off in the other room. It had to be Carter. She jumped up and raced to her phone, which rested on the coffee table. "Carter?"

"This is Joe's Repair Shop," came a voice with a thick Texas drawl. "We got a Model T in here ready to be picked up."

She slumped in her seat, her exhausted brain not understanding. "Sorry. You must have the wrong—"

Wait a minute. A Model T? She thought back to when the ring tone she'd just heard—a *quack*.

"Carter, you goon." Toni laughed, and a lighthearted feeling coursed through her aching body like cool water on parched soil. Her raw nerves had definitely needed soothing. Talking to Carter would help. So would some food. She got up and crossed to the kitchen, where she put a bag of movie-theater popcorn into the microwave. The horridly bad for you, buttery kind. It was that kind of night.

"You holding up all right?" he asked.

She hit start then leaned against the counter to wait. "I'm okay for now."

"But?" Of course Carter heard the *but* in her voice.

"It was horrible," she admitted. She pushed off the counter and paced the tiny kitchen. "I've never seen my dad like that. He looked so frail. His face was deathly pale, and the tubes and wires and . . ." She shook her head. "Worst of all, I couldn't do a thing for him or for my mom besides *be* there. I'm the one everyone is counting on to hold the family together, and I can't do it." She lowered her face into the palm of one hand. "What if he dies?"

"He's not going to die," Carter said. His voice sounded so assured, so calm, she wanted to believe him. She wanted him to be there right now, holding her in a big hug so she'd feel safe.

"I hope you're right."

The microwave beeped, interrupting their conversation. Toni dug a plastic bowl out of the cupboard and emptied the popcorn bag into it. As she headed back to the couch, she told him about how hard it was to remember happy things about her dad, how the biggest memories she had of him after about age ten were when he was criticizing her. She paused at that, eyeing the popcorn and picturing what Dad would say if he could see her eating it now.

Better put that away, butterball. You don't want that fat to end up on your hips.

She pulled the blanket higher to cover said hips—ever since she'd *had* hips thanks to puberty, they'd been far bigger than she'd liked. She had a nice waist, though. Put her in a Cinderella dress, and no one would know that she had elephant legs beneath the skirt.

"Hey, Ton?" Carter's voice broke through her thoughts, making her realize that she'd stopped talking and had zoned out.

"I'm here. It's just . . . man, I hate this."

"It's got to suck," Carter agreed, although she knew he couldn't have any real clue what she meant by *this*. So much sucked in her life, from the heart attack to her crappy adolescence, filled with her dad's never-ending attempts to make his daughter better by tearing her down.

She didn't know what else to say; she couldn't tell Carter about some parts of her past; he was a guy and wouldn't understand. Thankfully, he changed the subject, and soon they were talking about several movies that would be coming out in the next month and what they thought of the trailers. They debated and laughed—sometimes so loud that she worried her neighbors would be woken up from it. She got up and made more popcorn whenever she ran out. After devouring several bags—she had to count to believe she'd really eaten that many—she looked at the clock and groaned.

"It's almost four. You've got to be exhausted. I should let you go so you can get a couple of hours of sleep before work."

"It's Saturday," Carter said with a laugh. "They do abuse high school teachers, but they don't make me be Mr. Mackenzie on weekends. And art teachers don't have mounds of research papers to correct."

"Oh yeah."

"But it is a little late."

Even though Toni had been the one to point out the time, she flinched at the comment. "I say we both get a little sleep. I'll pick you up at eight, and we'll go to McDonald's for breakfast. Deal?"

"Deal," she said, even though she'd have preferred six or seven o'clock; she wouldn't be able to sleep anyway.

"See you then."

Toni hung up and stared at the phone, wishing she could call Carter back, wishing they'd decided to go to Denny's instead because it was open 24/7. Her apartment felt eerily empty and cold, more so as memories of her father and the hospital returned, along with a torrent of emotions. Stress built up in her until she couldn't take it any longer.

Her stomach felt heavy as a rock; eating so much popcorn had felt good in the moment—it *had* released her stress—but it was all back now. She could do one more thing to relax, and then she'd be able to sleep until she got to see Carter again.

She threw off the blanket and hurried to the fridge, one arm covering her middle. Throwing the door open, she talked herself into calming down; in just a minute or two, she'd feel better. The emotion would be out, gone. Toni searched through the shelves and was relieved to find exactly what she'd been looking for: two cans of diet Dr. Pepper.

Hands trembling, she opened one and guzzled it down as fast

as she could. The rush was about to come. Quickly she opened the second can and gulped down its contents as well. Then she stood by the sink and waited. She didn't know why, but for some reason, soda always encouraged food she had indulged in to come back up, and with it came her emotions.

She clung to the edges of the sink, feeling the unease in her middle. She eyed the plastic spoon she kept by the sink in case she'd need it. Fingers didn't work anymore.

Steady, steady . . .

Relief was on its way. With a surge, the popcorn and soda—and stress and anger and sadness—purged from her throat, into the sink, her stomach contracting until it was all gone.

When it was done, she stood there, trembling for a minute, before ripping off a paper towel and wiping her mouth. Even with the shakes, she felt so much better.

What a relief. When she first started purging, it was just to keep the weight of her indulgences off. She hadn't realized until later how great it was at relieving stress—some days it even gave her a rush.

She'd be able to sleep now. She went to her bathroom sink and brushed her teeth then swished some mouthwash to get rid of the lingering taste of stomach acid. Then she looked at herself in the mirror, smiled at the fact that the popcorn was *gone*, took a deep breath, and went to bed.

Chapter 7

After hanging up, Carter sighed hard, keeping his hand on the phone as if he might just call Toni back just to hear her voice again. He rested his head against the couch and ran his fingers through is hair. His drawing tablet sat beside him on the cushion, showing Toni in an arabesque, a dreamy look on her face, with a half-smile.

Mona Lisa, eat your heart out.

He'd added fairy wings, making her look like she really was about to take flight. Maybe he'd add color to the picture—something pastel, maybe a pale peach. If he uploaded it to one of the sites he used to sell graphics rights to his images, he bet he'd get a lot of takers. Maybe one day, he'd see this image on a poster or a book cover.

With a sigh, he turned off the tablet and headed to bed, but when he climbed between the sheets, he stared at the ceiling, thinking about Toni. He'd left his phone on his night stand, sound on, in case she needed to reach him before breakfast. An alarm on it would wake him up an hour before he was to pick her up to give him enough time to shower so he'd look—and smell—the part.

What part is that? He demanded of himself. *Best friend? You don't want to look* that *part.*

An hour later, he still lay wide awake, images of Toni on her pointe shoes floating through his head. He nearly drifted off twice. Both times, the peach-colored fairy of Toni flew toward him, wearing the smile he'd seen whenever she talked about men she found attractive. But this time, the smile was directed at him. Just as she reached in to kiss him, he startled awake.

Enough. He threw the covers off and got up. *Might as well do something.*

As he left the room, he avoided looking at the prom picture that still sat on display on his bookshelf. Luckily Toni had never been in his bedroom; she would have thought him crazy to still have that old picture up. Heck, he thought he was crazy. But even with their outdated hair styles and clothes, the picture felt a bit like home to him.

Great. He'd passed the picture without looking at it, but he'd still thought of it as much as ever. He whirled around, stalked back to the bookcase, and snatched the picture. In one quick movement, he opened his night stand drawer and shoved it in, then kicked the drawer closed. He *had* to stop thinking of Toni as anything more than a friend. Not as a woman, not as his fantasy, not as anyone he'd ever be able to call his own, not someone who would ever say she loved him.

He deliberately changed into his workout gear and went outside to brave the cold for a real run. In spite of the somewhat cold air and slick roads—and his classic rock play list thrumming into his ear buds—his thoughts drifted to high school. And Toni.

She'd had always been a shy teenager, without what you could call a "real" social life. As the end of their junior had approached, she hadn't ever been asked to a date dance, and she'd gone to one girls' choice dance at the prodding of some friends to join their group. Back then she rarely mentioned dating, but one night as they studied geometry, when their junior prom was a month away, she confessed how much she wanted to go.

"I know the chances of getting asked are pretty much nonexistent," she'd said with a sigh as she doodled in the margin of her homework. "But it's prom, you know?"

"Yeah," he said. *I was so eloquent even then.*

Carter had admitted sometime before that study hour that he didn't like asking out girls, although he never mentioned why—that he constantly hung out with the only girl he had any interest in anyway. So Toni knew Carter wouldn't be going to the prom, either.

"Hey, I have an idea," Toni said, sitting up excitedly. "On prom night, let's have a party. We could go out to a Mexican restaurant and eat nachos till we're sick. Then we can go to a movie."

A night out with Toni? Like he'd object to that. "Hmm," he said, not wanting to show how eager he was. "Not a bad idea."

She closed her text book with a thump and turned to him. "Even better, let's rent a couple of classics, like *The Philadelphia Story*." She grimaced. "If you're not sick of it."

They'd watched that movie several times together, and frequently quoted lines from it. "Hey, how could I ever get sick of watching Katharine Hepburn in a swimsuit?" Carter said, looking up from his homework with a grin.

Toni nodded. "I know it'll take me several more times of seeing it before I get tired of Jimmy Stewart or Cary Grant." She leaned against the couch and got a starry look in her eye.

"Let me guess," Carter said with a smirk. "You're imagining Jimmy Stewart kissing Katherine Hepburn again."

She rolled her head toward Carter and smiled. "Golly."

Which was exactly what Hepburn said after Stewart's kiss. Carter cleared his throat and went back to work on his math homework. What would it be like to have a girl say something like that after one of his kisses?

Forget kisses. Forget that movie.

Carter decided to leave the subject of the movie. "Then let's do it. That is, *if* you don't get asked to prom," Carter said, looking at the text book. He'd almost said, "It's a date," but that might have sounded wrong.

"Yeah, right. Like I'm going to be asked to prom." Toni laughed, but Carter sensed disappointment in her voice. She went back to doodling, her eyes losing the sparkle they'd had a moment before. "That's about as likely as me being Miss America."

They didn't watch Cary Grant and Katharine Hepburn on prom night, because Carter took her to prom. All night he reveled in treating her like a queen. She practically beamed all night with her red taffeta dress and fancy up-do. It would have been the best night of his life if Toni had shown the slightest hint of feeling more for him than friendship. But she didn't show anything like that on prom, giving him a friendly, if long, hug on the doorstep. It showed her appreciation and affection, but it was the hug of a best friend nonetheless.

She hadn't shown anything more than that since, either. He was getting pretty sick of best-friend hugs, he thought as ended his run. He reached his apartment and slammed the door with a smack.

After a quick shower, he dried off and got dressed then put on his glasses and headed to the sink to shave. He thought of the times he'd comforted Toni after a breakup. Hearing about her latest date, the cutest guy, her relationship issues. He pulled the razor in short, quick strokes, angry at himself for putting up with it.

A sting and a spot of red made him stop shaving so recklessly. He set down the razor and grabbed a piece of toilet paper to stop the bleeding. He could stop putting up with it. But what was the other option? Not have Toni in his life at all?

He'd stop hearing about her boyfriends, sure, but he'd no longer have late-night phone calls like the one last night. He wouldn't be able to text her whenever he felt like it or laugh at a link she'd shared on Facebook. She knew his sense of humor like no one else.

Carter rested his hands on the counter and stared himself down in the mirror. Enough of self-pity. Toni genuinely needed him, so he'd be there for her. "Ok, buddy," he said to his reflection. "Get yourself together. You gotta be there for her. She's counting on you."

It took him another three minutes, but he finally calmed down enough to keep getting ready. He turned on the television in his room, though, so he could drown out his thoughts with the voices of the morning news anchors. No sense in torturing himself more.

No more thinking about Toni until I see her, he decided, picking up his razor and lifting his chin to shave beneath it.

T oni had answered concerned texts and emails from her siblings—mostly saying that no, she didn't have an update, and that yes, she'd be sure to pass one on when she had one. Finally she and Carter were talking over hot cakes and sausage at McDonald's. He'd managed to wipe that morning's frustrations out of his mind so he could be the friend—ugh, the friend—Toni needed.

Toni wore her faded high school dance company sweats, and she had pulled her hair back into a pony tail. She looked seventeen again, and between the sweatshirt with their school's logo on it and her face without makeup, he couldn't help but remember moments from high school. For a second it felt like they were still the old Toni and Carter, hanging out over fries. Only this time it was pancakes and sausage.

Knock it off, he ordered his brain as he stabbed a piece of sausage. He shoved down the feelings and took a bite of the sausage with a bit for force than necessary.

"It doesn't bite," Toni said with a laugh, nodding at the sausage, which Carter had nearly attacked.

He looked at the plastic fork in his hand, chuckled, and set it on the foam plate. "Guess I'm hungry."

Not entirely a lie. I'm just not telling her what I'm hungry for. Dang, how do her lips still look like they've got lip gloss on them even after she just ate? He found himself picturing—surely for the thousandth time or more—what it would be like to kiss Toni.

"Hey, earth to Carter." Toni waved a napkin in front of his face, and he looked up, feeling sheepish that he'd let his thoughts and emotions get the better of him yet again.

"Sorry," he said. "I think I'm just tired. I can't focus." He reached two fingers under his glasses and rubbed his eyes as a yawn overtook him. He was tired, of course. That was true. And it served as a good excuse for his distraction this morning.

She grimaced. "My fault. I'm sorry."

"No, don't you dare apologize," Carter said, adjusting his

glasses now that he'd knocked them out of position. "It's not your fault that your dad's in the hospital. Besides, if we'd gone to the studio party, chances are, we would have stayed out late talking anyway. Maybe had pie at Village Inn into the wee small hours of the morning. We'd both still be wiped."

"True," she admitted, making trails in her syrup with her fork. "I could really use some banana cream pie." She shrugged and tossed the fork on to her foam plate, which was empty besides a few crumbs and syrup trails. She must have been hungry. She'd eaten more than Carter could.

"Thanks again for letting me talk it all out last night," Toni said. "I really needed someone. I'm so glad I have you."

Carter found his throat tightening. He swallowed to clear it then put on a grin. "Hey, I asked for it." He held out his arms. "You know me, always ready and willing."

Toni looked out the window. A smile suddenly crossed her face, and she bit her lip.

"What's that for?" Carter asked.

Toni jumped. "Huh? Oh, nothing. I was just thinking."

"Obviously. About what?" He knew that look all too well—and didn't like it. He'd seen it when Toni first fell for Keith their senior year of high school, and then when David entered the picture in college, followed by Paul, and, of course, most recently, Andrew almost a year ago. He braced himself for what he knew was coming. Probably something about that new guy at the studio.

"I just saw someone in the parking lot that looks like Clint," Toni said with a poorly hidden smile.

"Where?" Carter asked, looking out the window. Toni pointed to the far side of the parking lot, where a man with dark hair and an obviously good build unlocked his car. Muscles aside, the guy couldn't have been more than five three. Carter looked back at Toni, one eyebrow raised. "That guy looks like Clint? I hate to break it to you, but he's *short*." Had to find some fault with the guy.

"So Clint's short," Toni said with a shrug, going back to playing with her fork and syrup. "He's actually a little taller than that guy. But most Latin ballroom dancers are on the shorter side. It's the Modern ballroom dancer—the ones who do the waltz and tango and whatnot—who are tall and lanky.”

"I thought you only liked guys you could wear heels around.”

Careful, Carter warned himself. *Don't push too hard. She'll realize you're jealous.*

"I could probably wear heels around Clint." Toni's eyes turned dreamy. "But he's cute enough that even if I can't, I could make an exception in his case." She gazed out the window, so she didn't notice Carter stabbing a fork into the top of the hotcake tray. His heart beat faster, and his stomach twisted as he imagined Toni in Clint's arms. Why didn't she ever get that dreamy tone and look over him? He wasn't exactly ugly.

I'm not short, dark, and handsome, either.

Toni's voice interrupted his thoughts. "I'd bet Clint could make a girl say, 'Golly.'"

Carter couldn't answer that one. Instead, he clenched his jaw and tried to breathe normally, fighting the urge to go to the studio and break Clint's nose for no other reason than that Toni found him attractive.

She turned from the window and shook her head. "It doesn't really matter what I think about Clint, though. I don't think he even knows I exist. He's been at the studio for two months already, but we've had maybe two conversations, and in both, I blubbered like some junior high girl. It's probably better that he doesn't know who I am. It's getting ridiculous." Her smile clearly said that looking ridiculous didn't bother her too much.

"So why don't you ask him out?" Carter asked, apparently a glutton for punishment.

"No way," Toni said, waving the idea away with both hands. "I'm hoping he'll ask me out sometime, when I can keep from blushing the second he walks in the room. I swear, his eyes could melt ice."

Most of the time Carter handled these conversations well enough, encouraging her when she needed it, rooting for her, asking what the guy was like. But for some reason, he couldn't do it today. Maybe it was the sleep deprivation, or maybe he'd reached his limit after all these years.

He pushed his tray away and tried to do the same to his feelings for Toni. Pushing them off was getting harder and harder.

Fortunately, Toni didn't seem to notice his distance.

She glanced at her watch. "Oh, I should be getting to the studio."

"Why?" Carter asked, unwilling to let her go, even though another man occupied her mind. "You don't teach today, do you?"

"No, but my Jazz II class is supposed to learn more of their recital routine on Monday—and the recital's only a couple of weeks away. I haven't got the kinks worked out yet. Then this afternoon the studio's professional company rehearses."

"I've always wanted to see you at work," Carter said, sitting back and scrutinizing her.

Toni laughed. "You've seen me dance plenty of times. You know what I do."

"Yeah," Carter admitted. The truth was, he had never missed a performance. "But seeing you or your class dancing on stage is different than seeing you bossing a class around or rehearsing or—*choreographing*. That's the right word, isn't it?"

"That's what we call it," she said with a laugh, then looked up at him. She had dark circles under her eyes, and suddenly he knew why she really needed to go the studio. She needed some alone time. Working on routines and going through technique exercises sometimes gave her an escape, like drawing did for him.

Carter had always wanted to go to the studio and sit behind the one-way mirror to watch her, but he knew she wouldn't appreciate that, so he stayed away, especially at times like this, when she expected privacy.

"Before we leave, though, I need to use the ladies' room," Toni said, and scooted out of the booth. With trepidation, Carter watched her go. About a month ago he had noticed how little Toni ate, and the times she really did eat, she always excused herself and headed to the bathroom.

He had no idea how long it had been going on, because it was only recently he'd realized that her behavior had warning signs all over it. During lunch one day at the high school, Janet Miller, a science teacher, had told him about her concerns about a bulimic student. Before that, Carter hadn't known much of anything about eating disorders, but after that conversation, he noticed

Toni's odd behavior around food. He went back to the teacher and asked for more details. It didn't take long before he was convinced that Toni had a problem.

When she disappeared around the corner, Carter stood and softly followed her steps. He listened at the door for any sounds, hoping his fears wouldn't be justified. They were. When the sink began to run, Carter jumped up and virtually ran back to their booth as if nothing had happened. Toni emerged seconds later and offered him a breath mint.

"No thanks," he said quietly, knowing why she wanted to freshen her own breath.

Chapter 8

Back at her apartment, Toni put on her dance clothes and replaced her sweats over them, then touched up her makeup and hair to look a little better, just in case Clint showed up at the studio too. She couldn't remember for sure, but she thought the junior ballroom team practiced Saturday mornings. The thought made her smile as she grabbed her dance bag and headed out the door.

When Toni arrived at the studio, she tiptoed past Allen's office, with its big window opening to the front desk, so he wouldn't notice her. He sat at his computer, probably looking over costume orders or something. Behind him were three framed posters of famous dancers from totally different styles: Martha Graham, Mikhail Baryshnikov, and Bob Fosse. The latter was Allen's personal idol.

A heavy beat came from the big studio room on the left—a samba, from the sound of it. The junior ballroom team. And Clint. She grinned. He was here. And with the loud music, Allen would almost certainly not hear her walk past. Toni paused to look through the one-way mirror at the ballroom team—or, rather, their coach.

Clint was at the front, calling out directions and comments to specific dancers. "Good! Keep that line straight. Jeremy, stop making Chelsey lead. That's your job. Okay, everyone, samba walks to the next formation—yes. Good."

He was good. And hot. Clint turned off the music, drawing the attention of the dancers, who were roughly junior high age. "Looks like we need a bit more work on your samba walks. Watch me. Notice how my head stays level; I'm not bouncing up and down. All the movement of the walk itself is waist down. I can't add spice with my arms, but all action is below. See that?"

Oh, she saw it. He had the best Cuban action she'd ever seen.

He clapped again to get their attention. Toni took a step backward in case he could see her outline through the mirror. "Everyone, line up on the other end, and let's do samba walks across the floor."

He turned the music back on and counted out the syncopated rhythm, "Ready, go. One, and two. Three, and four!"

As the teenagers headed across the floor, Toni's view of Clint disappeared. She shook her head. Time to get to work herself, anyway. She headed down the hall, which was flanked by four dance rooms. The smaller two were toward the back. By the time she'd passed the one-way mirror into Clint's class, she dared to draw a breath of relief, only to hear Allen's office door click open. She stopped short. She grimaced, waiting for his voice.

"Good morning, Toni," Allen said. "After hearing about your dad, I didn't think I'd see you today."

She pivoted around and put on a smile. "I won't spend too much time here today," she said over the music. "Just enough to work out a few bugs in one of my class's numbers."

He nodded in that aggravating patronizing way he had, as if he were her father—which he often tried to act like. Hence the constant jabs about when she'd get married, and how she needed to be more responsible, and whatever else he decided was his pet topic of the day.

Toni hitched her dance bag a bit higher on her shoulder and smiled, taking a step backward. "Good to see you. I hope the party went well."

"Actually," Allen said as he stepped forward.

She wanted to groan—to escape. But this was her boss, after all. "Yes?"

He walked closer. "I know you don't enjoy coming to studio parties."

"I would have come if it hadn't been for my dad," Toni said hurriedly. "I swear. I had a date and everything."

"I know, I know." Allen nodded several times, wearing a slightly sad smile. "But the thing is, I know you don't like them. They're a bit annoying to you, aren't they?"

Like she was going to answer *that* honestly.

"I just hope you can see one day that I don't put on these socials just to give the staff a good time." He slapped the back of one hand against the other as if making a strong point. "They're important for studio morale, a chance for each person to become a closer part of the studio family. Now, I know you had a good excuse this time, but please keep this in mind for the next social."

She had no desire for the staff at the studio to become a giant group of brothers and sisters, with Allen as their dad. Heaven forbid. Especially if that meant Clint saw her as a sister. No way. Toni took a deep breath and forced a smile. "Will do. I'm sure I'll be there next time. No worries."

"Good." Allen looked ready to head back to his office, but he turned around to face her again. "I didn't ask—how is your father doing?"

She had talked it out so much with Carter that now she could talk about it without crying again. "He's stable for now, but he'll be in the hospital for a while."

Allen ran his fingers through his slightly overgrown blonde hair, which Toni thought he kept long to give the impression that he was twenty years younger, back in his dancing prime. He was still in good shape, but he couldn't pull of the same moves and technique he once had, and his face showed the signs of decades of dance. Plus, his hairline was receding. He was nowhere near bald, but his forehead was significantly larger than it had been when she was hired three years ago.

"If you need someone to take your class, or if you need to be at the hospital or whatever, just let me know," he said. "I'll try to get Jill or Amy to fill in."

With a final smile, he walked back down the hall and ducked around the corner, back to his office. She heard the door click behind him, and only then let out a breath and headed back down the dimly lit hall toward the last dance room on the right, one that was almost always available at this hour on Saturdays.

As she reached for the doorknob of the back room, the samba music cut off, and Toni heard Clint's voice calling out to his team.

"All right, everyone. Great practice today. You're excused, but if you want to go over the routine again, I'll leave the music playing."

For a minute Toni wanted to go back, to peek through the mirror again to watch Clint, but she knew his students would be coming out any second, and she wasn't about to be caught watching him. Sure enough, the door to the big studio room opened. Toni jumped, grabbed her bag a little closer, and quickly opened the door to the room she'd be working in. She closed the door safely behind her as if she had been pursued then leaned against it, feeling her heart racing. Toni couldn't decide whether she hated or loved that weak, flushed feeling Clint sent through her.

She shook off the rush as best she could; she needed to focus, to practice. She crossed the wooden floor as she dug into her bag for her iPhone and looked up her warmup play list. She plugged it into the speakers and pushed play. The beat began, and she sighed instinctively, her body already starting to relax. This was where she found the most satisfaction. She dropped her bag on the floor, took off her sweats so she could move better in her leotard and spankies, and left her feet bare.

At the center of the room she started with neck stretches, then arm warmups, and then her torso, gradually working down her body to each muscle group. After a long night of tension, the familiar relaxing music and her warmup routine released the stiffness better than a hot bath could have. By the time the three songs on the play list ended, she felt miles away from her emotions of last night.

She switched to the play list she used for floor exercises and began to do what, to an outsider, might have looked like boring drills—leaps, kicks, and four types of turns across the floor, again and again. For Toni, feeling her body perform familiar movements with precision thrilled her, yet she constantly strove for even better technique.

Soon she had more energy than she should have had with so little sleep. Toni wiped beading sweat from her forehead and headed to the sound system yet again, this time putting on the music she had picked out for her class's lyrical jazz routine. As she went through the combinations, she focused on the rough parts, picturing the moves or rhythms that would make the dance appear seamless, trying to envision a group of fourteen girls performing sections in waves and different formations and groupings. Every so often, she stopped the music, worked out the problem sections, then replayed it to make sure the changes fit.

When she had fixed the entire dance, she played the piece from the top to make sure it all worked. It did, perfectly, sending the thrill of creation that always went through her when she had finished a good routine. She did a little hop of excitement as she went back to the sound system to try it a few more times. She had been at the studio nearly an hour, and she still didn't want to leave.

This time when the class's song ended, another lyrical piece began, and Toni kept dancing, feeling the beat and emotion of the music as she danced. She improvised, only half aware of her movements as she leapt and turned, gracefully flying, dropping, rising again, then collapsing and leaping again. She went into a layout, and as she stretched her lower body one way and her head and upper body the other, she saw Clint standing by the open door. The layout—and the moment—fizzled, and Toni collapsed on the floor with a yelp.

"Sorry, I didn't mean to startle you," Clint said with a smooth smile as he came in. "I really liked that last combination. Could you show it to me again?"

Toni scrambled to stand up. She pulled out her loose ponytail and, with trembling hands, smoothed it out and replaced it. "I don't even remember what I did. I was—I was just improvising." She mentally kicked herself. Why couldn't she even make a coherent sentence around this guy?

Because he was hot and an amazing dancer. That's why.

"I'm sorry to interrupt such a great creative session, but I was wondering if you had change for a twenty," Clint said, waving a bill. "I wanted to get something to eat from the machines."

Toni hurried to her bag, feeling like a circus clown stumbling over her feet. A quick search uncovered a couple of dollar bills in her wallet and a few stray coins floundering at the bottom of her purse.

"I don't have enough," Toni said, sincerely sorry that she couldn't help him. She reached for the dollar bills and nearly tripped over her discarded sweat pants as she crossed the room and thrust the money in his direction. "Here, take these and get a snack. You can pay me back later."

Clint crossed the floor and met her half way to take the money. "Thanks," he said, flashing the smile that sent a ripple of goose bumps up Toni's spine. "I owe you," he said, adding a wink at the end, which made Toni's knees so weak she didn't dare walk. He went out and closed the door behind him, and Toni turned to the wall of mirrors, wondering why she'd always thought that winks were lame and stupid, only to totally fall for one from him.

Her reflection betrayed the fact that her face had turned bright red, but that could have been as much from an hour of dancing as from the encounter with Clint. She was most conscious of the grin splitting her face. She let out a squeal at the idea that maybe, just maybe, Clint thought her attractive—he at least knew she existed, which was a start. Then she realized that he might still be watching her from the other side of the mirror. Her face fell into what she hoped was a neutral expression as she headed for the sound system, hoping against hope that he hadn't seen her reaction.

She fumbled with her ponytail again, and decided she was too worked up to dance anymore. Might as well put the music away and go home for a shower. But as she unplugged her iPhone from the speakers, the studio door opened again, startling Toni so much that the phone slipped from her hands. She had to do a juggling act to rescue it before it hit the floor. She managed to salvage it and click the screen off before turning to the door, already flushed at the thought that Clint had come back to talk to her again.

It wasn't Clint. Instead, Allen stood there, leaning against the doorjamb. "Your mother just called from the hospital. She wants to you to go down right away."

All thoughts of Clint evaporated, and Toni's heart fell to her stomach. Her phone had been set to her playlists; she hadn't checked her calls, and with the music blaring, she wouldn't have heard them anyway. Then she remembered she'd put the ringer to silent—and mentally kicked herself.

"Did she say anything else?" Toni asked. "Any news on my dad?" She hurriedly packed up her things, throwing on her sweatshirt as she spoke, and then stuffing her ballet slippers and other items into her bag.

Allen shrugged. "Nothing more than to pass on the message that you needed to come to the hospital."

"Thanks," Toni said. She slung her bag over her shoulder, found her car keys in a side pocket, and headed for the door.

"Uh, you might want to put on some shoes," Allen said with a laugh, pointing at her bare feet.

"Oops," she said, cursing her recent forgetfulness as she grabbed her white sneakers and thrust her feet into them. In the summers, she often made the short trek from the studio to her car in the parking lot in bare feet. But in December, with layers of snow and ice? Not the best idea. Shoes on, she hurried toward the door, where Allen stopped her.

"You will be back for the company rehearsal this afternoon, won't you? We've got a performance Wednesday."

Toni tried not to show her frustration. "I'll do my best to be there, but family comes first at times like this. If I can't come, I'll text you, and you guys can change the formations so there isn't a hole." She didn't wait for Allen's response, and instead rushed past him and out to her car, realizing in hindsight that Clint was sitting on a couch in the lobby area as she'd passed.

Toni drove to the hospital, parked, and ran inside. She arrived at the ICU out of breath, confirming before she went in that her father hadn't changed rooms. She forgot at first to ask for Ralph Harper, which was the name on his wristband. He'd had always gone by his middle name, Peter, so Toni found herself flustered for just a second and had to correct herself when she asked whether he'd changed rooms—or maybe whether he was back into surgery or something. He hadn't, which made Toni annoyed with herself for losing valuable minutes.

She hurried through the double doors and down the hallway to her father's room. Her mother saw her coming and met her at the door, closing it behind her. Toni tried to look into the room through the little glass window in the door to check on her dad. There was no team of doctors and nurses working around him. For the small square she could peer through, he looked just as he had the night before.

"What's the matter?" she asked. "Is he worse?"

Her mother smiled with raised eyebrows. "Heavens, no. What gave you that idea? He's sleeping, so I thought I'd talk to you out here."

Toni stammered. "Allen said to come right away. I assumed that meant you had bad news, and—"

"No," she said with a shake of her head. "It's just that Dad's been asking for you. He's a bit drugged up with medications, but every time he starts being himself again, seeing you is the first thing he asks for. I didn't mean to worry you."

Toni glanced over at the closed door. She thought over the past week and wondered if she had done something he could blame the heart attack on. "He asked to see me? Why?"

"I don't have the slightest idea." Her mother shrugged. "He insisted I call you, and I when I got your voice mail, I tried the studio. He just fell asleep, and I'm sure he'll be out for at least a couple of hours. Why don't we go do something while we wait for him to wake up?"

"All right," Toni said, taking one more curious look at the wooden door before going back down the hallway with her mother.

"What would you like to do?" her mom asked. "Are you hungry?"

Toni shook her head. "Not really. Do we have enough time for us to go to my apartment so I can take a shower and make myself look human?"

"I think we can manage that."

As they headed toward the elevators, her mother reached

into her purse and withdrew a snack-size bag of potato chips. "Here. Thought you might like to have an emotional boost. I know I need one, although mine has a different form." Toni took the chips reluctantly, and her mother pulled out a chocolate bar with almonds for herself. "These will keep us going until we get back."

"Thanks," Toni said, but wished her mother hadn't taught her that food was just the thing to make you feel better. Her mother had no problem with eating junk food; she had a turbo-charged metabolism that wouldn't let her gain two pounds if she tried. Toni, on the other hand, loved to indulge, but had to do so carefully; pounds loved to stack up on her hips even with her rigorous physical schedule.

Toni had learned to be constantly aware of what she put in her mouth and how much fat each bite contained. She had entire calorie books memorized; she could spout off the number of fat grams in any store-bought cookie, fast-food chain menu, or bag of potato chips. But at emotional times like this, she often caved anyway.

She'd get rid of the evidence before seeing her father, of course. She'd gotten good at that over the years. If she carelessly left a wrapper out—or even on top of the garbage can—she could be sure to get pointed remarks from him.

This time, she could easily eat the chips without him knowing about it, but she still didn't want to eat them. She shouldn't. Not after the bags and bags of popcorn last night, land not after the breakfast with Carter, even though she'd taken care of both afterward.

The walk to the parking garage felt long, giving Toni plenty of time to think about how she deliberately dressed in loose clothing around her dad so he couldn't tell what her figure really looked like—and then comment on it.

Thanks to her dad, she'd reached the point that any time a man commented on her great body, she immediately wrote him off. If he couldn't see beyond her legs and flat stomach, she wanted nothing to do with him. Which was probably why she was single. No way would she marry another version of her father. Toni had always suspected she had nice eyes, but no man had ever said so. It was always her great figure.

When they reached her car and headed to her apartment, they drove in relative silence, Toni ignoring the bag of chips, and her mother eating her chocolate bar. Toni took the chips with her, just in case she'd want them later. She could eat them in private.

As they entered her apartment, Toni motioned toward the couch. "Make yourself at home," she told her mother. "I'll be just a minute."

Toni headed for the bathroom, where she locked the door and stepped onto the scale. Two pounds up. Probably the popcorn and McDonald's. She knew better than to eat that late, even when she got rid of it. Apparently, she hadn't gotten rid of it soon enough.

In frustration, she stepped off the scale and noticed the unopened potato chip bag where she had tossed it on the counter. She snatched it and emptied it into the toilet, desperate to get rid of the fat-laden crap while she had control. Being presented with food when she wasn't prepared for it sucked.

She gave the toilet a determined flush, and the potato chips disappeared. "I've got to stop doing this," she whispered to herself. "I won't throw up anymore."

But she knew that those two pounds would haunt her until she did something about them. She went back to the scale, this time minus her heavy sweats, and the digital readout displayed a few tenths of a pound lower. At least partially satisfied, Toni brushed her teeth then took a quick shower.

"Feel better?" her mother asked as she emerged wearing her soft bathrobe and a towel turban on her head.

"Much," Toni said. "What time is it?"

"Twelve-thirty. I'll call the hospital to be sure Dad's not up yet, but I'd imagine you have time to get ready." She stood and headed toward Toni's kitchen, which she knew as well as her own. "Want me to fix you anything to eat?" From the fridge, she pulled out bowl of leftover chocolate pudding.

"I'm not hungry. Had a big breakfast." She snagged her water bottle from the counter and filled it up from the fridge's dispenser. "Feel free to eat whatever you find," she added. As if her mother hadn't planned on doing that very thing.

Water bottle in hand—one of her trusty weapons for flushing unwanted pounds—Toni returned to the bathroom. She dried her hair and put on some makeup. She decided to wear on an oversized sweater, one that didn't show her figure. Baggy clothes were best for dealing with her dad; He was less likely to comment on her ribs sticking out or how he shouldn't be able to see her collarbones. After a final once-over in the mirror, Toni came out and announced she was ready.

"Then let's see what Dad wants of you," her mother said, scraping chocolate pudding from the mixing bowl. With the spoon upside down, she licked off the last bit. As she put the spoon and bowl into the dishwasher, Toni smiled, glad her mother had gotten rid of the sugary temptation.

When they got back to the hospital, Toni hesitated going into the hospital room. Dad had been asking for her. What would he say? What would *she* say to *him*? Could she handle seeing him again with all those tubes and wires? Would he have the strength to give one of his patented lectures?

Her mother went in first, opening the door slowly and peeking around it. Toni waited on the other side, biting her lower lip, as her mother disappeared, and the door clicked closed. A few minutes later, the door opened, and her mom came out. "He's awake. Still wants to see you."

Toni nodded, but before she could enter the room, her mother pressed another small bag of chips into her hand. "Here."

Toni smiled at her mother's attempt to calm her nerves and thanked her with a hug. But a fatty snack food would prompt nothing from her dad but snide remarks—and possibly a well-intentioned sermon about heart health based on his own situation. Toni slipped the bag into her purse with the determination to get rid of it at the first opportunity.

She stepped inside. His eyes lit up, and he reached his arms out to her. "Dumpling."

At hearing her old childhood name, a small lump formed in Toni's throat. "Hi, Daddy." The old way of addressing him popped out in reply. She leaned over carefully to avoid pulling on his IV or any monitors and gave him a gentle hug. His once-strong arms could barely squeeze at all, and when Toni pulled back, they fell to his sides.

"You're a bag of bones," he chided her. So much for the sweater as camouflage. "A man wants some meat to hang on to when he gives his woman a hug. You need to put on a little weight."

Toni tried not to get defensive; she'd heard this enough times to let it slide right off her back. "You've always been the one to say I needed to lose my baby fat, or no man would ever look at me."

He waved the idea away. "I never said that," he said, his voice weak and hoarse. He had a healthy growth of stubble, a rare sight. "Just wanted my little girl to be as healthy and pretty as she can be, that's all. To live up to her potential. Besides, you'll have to put on a few pounds if you plan on finding a husband and giving me some more grandchildren. Don't forget, you're not getting any younger, and the number of single men—"

"Is slim pickings at my age," Toni broke in. "Believe me, I know." She looked away to bottle up anger simmering under the surface. At a time he was supposed to be healing from surgery, her father shouldn't be made upset. She sat on the chair beside the bed. For a few minutes she watched the talk show on the wall-mounted television, although the volume had been turned down so far she couldn't hear more than a murmur. Her dad coughed lightly, but even that movement sent spasm of pain through his face. Toni stood, braced to act.

"What should I do? I'll go get Mom."

Before she could race out, Dad took her hand in his and convinced her to sit down again. "I'm fine, dumpling. They say the pain will be with me for a while yet, and there's not a whole lot anyone can do about that."

Toni stood. "Should I ask a nurse to bring some more pain medication?"

He shook his head and put what little pressure he could on her hand to keep her there. "I've got a pump here for that, but I'm not using it much. I don't like the idea of putting junk into my body."

Trust her father to consider pain meds after major surgery *junk*.

She'd been in the room for five minutes but hadn't brought up whatever it was he wanted to talk about. While she didn't relish the idea of putting herself in his sights, she might as well get it over with. "Mom said you wanted to see me."

"Right." He trained his eyes on her. "Come close. Let me look at you."

Great. Another hug, another criticism. *Get it over with.* She leaned close for a hug but stopped her when their faces were about six inches apart.. He gazed into her eyes.

"Huh. Brown." He lowered his hand as if he'd finished whatever he was doing.

Toni sat on the chair again, confused. He wanted to *look* at her? "What was that about?"

He dad's mouth softened into a slight curve. "When I was in recovery, I pictured the family's faces to keep from thinking about the pain. I started with your mother. Then I went on to Kevin, Josh, and Brandon, but I never got to Sam, because I got stuck on you. No matter how hard I tried, I couldn't remember what colors your eyes are. I kept thinking blue or green, but that didn't seem right."

He squeezed her fingers lightly and closed his eyes as he took a long but shallow breath. Toni kept holding his hand as she watched him, unsure what to think about her dad not knowing that she had brown eyes. For someone who made a point of noticing details and commenting on them, that was a pretty big one to miss.

After a few minutes, when she thought he had drifted back to sleep, he opened his eyes and crumpled his eyebrows. "You don't look well. Too pale. Go get some lunch, okay?"

"I'm fine—" Toni began.

"You don't *look* fine," he repeated. "Promise you'll eat lunch."

"Fine. I promise." *I'll eat some celery sticks.*

He nodded and closed his eyes again. Within a few minutes, his breathing had grown deep and even. This time he really was asleep. Toni slipped her hand from his. As she stood, the door opened, and her mother came around the curtain.

One look at her husband, and Toni's mother whispered, "How are we doing?"

"He just fell asleep again." Toni nodded toward the hallway. "Let's get some lunch. I promised him I would, and if you're with me, you can vouch for my doing it if I'm not here when he wakes up."

Her mother chuckled. "Bag of bones?" she whispered. Toni rolled her eyes and nodded as they went out of the room. With the door closed tightly behind them, they headed toward the cafeteria. "Your father's right, you know. You look terrible. Put on at least enough to look like more than a walking skeleton, for heaven's sake. Men don't like women who are too skinny."

"I don't look like a walking skeleton." Toni tried not to grit her teeth. Instead, she clenched her hands, digging her fingernails into her palms.

Her mother shook her head. "*Practically* a skeleton then."

"I'm a dancer. Dancers have to stay trim. I'm on display every day at work and on stage when I perform. I *have* to watch my weight. Have you ever seen a successful dancer who had saddle bags or a gut?"

They entered the cafeteria, and Toni's mother shook her head as if to chase away the subject. "What do you want? My treat."

A quick look at the menu made Toni's stomach growl. Fries and a burger sounded awesome. But her scale's readout flashed in her mind. "A salad. No cheese, no dressing."

"Anything to drink?"

"I've got my water bottle." Toni gestured toward her oversized purse.

"That's it?" Her mother turned around, one hand firmly planted on her hip and one eyebrow arched. "I said, what do you want for lunch? I will not tell your father that you ate if all you're having is plain lettuce."

"Fine. Get me . . ." Toni scanned the menu.

Mom turned and placed their order without waiting for Toni. "She'll have a large crispy chicken salad with ranch dressing, and a large cheese fry."

Toni looked at her with frustration. "Cute, Mom." She tried not to think about the deep-fried chicken and what it would do to her thighs.

"And a large chocolate shake." Patricia looked at her daughter and grinned with a bit of triumph. "What? I know you. If I forced you to add something to your bowl of iceberg lettuce, you'd pick fat-free frozen yogurt or a plain piece of bread. Ridiculous. So I decided for you. And you *will* eat it all, or I'll tell you father that you didn't have any lunch." She lifted her eyebrows in a smug expression and turned to pay the cashier.

It's moments like this I remember why I moved out. The constant focus on food at home had always driven her crazy, which was why, after nine years of living on her own, she still dreaded family get-togethers like Thanksgiving, when everyone would notice how much—or how little—she ate, and she snuck food into her napkin to make everyone think she'd eaten more than she had.

When they sat at a booth with their trays, Toni decided to put a stop to the food issue at least for the moment. She'd eat everything her mother got her—including the chocolate shake and the fried chicken pieces in her salad—and deal with the effects later, in the bathroom.

I'll stop doing that tomorrow. Not now, after a lunch like this.

After lunch, back in her dad's hospital room, they chatted as a family. Every time Toni eyed the door and tried to excuse herself to go to the restroom, her mom pulled her back into the conversation and gave her the look.

It wasn't until her mother took her own trip to the restroom that Toni jetted out and ran down the hall to find a different bathroom. She got rid of at least some of the lunch—whatever hadn't been absorbed into her system.

She wiped her mouth with some toilet paper, flushed, and went to the sink to rinse her mouth. Just as she dug around in her purse for a breath mint, her phone dinged with an incoming text. Carter.

*Up for an art lecture tomorrow @ noon? About Michelangelo. They may show pictures of male nude sculptures. *eyebrow waggle* What do you say?*

She laughed in spite of herself. Toni popped a breath mint into her mouth and replied.

How can I pass up an offer like that? You're on.

As she headed back to her father's room, he texted the address at a university lecture hall. She grimaced; university lectures were often stuffy academic things, not nearly as interesting as, say, some of the docent-led tours they'd taken of museums. But it was a chance to hang out with Carter and relax. She'd take it.

She slipped her phone into her purse and looked up to push open the ICU doors, only to have her mother reach them at almost the same time, coming from the elevators.

Her mother scowled and planted her fist on one hip for the second time that day. "Where were you?"

"Don't worry about it," Toni said, pushing through the doors. "Carter was just asking me to go to an art lecture with him tomorrow." Toni had only slightest pinch of guilt. She'd told *part* of the truth, right?

Yet another thought worried her the moment the words escaped her lips, and she wanted to call them back. Tomorrow was Sunday. Would her mother chide her for not attending services?

Then again, did her parents still go to church every week? She doubted it; her mother still had a cross-stitched scripture hanging in the kitchen, but her Bible no longer sat on the coffee table for regular reading. When Toni had been a little, they used to send her to Bible study groups, but she hadn't gone in she didn't remember how long.

"Have fun at the lecture," her mother said, and walked ahead with brisk steps.

Toni smiled to herself, relieved that there wasn't yet one more thing to stress out about. She could enjoy her time with Carter tomorrow without her mother's disapproval causing any guilt. And Toni fully intended to.

Chapter 9

The lecture on Munch's *The Scream* would start any minute. Carter sat at the back of the lecture hall, saving a spot for Toni. He glanced back at the door again, hoping to see her. A professor began the lecture, some Ph.D. who looked like a walking cliché, complete with glasses he could have stolen from Radar on MASH and a tweed jacket with patched elbows.

Carter had a notebook open to a blank page where he fully intended to take notes, but within five minutes, he was pretty sure he wouldn't be learning much, let alone anything he could pass along to his students. The speaker went on about how the painting showed "universal angst" and "an emotional crisis." It was so general, it may as well have come off of Wikipedia.

Carter used his pencil to doodle on his notebook just as Toni slipped into the room and took the padded theater seat beside him.

"Sorry I'm late," she whispered as she shrugged off her coat.

"You didn't miss much." Carter stopped himself from saying that this lecture was pointless; if the guy turned out to be as long-winded as Carter guessed, he'd get to be with Toni for at least an hour, and maybe they could go out for lunch afterward. He'd even take a boring lecture on The Scream—although how exactly did one make *that* painting boring?—if it meant time with Toni.

For a few minutes, the only sounds besides the lecturer were people shifting in their seats and Carter's pencil on his notepad.

Toni stifled a giggle, making Carter look over. She pointed at his caricature of the speaker and bit her lip to keep from laughing.

His doodle was exaggerated, but it had a certain *je ne sais quoi* that captured the professor, complete with a large bald head, glasses, and mustache that may as well have belonged to a walrus—or at least that guy on *Mythbusters*. He leaned toward Toni.

"Accurate, no?"

"I'd hate to see how you'd interpret me."

"I hope not," he said murmured under his breath. Then, feeling heat rise up his neck, he kept doodling, hoping Toni didn't guess the truth. Sure, she knew he'd used her as a model for his freelance stuff, but she knew nothing about how he'd sketched her off and on for years. How he still had some of those old pictures he drew back in algebra class. No one should know that. It was borderline pathetic—or worse, it sounded creepy, even to him. But he couldn't get himself to throw all the old pictures away. Or stop himself from drawing a new one every so often, like the night he stayed up waiting for her to call.

"Did you say something?" she asked.

"Never mind. Shh." He nodded to the speaker, who was now elaborating on the four versions of the painting and their differences in color. Still nothing Carter was interested in. He'd hoped to hear something about putting emotion onto the page, or at least about the spare strokes used for the man, who was almost skeletal. Or about the perspective, which was so different from the norm.

Toni settled into her seat and seemed to be paying attention. Carter turned the page and scribbled a few notes about the lecture to look like he cared—and to distract himself from the memories of the pictures he'd made. He wasn't *about* to tell her about those.

The first few had been something he'd intended to give her as gifts, but he'd never dared. Since high school, he'd done a few more pieces, some sketches, a few watercolors, all tucked into a big file folder in his office at the high school, with the exception of the large painting on his easel right now.

He no longer pretended to himself that they were gifts. Drawing and painting Toni—almost always in a dance setting—was simply a way of capturing something of her for himself, something no one could take away, not even her.

Each time he worked on the painting with Toni untying her pointe shoes, he wondered what she'd think of it—and of him—if she ever saw it. She never would see it, of course.

The professor droned on, and Carter found himself needing something to distract him from thoughts of Toni and his pictures of her. The lecture certainly wasn't doing that. He reached into his messenger bag and pulled out a two-pack of Snickers. He leaned back in his seat, opened the wrapper, and offered one of the Snickers to Toni. She raised her eyebrows, her mouth pulled down in disgust.

He leaned over to whisper. "What? It's not moldy or anything."

Toni glanced around as if making sure no one was watching or listening then whispered too. "It's also just about the highest-calorie candy bar you can find. No thanks." She sat back and listened to the lecture—or pretended to.

"Hey, it's got peanuts—that's a healthy protein, right?"

She didn't turn her head at that, but she looked at him out of the corner of her eye and then shook her head, muttering something he couldn't make out. She stared straight ahead, arms folded.

On impulse, Carter reached for her wrist and held it up, wrapping his fingers around it. His thumb went to the first joint of her pinkie. "Look at this."

Toni's forehead creased with confusion, and maybe something else—frustration? She yanked on her arm, but he didn't release it. "What are you getting at?" she whispered angrily.

"That a Snickers couldn't hurt. That you could use a few extra calories. I shouldn't be able to wrap my hand around your arm as if it's a twig."

At the look of pain that descended over her face, he let go and tried to backtrack. "I'm sorry. I—"

"You were just trying to be my father." Her whisper sounded

venomous. She glanced warily toward the front of the hall as if she hadn't realized she'd spoken as loud as she did. Two people from three rows up turned around and gave her a look.

She stood, grabbed her coat and purse, and walked out of the hall. Carter eyed the room and the many people looking back at the commotion. He swallowed and ducked out to follow Toni.

He caught up with her halfway down the hall. "Look, I'm really sorry."

Toni didn't say anything, just raised her left eyebrow and hugged herself.

"I didn't mean anything like what your dad says. I just worry. You're getting smaller and smaller. It can't be healthy."

Without a word, she shook her head and stormed down the hall.

"Toni, wait. Please."

Her step slowed then stopped, but she didn't turn around.

Carter jogged to catch up. He went around to face her and tried one more time. "I'm concerned. That's all. I'd like to know that next time there's a wind storm, my best friend isn't going to blow away like Mary Poppins."

Toni cracked half a smile. She let out a deep breath and shook her head. "I'm sorry. I shouldn't have reacted like that."

"Let's get out of here," Carter said, hoping to lighten the mood and change the subject. "That lecture was pointless. I'd rather walk around the museum or get some lunch. You game? My treat. It's the least I can do for putting my foot into my mouth."

She walked forward, hands in her coat pockets. Carter followed, noting how her face was softening.

"Keep it up, and you may have to get your foot surgically removed from your mouth," she said, her smile a bit wider now.

"Up for lunch, then?" Carter asked hopefully.

"Nah. Let's walk through the museum on campus."

"Deal." As they headed toward the exit, Carter opened his notebook and ripped out the scribbles, ready to dump them into a garbage can by some vending machines.

"Oh no, you don't," Toni said, snatching the pages. "These are works of art."

Carter snorted. "Sure. That was totally the right term."

She looked the pictures over and laughed as they headed out the door and down the hall. "I'd like to see you at work sometime. It's one thing to see your students' stuff or some of your paintings on display—"

"Or a bunch of doodles on a notepad."

"Exactly. But it's quite another to see you teaching students how to draw and paint, or to see you behind the easel yourself. I never have seen any of that, you know. Just doodles. I'm keeping these, so you know." Before Carter could protest, she folded them in half and slipped them into her purse, the cavern from which nothing could be rescued.

When they reached the door, Carter held it open for her then followed her out into the wintery afternoon. "Tit for tat. I've never seen you at work in the studio."

"It's not exciting, I swear. Most of it is doing warmups and calling out floor exercises—and then teaching choreography one or two counts at a time. Thrilling." She rolled her eyes as she walked, the snow crunching beneath her feet.

"And somehow, I doubt you'd be impressed seeing me working in a classroom that looks like a cyclone hit it, with loud, obnoxious teenagers and my hands covered in paint."

Toni paused in her step and turned to face him. The cold air made her breath come out in puffs. She took Carter's hand and turned palm down. The top of his hand had flecks of dried in the lines of his skin, under half his fingernails, in the cuticles. It wasn't like he didn't wash up; it was almost like art had claimed him and left a permanent mark. Did she mind that his hands looked like those of a grease monkey?

With one finger, she traced lines on his hand, almost as if she was connecting the dots of paint. At her light touch, Carter's hand felt like it was on fire. He swallowed, hoping she didn't notice his breath hitching.

"I think I could handle seeing your classroom." She smiled and wrapped her hand around his as they headed toward the campus museum.

He squeezed hers, and she squeezed back playfully. He stole a glance at their hands, entwined. Toni had taken *his*. They were walking hand in hand. But she was laughing as she talked—his emotions were so crazy that he couldn't focus on her words. He walked, nodding in and adding *uh-huh* and *yeah* in the right places, but wondering what it would be like to walk like this, hand in hand, and have it *mean* something.

If it did, he'd be able to trail a finger down her cheek, and she'd get goose bumps from *his* touch. He'd lean forward, their faces inches apart, and she'd close the distance.

Then they would kiss.

But all of that was a dream. He cleared his throat as if that might clear his mind.

Their stroll through the museum was quiet, but under the circumstances, quiet was appropriate, so Carter doubted that she'd notice something was off. Normally he loved taking his time at exhibits, stopping before every painting or sculpture, reading the placard and really appreciating what the piece had to offer. She didn't seem to notice that he wasn't doing that today.

On their way back to the parking lot, Carter wondered if it was time to tell Toni how he felt and see what happened.

Way to ruin the best relationship you've ever had.

If and when she didn't feel the same, their friendship would crumble. On the other hand, he'd marked time for years. If he didn't act, he'd be stuck in limbo hell.

She'd joked that at her wedding, Carter would be her "maid" of honor. He still didn't know how he'd be able to stand by and watch her marry someone else. Maybe he'd develop appendicitis on the morning of her wedding and land himself in the hospital.

If something drastic didn't happen, he'd have to show up, giving the bride a hug, wishing her all the happiness in the world. He'd shake the groom's hand and smile, trying not to say anything like, "So help me, if you hurt her, I'll hunt you down."

And then he'd have to walk away. No husband would want another man hanging around. This friendship would end, relatively soon, one way or another.

"Where do you see yourself in ten years?" Toni suddenly asked.

"Hmm," he said, kicking some snow out of the way and then looking at the sky above them to buy time.

Her question wasn't out of the blue; over the years, they'd speculated about the future.

And not once had he been completely honest. At twenty-one he'd said something about studying in Paris and becoming a world-famous artist, while in reality, he didn't care about being famous so much as being able to make a living doing what he loved—making and teaching art.

The truth? He'd pictured himself married to Toni. They'd have two or three miniature versions of themselves running around. Here he was at twenty-eight, not an inch closer to that image than he'd been at twenty-one.

"Where do *you* see yourself in ten years?" he countered, unwilling to be the first to answer this time. But the moment the words left his mouth, he wanted to call them back. Maybe he didn't want to know her dreams, because he probably didn't figure into them.

Toni considered. "I don't know. A few years ago, I would have said I'd like to be part of a professional touring company, but I don't think I'd enjoy that much anymore—traveling all the time, living out of a suitcase, no constants in your life. I'm creating new dreams now."

Against his better judgment, Carter decided to ask the obvious follow-up question. "What are your new dreams?" His heart rate sped up a bit. Toni slipped on some ice, and Carter held on so she wouldn't hit the sidewalk.

"Whoa. Slippery. Thanks."

As they kept walking, Carter wondered if he could let the whole conversation die and pick a new topic—maybe suggest they go to his place and watch an oldie like *Singing in the Rain.*

But apparently Toni had other ideas. "This may sound silly, because it's not where I actually think I'll be in ten years."

"Oh?" Carter kept his voice neutral. At this rate, he'd deserve an Oscar.

"My ultimate dream." Toni squeezed his hand and laughed. "I don't think it'll happen."

"Why wouldn't it happen?" he asked. "What is it? Dancing on Broadway? You could totally do that, you know."

"No." She paused in her step and looked at him. "It's simpler than that." She shrugged and stared off into the distance, over his shoulder, a wistful look on her face. "I'd live in a beautiful house with my adoring husband and children—at least two."

"Two husbands?" Carter asked with a grin.

She elbowed him. "Kids. One of each at least. I'd have my own dance studio in the basement. I'd teach out of it."

They walked a few paces in silence. Her supposedly dream sounded pretty close to his own. "Why is that so unlikely to happen?" he asked, adding a basement studio to his own picture.

Toni shrugged and hunkered further into her coat. When she spoke next, her tone was sarcastic. "Oh, I figure by the time I actually get married, I'll be so old I won't be able to have kids, and my arthritis will be so inflamed I'll be past doing pliés. And that's assuming a hip replacement doesn't do me in first." She tried to laugh, but her voice caught.

Carter noticed the change in tone. He stopped again and turned her to face him. "What?"

Her eyes sparkled with tears. Toni wiped at her cheeks and shook her head. "It's just that the older I get, the more likely it is that I'll never get that dream life. That no man will ever find me desirable. My dad keeps saying I'm too skinny, and that men don't like to hug a bag of bones. When I was a kid, he was always on me to lose weight. But in the last few years, it's both—I'm never in that perfect medium he thinks I should hit. It's always either, 'Toni, you're too fat' or he goes the other way with, 'Toni, you need to eat more.'"

She grunted and walked over to where their cars were parked, two spaces apart, hands in her pockets. "Maybe he's right either way. I'm always too *something*." She viciously kicked some pebbles out of her way as Carter took a couple of quick steps to catch up. "I'm so *sick* of hearing about my body. I've always gotten compliments on it—even from boyfriends." She stopped by her car and leaned against the driver-side door. "I'd give a lot for a man to say my *face* was beautiful. And even more if a guy thought that what I had between my ears is worth something. For someone to care about more than my damn body."

"I care," Carter said softly. He stepped closer and put one hand on her shoulder.

"I know you do." She struggled to smile then stepped into his embrace.

Carter instinctively put his arms around her and tried not to breathe in her perfume too much. *I'm here as a friend, as a comfort. I can't let her down.*

"I wish more guys were like you," Toni mumbled into his shoulder.

I'm right here, Carter thought. *Give me a chance.* He hugged her, noticing how painfully thin she was. *Bag of bones isn't too far off.*

Toni rose onto the tips of her boots and kissed his cheek, then returned to her spot, where she fit perfectly in his arms. His skin warmed to the touch of her lips. It was all he could do not to lift her chin and kiss her lips with his own.

But maybe this was the time to speak up, to let her know how he'd felt all these years. *He* could make her dream come true. He swallowed hard and took a deep breath, but at the last moment, he didn't dare risk losing Toni. He rubbed her back and clamped his mouth shut again.

After a few minutes of sniffling, Toni sighed, letting out her emotion, then pulled back again and gazed at Carter with a look of gratitude.

Not love.

"Now you tell me about *your* ultimate dream. Do you still see yourself as a famous artist living out of a penthouse in Paris? Or is it Rome now?"

Carter couldn't take his eyes from Toni's. He wished she could hear his thoughts, know his feelings. "My dreams aren't too different from yours. I'd love to settle down with a wife, be a dad, have kids." His gazed into her eyes.

Figure it out!

"Hey, here's an idea," Toni said with a laugh. "In another ten years if we're both single, let's get married. What do you say?" She put out her hand as if to seal the deal, but Carter just laughed sardonically. Great. She was making a mockery of the one thing he hoped for.

She lowered her hand. "What, am I that repulsive?"

"Of course not." Carter's mind was spinning. What could he say that was both true and hid the truth at the same time? "I can't see either of us marrying without—" He cut off, but Toni smiled, seeming to know what he meant.

"Without what, romance? Falling madly in love? All that stuff is highly overrated. Trust me, I've been there." She shook her head derisively.

All that stuff was hard to deal with when the object of your feelings didn't return them. He'd been *there*. "Do the math, Toni. In ten years, you'll be thirty-seven. You may not be able to get in two or three kids."

"Then I'll settle for one." She punched his shoulder. "We could even adopt kids to avoid the whole 'we're not in love' issue."

"Oh, right," he said, rolling his eyes.

She raised her eyebrows provocatively. "Fine. We can be married . . . with benefits." She laughed.

His face went hot; he had to turn around so she wouldn't see his reaction. No way did he want her guessing how much he wanted to hold her, wake up beside her—make children together.

He leaned against the car and laughed along. With any luck, it sounded natural. Instead of shaking on the deal or giving her a direct answer, he opened her car door so she could get in. And so he could escape.

She sat down and put her purse on the passenger seat. "Thanks for inviting me."

"You bet. Talk to you later."

Carter watched her drive off. When she waved, he lifted one hand and did the same.

You're killing me, Toni.

Chapter 10

As he got ready for work Monday morning, Carter kept replaying Toni's "brilliant" idea. He made the mistake of pondering it while shaving, which led to three painful nicks.

Why did the thought of Toni joking about their future frustrate him so much?

What if Toni *hadn't* been kidding—that she really wanted a backup plan? Would he have shaken her hand? No. As much as he'd give his right arm to have Toni as his own, one thing mattered more: for Toni to be happy with someone she loved.

He could only hope that he'd be that person.

As he rinsed his razor, the picture of his ideal future came to the foreground of his mind, as it had before. They *could* be happy together. Their dreams and aspirations—not to mention opinions on just about everything—were so compatible. He could almost convince himself they were made for each other. But he didn't want her to settle for him because no one who made her heart flutter had ever proposed.

When he arrived at school twenty minutes later, he locked away his emotions. They didn't belong in the classroom with his Mr. Mackenzie persona. Hiding his feelings wasn't hard; he had plenty of years' experience hiding them from Toni. The skill had simply proved useful as a teacher, too. By the end of the day, when his last student out of the room, he could guarantee nothing, but during school hours he had his problems tightly reined in.

During his AP art class, he wandered through the room, watching over the shoulders of several students as they worked. He had always loved working with AP students; they had the drive and motivation to create art, while by and large, his beginning classes consisted of students who wanted an easy A for an elective requirement.

He walked the aisles between the long rows of tables. These students had talent. In many cases, he'd found it lying under mental dust just waiting to be discovered. He loved finding students with rough potential then watching them blossom as they learned the basics of drawing and moved on to more complicated techniques.

At the end of a row, Darrin asked for help mixing the right shade of brown paint for part of a landscape. Carter reminded Sabrina about keeping her light source and shadows consistent. After moving to the other side of the room, he stopped to look at a drawing that Keri, one of his most frustrated students, was working on. She must have sensed his presence, because she stopped and looked at him over her shoulder.

"Any better?" she asked hesitantly.

How to answer that one? Keri had so much promise, so much skill. Carter had seen that easily two years ago. She'd progressed quickly at first, and now, any time he asked for a simple sketch or doodle, she produced stunning work. But when he requested a more complicated assignment on something specific—say perspective or movement—her hand froze up, and she produced work that looked lifeless and flat, as if a machine had spit it out. Yes, the technical elements were there, but nothing of Keri was.

Carter sighed and grabbed a chair to sit beside her. He eyed the drawing, trying to decide how to help Keri, when nothing else had worked yet.

"It's really bad, isn't it?"

"From a technical standpoint, it's great."

Keri's forehead wrinkled, and her eyes flicked to her sketch.

"It's like you're holding something back, trying so hard to stay within the lines of what's good that you never venture into new territory."

"But aren't we supposed to be learning the rules?"

"Sure, so you know why they exist, and so you can know why and how to break them later. Picasso painted regular human figures before he shattered that mold and did his own thing."

Keri turned back to her sketch pad and bit her lip for a few seconds. "I don't know how."

"Don't be afraid," Carter said. "Really. You know the rules. You've practiced them. Now go break them—or at least bend some a little. Put some of yourself into that." He tapped the page, which bore a drawing of an old women with weathered skin, wrinkles, and a flyaway bun. She held a carpet bag in one arm and an umbrella handle in the other.

She didn't look convinced. "Put myself into it." Her words were part statement, part confusion, and part *are you insane?*

"I want to see some emotion on the paper. Real emotion. *Your* emotion." Carter tried to find a better way of explaining it. Then he realized they'd been talking about it already. "You need to show what's really inside you. That's what being an artist is all about: bringing what's inside you into the open so others can see it."

Keri shook her light-red curls. "That's scary."

Carter laughed. "It can be downright scare-your-pants-off terrifying. But if, deep down, you want to make art . . ." He paused, and she nodded enthusiastically. "Then don't let yourself be afraid of getting your heart stomped on by critics or anyone else. If you truly love and want to create real art, then to keep getting better, you have to be willing to risk."

Carter took off his glasses and leaned a little closer to the drawing to see the details better. "Like with this woman," he said. "Who is she supposed to be? By looking at her, I don't believe she's real, that she has a history or personality. Is she homeless? A mother? What has she gone through?" When Keri opened her mouth to protest, he spoke over her. "We don't need to know, but if *you* do, she'll show up a fully formed and be totally believable."

"Okay," Keri said. "I think I get it."

"Just remember: if you know her, she'll be real to us."

When Keri didn't respond, he looked over at her. She was staring at him.

"Did you hear me?"

"You should totally wear contacts."

"Excuse me?"

Keri laughed. "I'm sorry, Mr. Mackenzie. I've just never seen you without glasses before. Seriously. You look a lot better like that."

Carter coughed awkwardly and replaced his glasses. The clean-up bell rang, saving him further embarrassment. Carter stood up and shoved his chair under the table. "All right, class, clear your work spaces."

T oni slept in Tuesday morning, visited her father then went straight to the studio, where she taught three classes: two Jazz classes and then a beginning adult hip-hop class. The latter consisted mostly of mothers of younger students. She ran through a cool-down with the adult hip-hop class before heading to the sound system in the corner.

"Good job, everyone," she said. "I'll leave some music on for a few minutes for those who want a longer cool-down." The next class in this room wasn't for another fifteen minutes, so she often let her adult students hang around a little longer. For many of the women, it was their one fun night out of the house every week.

Toni snagged her water bottle and the clipboard with the class roll on it and headed to the front desk to turn it in.

"You're really good," Clint said from behind her.

She whirled around. Her eyes darted to the two-way mirror. He'd been watching her class? "Oh, uh, hi," she stammered. "Thanks, Clint." She brushed away some hair that had escaped her ponytail. "It's just a beginning class, mostly with moms who haven't danced before, but I think they have fun with it. Were you—watching long?"

He shrugged and smiled mischievously. "Just the last twenty minutes or so."

So basically, half of the forty-five-minute class. Toni's mind raced through the last half, hoping she hadn't said or done anything embarrassing. She handed the roll to the receptionist then turned back to Clint and took a drink from her water bottle, somehow not knowing what to do next.

Awkward. Better to go back in to her remaining students than stand around looking desperate and tongue-tied. She smiled her goodbye and took a step toward the door, when he spoke.

"Hey, Toni?"

She spun around, her cheeks flaming instantly. He remembered her name? "Yeah?" she said. *Voice sounds natural. Good. But my face must be bright red.*

"You free for dinner tonight? I still owe you for helping me out the other day, remember?"

Toni glanced at the clock, even though she knew full well that on Mondays she taught until seven. "Sure. I mean, now that my classes are over, I'm free." She brushed back more flyaway hair, painfully aware that it had to be straggly and gross from hours of sweat. "Dinner would be a treat. I don't usually get much dinner on weekdays."

"Then it's a date."

A date. Her heart did a little tap dance as Toni grabbed a piece of scratch paper from the desk and scratched her address onto it. "It's pretty easy to find." She handed it over with a promise to be ready by eight.

Clint looked the paper over and tucked it into his jeans pocket. "See you in an hour then." He flashed his knee-buckling grin.

She watched him walk out, butterflies going crazy in her chest. She didn't look away until the darkness outside enveloped him. That's also when she started breathing again. She hurried back to into the hip hop studio, where a student or two still lingered as they tied their street shoes.

"Are you done with the music?" she asked absently, unplugging it before anyone could answer. She threw on her shoes and raced out, figuring that if she hit the traffic lights right, she could make it home in fifteen minutes, leaving her almost forty-five to get ready.

Toni could hardly sit still the whole way home. Maybe it was the dancer in her, but when she felt strong emotions, she had to move. She turned up the radio then used the steering wheel as a drum and bopped to the beat, singing at the top of her lungs to a song that had been in the top ten during her senior year. She felt ready to burst if she couldn't tell someone her great news. When the song ended, she grabbed her phone and called Carter. It went straight the voice mail.

She grunted with frustration, even though this wasn't a surprise. He was probably at the high school. She left as quick message for him to call her back, and hoped he'd notice he had a message before Clint picked her up. Calling him again wouldn't do much good if he had on his headphones; he wouldn't hear it.

Afraid she'd miss him calling back, Toni held her cell in her left hand as she drove. She reached her complex, parked, and had just gotten inside when he called her back.

"Hey, what's up?" he said. "Saw you called. Is something wrong? How's your dad?"

"He's about the same. He's out of ICU. I called about something else."

"It's Monday. I'm guessing you don't need me to fill in as your date on a Monday, do I?"

"No. Actually, that's just it—I've got my own date tonight." Toni squealed despite herself, and her voiced raced on as she kicked off her shoes and headed to her bedroom. She fell onto the bed and grinned as she gave Carter the news. "*Clint* came to the studio tonight—I'm pretty sure he doesn't teach on Mondays—and he waited for my class to be over. Then he asked me out for dinner."

She hopped up and hurried to her closet to pick out just the right outfit. "I can't talk long, because he'll be here at eight, but I had to tell someone who would be as excited as I am." She looked through her hangers, pausing here and there—the green sweater, or the red blouse?—and then laughed. "Hey, if this works out, you're off the hook at forty.

"Great," Carter said. "You'll have to tell me all about it." He sounded a little tired, but that was to be expected on a Monday night after dealing with grouchy teenagers who didn't want their weekend to be over.

"Oh, don't worry; I'll give you every detail." Toni settled on a royal blue top, her most flattering jeans, and ankle boots. As she set the items on her bed, her words started spilling out on top of one another. "I'd have to tell *someone* about it, and who else would care like you do?" She glanced at the clock on her night stand and grimaced. She had thirty-five minutes. "Shoot. I still have to shower before gets here. I'd better go. Talk to you later. Bye."

Chapter 11

The line went dead. Carter sat on his desk and stared at his phone, hating how happy Toni sounded about that Clint guy. "The Smurf's got her," he said under his breath.

He returned to his easel and picked up the brush he had been using on the oil of Toni—tonight he was working on her face, but now he couldn't go on. He sat back on his old stool and stared at the painting, letting the brush in his hand sag between his legs. He'd never get those eyes right. He couldn't capture the spark in them. He hadn't gotten them right on any of his drawings, either. Or the curve of her neck, for that matter. Toni had the most elegant neck. He tossed the brush aside and began to clean up; he wouldn't be able to work anymore tonight.

The next day, Carter dragged through his classes, wanting the school day to be over, but dreading the last bell, because that would mean Toni would call and tell him about her date with Short Romeo. Carter kept using that name when he thought about Clint; since they'd never met, he couldn't come up with anything about Clint that Carter had over him besides height. It didn't matter that Carter himself was a hair under six feet, hardly tall.

"That's the cleanup bell. Get your stations looking good."

In ten minutes, the school day would be over. Maybe he'd

stick around to enter grades or clear out the storage closet that was getting messy. He could stay really late, painting as he had the night before, but he rejected that idea quickly. Working on Toni's face while listening for the phone so she could gush about Clint didn't hold much appeal. And he would listen for the phone, not drown out sounds with his headphones. If Toni needed someone to talk to, he'd be there for her. Even if it meant listening about her rave about the twit.

An hour after school let out, he headed home, stopping off at a drive-thru for a hamburger so he wouldn't have to cook. Most days he didn't mind bachelor cooking, but on days like this, when he felt like he'd be alone forever, he hated making food for no one but himself. So fries and a burger, plus a giant shake, would fit the bill.

Carter couldn't remember Toni's teaching schedule exactly, but knew that on Tuesdays and Thursdays she taught advanced classes, and that those ones often started later than those for younger students. Some nights she finished teaching somewhere around nine or nine thirty. She'd probably call well before those late classes began.

When she didn't call by seven, he stopped watching the clock, figuring she'd be teaching classes then. When the ten o'clock news came on he started to fidget again.

She'll be getting home any time now and she'll call, he thought. His mind went through his options. *She'd feel terrible if I were already in bed and she woke me up, but if I were asleep I wouldn't have to answer the phone and listen about their date for two hours. On the other hand, if I don't answer she'll feel bad, and besides, I'll have to hear the story sometime anyway. It may as well be sooner than later.*

In the end he decided to stay up. But the late talk shows all ended, and the phone remained silent. Had he been awake at midnight, he would have tried calling her to make sure she got home safely, but he had fallen asleep on the couch.

Chapter 12

After Toni's night out with Clint, she fully intended to call Carter and gush all about it, but never did. After a big dinner—one in which Clint said how impressed he was with how much Toni could eat—she had to do damage control in the bathroom. She collapsed in bed and slept till morning.

She didn't call Carter before her evening classes the following day, because she was busy in one of the smaller studio room; Clint was showing her some rumba moves.

And she didn't call after her Tuesday night classes because she and Clint went out for ice cream after work. By the time she got home it was late, and besides, Toni had floated into her apartment in a blissful oblivion beyond a need to talk anything out.

She lay in bed for an hour, half trying to sleep, half replaying her time with Clint and every nuance of the evening, down to the doorstep kiss—short, his lips lingering on hers for just long enough to make Toni want a lot more as he pulled away, grinned, and walked off.

For the next two days, though, she didn't see or hear from him, which nearly drove her crazy. She cleaned her apartment to distract herself, questions flashing through her mind. She scrubbed the toilet. Had Clint decided he didn't want to see her anymore? She wiped down the mirrors. Had she done something to turn him off? She swept and mopped the kitchen floor. Maybe he just had a busy schedule.

As she scrubbed the tile in the bathroom with a toothbrush, she glanced at her cell phone, which was perched on the counter by the sink so she'd be sure to hear it if he called or sent a text.

I have his number. I could call him instead of waiting.

But she shook her head, brushed a stray bit of hair out of her face, and went to task on the tile. Her grout had never been so clean.

No way would she call him; she'd look as desperate to Clint as, well, as she actually she felt.

Her father's condition continued to improve—he had been released the day before—so she didn't even have his health to take over her thoughts or a visit to the hospital to occupy her time. As she rinsed the shower clean, she realized that the only way to have a fighting chance to guess what Clint was thinking was to ask another guy.

Which meant calling Carter. Something she was supposed to do after her first date with Clint. Which she'd forgotten to do the following afternoon. She had Clint's rumba lesson to blame, though. How could a girl be expected to think straight when a hot guy was teaching her how to move her hips just right, and as he led her through the steps, first pushing her away, then pulling her back in, all the while with his eyes locked on hers? No way. Clint was good at the rumba—the dance of love, as he called it. He sure got her heart pounding, and not because of the exercise.

Yet she couldn't get herself to call Carter, not yet. Not this time. Maybe her reluctance had something to do with their agreement about turning 40. Maybe it was just paranoia. Maybe it was Carter's joke about Clint being short. Whatever the reason, she didn't feel comfortable telling Carter about Clint. Yet.

Friday morning Toni came in early to choreograph more of her hip-hop routine and come up with some new practice combinations for her jazz classes. She planned to work in the back studio again, but as she reached for the doorknob, a loud bang and yelling caught her attention from the studio on the other side of the hall.

She peered through the two-way mirror to see Clint stalking around the room, alternately kicking a trash can and pulling his hair. Toni waited for a minute. Should she open the door? Quietly go into the other studio and blare her music so he could have his privacy freaking out over whatever it was?

But Clint started to calm down. His nostrils still flared, but he was no longer kicking the trash can or yelling. When he turned sideways to Toni, staring at the front of the room into mirrored wall as if he could burn holes through it, she ventured to open the door.

"Hey," she said with a broad smile and her best cheerful voice. She immediately regretted it. She hadn't heard from him in days, and the next time she sees him, he's pissed off?

Wise move, she chided herself.

She smiled even bigger. "I didn't expect to see you here this morning."

Clint's eyes darted to the hall and then back to her. "Was I bothering you? I didn't know you were working."

"No, I wasn't—yet."

He didn't seem upset or annoyed by her intrusion, so Toni ventured a single step into the room. "Are you all right?"

Clint laughed to himself. "I guess you heard me, huh?"

Toni nodded with a wan smile. "It was kind of hard not to."

He let out a long breath. "Don't mind me." He raked one hand through his hair again. She had an unruly urge to walk over and smooth it with her fingers. "It's just that after being together for two years, Sharla up and dropped me."

Toni's heart hit her stomach at the mention of another woman. "Sharla?" she asked, hoping her voice sounded totally casual. Maybe she'd misread all of Clint's signals. Maybe this explained why he hadn't called. Their two dates—weren't. And her rumba lesson was just that—nothing but an innocent lesson.

"Sharla's my dance partner. *Was* my partner," Clint corrected himself.

Not a girlfriend, then. Toni's heart began to beat again. "What's wrong with her?"

"She's moving to Oregon next week. Somehow didn't get around to telling me that was a possibility until practice this morning. We were supposed to be getting ready for a competition, but that's obviously not going to happen anymore."

As he went on, and resumed his frantic pacing, anger returned to his face. "She could have at least warned me a few weeks ago so I wouldn't have spent so much time on the routine. Fine, she said that she wasn't sure about it until she got the job offer, but she could have told me she was applying and interviewing. I wouldn't have dished all that money on professional choreography. I spent hours finding just the right music for our solo performances. I swear, I could just—" He kicked not the trash can, but wall and let out a yelp of pain. "Oh, that hurt."

Toni bit her lips together and tried not to laugh, but despite her efforts, a huge smile broke onto her face. She covered her mouth as a giggle escaped. Clint snapped his head in her direction. "I'm sorry," she said. "That was kind of funny. I think the wall won."

Clint's face softened, and his face broke into a smile too. "Go ahead. Laugh. I deserve it." He let out another breath. This time he sounded tired rather than angry.

"What are you going to do?" Toni asked.

He shrugged. "I guess I'll start by writing off the next few competitions. Then I'll tell Gary that we won't be doing the filler number I'd promised for the spring recital. And after that, I guess I'll cross my fingers and hope I can find someone else that I can work well with."

Toni tried to think of something that might make him feel even a little better. "Could I hear some of your music? Were you guys doing all the Latin dances?"

"Yeah. But the rumba's my favorite." He headed for the stereo system and fiddled with his phone player to cue the music. He turned up the volume then turned to her. His eyebrows went up and down suggestively, and he a lowered voice for effect. "Remember, rumba is the dance of *love.*"

The music started, and as if unconscious of his doing it, Clint began marking through dance, leading an imaginary partner through each move. Toni moved back to the mirrored wall to watch. Clint's hand went up, and Toni could tell his partner was supposed to go into a series of turns. Clint looked up, caught her eye, and paused.

"Hey, come over here," he said, waving her his direction.

"Why?" Toni wasn't sure whether to be excited or terrified at the look in Clint's eye. Her heart was beating fast enough it could have been either—or a bit of both.

"Let me walk you through some moves. I don't suppose you brought any heeled shoes with you?" He'd explained last time that even a small heel was better for ballroom dancing, because it forced your weight forward. Even the men used a short heel, although the women typically had four-inch numbers.

"Nope. Sorry. Sneakers it is today. But remember, the only rumba I know is what you taught me the other day—the rumba walk and a couple of basic steps. And I don't know how to follow." Even as she filled her words with caveats, Toni took one tentative step forward and then another, drawn to Clint's outstretched hand.

He took her left hand in his and drew her close, holding her right hand in his left. She gulped, but she also didn't want to pull away from his touch. She could almost feel his breath.

She could almost see over his head, though. *Man, he is short. No fault of his own.* Maybe it was a good thing she didn't have heels on.

"Following is easy," he said. The music was still playing so he moved to it, showing her gently. "Now remember, give me some pressure back. Can you feel the rubber band?" Clint gently pushed her hand away and brought her back.

Last time he'd explained that if there was enough tension between your whole arm and your body, you could feel exactly where you were supposed to go when the man led you around, sort of like a tight rubber band.

He pushed her out and brought her back again. "Good! Better than last time. You reacted just a hair after the fact."

"Okay, I think I remember," Toni said hesitantly.

"Good. Let's try some more moves then." Clint did a quick refresher of through the basic step then moved on to the underarm turn and a few other moves. Then he brought her to one end of the studio, and, standing side by side they did rumba walks across the studio floor, their toes sliding forward, pushing off, hips rolling with each step.

Clint gave her pointers on how to land on a straight leg and release her hip for just the right hip action. To her surprise, Toni wasn't embarrassed at his corrections, instead feeling the familiar thrill of pushing herself to learn new ways of controlling her body and expressing herself.

He went to cue the music again. "Can you believe it's been an hour?" he asked over his shoulder.

Toni looked at her watch. "No way." They'd actually spent well over an hour dancing together. It was closer to an hour and a half since she'd first heard him kicking the garbage can. She turned back to the mirror and did rumba walks. "I had no idea even the simple moves had so much to them."

Clint joined her in doing rumba walks toward the mirror then took her hand and led her into some of the moves they'd gone over. "Ballroom is just like any other kind of dance. There's a whole lot of technique involved. Any dance background makes it easier to do well, of course." He glanced down at her movements. "Your hip action has some real potential."

Coming from anyone else about any other aspect of her dancing, Toni would have considered a comment about "potential" an insult. But from Clint and a comment connected to a brand-new kind of dancing, all she could do was smile. She decided not to think too hard about the fact that he was watching her hips. "You think so?"

He dropped their hands and jogged over to turn off the music. Then he came back over and took her by the hand. "Here, let me teach you the opening combination for the solo I was telling you about." He led her to the center of the floor and turned her around so her back was to him, with both of them facing the mirror.

"Now cross your arms at your waist."

Toni did as she was told. Clint wrapped his arms around her and took her hands. She tried to breathe normally; she had never been so close to Clint, and his cologne affected her so much, she was sure he'd sense her trembling.

"We start like this and hold the first four counts," he said into her ear. Clint leaned slightly to the left, his leg bent as he led her into a turn. "And I bring you around like this."

Now they were doing the basic rumba step. "Away on two, back on three," he continued. He drew her back into dance position. "Draw it to the side, four, five." He stopped. "Got it that far?"

"I think so," Toni said, glancing in the mirror to see how red her cheeks had become. They felt like flames.

"Let's try it from the top and then we'll go on," he said, cuing the music

Toni tried to concentrate on the moves—and block out his cologne. Eventually she managed to focus at least partially on the steps, her hip action, the "rubber band" feel of the push and pull. He taught her another eight counts of the routine, and then another eight.

Soon they moved around the floor in unison in turns and spins and more. With the music, the rumba came alive, and the thrill of dance coursed through Toni. It was as if she'd always been able to dance like this.

"Do you want to go on?" Clint asked, pulling back after they'd reached the end of what she'd learned.

"Definitely."

As Clint went to turn off the music, Toni reviewed the last sequence again, watching herself in the mirror. He returned and stood beside Toni on her left. She held his right hand, in the position they had ended the last combination.

"This next part is tricky at first, but audiences love it," he said. "First I lead you into several turns. Just keep your palm up, and your forearm at a right angle to your upper arm. Don't let it move back like this. And don't forget to spot. When you've crossed me, I take your hand down and lunge over like this. You fall on my arm, arched back. Lean far enough that you can look at the back wall. And don't worry—I will catch you."

"It feels so awkward," Toni said, trying to turn around and around with Clint's hand guiding her. She pulled away and blew out a breath. "Shoot. I've always considered turns one of my strong points, but I've never done them with someone else like this. It confuses my body; I don't know where I'm going."

"All you have to do is concentrate on the form, and I'll lead you where you should go. Want to try it again?"

"Just once more today." Even as she said it, she knew she wouldn't be stopping after one. She'd have to stick around until she nailed the turns. They went over the move—four counts of rapid turns, followed by the backward arch over his arm—several times before it felt right to her.

"Looking good," Clint said after probably the tenth try. "I think you're ready to do it with the music."

"Okay," Toni said, trying to psych herself into it.

As always, the music added a powerful element to the dance. And as Clint and Toni started the routine from the top, a new electricity sprang between them. Toni almost had to catch her breath with she saw the intense look on Clint's face, which bordered on passionate, and she had to remind herself that he was just getting into the dance. He was a ballroom performer, and this was how the rumba was done.

Even so, his eyes sent little thrills through her. When the new combination came, he drew her in, turned her around and around—she spun and spotted perfectly—then fell back on his arm, head thrown back. The whole sequence couldn't have been smoother.

Clint didn't move for several counts, so Toni began to bring her head back up slightly to ask how she did. His face was closer to hers than it had been as they practiced. Much closer. They looked at each other in silence, catching their breath. Clint leaned in, and he brushed her lips with his ever so lightly.

Shivers went through Toni's frame, but Clint pulled back quickly helped her to her feet, shattering the moment. "Sorry. I shouldn't have done that." He headed to turn off the music.

Toni strained to find her voice. "No, Clint, don't apologize."

He'd unplugged his phone. Now he turned around with it in one hand, a smile creeping over his face. "Really?"

Toni didn't manage a word, but she nodded and smiled back. Clint's thumb ran along one side of the player as if he was unsure what to say or do next.

She decided to break the silence. "I suppose that's a long enough lesson for today." She went to the door and picked up her dance bag. As she reached for the door handle, Clint stopped her.

"Toni."

She turned around. "Yeah?"

"Let's do this again sometime."

Toni's face broke into a big smile and nodded before going out and closing the door behind her.

Chapter 13

Three of Toni's four brothers made it into town to visit Dad. He was doing much better, but he was still weak. Her brothers had taken off work and come as fast as they could, thinking that he'd still be in the hospital, which was why Brandon and Josh didn't bring their families but came alone for the emergency visit.

Kevin had come with his wife and baby; he only had a couple of hours to drive. Sam couldn't get away, even though he was the only brother not married. With most of the family in town, and with Brandon leaving soon, the family decided to have a special dinner to celebrate their father's homecoming.

The night before, Toni came home from a date with Clint—and a delicious goodnight kiss. She'd kept her phone on vibrate all night, so it wasn't until she pulled it out of her purse that she found a message from her mother.

"We're eating at five thirty tomorrow," her mother had said. "I figure that's about as early as I can get dinner ready. Would you tell Carter, too? Dad considers him to be part of the family, and he'd love to see him, especially after all he did for us while Dad was in the hospital."

Toni's eyebrows came together. What exactly had Carter done for her family, and why didn't she know about it? The thought sent a stab of guilt through her chest. Carter may have done more for her parents during a hard time than she had.

Falling to Pieces

And I never did call Carter after my first date with Clint. Or the second. Or . . . Shoot. I haven't talked to him in almost a week.

Not since last Sunday's art lecture. That had to be a record for them. She hadn't called Carter, but why hadn't *he* called *her* at some point?

Her mother's message continued. "Josh and Brandon are dying to see Carter too, so be sure to bring him. Love ya tons. I'll see you tomorrow, my Antonia."

At the nickname, Toni shook her head. She glanced at the clock to see whether she should still call Carter tonight to pass on the dinner message. Just past ten thirty. He might be asleep, but he might not be.

As she headed to the bathroom to get ready for bed, she thought again about how odd it was to have gone so long without seeing or at least speaking to Carter. She felt odd about it, yet she couldn't quite put a name to the feeling. Sad? Guilty? Jealous? No, not jealous, unless he had some new girlfriend who would take up all his time and get jealous of Toni, making Carter pull away more. It was bound to happen, and while she'd braced herself for the eventuality, she didn't have to like it.

She put on her favorite pair of pajama pants—pale green and soft—plus a fitted tee. By the time she'd brushed her teeth and flopped onto her back on the bed, she knew the real reason she hadn't talked to Carter in nearly a week: Clint.

And it wasn't only because she'd spent so much time with him.

She turned her head to look at her cell phone, which lay on the bed just out of reach. As much as she had always loved pouring out her heart to Carter about her dates, this time felt different. But why? Did she have stronger feelings for Clint than she typically did for the men she dated? Toni scrunched up her face. No, that wasn't it.

Then what?

She grabbed her phone and went to her favorites list, where Carter was listed first, above her parents and the studio. Her thumb hovered over his name, but she couldn't get herself to tap the screen. Not yet.

And then she realized what she was feeling: dread. The

thought of telling Carter about Clint made her uneasy. How could she tell him about learning the rumba? What about the stolen kiss in the dance studio? Or the ones on her doorstep several times since?

The question of why remained. She'd told Carter those kinds of details before. It wasn't like he was a regular guy. He was her best friend.

Maybe we've grown up. Maybe it was no longer appropriate for a woman to tell her private moments with one man to another.

On the other hand, the feelings Clint evoked were hot—intense. She didn't trust herself to *think* too much about them. No way could she verbalize them.

Her thumb still hovered over Carter's name. *Call him. Just pass along Mom's invitation to dinner tomorrow.*

But she wouldn't be able to keep the conversation to that; she'd have to tell him *something* about Clint, especially after this week of silence. Glancing at the top of her phone screen, she checked the time again. Nearly eleven. Carter had probably gone to bed already.

An idea struck her. She could send him an email and then go right to bed. That way, if he was already asleep, he'd find it first thing in the morning. And if he tried replying right away—even with an instant message—she could pretend she hadn't seen it, because she'd gone straight to bed after sending the email.

She hurriedly ran out to the front room, where her laptop was on the coffee table. She crafted a quick email about dinner.

Hey, long time no talk. Hope you're not sick or anything. My dad's coming home today, so we're having a big dinner at the house. My parents and my brothers all want you to be there. Five thirty. Talk to you later!

Toni clicked send and ran back to her room so she could honestly say she never saw a reply. But when she reached her room, she realized that any email would still come through on her phone. And Carter could text or call. She snatched her cell from where she'd abandoned it on the comforter and set it to do-not-disturb mode so he couldn't get through. In two quick movements, she opened her night stand drawer and put the phone inside.

There. Now I won't know if he tries to reach me tonight.

She stared at her night stand for a few seconds, realizing that she'd become oddly paranoid.

Fine. With another swift move, she opened the drawer and removed the phone. She shut the drawer with her foot and put the phone face-down on top of a book resting on her night stand. Good enough.

After letting out a deep breath, she slipped under her covers and turned out the lamp. Maybe Carter wouldn't show up to dinner after all. If he went on a morning jog and then did something like visit an art museum or another lecture, he might not bother checking his email until it was too late. Carter was the only person of her generation she knew who wasn't so attached to technology that he had to read emails as soon as they arrived.

They both knew that. She cringed, rolling onto her back and groaning as she stared at the ceiling. Carter would *know* that she'd emailed to avoid calling or texting. Plus, her little email ploy didn't fix the fact that she would still have to face Carter enough to tell him about Clint. She closed her eyes, trying to relax, but unable to. After all, she'd have to find a way to talk about kissing Clint.

Hmm. Kissing Clint. She smiled at the memory and breathed deeply, reliving it.

She remembered dancing close to Clint, feeling his heartbeat against her hand when she pushed off his chest. Breathing his scent. Seeing his mesmerizing gaze lock onto hers. The deep beat of the music enhancing the mood, the moves powerful and sensual.

When she fell onto his arm and she looked at him, something flashed, and suddenly it was *Carter's* face inches from hers, heat in his eyes, his lips ready to kiss her.

Her eyes shot open, and she found her heart thumping against her rib cage like a drum. Toni covered her face with both hands. *What* was she thinking? What was *Carter* doing in her half-awake fantasy?

What is wrong with me?

Chapter 14

Toni slept in until after ten—something she rarely did. When she finally got up, she went about her day as she usually did—taking a shower, blow-drying her hair, avoiding the kitchen. She was applying mascara when she realized she'd neglected a key part of her morning ritual: checking email.

Wand shoved back into the tube, she stepped into her bedroom and peered at her cell, still lying face down on her night stand. Still in do-not-disturb mode. It hadn't beeped or dinged all morning. No wonder she'd forgotten about it.

And about Carter. And Clint. And Carter's lips ready to kiss hers.

Shake it off. She couldn't go there, even in her fantasies. Not Carter. He was like a brother, for crying out loud. Besides, she had Clint to give her toe-curling kisses.

Even so, she walked over and picked up her phone, just to see what she'd missed. Twenty-one emails, most of which were probably retailer lists she'd subscribed to. Two texts. A missed call and a voice message.

Biting her lip, she opened the texts first. Both were from Carter.

Thanks for the invite. I'll be there.

The second text gave her heart a twinge.

Going to see the new exhibit at the university museum this AM. I'd love to see you there. If you can, meet me by the gift shop at noon.

Falling to Pieces

Noon. She had plenty of time this morning, and nothing she had to do. But the thought of going to the museum and walking beside Carter when he expected to her to dish—and after she'd had such an embarrassing dream about him—Had it been a dream?—she couldn't go. She wanted to, and normally would. She threw her phone onto the bed and went back to the bathroom to finish her makeup.

Stupid that anything ever had to change. She'd managed to keep her best friend as the one unchangeable for her entire adult life. So much in her life was out of her control, but she had always been able to count on Carter. Why was she being so ridiculous about him now? She couldn't afford to let anything come between them, to let anything change.

She gazed at her reflection. "So go then," she ordered herself. She tucked the mascara tube into her packet bag and put both hands against the counter, trying to feel stronger. "You know you want to. You know you'll regret it if you don't. If nothing has changed, it's no big deal."

She pushed off the counter and straightened, but her shoulders slumped. She would regret not going, because she simply couldn't go and face Carter. Not after a week of silence. Not after last night's "dream." Not with details about Clint and his moves and his cologne and his kisses. She'd see him later today, but it would be at her parents' house, with her brothers there as a buffer. Carter would have no opportunity to ask her to spill about Clint.

Noon rolled around, and Toni knew for certain that Carter was waiting for her by the museum gift shop. Sitting on the front room couch, with her computer on her lap, she eyed her purse hanging on a hook by the door. She could still make it. He'd wait for her to get there late. But then she shook her head. No dice. She grabbed her phone and sent a quick text saying she had to help her parents, so sorry, she wouldn't be there.

As she clicked send, she sighed. *Guess I'd better go help Mom and Dad so I'm not a total liar.* Just half of one.

She arrived at her parents' home around twelve thirty. Dad rested on the old living room couch, which still looked nice despite its age and occasional lump. His face hadn't quite regained its color, and Toni was more aware than ever of the wrinkles along his forehead and framing his mouth like a pair of parentheses, but he appeared to be in good spirits.

"Hey, dumpling," he said, holding out his arms for a hug. "We didn't expect you here for a few more hours yet."

"Hi, Daddy." She couldn't call him "Dad" when he called her "dumpling." She came over and gave him a gentle hug, still afraid of hurting him, then sat on the edge of the couch and took his hand. "I thought Mom could use some help in the kitchen. How are you feeling?"

"A bit better, but that's not saying that much," he said one-shouldered shrug. "I have to take a meal's worth of pills every day. I hate the thought, but they aren't giving me a choice. And they're making me get up to walk around a lot, too—they expect me to be able to walk around the block by next week. After cracking my chest open. Can you believe it?"

"This from the man who used to run three or four marathons a year," Toni said. "You'll get around the block. Think of it as training for a race."

Mom came over from the kitchen, wiping her hands on her apron. She stood at the head of the couch and put a hand on her husband's shoulder. "They say he should be back to normal in a few more months. Good thing he's been such a healthy person, or this would have taken his life." She leaned down and kissed his temple. "Glad you're still here with me."

"Me, too." Her parents smiled at each other. Mom squeezed his hand and headed back to the kitchen. Dad let out a sigh. "I'll be glad when I'm up and around again, and *running* around the block."

"You take it easy," Toni said, realizing that she was practically contradicting her previous words. "Don't push yourself before the doctor says you're ready."

He took her hand between both of his and patted hers. "Don't worry about me. You're the one who needs to be worrying about doctors. You're too skinny. Now go on. Go in the kitchen and eat something. It's hours yet before dinner, and I'm betting you haven't had a bite since you woke up."

Toni pulled her hand back and looked away. She'd eaten today. Or at least, she'd had a drink. But it was a protein shake. Or half of one. Maybe half. Regardless, it wasn't any of his business what she was and wasn't eating. "I'm not hungry."

Her dad looked across the room, over Toni's shoulder, and spoke someone. "You take her in there and make sure she eats something, all right?"

"I'll see what I can do."

Carter. Toni whirled around to see him sitting in one of two red wingback chairs at the other side of the living room. "What are you doing here? I thought you were at the museum."

He grinned. "Thought I'd help out here. Turns out that museums are more fun when you're not alone."

"Oh." Lame answer, and she knew it. He'd seen her dad's surprise at her early arrival. He had to know she'd come here to avoid being alone with him. She'd never had felt awkward around Carter before, and she hated it now.

If she didn't think a real relationship was a possibility with Clint, she should drop him so her friendship with Carter could relax and get back to the way it was before. But as things were, she really liked Clint, and hoped something serious might develop.

She'd had boyfriends before, she'd but had never run into problems about them with Carter. Why now?

Maybe because we're getting older, and it's about time we grew up already and stopped pretending we're still high school buddies?

When neither she nor Carter said anything for a second, her dad chimed in. "Go on, dumpling. Get something in your stomach and then help your mother like you said." He pushed her arm with what little strength he had, urging her off the couch.

Reluctantly, Toni stood and headed for the kitchen. Carter followed. Her throat tightened, and something in her chest twisted. Was she glad he was coming? Or did she dread talking to him?

Find safe territory—some topic besides Clint and our dates from the last week.

They entered the kitchen, where her mother was clanking dishes and joking with Josh and Brandon. She didn't hear Kevin's voice, and hoped he wasn't in there right now—he always cracked the most embarrassing jokes about her and Carter, and that generally set off the other brothers' jokes.

"Hi, guys." Toni waved to her brothers. Brandon and Josh each came over and gave her a big hug, nearly smothering her. They were tall, former football players, and loved making her lose her breath when they hugged her. She wouldn't have been surprised if they tried giving her a noogie with a knuckle to her head.

"How can I help?" she asked.

"Here," her mom said, plopping a bowl of bread dough in front of her. "Punch that down and form the rolls." She crooked a finger at Carter. "Are you here to help? Come over and chop some veggies for the salad." She pointed at a spot on the counter that had three kind of lettuce and a variety of bright-colored vegetables, as well as her mother's famous wooden salad bowl.

Toni went to the kitchen sink to wash her hands before punching down the dough. "Where's Kevin?"

Please let him not be here. I can't take Carter romance jokes.

"Oh, he's around here somewhere," her mother said as she headed out of the kitchen. To get something from the storage room downstairs, no doubt.

Toni was about to turn off the water when a masculine arm reached for the sprayer and turned it on for a second, hitting Toni smack in the face. She gasped and whirled around. "Kevin!"

"Hey, sis." He grinned.

Toni grabbed a dishcloth and wiped her face. "Nice to see you've still got the maturity of a twelve-year-old."

Kevin squeezed the trigger one more time, laughed at Toni's resulting yelp, then turned off the water and leaned against the counter. "Hey, Carter, you got a woman yet? Or are you and my kid sister finally looking for rings?"

Toni groaned. She twirled the dishcloth then smacked Kevin with it. "Not funny." She tossed the dishcloth to the counter. Then, before Carter could say anything, she tried to change the subject before Kevin could get traction with it. "That goatee looks terrible on you, Kev. It's as if some rodent attacked your chin and died there."

"I like it. What do you guys think?" he asked, tilting his head as if posing for a picture as he stroked his whiskers.

"I like it," Josh said. "I'm tempted to grow one myself."

"I'd wear one if Melissa didn't hate them," Brandon added.

It didn't escape Toni that Carter didn't say a word about either the goatee or Kevin's ring remark. Carter kept his eyes down as he intently peeled a cucumber. But Toni's eldest brother wouldn't be dissuaded from his original question. Kevin walked over to Carter and draped an arm around his shoulders.

"What do you think about my beard? I think it makes me look rather distinguished."

Carter laughed with a shake of his head. He picked up a few stray peelings, tossed them into the scraps bowl, and began slicing the cucumber. "Get real. You don't think it makes you look distinguished. That's an old man word. You think it makes you look ten years younger, more virile."

Josh and Brandon burst out in belly laughter and hit the counter with open palms, despite Kevin's looks of warning and the sudden crossing of his arms across his chest.

"Come on," Josh said between breaths. "You know it's true."

Toni went over to the bowl of roll dough and concentrated on punching the lights out of it so she wouldn't laugh—or blush as she hoped Kevin's joke about rings was laid to rest for the day. Somehow it bugged her more today than his snarky remarks usually did. Probably because things were oddly strained between her and Carter right now; they couldn't laugh stuff off together. And possibly because of that stupid agreement about turning forty and getting married.

That would be in twelve years, assuming it was real. But it *wasn't* real—only a joke, right? It still made her feel weird around Carter. She wished she'd never brought it up. Toni hated change, and she'd successfully created just that.

When Josh and Brandon's laughter—and Kevin's threats—died down, they heard their father's voice calling from the living room.

"Hey, boys, come in here for a second."

Carter sliced the last of the cucumber, dumped the pieces into the bowl, and wiped his hands on a dishcloth before heading toward the living room with Toni's brothers.

Toni attuned her ear to the other room, hoping to hear something. All she made out was, "No, Carter, you stay in the kitchen."

A moment later he returned, blushing slightly. Maybe he'd hoped to avoid being alone with Toni. She couldn't blame him. Where was her mother? A trip to the basement never took this long.

Carter resumed his slicing in silence. After a moment, Toni continued forming dinner rolls. She concentrated spraying a cookie sheet with nonstick spray and them forming the rolls, as if it were as complicated as taking the SAT. Stupid how much she dreaded being alone with Carter today. Or, more specifically, of Carter bringing up Clint and having to dish.

She decided to break the silence with her own choice of topic. Kevin's immaturity would do. "You'd think that after all this time, they'd stop hoping sparks will fly if they leave us alone," she said with a forced laugh, avoiding Carter's eyes.

Carter finished tossing the salad. He rested the salad's wooden spoon and fork on top then leaned against the sink, not saying a word. The two of them stood there in awkward silence, made worse by the fact that the only coming from the living room was whispers.

"So," Toni said, trying her best to keep her voice light. "What have you been up to the past week?"

Crap. Now he'll ask what I did this week. Smooth move.

"Oh, nothing too interesting," Carter said, adjusting the angle that the salad's utensils sat in the bowl—and clearly avoiding Toni's eyes. "Work was typical. Took on a new freelance client. Did a little work on a new painting."

"What's it of?" Toni asked, grasping at a conversation topic.

Carter smiled suddenly, as if he was somehow relieved. "A landscape. I took some pictures of the Seattle skyline at sunset when I visited a few years ago, and now I'm working on a piece based on them."

"Your work is great no matter what," Toni said. "But I have to admit, I've always loved your portraits better than anything else." She draped a cloth over the rolls so they wouldn't dry out as they rose.

"Portraits, huh? I haven't done that many good ones. They aren't my forte, really." He eyes sketched toward her and then away again. He seemed to be looking around for something else to do, anything but look right at Toni for any significant length.

Why was Carter acting so weird? Toni chewed her lip in thought as she covered the second sheet of rolls with another cloth. It was almost as if he was embarrassed about his art, which was a ridiculous thought. He was excellent, and he knew it. He'd never been shy about letting her see his latest works in progress or even some of the logos and mascots he'd created for corporate clients. Was he somehow losing confidence in his abilities?

Toni grabbed the empty dough bowl and took it to the sink, close to where Carter stood. He took a step away, even though he hadn't been in her way to begin with.

Ordering herself not to over think things—but hating how awkward things felt with her best friend—she cleared her throat. "Remember the old fisherman?" she asked, putting the bowl in the sink and rinsing it. "That's one of my favorite—pencil, wasn't it? And he was so real—the leathery skin, the wrinkles, the—"

"Tell me about Clint," Carter said suddenly. He turned to her, bracing himself against the counter as if he dreaded hearing a word. If so, why did he ask? But then, why would he dread it?

"Well, let's see," Toni said, deciding where to start—and where to stop. She grabbed the same dishtowel she'd whipped Kevin with and twisted it in her hands. She couldn't exactly tell Carter that Clint awakened passions inside her that she hadn't known existed, that kissing him was so much like something out of a movie that she could practically hear the background music. For one thing, her mother and brothers could return any second, and for another . . . well, things had changed.

She shrugged. "He took me out to dinner after classes one night. That was fun. But you knew about that beforehand." She turned to smooth the towel over the rim of the sink.

"Where did you go?" As always, Carter asked the "right" questions. But if she didn't find a way to cut him off, he'd ask questions that *used* to be right but that today would feel so, so wrong.

"Oh, just for pizza." She set to hand washing the few dishes in the sink. "The next afternoon I met him at the studio, and he taught me a little of the rumba. I learned some of his competition routine too. Now that is a fun dance." Dance. That was a safe topic.

"Anything else?"

Usually Carter asked about hand-holding and kissing and especially the doorstep moment. This time the exact words weren't there, but she knew what he meant. No *way* would she discuss making out with Clint. Not here, not with Carter. Maybe that was a sign that her best friend situation was gradually changing in the healthy way her mother had always warned her it might.

You two will gradually drift apart, sharing less and less, especially when one of you finds that special someone.

Had Toni found her special someone? Maybe that was why she didn't feel comfortable talking to Carter about kissing Clint. "Let's see . . . anything else . . . well, we've been out a few more times since." She shrugged and turned off the water. "We'll have to see where it goes."

Toni picked up the towel and began wiping a pot dry. Carter raised an eyebrow, expectantly, as if she was supposed to go on. She swallowed and ignored the look. Sure, she usually did go on for a lot longer than this, and in excruciating detail. What her date had said or did, how she reacted to it, or what she hoped or worried about the relationship. At the very least, Toni usually asked questions about what Carter thought a guy must be thinking, what he might have meant by saying or doing this or that.

As Toni set the pot aside, she hoped that Carter would assume that Clint meant nothing to her, but she had a feeling that the flush on her cheeks betrayed her, saying otherwise. They both knew she'd left out a lot—she'd been vague at best. He had to wonder why. Well, let him.

"He kissed you, didn't he?" Carter said, clearly trying to sound playful.

Toni's cheeks flamed. Her mind raced, but she couldn't come up with anything to say besides, "Yeah, he did." She crossed to the salad bowl and began tossing the salad within an inch of its life. She simply wanted to stop talking about Clint. Anything to get that look off Carter's face.

"So, have *you* gone any dates recently?" she said, sprinkling croutons over the salad.

"No. But my mom's trying to set me up with a girl who moved into their neighborhood. She introduced us today."

"And?"

He shrugged. "Neither of us likes the idea of blind dates, but we agreed to go out once to keep the peace with our mothers."

Toni carried the salad to the table, even though dinner was still at least half an hour away. "What's she like?"

Carter poured some croutons into his palm from the box had set down. "I only saw her for a few minutes, but she seems nice enough. She's about your height, sandy blonde hair. Elementary school teacher. We're going out on Friday." He popped a crouton into his mouth.

"You'll have to tell me all about your date," Toni said, vaguely aware of echoing what Carter had said to her about Clint.

Several minutes more of whispering coming from the living room—during which time it became clear that Toni's mother had gone in to talk with the boys. That could mean only one thing: that Toni and Carter were right in assuming her parents were trying to give them some alone time.

Only after Toni baked the rolls did they all return to the kitchen to eat. They all sat at the table, which was extended with two leaves, and dinner was served. As the food was passed around, Toni put a small dab of mashed potatoes on her plate then passed the dish to Carter, who sat at her right.

"Oh come on, you can eat more than that," he said, plopping a huge fluffy mass onto her plate. Toni laughed, grabbed her spoon, and scooped some up to aim for Carter's plate. He was too quick for her, though. He picked up his plate, and the potatoes landed on the table cloth with a splat. With a smug look,

Carter took the serving spoon and added another big pile onto her plate before passing the serving bowl to Josh. "And you *will* eat it all," he said, his voice taking on a more serious tone. "You need it."

Toni clenched her jaw, her expression stony. Carter, too? How *dare* he?

Carter coughed and hunched into his chair, suddenly looked like he regretted saying anything.

Good.

Toni took her spoon and deliberately shoveled all of her mashed potatoes onto his plate. When nothing of remained on hers but white streaks, she glared at him. "Don't you *dare* tell me what or how much to eat."

"Already fighting like an old married couple," Kevin said with a smirk.

"Get off my back," she shot back. "My life is none of your business."

Her dad broke in, interrupting the argument. "Now, now. Sweetheart, no one's trying to put their noses into your business."

She folded her arms and rolled her eyes. *Sure they aren't.*

"But Carter's right," he went on. "You're too thin. You don't look well."

Toni had had enough. She pushed her chair back and stood. "Let me guess what comes next. I'm a bag of bones, right? I am *sick* of hearing, 'Toni's weight this' and, 'Toni's weight that.' It's no one's business but mine what I weigh or what I eat. So back off already. I'm not some fat thirteen-year-old girl anymore. You should at least be happy about *that*."

She stormed away from the table, grabbed her purse, and left the house, slamming the door behind her.

Chapter 15

On Monday as Carter taught his classes, he couldn't dismiss thoughts of the walls of the Harper house shaking as Toni slammed the door behind her. But even if his thoughts stayed on Toni, he buried his emotions in front of his students, as he always did. Lately, however, leaving his feelings at the classroom door had gotten much harder. The stress had him snapping at his students more than once.

He kept replaying Sunday's dinner over and over—while he demonstrated perspective to his beginning class, as he demonstrated a coil pot to his ceramics class, and as his AP Art students worked silently on their portfolios. Through all of it, he wondered what he could have done—or should have done—differently.

When lunch came after third period, he snagged Janet Miller, the health teacher, in the faculty lounge. A few weeks ago, he'd seen her putting together a PowerPoint about eating disorders. The bullets listing common behaviors and warning signs had lodged themselves in his brain. It was why he'd listened for sounds in the restaurant's bathroom when he'd taken Toni out for breakfast. Why he'd tried to encourage her to eat the damned mashed potatoes.

Janet sat at her usual table, laptop open as she forked mouthfuls of a salad into her mouth. After Carter warmed up his lunch—a frozen dinner that had been on sale—he pulled up a chair at the same table. Janet glanced over and smiled before going back to her lunch.

"So," Carter said, hoping to start up a conversation. He felt suddenly awkward. "How did your lesson on eating disorders go the other day?"

She tilted her head back and forth. "Pretty well, I guess. I worry that the kids who really need to hear the stuff aren't the ones who listen to it, you know?"

"Yeah, I bet." Carter peeled the plastic cover off the tray. The smell turned his stomach. Or maybe it was less the smell and more the idea of what he was about to ask. He suspected Toni had a problem. Now he'd be getting validation—or not—for his concerns. And then what?

"If I learned about that in high school, I was probably one of the ones who didn't really get it."

Janet nodded and closed her laptop, turning in her seat to face him. "It's easy to ignore the whole topic if it doesn't affect you or someone you care about. Actually, it's easy to ignore if you're the exact person who should be listening. That's what makes this unit so hard to teach."

Carter pushed his lunch aside and leaned forward. "I didn't see a whole lot of the PowerPoint, but now I'm curious. What if a woman—an adult, not a teenager—shows signs of an eating disorder?"

"It's a dangerous condition no matter who has it," Janet said. "It's becoming more prevalent in middle-aged women as they get older and panic over changing metabolisms and body shape. We live in a sick society. Eating disorders can hit anyone—men, too—at any age."

She took another bite of salad and chewed away as Carter thought about her words. What if Toni had been suffering with an eating disorder since high school—and he'd been blind to it all these years? He could be reading more into things than there was.

"I'm probably overreacting, but I have to ask—I don't suppose it's a real concern when a friend eats a big meal and then happens to go to the bathroom to throw it up, right?"

One of Janet's eyebrows went up. "Unless your friend has the flu or is pregnant, I'd say that's a problem."

For a split second, Carter considered whether Toni could be sick. She looked a bit tired at times, especially while her dad was in the hospital, but who wouldn't under the circumstances? The second option ran through his mind. Could she be pregnant?

Is that why she's been acting so off? No way. That's not Toni, and you know it.

"She probably does have a problem." He said with resignation as he swore silently.

"I'm so sorry." Janet smiled her sympathy.

"Thanks." Carter had lost any appetite. He picked up the tray and tossed it into a garbage can.

On his way back to his classroom, he pulled out his phone and considered calling Toni right then—he wanted to confront her about purging and who knew what else she was doing. But then he thought better of it. The next time they talked, it couldn't be about food, not after she'd stormed out over mashed potatoes. If he called now, she'd never talk to him again. The cell went right back into his jeans pocket.

He spent the rest of the lunch period sitting at his desk, doodling on scratch paper to get rid of his restless energy.

The last period of the day felt like it went on forever. Carter spent little time lecturing. He went over upcoming assignments and answered a few questions, then got the class to work. Thank heavens they were more advanced students who took the class seriously and could work for the whole period without causing trouble.

Carter walked up and down the aisles between tables as he usually did, but instead of checking to see if anyone needed help, or commenting on students' progress, he wandered aimlessly. His emotions had come straight across the threshold and were swirling inside his chest.

He *knew* that Toni had an eating disorder. He'd heard her purge; she probably binged, too. He'd been there when she refused to eat, meal after meal. Sunday was just one example of many. But now that he thought back, he could identify many other times she'd made excuses for either not eating at all or for going to the bathroom after eating, always with some ready story to explain it all. She wasn't sick, but she was thinner than she used to be. What if she wasted away, and he lost her altogether?

And why hadn't he seen it before? Could he have helped her, stopped this whole thing, years ago?

How could he help her now? His first thought was to strap her down and force a hamburger down her throat.

Food issues aside, what if he'd told her years ago how he felt? Would they be married today? Would she have the same problem, or would he have been able to love her through it, helping her get over whatever it was that drove her to bulimia? What if, whatever it was, never would have happened if he'd just spoken up and gotten a ring on her finger?

What if he'd spoken up years ago and lost his best friend?

He blew out a sigh and shook his head. Too many factors. Too many unknowns.

"Hey, Mr. Mackenzie, are you all right?" Keri called as he passed behind her.

He paused in his step. "Need some help?"

"You tell me." She sat back and looked at her drawing critically. She snapped some gum then looked sheepish; gum wasn't allowed in class. Keri cleared her throat. "Is this one any better?" She'd scrapped her first attempt at the portrait of the middle-aged woman. This drawing looked entirely different—in a good way.

The woman no longer looked like a mannequin. She had life—pain mingled with joy in her face, especially around the eyes. He sensed a smile hovering beneath the surface, not quite there. Carter pulled back in surprise. "Wow. This both is and isn't the same woman you drew before. Where did she come from?"

Keri shrugged, but she was obviously pleased, biting her lower lip as if to hide a grin. She flipped her hair over her shoulder. "Just took your advice. You told me to put some of myself into it, go out on a limb and risk something."

Carter took off his glasses to get a better look at the wisps in the woman's hair. Keri had made fine pencil lines around the woman's eyes that would become deep wrinkles in years to come.

The woman looked so lifelike that one had to believe she really would age.

Keri laughed. "It scared me to death, but it worked, I think. I took a risk."

"This piece needs to go into your portfolio." Carter his glasses back on and stood back to look at the whole picture.

"How did you know that's what I needed?" Keri asked. "When did you first risk something big?"

Her comment couldn't have been more perfect had she known his thoughts about telling Toni his real feelings. He hadn't taken that one big risk. He'd never dared. "I, well . . . no. I guess not." *His* art had never felt like a risk. He'd read about the risk theory and knew teachers who'd used it and found it successful. It worked for many blocked students. But suddenly he felt like a fraud.

Keri leaned back in her chair. "It's a great feeling, you know? Risking something. It's a rush. My mom used to always say that if you don't try, you've already failed, and now I know what she meant." She screwed her eyes up and leaned toward him. "You should totally take a risk. It's awesome."

Carter coughed to clear a knot forming in his throat, turning it into a laugh that sounded forced to his ear. "Get back to your work, Miss Harris." He walked away before Keri could say more, but her challenge rang in his ears.

If he never risked his friendship with Toni by confessing his real hopes, would he ever get what he really wanted out of that relationship? Out of *life*? How much longer could he stand around, waiting for her to come to her senses? Would taking the risk of telling be worth the possible result?

The bell rang, and students ran around like energetic puppies as they cleaned up and grabbed book bags.

"See you tomorrow," Carter called as they filed out the door.

He sat on the edge of one of the tables and thought about Keri's challenge. She almost surely meant something related to art, but he knew his great risk wouldn't have anything to do with pencils or oils.

It meant of finally taking that big step. It could work; Toni and Clint hadn't been going out that long. Maybe he wasn't competition yet. Except that Clint was, in her words, "hot."

Carter could wait for their relationship to end. *What if it doesn't?*

He needed to act, and the sooner the better. If he waited much longer, if she and Clint got serious, Carter might be too late. He could lose Toni forever.

I may lose her if I tell her how I feel. But I'll lose her to some man if I don't.

He made up his mind. He didn't know exactly how or when, but he'd tell Toni that he loved her—and not like a best friend.

Chapter 16

It was Wednesday, and Carter was coming out of a florist's shop with a bouquet of peach roses—Toni's favorite. He got in his car, setting the flowers on the passenger seat, then sat there, not starting the car, trying not to throw up.

Since Keri's challenge and his decision, he'd waited a couple of days before pulling the trigger. He'd sent Toni a few friendly texts and left some voice messages. Apologized for the mashed potatoes incident. Sent her a picture of a caricature of himself one of his students had drawn.

Today was the day. He figured she'd forgiven him and softened up a bit. He'd stayed after school to help some students with their projects. Then, after getting something to eat—mostly so he wouldn't pass out from nervous energy—he went to the flower shop. By that point the sun had set and the darkness of winter had fallen thickly.

Now he sat in his car, too nervous to think clearly. He finally managed to get himself to turn the key and drove, meandering, through the dark city streets. Eventually he found his way to the dance studio, but he passed it three times, waiting for Toni's classes to end. He couldn't get himself to go home or do anything else.

He'd practiced aloud, trying different ways of telling Toni he loved her. Asking her out on a date wouldn't be enough. They'd gone on several official dates through high school and college;

that wouldn't get the message across.

He ran through the options of how to tell her he loved her. He considered going with the direct method: handing over the flowers with a card that said, *I love you.* After she read it, he'd go into his speech. Or maybe it would be best to talk to Toni about their years of friendship and work up to the big revelation. The falling snow turned into a slushy rain as the clock on the dash changed to seven. She'd be heading home soon if he didn't hurry.

Or going out with Clint.

No, not Clint. Toni hadn't dished about goodnight kisses and dreamy eyes. Maybe the hot Clint hadn't measured up while on a real date. Carter could hope.

He let himself pull into the parking lot, but purposely parked away from the studio windows so she wouldn't see his car right way. He didn't want to be noticed, not yet. When he decided to be seen, on his terms. As he took the key out of the ignition, his mind went blank. Two hours of speech planning, gone in a heartbeat.

What would he say? Could he really march in there and declare his love? What about all of the people in the studio? Could he sneak her to a quiet, private area?

And how would Toni respond? Whether it was to turn him down or to confess the same feeling, his life was about to be changed forever.

He sat in the car with his head against the headrest, staring at the fuzz on the car roof. What could he possibly say to the woman he had loved for as long as he had known the meaning of the word? Instead of rehearsing speeches again, he whispered under his breath.

"Here goes nothing," he said, even though *everything* hinged on this moment.

*

After Toni's classes ended and her students had dispersed, Clint came into the studio room she was teaching in. Toni was turning off the sound system when he came up. She saw him in the mirror just as he wrapped his arms around her and greeted her with a light kiss.

"Looking good," he said. "I love watching you dance."

Toni turned to face him and wrapped her arms around him too. "And I love dancing with you," she said with a smile, then planted a quick kiss on him. Nothing too heavy in public.

"So, you done for the night?" Clint asked, watching the last of her students head out.

"All done," Toni said. She slipped her shoes on and put her bag over her shoulder. "Did you have something in mind?"

Clint gestured to the bench by the door. A box sat on top of it. "Look in there."

Toni gave him a suspicious look but retrieved the box. "What is this?" she asked, sitting on the bench and holding the box out.

"Open it and see." He sat beside her and waited for her to open it.

Toni took the top off and looked inside. She lifted a sheet of tissue paper. Inside the box lay a pair of silver Latin ballroom shoes with a line of rhinestones up the front strap. Her eyes grew wide. They were her size. And extremely expensive. "Clint, I can't accept—"

"Yes, you can." Clint took the shoes out of the box and handing them to her by the straps. "Try them on."

"These must have cost—"

Clint just shook his head and pushed the shoes into her hands. "Take them. You'll need something to wear if we're going to keep dancing together. Try them on."

Toni acquiesced, feeling a thrill of excitement as she removed her sneaker to put them on.

"Since you're free now . . ." Clint waved his smart phone as he headed to the sound system. "I was just wondering if you'd like to rumba for a while." His eyebrows went up and down suggestively.

"Sure." Toni finished buckling the shoes; he cued the music.

"You've learned most of the routine Sharla and I were doing. I thought maybe we could tell Allen that he'll have the number for the recital after all. What do you say?" He held out his hand so they could take the floor.

Toni's eyebrows shot up, and her hand froze on the buckle. "You want me to rumba in front of all my students' parents?"

"You make your students perform out there."

Toni began to protest. "Well sure, and I perform too, all the time, but only with material I'm not a beginner at."

With both shoes on, she stood and looked at herself in the mirror. She liked the way the shoes made her look and feel—taller, sexier, *thinner*.

But perform the rumba? "I don't know. The recital is only a few weeks away. I hardly know anything about the rumba." Even so, she found herself trying out the basic step to see how it felt with the right shoes.

"Oh, come on," Clint said, coming close and taking her into dance position. He led her through several moves. "You already know most of the routine. Your hip action is getting really good, and I think by putting in a little extra time, we could, you know, make a pretty good couple."

He smiled knowingly at that, as if he meant that they'd be good as a couple in more ways than dancing. That smile was enough to melt a polar ice cap. Toni tried to catch her breath. Clint released her hand and did rumba walks, watching himself in the mirrored wall. "But if you really don't want to, then I won't pressure—"

Toni jumped in. "I didn't say no. How about if we tell Allen that we'll *try* to put something together, and we'll let him know for sure in a few weeks? That way, if I don't feel comfortable performing, I can pull out and not make a fool out of both of us." Toni felt a rush of excitement mixed with nervousness at the thought of performing a ballroom routine with Clint, and she knew her face showed it. She couldn't stop grinning.

Clint returned the smile. He walked over to the door, kicked it closed, and turned off the overhead lights. Only the glow from the outside street lamps washed across the floor. They were alone, and the studio suddenly seemed quiet, romantic, and secluded.

"Come here," he said, holding out his arms. "You look like a scared little girl. Maybe I can chase away your fears."

She stepped closer, intending to settle into dance position, but instead, Clint put his arms around her, sending the now familiar jolt of excitement through her. With Toni wearing four-inch heels, he seemed shorter, but a glance at the mirror showed that even with the heels, she wasn't *quite* taller than him. They were about the same height.

He brushed away a stray piece of hair from her face and leaned close. He gave her first a soft kiss, then another, stronger kiss, which sent warm tingles through her entire body. He finally pulled away, nearly taking her breath with him.

"You have no idea what you do to me," she said a little shakily. She hadn't been kissed her so passionately in . . . probably ever.

"I'll take that as a compliment." Clint leaned in and reached for the side of her face for one more kiss.

Chapter 17

Carter stood in the parking lot, watching through the floor-to-ceiling glass windows of the studio, his glasses spattered with rain and blurring his vision. The bouquet hung limply from one hand and his car keys from the other.

He assumed he was hidden by the shadows of the other cars, but if not, it wasn't as if Toni would see him there. She was very much occupied with a dark-haired man kissing her. Of course she'd kissed men before; he knew that better than almost anyone. But seeing it—worse, seeing her respond to it—sucked the air right out of his lungs.

That was Clint. And this was most certainly nowhere near their first kiss.

One week. He moves fast.

Carter tried to turn away, but the image of Toni running her fingers through Clint's hair, of Clint holding her, moving his hands lower than he should

This may as well have been a train wreck; he couldn't look away. His throat grew hot and tight, and his heart pounded in his chest.

Of course she and Clint were an item. Of course she didn't care for Carter like *that*.

Did she even *remember* that he was a man? Maybe she thought he was gay—since he was an artsy, tidy type.

They broke off the kiss, and Carter managed to suck in air. It was over. But no. Clint merely stroked her cheek with his thumb as Toni gazed into his eyes with longing.

No more.

Somehow Carter managed to take a step backward, toward his car, and then another. Not until he unlocked the door and opened it did he realize that the bouquet had slipped through his fingers and landed in a puddle.

With waves of emotion crashing over him, Carter got into the car and looked at the steering wheel to finally break eye contact with the make-out session he'd stumbled upon. His breath came hard and fast.

And here he'd thought he'd dealt with the idea of Clint, tucking it into a neat package and locking it away as he had always done with Toni's other boyfriends.

Too bad he'd discounted how far their fledgling relationship could have progressed in such a short time. He hadn't prepared himself for the sight of Toni melting in Clint's arms. Every nerve ending in his body flamed with pain. He could only imagine what it would be like for Toni to want him that way. To run her fingers through his hair. To gaze at him the way she'd looked at Clint in that brief moment between kisses, before they plunged back in for more.

Many times, Carter had imagined what Toni looked like when she felt drawn to a man. He'd painted his image of it many times. But in those pictures, *he* had been the one she was looking at. He'd always thought her eyes were never quite right in his pictures. Now he knew for certain, because he'd seen the look.

It just hadn't been directed at him.

And therein lay the rub.

Carter put the key into the ignition but made the mistake of looking up again. He couldn't help it; his eyes were drawn to the windows like a light in the darkness. Clint separated from Toni, this time, apparently for good. Their fingers lingered as he walked away. No, not away. To start some music.

I can't watch this. I can't.

And yet Carter did. He couldn't look away as the two began to dance what he could only assume was the rumba routine Toni had mentioned. The warmth in the car had fogged up his glasses. He could hardly see, but even without clouded lenses, his vision would have been blurred by his tears. He could see enough to feel like he was bleeding inside: two bodies moving together in passionate, fluid movements.

With a quick swipe, Carter took off his glasses and wiped them clean. He had to leave. No more torturing himself. He turned the key and drove out of the parking lot, nearly sliding into a passing car as he pulled onto the road.

He found what little refuge he could by driving as fast as he could through the wet and dark city streets until he reached the high school. Time for some painting. Not of Toni. Something crazy and wild and illogical, with clashing colors.

Something to get the emotion out before it ate him from the inside out like acid.

Chapter 18

Carter painted until late into the night, going home for a couple of hours so he could take a shower and get something to eat. He went through the school day on Thursday like a zombie. His eyes were bloodshot, his thinking muddled.

When fourth period rolled around, he was grateful that he didn't have Keri in class until the following day. No way could he face her the day after he'd tried to take up her on her challenge. He stumbled home, managing to respond to a couple of Toni's texts with one-word replies.

Friday was much the same, except that Carter spent most of the night at home drawing on his tablet instead of painting frenetically in the art room.

Every time his phone vibrated in his shirt pocket, he tensed, wondering if it was a text from Toni. When school got out, he checked his phone. Sure enough, Toni had sent several texts. The last twisted the knife already in his gut.

Hot date with Clint tonight. Wish me luck!

Somehow his thumb typed out a single word: *Luck!* And then he sent it. Good thing texts didn't include vocal tone. Or what he looked like.

As he headed home from work, he found himself dreading the prospect of spending Friday night alone—as he would until

Toni and Clint broke up. If they ever did. It wasn't until he pulled into a spot in the four-plex parking lot that he remembered.

It was Friday. His mother had arranged that blind date. *For tonight.*

After the debacle of Wednesday night, he'd totally forgotten about it. He had no desire to even go on a date with some stranger, but he figured it would be better than sitting home alone, doodling on his tablet for the second night in a row.

I need to call my guy friends and hang out with them. Do manly stuff.

Except that they were all married with kids. Most had moved far away for school or work. The two who lived close by were almost certainly having their own date nights with their wives.

And he had a blind date tonight, set up by his mother.

I'm such a loser. He got out the car and trudged up the single flight of stairs to his apartment. He'd rather go to an action movie—alone—than on a date, but he knew that the next time he visited his parents, he'd never hear the end of it from his mother.

She could have been your soulmate, she say. *How could you not go out with her?*

Might as well go and get it over with. He'd pick up what's her name—Brooke, he thought it was—and they'd go out to dinner and maybe a movie. Then he'd drop her off, and his duty would be over. But he hadn't even made contact with her yet. Their mothers had agreed on Friday, and that was it. He glanced at his watch—4:30. At least he could give her a couple of hours' notice.

He locked the apartment door behind then went to the fridge, where the name and phone number of the girl were attached with a magnet. He took it off the fridge and pulled out his cell. Brooke Williamson.

With a queasy sensation rippling through his stomach, he dialed her number. Carter rarely went out dates, let alone blind dates. Even though the woman had already agreed to go out with him, he felt like a sixteen-year-old boy asking out a girl for the first time. As the phone rang, he whispered what he'd say, practicing it so he wouldn't stumble.

Not that I want to impress her. I just don't want to look like a fool.

When someone answered, he managed to ask for Brooke.

"Speaking."

Oh. Did she have a roommate? Did she live at home? How old was she?

He probably should have found out some basic about his blind date. Not that it mattered; it wasn't like he'd see her again after tonight. "This is Carter Mackenzie. I don't know if you've heard of me, but our mothers—"

Brooke laughed lightly on the other end. "Oh, of course. Let me apologize right away. This is all my mother's doing. Her biggest worry in life is that I won't give her grandchildren."

Her tone instantly relaxed Carter. Good. This wasn't a woman who would be hinting about wedding colors and bridesmaid dresses over their dinner. Now that Brooke had broken the ice, he couldn't help but laugh along.

"Believe me; I know how that feels," he said. "All of my siblings—including the one five years younger than I am—are married." Carter hadn't talked about single life—and his mother's wish for him to marry—with anyone for a long time. He couldn't exactly talk about it with Toni. "Thought I'd call so we could plan tonight."

"Of course," Brooke said, sounding animated. "Ideally, we should plan something spectacular. If your mom is anything like mine, she'll interrogate you tomorrow. Then both of our mothers will get together to discuss our date as if they had been there, looking right over our shoulders. When they run out of material, they'll decide where the wedding will be held. We really should give them something to discuss."

Carter couldn't help but laugh again. He wiped one eye, which was tearing up from laughter. Such a relief to know he was going on a date with someone who took the setup as seriously—or not—and he did. They both knew precisely where they stood.

"There is one small glitch with tonight that my mom didn't know about when she planned tonight," Brooke said.

"What's that?" Carter asked, wondering if she would back out after all.

"The fourth grade has an evening for parents on Friday. I really need to be there."

That's right; she was a school teacher. "So should we reschedule or just cancel?" Carter asked.

"Neither. If we put it off, my mother will have a coronary. She'd be afraid that this one date would have sealed my destiny or something. You're welcome to come along, as long as you don't mind a bunch of ten-year-old kids cracking kissing jokes. The musical presentation is about forty-five minutes long, and that's followed by refreshments and an art gallery with the students' work. The whole thing shouldn't go past eight, and we could go get something to eat after that." Her voice sounded apologetic. "I know it's not the most exciting thing to do for a date, but—"

"I'd love to," Carter rushed in, surprised that he meant it. "I don't know if your mom knows or told you or whatever, but I teach high school art. Seeing your students' work would be fun."

"I have to warn you—it's not like they're junior Picassos. One of the boys drew a picture of a furry orange monster picking its nose."

Carter bellowed with laughter. "Oh, that's awesome. I have to come now." He sat on his couch and rested his right foot on his left knee, feeling more relaxed over a date than he had in months. "In college, I considered going into elementary education. I like the idea of getting to work with the students using scissors and paste and encouraging children's creativity. Seemed like the ideal job. Then I decided I wouldn't have the patience for young kids and went the secondary ed route instead."

"Basically, you traded noisy kids for teenage hormones and drama."

"Maybe a bad choice, in hindsight."

"Hardly. I'm glad you won't be suffering too much tonight."

"What time should I pick you up?" Carter got out his phone and clicked over to the calendar.

"Oh, I have to be early, so—"

"I don't mind coming early," Carter said. "I can come get you whenever."

"I'm already at the school," Brooke confessed. "I was planning on just staying after class until the show starts. I have some work I should catch up on anyway. Would you mind meeting me here? It's Aspen Elementary, just a few blocks north of your parents' house."

"My old stomping grounds," Carter said. "It'll be fun to see the old school."

"Then you know your way around, too. I'll be in the gym after five o'clock. The show begins at six."

"I'll be there." Carter was about to hang up when he realized he had no idea what Brooke looked like. "How will I recognize you?"

"Oh, good thinking." Brooke laughed again, clear and light. "Are you calling from your cell? How about I text a picture?"

"Good idea. I'll do the same."

When he hung up, he heaved a big sigh of relief. There hadn't been the tense experience he'd expected, but it still had drained him. He checked the time on his phone. If he wanted to have a chance to talk with Brooke before the evening began, he'd need to leave in about an hour. In another five or six hours, the date would be over. He and Brooke would shake hands, say goodbye, and he could beg his mother to shred her matchmaker card.

His phone beeped, and only then did he remember to look for Brooke's picture. Sure enough, she'd sent a slightly blurry cell-phone image. She had long, light brown hair. A broad smile, and a pretty green sweater. He couldn't make out her eye color or much else, but she was pretty, definitely. He made a note of the sweater, so he'd have something concrete to search for when he got there. Instead of taking a picture of himself right then, he searched him phone camera roll and found one Toni had taken at a movie. It wasn't the greatest picture, but he didn't hate it. At least Brooke would have a fighting chance at recognizing him.

After showering, shaving again, and putting on a light blue shirt and khakis, Carter drove toward his old elementary school. He got there around five thirty—exactly when he'd planned to. He parked, and with satisfaction, noted the time as he got out. He headed toward the doors and clicked his key fob to lock the car. He was early enough to meet Brooke and chat for a few minutes, but not so early that they'd have a whole—potentially awkward—hour to kill. Not that he expected the night to be awkward, after having such a relaxed, carefree phone call.

As he walked in, he was struck by how different the elementary school felt compared to what it had been like when he was a student here. Smaller, for one, but then, he was a foot taller now. And older, which made sense. But it was also so different from the high school. The halls were cleaner, the drinking fountains hung a little lower in the halls, and bright billboards with smiling cartoon characters hung everywhere. He tried to picture what some of his students would say if "Bee Smart—READ" and a bumble bee with a book were plastered by the high school cafeteria door. At best, by the end of the day, the bee would have a marker mustache.

He opened an auditorium door and went a few feet inside, near the stage. Two teachers, neither of them young enough to be Brooke—and neither wearing a green sweater—stood in at the front of the room, which had rows and rows of folding chairs for the audience. A large group of students sat on the deep-set, carpeted stairs that ran the length of the stage front. Carter stepped into the gym a bit more to see the students and teachers, hugging the wall.

Both teachers tried unsuccessfully to control the excited nine- and ten-year-olds, but the students' excitement for performing got in the way. Boys teased girls by pulling at their costumes, and girls retaliated by yanking away props. Still others sat in deep concentration, maybe going over lines.

What kind of musical production would this be? He'd expected a bunch of students standing in neat rows as they sang songs, but obviously there was more to this. He hadn't realized that all the students would be here early; maybe he wouldn't get much of a chance to talk to Brooke beforehand after all.

He looked around the room, searching for Brooke, when a feminine smell passed by him on the left, along with a blur of green. Brooke. She'd come from the backstage doors and now headed for the other two teachers. She moved with a purpose, clearly not seeing him. A boy, with blond hair that stood up like a balloon had been rubbed against it, was poking and otherwise teasing two girls on the step in front of him. When the girls saw their beloved teacher, they flew to her for cover.

"Miss Williamson, Ethan won't stop bugging us," the one with yellow curls whined.

"Yea. And he keeps saying he's going to kiss me at recess

tomorrow if I don't let him hold my veil. But if I let him, he'll *rip* it." Her voice implied that the demise of her veil would be a tragedy akin to death.

Brooke leaned down and rested her hands on her thighs so her face was even with the girls'. She spoke in a conspiratorial sort-of whisper, which Carter could easily hear. "Let me tell you a secret."

"Really?" The dark-haired one said.

Brooke nodded. "But you have to promise not to say anything about it to anyone else—especially not to Chad or Kyle or any of the other boys."

"Like we'd tell them a secret," the redhead said. They both rolled their eyes at the idea.

"Well, you see, the secret is about *them*." Brooke smiled as the girls' eyebrows shot up.

"We can keep a secret," both girls said together.

"All right. I think can trust you," Brooke said. Carter couldn't help but smile as he watched her in action. She went on. "Do you know why boys tease girls?"

The blonde leaned in. "You mean like why Chad teases us?"

"And Kyle?" the redhead said. "They're jerks?"

"No. It's worse." Brooke paused as if for dramatic effect. "Boys tease girls, because . . ." Her voice got softer. "They *like* the girls they're teasing."

The girls' hands flew to their mouths in horror. "No they don't!" they cried, blushing in spite of themselves.

"What do we do?" the redhead said in desperation. "We don't want them to think *we* like them back." She shivered at the thought, as if she could already feel cooties crawling up her back. Carter laughed to himself. Maybe the girls really did feel fondly toward their persecutors.

Brooke's answer was matter-of-fact. "Just ignore them." She shrugged as she said it. Then she wore a mischievous grin. "Ignoring boys drives them *crazy*. And trust me. When boys get older, they learn to be nice to girls."

"Ignore them," the girls said in unison, as if Brooke hadn't said anything past that. They grinned at each other. They seemed to like the idea. "Awesome!"

"Thanks, teacher," the redhead said.

They almost headed back, but Brooke caught them. "Remember, you can't say a word." She put a finger to her lips.

The girls looked at each other again, tickled pink at having one up on the boys sitting behind them. "We promise," they chimed together.

"Now hurry up. We're running out of time. Your parents will start arriving in a few minutes." Brooke watched her students return to their places. She smiled as they ran off and took their seats.

She checked her watched, turned then noticed Carter standing by the wall. She came over, hand outstretched. "Carter Mackenzie, right? Good to meet you."

She had a good, firm handshake, Carter noticed. He liked that. It showed that she had confidence. "Likewise." The cell-phone picture didn't do her justice; her hair was a pretty light brown, and she had a smile that he knew had to draw attention to itself anywhere she went.

"Hope you don't mind being alone for just a bit," Brooke said. "I still have to help the other teachers set things up." She took a step back, but still faced him and bit the side of one lip, as if she didn't quite dare leave him.

"Don't worry about me," Carter said, waving her off and liking the thump of his heart in his chest. "You'd better go. They looked like they were in a panic a minute ago." He meant the other teachers but let the comment slide without further explanation. Let her assume he meant the students.

Brooke laughed. "When we tried to run through the opening number, we couldn't hear the recording that's supposed to accompany the singers. Mary Ellen and Maggie over there"—she indicated the other two teachers—"were sure the sound system was broken. Mary Ellen thought the night was doomed. I went backstage to check it out."

"You know about electronic stuff?" Carter asked, impressed.

"Not hardly." Brooke waved the thought away. "But I thought I'd see if I could figure it out anyway. Turns out the system wasn't even turned on. I don't know much about technology, but I *can* find a power switch."

Carter laughed with her. "You're a miracle worker."

She shook her head with let out a deep breath. "I just hope the performance goes well. We've had so many glitches that nothing will surprise me anymore." She raised a hand with one finger up. "No, on second thought, I'd better not say that. A few things would surprise me, and after all the work we've put into this evening, I couldn't take any of them happening. I have some stuff to take care of, and then I'll be right back. You can sit anywhere you like." She indicated the rows and of chairs.

"Can I help you with something?" Carter asked, following Brooke toward the two other teachers, where she was clearly going to take over, to the relief of the other two.

Mary Ellen heard his comment. "Oh, would you help *me*? The refreshments aren't out yet. Come here and help me put them on trays."

Brooke shook her head and waved her hands. "Oh, no. Carter, you don't have to do that."

"It'd be my pleasure," Carter said. Granted, he'd prefer to help Brooke, but helping Mary Ellen probably did help Brooke, albeit indirectly.

"Just come with me," Mary Ellen said, walking with determination toward opening in the folding curtain wall that blocked off the gym from the cafeteria.

Carter glanced back at Brooke, who wore an apologetic expression. "Really, I don't mind," he assured her. "Besides, this will give me something to tell my mother tomorrow—that I spent the evening with more than one woman." He waggled his eyebrows. "Won't *that* sound juicy?"

Brooke laughed—he liked the sound of that—and turned back to the crowd of unruly preteens. "Hey Miss Williamson, is that your *boyfriend*?"

The students burst into laughter, and several boys made kissing noises. As he followed the middle-aged Mary Ellen—leaving the students behind—he remembered one more reason why he'd decided against teaching elementary school.

Without answering the question, Brooke somehow got the group in control, and within seconds they were singing in unison. Carter glanced over his shoulder to see students acting out parts with costumes and props—all to a medley of Broadway show tunes. Shaking his head, he walked off, curiously intrigued by Brooke Williamson and wanting to know her better.

Chapter 19

As the evening went on, and Carter watched Brooke manage the production and then mingle with her students' parents, he couldn't help but be impressed, even if it meant that he didn't spend much time with his date. Brooke had a poise about her that Mary Ellen and Maggie simply didn't possess. On top of that, Brooke clearly knew and loved each of her students.

Carter wiled away the time, alternately watching Brooke interact with her students and their families and strolling past the artwork displayed on several cafeteria tables. He recognized the monster picture immediately and smiled. This was a drawing made by a kid—Aaron Hill, the placard said—who had no fears when it came to art.

Or, most likely, anything else, he thought. He pulled out his phone and took a picture of the monster. *Maybe I'll pull it out when I start feeling scared to take a risk.*

The single word—risk—brought back thoughts of his student Keri, her challenge, and the result of *that* challenge. Thoughts he'd hoped he'd banished for the evening flooded his mind: a wilted bouquet of flowers, standing in a rainy parking lot, standing in a cold puddle in the night. Watching Toni kiss Clint.

He cleared his throat—and, he hoped, the emotion that had tightened it—and tucked his phone back into his slacks pocket.

For the next twenty minutes, he distracted himself by intently studying the artwork and talking to Mary Ellen and Maggie.

No more thoughts of Toni tonight.

When the last of the students and their parents had gone, the other two teachers came up to give Brooke their thanks at the same time Carter decided to approach her, figuring he could claim her attention now.

"You're a lifesaver, as always," Mary Ellen told Brooke.

"Another successful evening," Maggie agreed. "I don't know how you do it."

"I didn't do all it myself," Brooke protested.

Mary Ellen tsked and then counted off on her fingers. "Let's see, you wrote it, you directed it. You led the rehearsals. You gathered the costumes and props. You cut all the music together. I'd say you pretty much did it yourself." She thrust Brooke's coat at her, which Carter hadn't noticed she'd been carrying.

Brooke took her coat. "What's this for? We still have to clean up."

The other two teachers exchanged glances and giggled. Maggie shook her head. "You've done so much already, and you're even on a date. Let the two of us finish cleaning up; we can handle it. You two go have some fun."

The next thing Carter knew, Brooke sat beside him in his car as they drove toward an Italian restaurant. "Those two have a mind of their own, don't they?" he said with a laugh.

"They sure do," Brooke said. "I wonder what Mary Ellen and Maggie would think if we told them this whole date is nothing but a favor out of familial duty."

Carter glanced over and grinned. "Maybe we should make up something to tell them."

"You mean aside from whatever story we'll concoct for our moms?" Brooke grinned back. "I could get on board with that."

"We can probably tell your friends and our parents the same story, with a few added details for spice. Those are for Mary Ellen and Maggie, of course."

"Naturally. Because I'd never tell those kinds of details to my mother even if they were real."

"Exactly."

The rest of the evening flew by. Even waiting for their food felt like no time at all as Carter and Brooke kept talking and laughing as if they had known each other for years. More than once Carter caught a look in Brooke's eye that took him off guard.

Is that what a woman looks like when she finds you attractive? He'd never seen that look from Toni, although he'd imagined it a thousand times if he had one.

I think she likes me. It felt good.

All too soon he brought Brooke back to the elementary school parking lot, where they had left her car. Carter walked her to her Saturn.

"I've never dropped a girl off at a car door," he said. "How does this affect the doorstep moment?"

Brooke fumbled for the right key then stopped as they got to her car. "Well, let's see—it probably doesn't change much of anything. I think I'm supposed to say I had a nice evening, and then you say we should do this again sometime, and—"

"Should we?" Carter broke in.

Her head came up. "Should we . . . what?"

"Do this again sometime. I enjoyed myself on a date for the first time in probably—oh, at least a year. Maybe ever." He shrugged. "The experience may be worth repeating."

"I'd like that," Brooke said. But then her face screwed up. "But what would our mothers say?"

"We'd keep it from them, so they wouldn't get any ideas. How about this: if my mom asks what I'm doing the day of our next date, I'll say I'm going on an outing with a friend."

"Sounds like a plan," Brooke said with a laugh. She reached for Carter's hand. She gave it a squeeze and smiled shyly. "Call me?"

It was just a handshake, but her finger lingered in his for a moment, and her eyes held his. She was interested, no question.

Carter felt as if he had been dropped onto a different planet. Or at least that he should be looking behind him for the guy this beautiful woman was really talking to. He finally found his voice. "I'll call you."

Brooke flashed a final smile at Carter before ducking into her car. As she drove away, he watched her taillights disappear, completely unaware of the chilly night air, even though he had left his coat in the car.

Chapter 20

About twenty times over the weekend, Carter picked up his phone, fully intending to call Toni to tell her about his blind date. That was their MO, and it had been for years. Right? Sunday afternoon, he managed to make the call without disconnecting. He paced the living room the entire time he left a brief message.

"So, hey," he said, painfully aware that his voice sounded strained. "Been meaning to tell you about a date I had Friday. Haven't talked to you or seen in you in a while. Um. So, yeah. Call me back when you can." He pressed end call and collapsed on the couch.

Bizarre that they hadn't called or texted or seen each other in days. It had to mean that Toni and the short guy were hitting it off. A male best friend likely threatened that. He couldn't imagine a boyfriend being okay with his girlfriend hanging out and confiding in another guy. Her past boyfriends either didn't know about Carter, or they didn't care. The fact that Toni had been silent over Clint told Carter that their relationship was likely different from her past ones.

The thought made him want to throw something.

Several hours later, when the sun was dipping into the west and splashing a wash of orange and pinks across the sky, his doorbell rang. Carter was sketching Toni again, this time in an arabesque, wearing the white costume with tutu and tiara that she'd worn in a ballet a couple of years ago.

He set his tablet on the couch and headed for the door. He answered it, only to find Toni on the other side.

"Hey. Long time, no see," she said with the same old smile that turned his insides into butter. He'd missed it.

But then Carter's eyes darted to the tablet. Toni had never seen his pictures of her. Not the paintings, not the sketches. Which amounted to a lot of his portfolio, including some work that had landed him several freelance jobs. He wanted to keep it that way—*had* to keep it that way. She'd think he was creepy and different, she'd know his real feelings, and it would ruin everything. Assuming Clint hadn't ruined everything already. Carter casually took a step toward the couch and tossed a throw pillow onto his tablet.

"It's been awhile. Want to go on a walk? We can catch up." He grabbed his coat from the back of a kitchen chair and headed out before Toni could say no.

As he closed the door behind him, Toni gave him a curious look, but followed along. Soon they were strolling down the city streets, and Carter's heart rate slowed down. Things were back to normal, for the most part. He felt relaxed again. Toni was chattering along about all kinds of things.

And she hadn't seen his tablet.

All too soon, her conversation veered into territory Carter would have been more than happy to avoid forever: Clint. She told of their first week of serial dating. Of the first time he kissed her. Of how *hot* he was. With each statement, a piece of Carter died inside. He gritted his teeth, remembering every second of their kissing he'd witnessed from the parking lot.

He didn't realize she'd stopped talking until she paused in her step and turned to face him. "You okay?" she asked, putting hand on his arm. Even though his coat was between them, his skin burned. You seem kind of out of it."

He shrugged, brushing off the question, and her hand. He kept walking. "So how are the two of you doing now? I mean, now that it's established that he's totally hot and that you two have chemistry."

Way too much chemistry.

Toni grinned. "Really well. It's almost like a dream. Did I tell you that we're working on a rumba routine for the spring recital?"

"I didn't know," Carter said. Odd. Toni never performed unless she'd perfected a routine. "How did he convince you to do that?"

Toni made a pleasant noise. "Let's just say that he's *very* persuasive."

I know how he probably persuaded her, too.

He'd seen their chemistry firsthand. But a relationship needed a lot more than a powerful chemical reaction to survive. Didn't it?

"Anyway, we're practicing a lot—almost every day. Usually before classes, in the morning," Toni went on. "Clint is *so* sweet."

Her voice dripped like corn syrup. Carter's jaw tightened. He didn't say anything, but he knew he didn't have to; Toni would keep talking now that things were back to normal between them.

Carter had been right; it was Clint that had kept Toni away. But not because of any boyfriend jealousy. Because apparently, Toni had been too busy dancing with Clint to remember her best friend existed—until today.

"He writes me love letters," Toni went on. Carter wondered how much he'd zoned out and missed. He tried to care but couldn't manage it. "Get this—yesterday, he left gourmet chocolates by my dance shoes. And a few days ago—or what, maybe a week ago? I forget—he gave me a brand-new pair of Latin ballroom shoes. They were gorgeous. Must have cost a *lot*."

Carter eyed her with one raised eyebrow. He didn't want to burst her bubble by suggesting that Clint was investing money in a relationship and would likely expect to get payment back in his own ways. He'd probably considered the make-out session in the studio as merely a down payment. Maybe he should tell Toni that not all guys had good motives.

And maybe I'm judging him too harshly. Sometimes a cigar is just a cigar, and sometimes a pair of ballroom shoes are just ballroom shoes.

He floundered for something to say and managed only, "So you can wear heels around him after all?"

Toni laughed. "Barely. I'm probably an inch taller in the shoes. But it works well enough for the routine."

They walked for a few minutes in silence—thank heavens. Carter noticed some bright green buds on the branches of some trees. If the frosts didn't get them, they might bloom early. Early springs following mild winters, like this one, always made him worry for the fragile blooms. You never knew what damage a spring frost could do. All too often the first the tender buds and blossoms crept out in promise of a new beginning, then a frost would follow close behind and kill them.

Carter wasn't sure if the analogy had popped into his head because he hoped that a frost would kill whatever existed between Toni and Clint, or whether he viewed their relationship as a blossom that could freeze and die.

Or maybe he and Brooke had something new and green poking through.

Toni jumped suddenly as a thought occurred to her. "I almost forgot—your blind date! How did it go?"

It was as if she'd read his mind. "I had fun," Carter said, glad he meant it and grateful for the change in topic. "Brooke's in the same boat I am as far as mothers go."

"Nosy and desperate for more grandchildren?"

"Exactly. She didn't take the date the least bit seriously. There was no pressure at all." Carter motioned with his hands to emphasize.

"That's refreshing."

"No kidding. She even cracked jokes about our mothers swapping stories about us and planning the wedding. I was able to actually relax on a date." Carter had a theory about dating: people didn't show their true selves on dates, so dating was by its nature was the most unreliable way to select a marriage companion. His theory had held water, until Brooke.

"What did you do? Go to a movie?"

"Not this time," Carter said. Sad that Toni could predict that with such accuracy. He proceeded to describe the evening, from the fourth graders' kissing sounds to helping Mary Ellen set up refreshments.

"And you had fun?" Toni asked in amazement. "Wow. What was her name again?"

"Brooke. I know it sounds crazy, but I did enjoy myself. So much that I'm going to ask her out again."

"That's just . . . great," Toni said, turning to him and taking his hands in hers. Her voice sounded dull, not excited like her words seemed to imply. Or was her dull tone his imagination?

Chapter 21

When Toni drove to work on Monday, Carter and Brooke were still on her mind, as they had been ever since she and Carter had talked the day before. She parked and went into the studio, heading again for her favorite room in the back, where she planned to fix the choreography of a section of a hip-hop number for one of the competition teams.

As she pulled the door open and headed down the long hall, she hoped—oddly—that Clint wouldn't be there for an hour. They were meeting then to practice their routine, but before that, she needed a little time alone, even from the eye candy of his body and the heat of his touch and kisses. She put the music on and began warming up on the hardwood floor, starting with plies and arm stretches.

When they'd talked yesterday, Carter had looked *happy* for once about dating someone. That was good, right? And if all went well between him and Brooke, who knew—maybe he'd finally settle down to the life he'd always dreamed of. He'd have miniature Carters and Brookes, but before kids, maybe he and Brooke would take a summer to live in Paris, one of Carter's dreams.

So why couldn't she feel happy for him?

I'd be losing my best friend, that's why.

She ignored the twisting feeling in her stomach that indicated something more to her unease than that and set to stretching her legs.

She remembered Carter's description of the date and laughed to herself when she pictured him trotting off behind Mary Ellen as fourth-grader kissing sounds followed him out of the room. His eyes had lit up when he talked about how easy the date had felt with Brooke—then Toni sighed. Carter's attentions had found a focus other than listening to Toni vent on yet another phone call or replying to her texts. That's what really bothered her, surely. She'd gotten used to being the center of Carter's life. Aside from his art, of course. She'd always been able to count on him to be there for her, to listen to her. To be her sounding board, her shoulder to cry on.

Now he had something else—*someone* else—to occupy his time. Would he come to her with questions about women the way she had always gone to him with questions about men? She hoped so, but she doubted it. Men didn't need to talk shop to sort through their feelings like women did.

Then again, she was glad of that. Toni didn't think she could handle listening to Carter go off about a woman he was falling in love with. It wasn't as if she was attracted to Carter. She nearly laughed at the thought. He was, well, *Carter*. She didn't see him as a guy. Who knew what other women saw when they looked at him, what he looked like without those glasses, and in swim trunks? He worked out regularly; for she knew, he had a six pack.

This is Carter I'm thinking about! Stop it! She shook off the mental questions—and images—and found herself picturing the rest of the date as Carter had described it: the two of them sitting in a restaurant for two hours, just talking. For a split second, though, the woman at the table, gazing lovingly into Carter's eyes, wasn't Brooke, but Toni.

Clint walked in right then, making her jolt out of her thoughts. Somehow, an hour had passed. She'd done her warm-up routine three times, a solo she's choreographed for herself ages ago, and a bunch of floor exercises. She hadn't touched the hip-hip routine.

She got up from a saddle stretch and went to meet him at the door, where he planted a long kiss on her. He pulled back and smoothed some wisps of hair that had escaped her pony tail.

"Sorry I'm late," he said.

He was late? She glanced at the clock by the door. He was ten minutes late. She'd spent seventy minutes stretching, messing around, and thinking about Carter?

"See," Clint went on. "I had to stand in line for this." He revealed a single Columbian rose that he'd held behind his back. "A rose for a rose." He leaned forward to kiss her again.

After he pulled away, Toni took the rose and inhaled the sweet smell as Clint dropped his bag and went to put on some music. She watched him take off his thick coat to reveal his defined arms and back, and she nearly pinched herself to make sure this was all real. That a guy as hot as Clint had feelings for her. That *he* thought her attractive too.

"Come here," Clint said as he walked to the center of the floor. "Let's try it from the top."

Toni put the rose beside her back and then pulled out her Latin shoes. "Don't you want to warm up first?" she asked, hopping on one foot as she put the left shoe. The silver sandals were nearly broken in now.

Clint gave her a deprecating look. "Not everyone needs to warm up."

Yes, they do, Toni thought, but went to him with a smile anyway. She was plenty warm, however, so she let Clint take her hands and lead her into the starting position.

Clint counted as they went through the dance without the music. But Toni's mind kept wandering, making her mess up. Try as she might, she couldn't picture Clint sitting across from her and just *talking* at an Italian restaurant for two hours. Which is exactly what Carter had done with Brooke.

Could Clint sit still and talk that long? She doubted it. They'd end up leaving the restaurant as soon as they ate and paid the tab, off in search of some place private where they could exchange what Clint called "*real* communication."

When Toni didn't respond to one of Clint's leads, he stopped dancing completely and released her hand. "Is something wrong?" With the back of one hand, he wiped away some new beads of sweat from his forehead. "You're off today."

"Nothing's wrong." Toni shook her head to clear away thoughts of Carter and Brooke talking "easily" for hours. Of knowing that Clint would never be game for as unconventional a date as Brooke had offered Carter. Not that Toni was big into hanging around grade-school kids, but to know for certain that Clint wouldn't give someone like Brooke the time of day, well, that didn't sit right with her. She cleared her throat, because clearing her mind certainly wasn't working. "Sorry. Let's try that part again."

"All right." Clint looked at the two of them in the mirror and began counting. "Five, six, seven—"

"No, wait," Toni said suddenly, pulling away. "Something *is* wrong."

Clint looked to her blankly. "What is it? Are you upset because I was late?" He gestured toward the rose, which now lay beside her bag. I thought you'd like the rose—"

"I love the rose," Toni interjected. "It's beautiful. It's not that."

"Then what?"

Toni's hands worried each other. She finally wrapped them around her waist. The silence between them felt like a deafening chasm. How could she have never noticed that the two of t hem never talked? Really talked?

"Let's talk," she managed.

Clint ran a hand through his hair and took a step in the other direction. "Great. Here it comes, The Talk."

"No, that's not what I mean," Toni said, walking after him. She put a hand on his shoulder, and he turned around. "I just mean that, well, you and I have never just sat around and . . . talked. I don't know much about you, and you don't know much about me."

"Come on, sure you do." He started ticking items on his fingers. "You know I grew up in California and that—"

Toni held up a hand. "Sure, I guess I know a few facts, but not many of those, either. I don't even know if you have siblings or what high school you went to." Clint opened his mouth as if to answer those questions, but Toni plowed on. "But it's more than that. I don't feel like I know *you*. I don't even know what kinds of music you like, who your favorite actors are, what you like to do in your spare time. Are you a Coke kind of guy, or Pepsi? Seriously, let's sit down right here and just *talk* about something. Anything." Toni pulled Clint down and sat tailor style opposite him. He sat reluctantly. "Come on, I don't bite."

"This *isn't* The Talk?" he asked warily.

"It's a conversation. Ever heard of one?" Toni took off the Latin heels and tossed them aside.

Clint rested his hands on his knees. "All right, what should we talk about?"

Now we're getting somewhere. "Okay, let me think." She clasped her hands together as a trickle of excitement went up her spine. She and Clint *could* be like Carter and Brooke. "What's your favorite book?"

He blinked. "I don't have one."

"Okay, then, what are *some* of your favorites? Or maybe favorite writers?"

"Seriously, I can't answer that. I've never read anything I wasn't assigned to read, and most of what I was assigned, I never finished. Thank you, Wikipedia."

Disappointment twisted in Toni's middle. How could he not like to read? Maybe she could introduce some awesome book and make him a believer. He probably hated reading because he'd only ever been assigned to read hard stuff.

Clint shrugged. "I guess I kind of liked *To Kill a Mockingbird* in high school."

"Me too!" Toni said. *Now we're getting somewhere.* "I loved how many different ways the mockingbird shows up in the story, how many different characters represent it, from Boo Radley to... what?"

Clint's eyebrows were pushed together. He looked completely confused. "What are you talking about?"

"*To Kill a Mockingbird*," Toni said slowly. "And the symbol of the mockingbird." She waved the topic away. "But we can talk about something else. What about movies? Name the two best movies you've seen in, say the last six months."

Now Clint's face lit up. "That's easy." He began rattling off titles, all movies that reportedly had tons of gore, language, and vulgar nudity. Toni hadn't seen them and had no desire to. "Have you seen any of those?" he asked after rattling off the list.

"Can't say I have," Toni said, wondering what topic she should attempt next. Their potential for future enjoyable dates had diminished considerably. She didn't mind the occasional action movie, but nothing that graphic. And she had a suspicion that Clint would balk at the idea of seeing romantic comedy or period piece.

"What about you?" he asked. "What are some of your favorite movies?"

"I doubt you've seen any of them," Toni warned, trying to keep a flame of hope alive.

Not all couples have the same taste in pop culture.

"Try me. I've seen my share of 'chick flicks' over the years."

Clint seemed like he was starting to enjoy himself, which pleased Toni, except for the fact that now *she* felt uncomfortable. But he'd said he'd seen some chick flicks, so maybe he was more open to her kind of movie than she'd thought.

"I've always loved *The Philadelphia Story*," Toni offered.

"The one about AIDS with Tom Hanks? I never saw it, but I heard it won a bunch of awards."

"No, that's *Philadelphia*. This is a much older film with James Stewart and Katharine Hepburn."

Clint leaned back on his arms and seemed to think hard for a moment. He nodded as if remembering. "You mean the guy from *It's a Wonderful Life* and that old lady who talks like a frog, right? Or I guess I should say *talked*. She's got to be dead by now."

Toni clamped her mouth shut before something she'd regret came out. "Yes, those two," she finally managed.

Clint shook his head. "Haven't even heard of it."

She didn't dare mention *White Christmas* or *Bridge over the River Kwai*. Toni decided to try a different approach. "How about this: where would you like your life to be in, say, ten years?"

"Let's see, in ten years . . ." Clint said, gazing at the ceiling. "In ten years I'll be—yikes, in my mid-thirties. Chances are I'll be past my dancing prime, but hopefully I will have earned the National Latin Championship title. If I have, then in ten years I'd probably be touring the country giving workshops, coaching other couples, that kind of thing. Professionals—especially if they've earned a national title—earn a *lot* of money that way."

Touring. And Money. Not exactly her picture of the future. "What about marriage? Or kids?"

Clint cocked his head. "Was all this a sneaky way of leading into a serious talk after all?"

"Of course not," she said with a groan. "I just want to get to know you better. We've really hit it off, but I don't feel like I know who you are inside, what your dreams and goals are."

He reached forward and brushed aside a stray piece of hair from Toni's face. "You are so different from other girls," he said. "So sweet, so innocent, but passionate, too . . ." He leaned forward and took Toni in his arms. He gently kissed her a couple of times, and soon the kisses became more powerful, until Toni wrapped her hand behind his neck. She felt on fire. Clint finally pulled away, and Toni had to look away to catch her breath.

"Come on," Clint said, standing up and reaching for her hand. "Enough chatting for today. Let's practice." He pulled her to her feet, and then in close for one more kiss.

"Thanks for being willing to talk," Toni said, whispering it with their faces nearly touching.

"Any time," Clint said. "This kind of talking is much nicer than the serious kind."

Chapter 22

Even though Carter's first date with Brooke had gone well—better than well—he had to psych himself into calling her for a second date. He picked up his cell phone, put it down. Wiped his palms on his pants—twice. He breathed in and out a couple of times.

This isn't rocket science, and you're not fifteen. She liked you enough to practically ask for a second date.

He finally grabbed the phone from the table, dialed, and closed his eyes as he waited for an answer.

"Hello?"

Carter barely registered that someone had answered before he started pacing and talking. He hoped his voice sounded natural. "Brooke, hey. It's Carter. I was wondering—"

"Carter? Carter Mackenzie?"

"Yes . . ." And suddenly Carter knew he wasn't speaking to Brooke. His step came up short, and his eyes popped open.

"My, how wonderful," a woman's voice said—a voice *much* older than he'd expected. "I talked to your mother the other day. Says she hasn't heard a *thing* about your date with my Brookey, so I filled her in on everything I know—not that Brookey told me much." She laughed. "All she'd say was that you went out for pizza and had a good time. Maybe *you* can tell me some more of the juicy details. So, do you like her? Do you think she's pretty?" Her voice lowered. "Did you *kiss* her?"

Carter was about to hang up, or maybe pass out—he wasn't sure which—when he heard a frustrated groan in the background, followed by what was clearly Brooke's voice.

"Mom, please give me the phone."

Carter sighed with relief. At least he wouldn't be at the mercy of Mrs. Williamson for long. She had taken him so off-guard that he just might have spilled every thought and feeling and moment from their date before he managed to rein in his surprise.

She's good—she should interrogate spies for the government. Good thing Brooke was there to fend off her mother.

"Carter? Sorry about that." It was Brooke's voice, and she was whispering, as if she'd hidden herself in a closet. "When I moved into the basement apartment, she swore she'd stay upstairs, but obviously that hasn't happened, especially after dates. It's safe to talk; I've locked myself in the bathroom."

The bathroom. Not closet. Didn't really matter where she was; somehow the thought of Brooke locking herself away from her mother made him smile.

"Anyway, she's not here. Thank heavens we aren't talking on land line, or she'd try to listen in."

Carter rubbed his forehead and sat on a kitchen chair with a laugh. This was starting to feel a bit too much like junior high.

"Anyway, I'm glad you called," she said.

"You are?" After the circus that was Brooke's mother, he hadn't expected that. His spirits improved immediately. "I mean, well, I promised to call, so here I am." He barreled on before he lost his nerve. "I was wondering if you'd return the favor by helping me out with a thing at the high school Saturday night. It's a semiformal dance, and they need adult help. They've already got two adults at the door to take tickets, but they still need a few chaperones. Since I don't have a wife and kids like most of the faculty, I get volunteered to do this kind of thing a lot. It gets pretty boring by myself, so I thought that maybe . . ."

Carter knew he was rambling, but he couldn't stop himself, for fear that Brooke would actually get a chance to answer and say no.

"I'd love to," Brooke managed when Carter had to pause for breath.

"Really? I mean, great. Since it's semiformal, I'll be wearing a tie and jacket, and you might want to wear a skirt or a dress, but it doesn't have to be anything fancy. I can pick you up at six thirty so we're there before the dance starts. Unless we want to go out for dinner first." He left the thought hanging.

"I'll enjoy myself regardless of what we do. This is me, remember? The one who dragged you to a fourth-grade production and still had fun?"

Carter laughed at himself. "I swear, I'm starting to sound like the eighth grader your mother sees me as, aren't I?"

"Hey, I'm the one locked in the bathroom talking to a *boy*."

Carter smiled broadly, feeling more comfortable by the moment. "So do you want to have dinner before the dance?"

"Dinner sounds great."

"Say five o'clock? And I'll do my best to look good when I pick you up, for your mother's sake."

"Oh, she already knows what you look like. Your mom has pictures in her purse—that's how they got scheming in the first place. My mom thinks that if you got rid of your glasses, you'd be a modern Rock Hudson. No matter that your coloring is all wrong for that."

Carter took off his glasses and looked in the mirror on the wall. "What did you say to that?" he asked, eyeing himself critically.

"Nothing. I went to my computer and Googled Rock Hudson."

Oh, right. He'd forgotten that most modern women weren't classic movie junkies like Toni, who'd shown him *Pillow Talk* with Rock Hudson their junior year. They'd watched it more than once since. Not as often as *The Philadelphia Story*, which would remain a perennial favorite. Toni insisted that really, you couldn't beat a movie with Cary Grant *and* Jimmy Stewart. And Carter certainly didn't mind watching a young Katharine Hepburn in a swimsuit.

He eyed his reflection while holding his glasses in one hand. His optometrist had insisted he try contacts and had sent him home with some, but he'd never worn them. They were still in his one of his bathroom drawers. Glasses didn't bother him, and based on his students' experiences, contacts seemed like a big hassle—falling out, tearing, making you blink all the time, or stuff slipping underneath and hurting your eyes. Besides, he'd used contacts for a few months during a semester of college, and with all the washes and disinfectants, it had been a total pain.

But maybe . . . He squinted at the mirror. His image was a bit fuzzy, so he leaned in closer, but that didn't let him see his whole face. He stood straight again. "Maybe I will try contacts," he said absently. "I didn't think they made much of a difference, and they seemed like a pain, but someone mentioned the idea the other day, and I've been thinking about it. I don't think my eyes are bad enough for Lasik, though." Carter could hardly believe he was asking a woman—one he'd dated *once*—for advice like this. Or that he expected her to be honest about it. Then again, he wasn't admitting that the "someone" who had suggested contacts was one of his students.

"I think you'd look even better without glasses," Brooke chimed in. "I mean, there are a handful of people who need glasses to look good. My uncle has really small, wide set eyes, so his glasses make his eyes look closer together and a bit bigger, more proportional. But in your case, I think contacts would make you that much *more* attractive."

He liked the sound of that: *more* attractive.

Brooke's voice was soft when she added, "I'd love to be able to look into your eyes without anything in the way."

Carter choked on his tongue and tried to come up with a response. His first thought was to laugh; Brooke couldn't possibly be serious. Why was she talking about looking into his eyes? Was she playing things up for her mother's benefit, in case Mom was on the other side of the door?

"I'll see you Saturday at five then," Brooke added, and hung up.

A little tingle began to simmer inside Carter at the idea that a woman could find him attractive—a beautiful woman like Brooke. If a beautiful woman like Toni felt no attraction toward him, then what had he been doing with his life for a decade? Pining for someone who would never look at him as anything more than a brother? A friend to watch old movies with?

An image popped into his head of Toni curled under his arm as they ate popcorn and watched *Wait Until Dark*. When the bad guy jumped out of the darkness, the bowl went flying, and Toni, well, she'd clung to him.

At the time, all thoughts of the movie vanished, and all he wanted was to hang on to her forever, but all too soon, the moment faded, she laughed, and they were settled again, leaning against the couch, for the remaining minutes of the movie.

He'd replayed that night more times than he could count, including what it would have been like to kiss her in the dark. How Toni might have turned into a girlfriend. Or how it could have pushed her away and ruined their friendship. He shook off thoughts of Toni.

No. No thinking about her now.

Chapter 23

Saturday night Carter spent more time getting himself ready than he had in he couldn't remember how long. He shaved twice, used the cologne that had been sitting on the shelf ever since breaking up with Laura, and he spent a half hour on his hair, trying to make it look like he *hadn't* done anything special with it. He noticed a dirty spot on his glasses and took them off to get rid of it. As he reached for a clean washcloth, he glanced at his reflection and stopped.

As he looked at himself again—he was doing that more often now—he wondered if he should trust the opinion of a hormonal high school girl and the mother of a woman desperate for a family wedding.

Then again, Brooke had encouraged him to toss the glasses, too.

Tentatively, he opened the bathroom cupboard and rummaged around until he found the two boxes of disposable contacts his optometrist had given him—one for each eye's prescription. Technology had improved, apparently, requiring only one solution, and the contacts could be thrown out after a month.

He opened the sealed packages, and, remembering the technique from his freshman year in college, inserted the right contact into each eye, surprised at how easily they went in after all these years. He expected his eyes to burn and water, but they hardly did at all, as if they had been waiting for him to put them in all along. He didn't dare take a good look at himself with his new look, so instead he plunged into his bedroom, where he spent another twenty minutes deciding which tie to wear.

After Carter picked up Brooke, and they were heading for the restaurant, it took him a few minutes to relax. She talked lightheartedly enough for both of them the whole way there, so by the time they were seated, waiter had seated them he had managed to relax and remember that this wasn't a date; it was an outing with a friend. A friend who happened to look amazing, wearing a peach-colored dress that flattered her already perfect figure and showed off her amber-brown eyes.

She wore her hair up, with a few wisps curling around her neck, something he had always been partial to. He'd always believed the neck to be one of the most beautiful parts of a woman. Which explained his crush on Audrey Hepburn along with his current attraction to Brooke.

Dinner was delicious, and the conversation comfortable. They reached the high school promptly at seven o'clock, but no students were in sight in the commons except for two ninth graders manning the refreshment table.

"It's uncool to show up at the beginning of the dance," Carter explained. "Of course, *we* have to be here the whole time, even if that means chatting with the punch bowl."

"Sounds like you've done this many times," Brooke said as Carter handed her a powdered sugar cookie.

"I've attended way more dances as a chaperone than I ever did as a student. Maybe I'll get to dance this time, instead of walking the walls."

Brooke grinned. "You can bet on it."

During the hour it took for the dance to get underway, Carter showed Brooke a few basic moves for the two-step. When Brooke felt she had the hang of it, she suggested getting their pictures taken by the photographer. "Come on. There isn't a line right now."

"I don't know."

"Oh, come on, it'll be fun," Brooke insisted, dragging him toward the cafeteria by one hand.

When they reached the photographer, Carter felt a little silly asking for pictures. But when the photographer, a woman about Brooke's age, grinned and motioned them on, he decided that Brooke's spontaneous personality was good for him. Brooke stood in front of him, and Carter put his arms around her waist. As he got into position, Brooke looked up and smiled at him. "No glasses. I like it." She smiled again, and the photographer snapped the picture.

"We weren't ready," Carter said. "We weren't even looking at the camera."

The photographer grinned. "It was a great shot. Trust me."

By eight-thirty, the commons had filled completely with boys in suits and young women in bright-colored dresses, some of the teenagers looking happy, some shy, and others miserable, as if they couldn't wait for the night to end.

"Let's go show them what we can do," Brooke said, holding out her hand. Carter took it hand and led her to the center of the dance floor. Their moves weren't anything spectacular from a technical standpoint—he knew enough about dance from Toni to know that this was the basic of the basic, but he and Brooke certainly outshone any of the moves the students were doing. Soon couples all around them had stopped to watch.

"Looking good, Mr. Mackenzie," a voice said from the crowd. Carter looked over and saw Mark, one of his students, grinning at him. "And I don't mean just the dancing." Mark nodded at Brooke.

"Yeah, she's hot," said Graham, the boy who'd been voted biggest flirt of the senior class.

Carter sketched a look at Brooke, unsure what her reaction would be to the attention, but she just grinned and drew a little closer.

When the dance ended, he led Brooke off the dance floor and back to the refreshment table for a drink, liking the way she let him be a gentleman. He handed her a drink, then got one for himself as a slow song started. Carter had always rolled his eyes at what the teenagers called "dancing" when a slow song came on—basically hugging as they rotated in a circle.

"Are you all right?" he asked over his cup. "I've got some

rather forward students.”

Brooke shrugged, but she still wore the smile of a woman complimented. “Just another version of the kissing sounds fourth graders make. Besides, it’s nice to be called ‘hot,’ even by a seventeen-year-old.” They listened to the slow song and watched the dance floor fill with couples, when Brooke set her drink aside. “Would you like to dance this one?” she asked with tilt of her head.

Carter set his drink beside hers and took her hand. “Sure,” he said, and led her out to a far corner of the dance floor as he tried to figure out how exactly to slow dance with her. Would she want to be in dance position, or in the teenager loose hug? Or, heaven forbid, try to hang on him like that couple over there?

When he found a spot and turned around, though, Brooke put her left hand over his right shoulder and held out her right hand for his left. Carter almost laughed at himself for worrying about what she’d do. Brooke was too classy for anything but this.

He took her hand and wrapped his other one around her waist in a relaxed version of the traditional dance position. As the song went on, though, he found himself gradually holding her a little closer, and soon she rested her chin on his shoulder. Part of him kept calling out that he was the shy guy who never dated, that he couldn’t possibly be enjoying this, that his date couldn’t be attracted to him, but he shoved that voice down and concentrated on enjoying the smell of her hair instead. When Brooke turned her head, it rested on his shoulder, and he leaned his own against hers. And wished they could stay that way all night.

After the DJ played the final song and the last of the students headed for the doors, Carter and Brooke headed to his car hand in hand. As they had on their first date, they talked like old friends, laughing at each other’s jokes and swapping stories. He released her hand and slipped his arm around her shoulder. At the same time, she put her arm around his waist as they walked, Carter thrilling to the idea that this woman—this gorgeous, smart, classy woman—genuinely liked being with him.

“Hey, Mr. Mackenzie!” A young woman’s voice called from behind them.

They turned to see a young woman dragging her date behind her. "Keri, is that you?" Carter asked. "I didn't see you in there tonight."

"Well, *I* saw *you*," she said. "Way to take my advice."

"Thank you, Miss Harris," Carter said, feeling his cheeks grow warm. "I'll see you in class on Monday."

Keri laughed and dragged her date in the other direction.

Brooke leaned toward him inquiringly. "What advice did you take?"

Carter coughed in embarrassment and started walking again. "Do I have to admit this?" Brooke batted her eyes, waiting. He groaned. "Okay, fine. She's the one who first said I should get rid of the glasses."

Brooke let out a slight laugh but covered her mouth and quickly smothered it when Carter shot her a look. "I thought it was a relative, maybe your mother or an aunt or something."

He shook his head, knowing his face was flushing bright red. Maybe Brooke wouldn't be able to tell by the lights in the parking lot.

She put a hand on his arm. "Hey, I don't care who it was. She has good taste."

Carter laughed, glad that what could have been an awkward moment was over. He put his arm around Brooke's shoulders again and started walking but came up short when he noticed Toni several yards away, walking toward the auditorium.

Without thinking, he called out to her. "Toni?" She stopped and looked around for the voice. She didn't seem to see him at first. "What are you doing here?" he asked.

Toni stopped in her tracks and looked around. When her eyes rested on Carter, they shot open and stared first—likely at his glassless face—then at the beautiful woman on his arm. "Um, hey. I didn't know you were going to be here tonight," she said, adjusting her dance bag on her shoulder. "I'm just—I'm here to finalize the lighting for my classes' numbers in the studio's recital."

"Right." Carter had forgotten that the spring recital was coming up. Toni's studio usually rented out the high school auditorium for the performance. After a brief silence, Brooke elbowed Carter in the ribs. *Right.* "Toni, this is Brooke Williamson. Brooke, this is Toni Harper, a good friend from way back."

Toni's eyebrows went up slightly, but she smiled and put out her hand. "It's nice to meet you, Brooke." She stepped back and pointed over her shoulder. "Well, I should probably be going," she said. "It's getting late, and they're expecting me." She backed up as she headed across the courtyard toward the auditorium doors. "It was nice to meet you, Brooke. See you later, Carter." She waved, and Carter and Brooke waved back.

But Carter didn't move until the door had closed behind Toni and she had disappeared into the unlighted hallway on the other side. His worlds had collided, and he was left reeling.

Brooke gently tugged his arm. "Who exactly was that? An old girlfriend?"

"Hardly." Carter shook his head and almost laughed at the question. "She's been a close friend since the middle of high school. We were best friends in high school." Why wasn't he admitting that he still considered Toni to be his best friend? "But it's never been more than that."

Not that I didn't want to move past the friend zone.

"Oh," was all Brooke said, in a completely neutral voice. They walked for a minute in silence, and then Brooke mused, "You two must have a pretty special bond."

"Yeah," Carter said, trying to figure out how to downplay Toni in front of his date. Bad form bringing up another woman.

"Are you still close? Do you tell each other relationship stuff?" Brooke had a teasing lilt in her voice, making Carter feel safe answering the question—she didn't sound jealous.

"Pretty close," he admitted. "I hear about her dates and boyfriends all the time."

Brooke looked up at him with a smirk. "So maybe she'll get the lowdown on everything that happens tonight?"

Carter drew Brooke a little closer. "I don't have to tell her *everything.*"

They'd reached Carter's car, which was parked by a light. Brooke leaned against the car and asked, "So what will you tell her when you talk over our evening?"

"I don't know yet." He took her hands in his and shrugged. "I don't know how the evening will end."

Brooke took a step forward and reached up to give Carter a hug. She pulled back slightly and looked into his eyes. "How do you want it to end?" She looked deeply into his eyes.

Carter had never seen that look given to him before, although he had dreamed of seeing it for more than a decade. His insides turned to jelly, and he had one coherent thought.

I'm so glad I wore contacts.

Lame thought, but Brooke *was* gazing into his eyes now, with no glasses in the way. Carter leaned in slightly then paused, as if he expected Brooke to pull away. Instead she leaned in even closer, so he closed the distance and kissed her. She kissed him back eagerly.

Chapter 24

Toni got halfway down the hall before her curiosity—and a twinge of something else—couldn't take it anymore. She dropped her bag and rested it against the wall then turned around and crept back up the darkened corridor. Through the tall windows bordering the courtyard, she watched Carter and his date talking at his car, clearly illuminated by a streetlamp.

Toni had never seen Carter with another woman, and, knowing that he really liked this one, was dying to see him in action. At least, that's what she told herself. But something else niggled at her. For one thing, she'd never seen Carter so put together as he looked tonight. He was always well kempt, but tonight he looked sophisticated, and, well, *handsome*. Part of it seemed to be the confidence he exuded around Brooke.

Another part was the fact that was missing his glasses. She wanted to put them back on him so no one else would know how good-looking he really was. *That* would keep him safe from other women. Even from nice ones like Brooke.

Carter leaned down to kiss Brooke. Toni shivered inexplicably and wrapped her arms around herself as she looked away. She didn't like watching Carter kissing anyone. But only because it meant that maybe he'd drift away, that she'd lose her best friend.

Right?

"Man, it's cold in here," she whispered. She headed down the lighted hall that led backstage. She took several strides away from her bag before she remembered it. She'd call him in the morning, demand lunch together, and then she'd grill him about the date.

She woke up the next day far earlier than normal—and too early for making phone calls. She spent an hour playing Sudoku and Minesweeper than finally caved and called Carter. They agreed to meet at Toni's favorite Mexican restaurant at eleven for an early lunch.

She arrived ten minutes early, before the place even opened, and when Carter came up the walk from the parking lot, again sans glasses—a look she was coming to appreciate more and more. She put on a broad smile and ran over and hugged him. They walked to the doors with her arm around his waist and his around her shoulders. It felt good, right. Like old times. Only better.

As soon as they were seated, they ordered; they'd been to this restaurant often enough that they didn't need to look over the menu. A bowl of chips and a cup of salsa were brought out, and then they were left alone. While they waited for their food—Toni had ordered a shredded pork chimichanga, and Carter beef fajitas—she leaned forward.

"Okay, so about Brooke last night . . ."

Carter smiled with a twinkle in his eye. Toni scowled mentally at that.

"What about last night?"

Toni grunted, leaned back in her chair and folded her arms. "Spill it."

Would he admit to kissing her? Toni was quite sure she'd witnessed their first kiss, because Carter would have mentioned it if he'd kissed Brooke before.

At least, I think he would have.

"It was a lot of fun," Carter said with a one-shouldered shrug.

Toni shook her head. "Seriously? That's all I get?"

The waiter arrived with their drinks. Toni stuck her straw into her Diet Coke and took a pull while Carter stirred his Sprite thoughtfully with his straw. "It's still pretty fresh. I don't want to kiss and tell—it'll make the whole evening seem less than it was."

"Kiss and tell, eh?" Toni rested her arms on the table. "There *was* some lip action, I take it." As if she didn't already know.

"You could say that." Carter twirled his straw some more then cleared his throat. "But I really don't want to talk about it. Not yet."

"Soon, though?"

"Mmmm. Maybe."

Why was he so hesitant this time? It wasn't like he'd never told Toni about past girlfriends—including the kissing parts.

They sat in a semi-awkward silence—because Toni could never feel entirely awkward around Carter; this was *Carter*, after all—until their entrees arrived. As they dug into their food, Carter changed the subject.

As he piled strips of steak and sautéed vegetables onto his first fajita, he said, "So how do the contacts look?" He tilted his head to one side as if posing for a picture.

Toni squinted for a second then shook her head. "Can't see them," she said, dead pan. "I can't tell *what* they look like."

He picked up a tortilla chip from the bowl and pelted her with it across the table. She yelped and laughed.

"Seriously, Toni. Your opinion means a lot. What do you think?" He set down the fajita fixings and held out his arms. "Better? Worse? Do I need plastic surgery to be pulled out of the depths of nerdiness? What?"

"They're great," she finally said, almost reluctantly. He wanted her opinion, and she had to be honest. She looked at his face, studying it. She'd never really looked at his eyes, not like this. "I didn't realize your lashes were so dark."

She scooped some refried beans onto her fork and casually tried to segue from the contact back to last night. "Were the contacts Brooke's idea?"

"Actually, no." Carter took a healthy bite of his fajita and chewed thoughtfully. He swallowed then continued. "I asked her opinion about tossing the glasses, but it was something I was already thinking about."

They both nodded and lapsed into eating their meals. Toni scrounged for another topic about last night, something more surface level that Carter would feel comfortable answering. "I'm assuming you and Brooke were chaperones at the high school dance?"

"Yep."

"And you had a good time?"

"A really good time."

Toni nodded and watched Carter eat for a minute before prodding further. "All right," she said, tossing her fork to the table. "Do I have to beat it out of you? Just spill it already."

Carter looked up, set down his fajita then sighed. "All right. I'll try to answer. What do you want to know?"

Try to answer. It was better than nothing. "Just start the beginning."

Carter proceeded to relate how they went to dinner then gave brief synopsis of the dance itself, mentioning that they had gotten pictures taken and that he actually got to dance for once. He stayed surface-level on his narration, though, finishing with, "When the dance ended, we left, ran into you, and then . . . I took her home."

Not quite. He was leaving out one big part.

"Anything else?" Toni asked innocently—then found herself looking at his lips and wondering for a flash of a second what it would be like to kiss them. She shook herself back to reality. "I mean, come on. That's not much of a story. You gotta give me something to work with here."

Carter folded his arms across the table as if in challenge to her. "Oh, am I supposed to give you some juicy details? Something like all the juicy details you've given up about Clint?"

"Touché," she said, but suddenly couldn't look Carter in the eye. She stroked the condensation on her glass as it the streaks were the most important thing in the world. "Guess I deserved that."

Neither said anything more for a couple of minutes. Toni thought of all the things she used to tell Carter about her boyfriends. About how lately she'd avoided telling him anything about Clint. How it all seemed so wrong to be holding back—or telling stuff. How it felt wrong for Carter to be looking so gorgeous without glasses and kissing nice, beautiful women.

Toni looked up, sadness washing over her. She refused to let the mistiness in her eyes turn into tears. "Carter, what's happened to us? I mean, we used to tell each other everything. We used to know every tiny detail about each other. Heck, I used to know which pairs of your socks had holes."

He tried to smile but didn't manage much of one. "I don't know." He set his fork down and leaned back with a sigh. Toni noted that he hadn't denied things changing. Not a surprise. They'd both have to be drunk and stupid not to sense it. "I suppose things had to change sometime. We're grownups now." His voice had an edge of regret.

She rubbed her fingers together, the moisture from her glass dissipating between them. Still unable to meet his eye, or she'd risk crying right there, she said, "You know how badly I handle change. Don't tell me things have to change after all these years. We've managed to make it work for so long."

A pregnant pause, followed by, "Made what work, Toni?" Carter's voice was tense and emotional. "We've fed each other's frustrations, wallowed in our miseries—especially in not finding someone to marry. So how are things changing? Well, maybe we're both growing up finally. For better or worse, we may as well admit that we've started to grow apart."

Toni nodded miserably but didn't say anything. A few tears tumbled down her cheeks, but instead of talking, she began eating in earnest. She let the food be her emotions, and she was eating them away. She'd nearly finished off the plate before saying anything more. When her plate was empty, the familiar discomfort of a fully stomach followed, and with it, the urgent need to purge. She wiped at her moist cheeks and under her eyes, where she knew her makeup had likely smudged. "I must look terrible," she finally said. "I need to clean up. I'll be right back."

Carter's hand shot across the table and grabbed her. "No, you don't."

Toni's face clouded as she looked at his hand around her wrist. "Excuse me?"

"Don't go in the bathroom. You look fine. Use the compact in your purse to check out your face and fix it if you have to, but *don't* go in the bathroom."

Stunned and confused, Toni sat down, and only then Carter's grip relax. "And exactly why shouldn't I go the restroom?" she asked in confusion. "I'm not a child."

"Because I know what you do in there, and I'm not going to let you do it."

He knew? *How?* Toni cocked her head and tried to play dumb. "I'm going to splash some water on my face to get rid of my red cheeks. Then I'm going to powder my face and reapply some lipstick—"

"I'm not stupid, Toni. You're going in there to throw up."

"Oh."

He did know. A surge of anger went through her at his efforts to stop her. She stood and dropped her napkin onto her place. "I'm going. This is none of your business."

Carter stood and blocked her way. "I'm not letting you go in there. You're sick. There's a name for what you do."

Toni rolled her eyes. "Oh please. I'm not bulimic." Even as she said it, her hand went to her purse, where she kept a bottle of ipecac for times when she needed a little help in starting the process. It was easier than carrying a wooden spoon around.

"You need help. You can't keep doing this to yourself."

Toni ripped her arm from his. "Who are you to tell me what I can and cannot do, Carter Mackenzie? You are *not* my psychiatrist. You are *not* my boyfriend. You aren't even my brother. And you sure as hell aren't my father." She pulled a twenty from wallet and threw it at the table. "There. That should cover my half and then some. This is *my* life. Stay out of it."

She stormed out of the restaurant without looking back.

Chapter 25

T he studio's spring recital was Friday night. Carter had spent the days since their fight at the restaurant waiting to hear from Toni, but he'd heard nothing. Not a call, not an email. Not even a measly text. He didn't dare contact her first, not after the bitter anger he'd brought out. Maybe in another week he could try to apologize.

Except he didn't know how he'd do that. It wasn't like he'd done anything wrong to be sorry about, and he *wasn't* sorry for trying to stop her from hurting herself. The only thing he was sorry about was that she was ticked off at him. That he'd hurt her. But she needed to hear it.

He'd stayed silent on the eating disorder for weeks. Actually, he'd almost forgotten about it because of everything going on with Clint and Brooke. But no way could he ignore it when Toni sat in front of him, wolfed down a meal on a plate bigger than her head, and immediately tried to throw it all back up.

The recital had been on Carter's online calendar for months, and he'd fully intended showing up like he always had. Tonight would the first time he'd miss a performance. Reluctantly, he deleted the recital from his calendar then called Brooke to see if she was up for driving an hour to a new exhibit he'd heard about.

Toni probably doesn't want me there anyway.

What he didn't want to think too hard about was another truth: that he'd would rather not see Toni dancing with the short dude. Carter had decided that his romantic feelings for Toni were going away—finally—as he let himself get closer to Brooke. Seeing Toni and Clint moving together sensuously in a Latin dance would only bring back all those old emotions and thoughts. Better to keep them on a shelf to gather dust. Where they belonged.

The trip with Brooke to the exhibit was pleasant, but he felt distracted the entire time. He wondered how long the recital was going, whether Toni had performed with Clint yet. Whether she'd gotten the flowers he sent in his absence. Whether she'd even read the card explaining that he couldn't come and wishing her luck.

When he dropped Brooke off at her place, she kissed him then held his face in her hands. "Is something wrong? Did I—"

He shook his head and took her hands. "You didn't do anything. I've just got a lot on my mind right now. I'm sorry."

"It's okay." She gave him a peck and squeezed his hands. "Let me know if you want to talk about it, okay?"

He nodded as she opened the door and went inside.

On the way home, Carter cranked up the radio in hopes of the rock music drowning out his thoughts. It didn't work. He tried silence. That didn't work either. He hardly slept that night, as images of Clint and Toni dancing—or kissing as they had the night he saw in the studio—insisted on taking center stage in his mind.

Around seven the next morning, he got up to watch television, and only then realized he hadn't taken out the contacts the night before. No wonder his eyes were killing him. He took them out, put on his glasses then went back to the couch. The only shows on were sports and infomercials. He tossed the remote aside and, in a bit of a daze, watched an infomercial about a miracle pillow. He wasn't impressed; even *that* wouldn't have gotten him to sleep the night before.

Around ten o'clock—several infomercials and kids' shows later—the doorbell rang. Carter glanced at the door and grunted. Probably someone trying to sell something or a high-schooler earning money for their team. He hadn't showered. His attention went back to the television, but the doorbell rang again. Maybe whoever it was had heard the show through the door.

He dragged himself off the couch and answered the door. Toni stood on the other side. She wore sweats with the studio's logo, and her hair was back in a ponytail. But why was she here? Probably to tell him off and end their friendship officially after days of icy silence.

"Can I come in?" Toni asked.

Carter didn't say anything, just nodded and stepped aside. He motioned for her to take a seat on the couch, and he sat across from her. Toni twisted a silver ring on her right hand until she spoke. "It's my fault that you didn't come last night." It wasn't a question. "I really wanted you there. I guess I assumed you'd come like you always have, and we'd be able to pick up where we left off, as if nothing had happened."

But a lot *had* happened recently. Everything was changing between them. They weren't the teenagers they used to be. They were growing up. Apart.

"I didn't think you'd want me there," Carter said.

"Why wouldn't I? I can't remember you ever missing a performance."

"You said to stay out of your life." Carter swallowed hard and avoided Toni's eyes.

She looked out the window, and her eyebrows pulled together. "I did say that, didn't I?" she said quietly. She looked back at Carter and tried to go on. "I'm not sure what got over me. I'm sorry. I really am. The whole food thing is such a sensitive subject right now, especially with my dad, and—" As her voice cut off, tears welled up in her eyes. She lowered her head so he couldn't see her face.

Softening, Carter reached over and took her nervous hands in his. "It's okay."

She looked up as a tear fell down each cheek. "Have I ruined our friendship for good? I didn't realize how much I count on you. You've *always* been there, and then suddenly you weren't. I assumed you'd come until the flowers arrived. I didn't think I could go on because you weren't there rooting for me."

"I wasn't sure you'd want me there."

Toni nodded. With a brighter tone that sounded put on, she added, "You can come see the show tonight."

"Since when does the spring recital go two nights?" Carter said a little disconcertedly. This wasn't over.

Toni wiped at her eyes, now smiling. "Allen hoped that the studio will draw a bigger audience, spread the word for future paid performances. I think he's stuck in his days of dancing in choruses of Broadway shows. He has a vision of the Rockies turning into a miniature New York." She laughed awkwardly then leaned forward. "Will you come tonight? Please? I just can't dance as well without you in the audience."

Carter sat back, thinking about the rumba and Clint. He forced away the knot of jealousy forming in his stomach. For his sake, for Toni's, and for Brooke's, he couldn't let those feelings resurface. Not now. The way to make sure they wouldn't come back was simple.

"I can't come," he said. "I wish I could."

"Come on, you've never missed seeing anything of mine—until last night. Why can't you? Do you have a date with Brooke? Bring her along."

"Toni—"

"Is there some other commitment you've already made?" Toni persisted. "You can come, but you don't want to."

"Are you saying I'm lying?"

Toni groaned. "It just seems like you're avoiding it. If you're still mad at me, say so."

The longer she stayed in his apartment, the more the old feelings kept wanting to return. He kept pushing them away by picturing Brooke. Kissing Brooke. Holding her hand. But then he was mentally kissing Toni.

He shook his head. "Look, I'm not mad."

"Then why won't you come?"

"Just let it rest." Carter got up and headed for the kitchen. "Want a root beer? Some chips?"

"No thanks," she said a bit too quickly.

Right. Dumb of him to bring up junk food coming off a fight about bulimia. He grabbed root beer for himself anyway and came back to the couch, hoping to find a way to chance the subject.

"Is it Clint?" Toni asked.

So much for changing subjects.

"I know I've hardly told you anything about him, but . . ." When her voice trailed off, Carter knew she didn't want to spill anything either.

But suddenly Carter had to know. "Are you guys serious?"

She seemed to consider the idea, but then shrugged. "Honestly, I'm not sure. I'd like to think we are, but . . ."

"Is he a good guy?" Carter asked. "I mean, if he doesn't treat you well, nothing will get me to go see you dance with him, because I'd have to jump on stage and use him as a punching bag."

Toni smiled at that, as if the idea of Carter beating someone up was funny. "Like I've told you, he's always bringing me flowers, chocolate, love letters . . ."

"Great. Then I wish you two the best." He leaned away slightly and looked into her eyes. "But if he's not the greatest guy since Superman, and he so much as thinks about hurting you in any way, he'll have one angry best friend wielding a sledgehammer at his front door."

Toni grinned and put a hand on his arm. Her touch felt hot on his skin. "You're the best friend a girl could have. So will you come? Clint knows that my best friend is a guy, and it doesn't bother him. He says he's looking forward to meeting you. He swears he's not jealous or anything." Toni watched Carter's face expectantly, hoping to see him change his mind. "Please come."

Carter could see her hopes, thoroughly mixed with very real pain at the thought of him not supporting her. He leaned forward and put his arm around her. "It means that much to you?" She nodded and wiped a tear from her cheek, which made him feel like a schmuck—here he was the one hurting Toni.

He opened his arms, and she scooted into his embrace. "I'm sorry," Carter said as he held her, ignoring his own issues to avoid hurting her further. "Why don't we go out for an early lunch, and I'll come tonight?"

Toni's eyes lit up. "You'll come? Seriously?" She threw her arms around his neck. "Thank you, Carter." Then, as a thought occurred to her, she pulled back. "But I don't think I can do lunch. Allen has notes about last night's show he wanted to go over with the teachers."

Carter nodded but knew better. Allen's notes wouldn't take all day. If Toni wanted to eat around him, she'd find a way. But pushing the point wouldn't help anything. "I'll see you tonight then. Break a foot."

"It's 'break a leg,'" she said, punching his arm. They both knew he'd said the wrong thing on purpose. No way could he have spent this much time around a dancer and not known it was *break a leg*. She picked up her purse to leave, and as she was about to stand, he took her hand. She turned back, eyes expectant.

"Get a little rest today if you can," Carter said. "You look tired, and you'll need all your energy tonight to wow the audience like you always do."

Toni's eyes looked a bit puffy today—they had at the restaurant before their fight, too, come to think of it. As if she'd just woken up. She looked tired a lot, and she had rings under her eyes.

She smiled, squeezing his hand. "You're sweet—and you worry too much." She leaned in and pecked his cheek. Carter closed his eyes and ordered his body not to respond to her kiss.

"See you tonight," he said.

Carter arrived at the auditorium early and took a seat dead center for the best view. As he glanced around the slowly filling room, high school memories came back—times he and Toni had come to school assemblies and plays in this very auditorium, or when he that had come alone to see her perform in dance company concerts. He half expected her to show up on stage looking seventeen again. The lights dimmed and came back on again, warning the audience to find their seats. Moments later, the recital began.

After attending so many dance performances over the years, Carter had gotten pretty good at knowing what to look for in a good dance, from choreography to technique to stage lighting and costumes.

As he waited in dread for the eighth dance on the program—Toni and Clint's rumba—he spent time distracting himself by critiquing the current dances on stage. When the seventh dance, a preschool tap number, ended, Carter sat up straighter and began rolling his program nervously. His heart raced, and he tried to keep his left leg from bouncing nervously.

Two figures entered the stage in the darkness, one dressed in black slacks and a tight black tee, the other wearing silver heels and a tight red dress with a high slit and fringe. The dress sparkled even in the dim light on stage.

The music started, and a single bright spot turned on over the dancers' heads. As the music and movements increased in intensity, gel lights from the sides went on, brightening the stage. Carter forced himself to watch everything, from Clint's arms wrapping themselves around Toni's slender frame to the intensity in every movement, the passion in his facial expression. Toni's expression matched his.

It's only a performance, Carter reminded himself. Except that he knew she really did have the hots for Clint.

A minute into the dance, though, Carter began to lean forward. Ballroom was one type of dance he hadn't seen much of, unless you counted his parents' occasional jitterbug in the living room. He found himself impressed that Toni had learned to dance like that—a style with totally different moves and technique—in such a short time. The audience loved it, too; they applauded at the end parts they particularly liked—a series of spins, a lift, a brief solo by Toni. At one point she began a move at Clint's side. He took her hand and led her in front of him in a series of incredibly fast turns, followed by a dramatic drop onto his arm.

The audience clapped and cheered, but when the music kept going—and the dance did not, the applause died down. Carter furrowed his brow. Was the dance supposed to end there?

He looked closer; Toni had gone limp. She no longer held her weight in Clint's arms. Instead, her limbs sagged, her head lolling to one side. Clearly disconcerted, Clint gently set her onto the stage floor then made a panicky motion to the tech crew at the back of the room to cut the sound. He stumbled off stage, calling for help.

The music cut off abruptly, but the lights stayed on, shining upon Toni's lifeless body. Without thinking, Carter bolted from his seat and hurriedly made his way over an endless row of legs to the aisle and to the outer hallway, where he broke into a full-fledged run down the hall. He leapt up the few carpeted stairs to the huge metal doors leading backstage, but someone had locked them, and the doors wouldn't open.

Carter whirled around and ran back up the hall to one of the side exits of the auditorium. He yanked the door open. The orchestra pit was covered by black dance flooring. Curious bystanders had gathered at the front of the auditorium, trying to get a glimpse of the unfortunate dancer on stage. Carter pushing people aside to reach the stage, where he jumped up and hurried to Toni. A man and two women from the studio knelt above her, trying to wake her up.

Unsure what else he could do, Carter ran to one wings of the stage, where he pulled the ropes for the curtain with every ounce of strength he had, to hide Toni from prying eyes. With the heavy red curtain blocking out the crowd, he hurried back to the stage, but before he could reach her, the man at her side stood and pushed him away.

"Stand back," he said. "We're waiting for the paramedics to arrive."

"I just—" Carter tried to reach her again, but other people from behind urged him back to the wing. He stood there, keeping a clear path for the paramedics to arrive, and watched helplessly. At least Toni's rib cage moved up and down. That meant something. But what had happened?

A few minutes later, paramedics rushed passed him with a stretcher, and soon they carried Toni past him and out a side door that looked like it was normally used for loading and unloading props and sets. They paramedics skillfully loaded her into the ambulance, and within seconds, the lights were flashing, and they were off to the hospital. When the ambulance had disappeared into the night, Carter noticed Toni's parents standing by the backstage doors he'd tried to open earlier. He had no idea how they'd managed to get back here but was glad they had.

He hurried over to them. Toni's mom sobbed when she noticed him and hugged him tight. "You're here," Patricia cried.

"She'll be all right," Carter said, trying to reassure himself as well as Toni's mother.

Patricia stepped back and gripped her husband's arm as he shook his head and said, "We need to get to the hospital."

Carter raised a hand. "Do you mind if I come?" But maybe that would be intruding. It wasn't like he was family.

She smiled weakly and reached out to touch Carter's arm. "Of course. We can even drive you if you like."

"Thank you, but I'll take my own car," he said. "I don't want you to worry about getting me home."

As they turned to the doors, Carter heard someone saying, "That was embarrassing. I didn't know what to do out there."

The Harpers had gone through the door, but Carter paused, his back to the voice, as he bristled and stopped to listen to Clint.

"Hey, it could have been worse," another voice said. "At least you caught her."

"At least *she's* the one who screwed up."

Short dude is a jerk. Carter tried to stuff down his anger and not smack the idiot right then and there. The Harpers were a few yards ahead and had stopped to look back. Carter waved them on. "I'll be right there," he said. "Go on without me. I'll meet you there."

He let the metal doors bang shut. At the sound, Clint and his buddy glanced over, and then continued their conversation. "Have you decided whether to dump her?" the buddy asked.

"As a girlfriend or a dance partner?" Clint asked.

"Either."

Clint tilted his head, considering the question. "I'll wait a bit before deciding on either count. She has the most incredible body, and when it comes to chemistry, she has real talent—if you know what I mean . . . she hasn't put out yet, but I think I may be able to change her mind." His grin made Carter's skin crawl.

Toni might care for this loser, but Carter wasn't about to let him talk about her this way. With two long strides, Carter reached him. He shoved his face close to Clint's, who backed away, holding his hands up.

"Whoa," he said. "What the heck? Do I know you?"

Carter moved in so close their faces nearly touched. "No, but I know you, *Clint.* And don't you *ever* speak like that about Toni again."

Clint's eyes grew two sizes, and he couldn't even stammer a reply. Carter wanted with everything in him to punch his lights out, but he held back for Toni's sake. She wouldn't want him causing a scene—or at least, any *bigger* of a scene. But he had to clench his fists and force himself not to give him a black eye, at the very least.

Carter stalked off, shoved the heavy door open, and let it slam shut behind him. He forgot the scene backstage, ran to his car, and drove as fast as he could to the hospital.

Chapter 26

Carter was frantically circling the hospital parking lot when his cell rang. A spot opened, so he quickly took it and answered Peter Harper's call.

"They took her back, and they're checking her over. She should be fine."

Good thing Carter still sat in his car; had he been standing, his legs might have dropped out from under him with relief. "I just got here," he said, unbuckling. "I'll be right in."

"No," Peter said. "Go on home. We'll be in touch when we know more."

Carter's eyes went to the emergency room doors. His heart told him to run in there and demand to know how Toni was doing, what was wrong with her. A small, logical part of his brain told him that doing so would be useless. No matter how close he felt to Toni and the Harpers, he wasn't family. He wouldn't have any rights to hearing about her prognosis or visiting her in the ICU if that's where she ended up. And Peter seemed to be basically telling him that they didn't want him hovering.

After a swallow—a pause to rein in his emotions—Carter found himself nodding. He rubbed his eyes with his free hand. "Please let me know that minute you find out anything."

"Will do."

Carter almost demanded a promise out of Peter Harper but thought better of it. Instead, he thanked Toni's father, hung up, and put the key back into the ignition. Not too long ago, he'd stayed up late waiting to hear from Toni. Tonight he'd be staying up to hear *about* her.

Three hours later, Carter had tried working on a freelance job for a sports-supply store and abandoned it in favor of streaming episode after episode of the original Star Trek. Peter finally called.

"How is she?" Carter demanded. His eyes burned with fatigue, and he rubbed them with his free hand.

"They think she'll be okay. They've got her on an IV for dehydration, and they'll be putting in a feeding tube—"

"Wow." He hadn't expected a feeding tube. "Do they know why she collapsed?" He forced himself to stop before he asked ten more questions.

"Looks like she hadn't eaten in quite a while. She was malnourished and dehydrated. Pretty simple, actually. She should be right as rain pretty soon."

Would she be fine, though? Could an IV treatment and a feeding tube cure the underlying problem? He doubted it, but he didn't know enough about this stuff. He hesitantly probed further. "She'll be totally fine after this?"

"Sure will," her dad said. "All she has to do is eat right, and she knows how to do that. She's just been overdoing it with dance and other exercise, and she hasn't eaten well recently. She'll be fine." A murmur came from the background, and then Peter said, "Patricia wants me to mention that the doctors suspect she has an eating disorder. But that's basically what I said, right? She hasn't been eating enough, and we can make sure she does. No need to worry."

Carter rubbed his forehead as he tried to figure out what he thought. On one hand, Peter's words made sense, but according to Janet at work, eating disorders weren't that simple. Sufferers needed lots of therapy for any chance of a full recovery, but eating disorders were highly resistant to treatment.

Why Toni couldn't force herself to eat a stupid hamburger—or, heck, a salad—was beyond him, but he was willing to admit that there was a lot he didn't know.

"Can I visit her?"

"In the morning, sure, but not terribly early. I'm sure she'd be happy to see you."

Peter gave him the room number, and Carter jotted it down, glad to hear that she wasn't in the Intensive Care Unit. Only after he found out that much—and that Toni would be all right—did he let himself go to bed.

After he turned off the light and collapsed into bed, his cell went off with an incoming text. Groggily, he opened his eyes and checked his phone, which was charging on his night stand. The text was one word.

G'night.

From Brooke. How had he gone all day and all evening without thinking about her? He rested on one elbow as he typed out a reply.

Sweet dreams.

He clicked send, feeling guilty for not being in touch with her at all. For not telling her that he'd gone to the recital without her. But why should he? It wasn't as if Brooke didn't know about Toni. He rolled onto his back and pressed his palms into his eyes.

How had his life suddenly gotten so complicated?

The following morning, Carter was glad it was Sunday instead of a school day, so he could go to the hospital first thing. He found the room without any trouble, but as he was about to go in, a nurse came out. Toni's door closed behind the nurse, and he hesitated, worried that the nurse would stop him and keep him out because he wasn't family.

He gestured toward the door. "Can I visit her?"

She smiled. "I should think so."

"Thanks," Carter said with relief. He began to move past her, but she held up a hand. He stopped and asked, "Is something wrong?"

"Just be extra sensitive with her feelings right now. She's pretty fragile."

Carter nodded. "Her father mentioned an eating disorder." As if he hadn't known already.

She seemed relieved that she could talk about Toni's condition, at least in generic terms. She began counting on her fingers. "Don't talk about how she looks, or how much she weighs, or anything about food. She needs to feel good from the inside, and that's the hardest thing facing her right now. This isn't about food."

"I can do that." He liked to see that this nurse—Jenny, based on her name tag—cared. Her advice helped, because he still didn't get this whole disorder thing or how it wasn't about food. Yes, it was—about food and a paranoia about being fat. What *else* could it be about? "Thanks for the advice."

"You'll do fine," Jenny said then walked down the hall.

When she had turned the corner toward the nurses' station, Carter gently pushed the door open. "Toni?" he said softly. "It's me, Carter. Can I come in?"

"Hi." Her voice was flat.

Carter inched forward into the room, where Toni lay motionless on her bed. She had an IV, and a tube filled with a white liquid went from a pump into her nose. "I came to see if you wanted to go on one of our Sunday walks," he said, hoping to lighten the mood. He had always been able to make Toni smile.

"Sorry to ruin your day." She didn't smile back, and she didn't say anything else for a few seconds. Carter racked his brain for something to say, but she finally took her eyes from her lap and looked at him with a face that looked drawn and pale. Her eyes were sunken. How could she have become so weak and sick so quickly? Or had he missed the signs?

She *had* looked unwell when she'd come to his place Saturday morning, but he'd figured it was because she'd been upset about him not coming to the performance Friday night. Maybe it had been more than that.

Toni lifted her arms—which looked like sticks—and dropped them again. "All right, I'm ready for it. Give me the lecture. I've had several versions already. Kevin called me long-distance from

California to chew me out and say that if Dad has another heart attack, it's my fault. So that was fun. Mom keeps asking why I'd do this to myself. And Dad's third lecture, the one about mono-unsaturated fats was especially riveting." She turned away and stared at the ceiling from her pillow.

"I didn't come to—"

"No, let's have it." She spoke without looking at him. "It's bound to come out sooner or later. You always told me to eat more, and you about attacked me in the restaurant when I wanted to get rid of my lunch." Her voice turned mocking. "'Toni, take care of yourself. Toni, don't throw up. Toni, you're sick. You need help.'" She finally turned to him, her eyes glaring. "Come on." Her voice rose a few notches. "I know you're thinking it. You might as well say it. 'Toni, you failed everyone who loves you. You owe your family better than this. Do you realize how much one day in a hospital costs?'"

Once again she stopped, but this time she turned her face to the far wall so he couldn't see her face, but he could hear her sobs. He'd never seen Toni so bitter.

He crossed the distance to her and stood by her bed, unsure whether she'd let him take her hand or hug her or touch her at all. "I came because my best friend collapsed and took a ride in an ambulance. Of course I worried. And I've missed you." When she didn't bite his face off, he sat at the foot of her bed. Her legs seemed tiny beneath the covers. He swallowed against a sudden tightness in his throat. "It scared me when you collapsed. Watching the paramedics carry you away . . . it felt like they were taking the best part of my life from me." He took her hand, and she didn't pull away.

"What about the restaurant?" Her voice was still quiet, but not as bitter. "Are you going to say that you were right? I said horrible things to you when you tried to stop me, and now look at me. You may as well say you told me so." Toni gestured around the room, her eyes resting on bag of fluid feeding her, stopping at her hands. "I thought you'd either come to chew me out or you wouldn't come at all."

Carter shrugged, remembering Jenny's advice. "That's not why I'm here."

"Then why *are* you here?"

"Friends support friends, remember?"

Toni glanced at their hands then looked at Carter as if she wanted to believe him. Her lips trembled, and tears welled up in her eyes. "You're not angry with me?"

Carter smiled as his own tears finally fell. He covered her hand with his other one, enveloping hers. "I never was angry, just worried. You're my best friend. It would take a lot more than a stupid fight in a restaurant to get rid of me. You should know that."

Toni clamped her eyes shut, but tears squeezed out anyway. "Thanks," she whispered. "I needed to hear that. My parents keep telling me how I've let them down. The doctor has them convinced that I'm anorexic. You know that's not true, Carter. You've seen how much I can eat in one sitting."

Carter bit his cheek, trying to find a response. True, she could eat a lot, but then she usually threw it all up. Hadn't they just talked about that? "Yeah, I know how much you can eat," he said flatly. "But maybe it would make everyone a bit happier—doctors, too—if you'd maybe eat smaller amounts more often. Maybe even put on a pound or two."

Toni snatched her hand away angrily. "Forget it. You're on their side."

Shoot. He'd just talked about the very things the nurse had warned him against. He felt as he were walking on ice that was thick in some places but paper thin in others, and he had no way of identifying the danger spots. He decided to take on a different subject. He cleared his throat and said, "How are you feeling?"

Toni rolled her eyes. "Like garbage. Better than last night, I guess, though. This thing," she said, indicating the tube in her nose. "Makes my throat sore. And I'm sure the stuff they're putting in me is so fattening that I'll be a jiggling blimp by the time I get out of here." She gave the tube a disdainful flick. "I want to yank the thing out more than once, but the nurse says that if I do, they'll restrain me during my 'feedings.' That's all I need—to feel like a mental patient."

What was he supposed to say to that? "What happens next?" Carter asked. "Do you get to come home soon . . ."

"Not until my weight goes up a little, and even then, the doctor may decide to send me to an institution."

"What?"

Toni shrugged. "That's what it would feel like. It's like rehab, but for people with eating disorder patients. You do group therapy and all kinds of other humiliating stuff. But since this is my first 'offense' I may get to go straight home as long as I promise to go to therapy on my own."

Carter hesitated before asking, "Will you?"

"Will I what?" Toni picked at lint on her blanket. She knew what he was asking.

"Go to counseling."

"Not you, too." Toni groaned. "I do not have an eating disorder, so I do not need counseling. I have good self-control, and I let it get the better of me for a couple of days when I got stressed-out over the performances. Now I know my limits, so this won't happen again. It's not like I'm in any danger of getting too thin. Look at my hips. They're huge."

Carter leveled a stare at her. "You have nothing on your hips but skin." He refused to take her bait by looking at them. He knew what they looked like. How bony they had become.

She folded her arms and shook her head. "Why did I think you'd be the one person who would understand and support me?"

Anything Jenny had told him flew out of his head as emotion took over. He stood and gestured at her body. "Look in the mirror and see for yourself. Your hips can't *get* any smaller, because you can't shrink bone! You're thin. *Too* thin. Just eat already." The instant he finished his speech, he regretted every word. He had just done everything the nurse had warned him not to do.

But couldn't she see it for herself? She'd have to be blind not to see that she was too thin.

"You think I can't get any thinner." Her voice sounded paper thin.

Carter's chest clenched, and he began cursing in his head.

"Then I really don't have any hope of ever having decent-sized hips." Toni pulled her blanket higher. "I thought you were my friend."

He furrowed his brow at that. "Hey, now Toni, come on. That's not what I meant. I—"

"After what you said at the restaurant, I don't know why I thought you'd be there for me." Her jaw tensed before she added, "Please leave." She didn't look at him, and her voice was laced with anger. "Now."

Carter had no idea what to do or say. He wanted to say so much, but chances are, he'd screw things up worse than he had already. He backed toward the door, but Toni wasn't finished.

"And don't come back. Ever."

He opened his mouth to say something, but nothing came out. His throat constricted, and his eyes stung.

Somehow, he turned around and pushed the door open. He took long strides down the hospital hallway, trying not think about what Toni had just implied about their relationship.

Despite what Jenny the nurse had said, he knew this whole thing involved food—eating it or not eating it. Binging and purging—or not. Wasting away on one hand or eating enough to stay healthy on the other. But he should have kept his mouth shut.

When he reached his car, he looked up to the floor he thought she was on and wondered if she could see him. Toni couldn't seriously mean for him to never come back. Maybe not back to the hospital.

After the doctors discharged her from the hospital, things would be different. They would. They had to be.

Chapter 27

T he next two days were a blur for Carter. He had no contact with Toni—the second time ever they'd had radio silence during their friendship. Both had been in the last few weeks. That didn't bode well.

Maybe she meant it this time—the "don't come back ever" part.

Tuesday night he decided to attempt to enter the land of the living again, so he took Brooke to a movie. He paid little attention to it even though it was a film he'd wanted to see ever since seeing the trailer months before. Afterward they went on a long walk in the crisp spring air, past the trees with buds getting ready to burst.

He was trying to enjoy the walk, like he'd tried to enjoy the movie, but he couldn't get Toni out of his head. Her words. Her weak body. Her collapse on the stage.

Her anger when she said to go away.

She looked so frail in that hospital gown. Did she weigh even a hundred pounds anymore? He remembered a time when she bragged about her weight because she was tiny but weight more than one would expect—but it was all muscle. No longer.

As Carter and Brooke walked through the dusky streets, she studied him from the corner of her eye, and when he didn't talk, she finally broke the silence. "Something's been on your mind all night. Want to talk about it?"

Carter ripped himself out of his thoughts and tried to focus on the present. "It's nothing you need to worry about."

"You didn't answer the question. Do you want to *talk* about it?" She squeezed his hand and added, "I know it's kind of a girl thing, but talking stuff out really can help. You won't lose your man card or anything."

Carter smiled briefly at that. He took a few more steps before answering. Should he tell Brooke? Talking about another woman to your girlfriend wasn't usually the best idea, but his friendship with Toni wasn't typical, either. He plunged right in the middle of the issue. "Why are women so concerned with appearances? Why do they obsess about the size of their hips, or how big their waist is, or whether their thighs jiggle?"

Brooke's eyebrows went up as if trying to figure out where all this had come from. "You're really asking?"

"Yeah. I don't get it."

"Lot of reasons. Some of it is self-imposed, a lot of it is how the media portrays and distorts beauty. Often it's pressure we put on ourselves or that people close to the person put on them." She paused in her step and looked at him. "Where did that question come from?"

They held eyes for a moment before Carter broke away and looked at a crack in sidewalk. "Remember Toni?"

"We saw her after the dance, right?"

"Right." Carter tugged Brooke's hand, and they kept walking. He found talking easier when he kept moving. "Saturday night she collapsed on stage."

"That's awful," Brooke said, brows furrowing. "Is she okay?"

"She's in the hospital being treated for dehydration and malnourishment. They say she's got an eating disorder or two. I've seen some signs lately that make me think it's true."

Brooke shook her head slowly. "I'm so sorry."

"I went to visit her the next morning." He could still hear Toni's voice telling him to leave.

"And?" Brooke prompted when Carter didn't continue.

"I've never seen her so angry. It was all I could do not to go get a double cheeseburger and shove the thing down her throat." Carter looked up at the emerging stars overhead. "I don't get why she's hurting her body to stay thin. She's so skinny now that it's not attractive, but she still thinks her hips are too big. Can't she see that she's killing herself?"

"It's not about small hips," Brooke said.

Carter almost missed her words. "What do you mean?"

"It's not about cellulite or pounds or fat grams or calories. It's not even about food. Eating disorders go a lot deeper than that."

Carter's eyes flicked over to Brooke and then back to the sidewalk as they strolled along. She had known an awful lot about eating disorders to say something like that off the cuff. He almost didn't dare say anything else, but finally mustered the courage. "Did you used to be…"

"No." She shook her head, and he sighed with relief. "But my mother was. Well, *is*. She was in and out of the hospital for years. I was the oldest, so when Mom was sick, I was the mom. At nine, I got my younger sisters and brother ready for school each morning. I packed our school lunches—usually peanut butter and jelly sandwiches and an apple. I did the laundry. If Dad worked late, or was with Mom at the hospital, or she was checked out in bed, I made dinner."

Carter put an arm around Brooke, and she drew close, resting her head on his shoulder. "I had no idea," he said. "That must have been so hard."

Brooke looked up with a melancholy smile. "It made me grow up. By my twelfth birthday, I could make one mean chicken enchilada." She stopped walking and turned to him again. "Whatever she's going through really has *nothing* to do with food."

He felt the blank look on his face, but he couldn't do anything about it. "Then what *is* it about?" He raked his fingers through his hair. "I thought if we could get her to eat regularly and keep it down, she'd be fine."

"That doesn't work, because the underlying reasons for the disorder are still there. That's like someone overweight going on a crash diet, thinking it'll fix their problem, but what happens the minute they stop dieting?"

"They gain it all back and more," Carter said. It was the reverse problem, he supposed, and that made some sense. "She needs new habits?"

With a shake of her head, Brooke said, "That and so much more. It's not just habits. It's about the tapes running in our heads, the lies we tell ourselves and believe."

"Okay . . ." Carter tried to process it all, even though he knew he didn't fully get it.

"With eating disorders, the problems usually have something to do with the person needing to control, absolutely, one part of her life. Or it's about perfectionism—trying to live up to an impossible standard. Either way, she doesn't feel good about herself, no matter how hard she tries. I'm willing to wager she pushes herself hard in anything she decides to do, am I right?"

"Oh yes," Carter said, remembering how hard Toni had always worked on her school work and dancing, always striving for better marks, better technique. Even when she reached a goal or got an award or other recognition, it never satisfied her for long. Somehow, she could always explain away any recognition or compliment and find the flaw in her performance.

Brooke nodded toward a bench next to a store. They walked over and sat on it. "Here's the thing. If Toni's anything like my mom and a ton of others I've seen, she wants to be perfect at everything. But she can't. This is one area she *can* be the best in—she can control what goes into her mouth."

"Or what doesn't."

"Exactly. Obviously, I don't know what her issues are. But I can say that controlling what goes in her mouth and where the needle on the scale points is one way she feels she can manage her life, the one area that no one else has any say over. And that can feel really, really good. Almost like a drug."

"It's like an addiction, then?"

"Yeah."

Carter leaned forward, with his arms on his thighs. "So what can I do? I've made a mess of things as it is."

"I doubt that. You guys are close." When Carter shook his head, she put a hand on his shoulder. "Okay, how did you make a mess of things?"

"I told her she was too thin and that her hips couldn't get any smaller than they already were."

"Ouch."

"I know that was the wrong thing to say—now. What do I do next? She basically told me to get lost and never come back, and she may mean it."

"I doubt she'll feel like that forever," Brooke said. "She was angry, and she said something she'll likely regret. She still needs support."

Carter held out his hands helplessly. "What does *support* mean? I don't know what to say or do. It's like all I *can* do is stand by and watch her kill herself."

Brooke put her arm around him as if to stop the gush of words. "You're right; there's a lot you can do. But don't stay away. Just being her friend may be what she needs. Sometimes family is the root of the problem, so they may not be her support system."

"Okay . . ." Carter thought through it all. "If she knows I'm still there for her, maybe she can talk it out around me, and eventually snap out of it?" At Brooke's cynical laugh, Carter turned to her. "What?"

She bit her lips together to stop the laugh. "Sorry. Just *being there* will help her chances of recovery, but in the end, the choice to change must be hers, and it must come from inside. More than that, it's a gradual process; there's no 'snapping out' of something like this. Chances are, she'll have to battle this for the rest of her life, one day at a time."

He leaned back on the bench and rested his arms on the back of the bench. "Sounds like an alcoholic or something."

"It's not too far from that." Brooke scooted close and rested her head on his shoulder. "Even after all these years, my mother has to remind herself to get something to eat if she's gone too many hours without food. She knows that a day without food could trigger the cycle all over again. She had to get a fasting blood test done recently and freaked out over it, terrified she'd slip back into her old habits."

Carter shook his head. "Sounds hopeless."

"There's always hope, and she may come through like my mom and be able to manage the disease." Brooke looked up and smiled at him. "Granted, instead of controlling her food, she tries to control her daughter's life, but that's another subject." Carter squeezed her shoulder, and she settled in next to him again. "Just keep being Toni's friend. Listen to her. Help her to see her inner value. Point out things she's accomplished by being herself, including things that are hard to measure or that people may not see. Toni needs to know she matters, no matter what. And that even if she royally messes this up, she is still worth something."

They lapsed into silence for several minutes as Carter processed everything Brooke was telling him. He'd never had a girlfriend who didn't look with suspicion on his relationship with Toni. Yet here Brooke was encouraging the relationship, for Toni's sake. "I wish I could have you standing behind my shoulder to coach me next time I talk to her. Or even better, standing in front of me so I can use you as a shield if she throws something."

Brooke laughed and patted his chest. "I'm sure you'll do fine. Just keep repeating to yourself that it isn't about the food. If the other issues get resolved, the food part is relatively easy to take care of but getting her to chew and swallow won't solve a thing."

Chapter 28

During Toni's entire hospital stay, Clint didn't come to visit once. At first, she told herself that he didn't know which hospital she was in, or that he couldn't get her room number because of privacy laws. That rationalization didn't last long. He had been right there when the ambulance drove away. He could have asked Allen or someone else—she'd gotten balloons and flowers from the studio.

She kept coming up with other excuses. Clint must be so busy training and coordinating his dance classes and teams. It didn't matter that because the recital over, the studio work load dropped off until summer classes started. Even that excuse evaporated as so much mist.

About two hours before her discharge, Clint finally made contact. She was eating a light lunch—blessedly, her last meal there. This one was made of real, if gross, food rather than the liquid they'd gradually weaned her off. The awful feeding tube was no longer in her nose and down her throat. She mostly pushed the food around her tray, but she knew the nurses would check to see how much she'd eaten, so she forced down a bite here and there. Her cell went off, and her mother passed it to her.

Toni's weakened arm reached out and took the phone; it felt three times as heavy as before. She checked the caller ID. Clint.

Finally. "Hello?" she said, eager to hear what had kept him from visiting.

"Hey, how's my beautiful woman?"

"It's so good to hear your voice," Toni said, leaning against the pillows. "I've missed you."

"Missed you too," Clint said. "I haven't seen your face for longer than I can stand. When do you get to come home?"

"Today, actually," Toni said. "I'm leaving in a couple of hours."

"Great. Maybe I can pick you up tonight, and we can have a night on the town. What do you say?"

Toni laughed and sketched a glance at her mother. "I doubt I'll be up to that. I'm still a little weak. Besides, I promised my parents I'd stay with them for a few days."

"Oh. Well, how long will it be before you can dance again?"

"Give me a week or so, and I'll be fine," Toni insisted. Her mother motioned out the door, likely on her way to grab something from a candy machine. After she left, Toni asked what had been on her mind. "Clint . . ." Her voice wavered slightly. "Why didn't you come see me?"

He breathed out hard. "Honestly? I couldn't handle seeing you helpless. And hospitals give me the creeps. Besides, I didn't want to ever remember you less than the energetic, hot chick I've always known you to be. I suppose that's a little selfish."

The hurt that had been festering wasn't quite appeased, but some of what he said made sense. She *was* glad he hadn't seen her with greasy hair and a feeding tube. Clint's voice reassured her, and she began looking forward to being held in his arms and dancing with him again. Besides, it wasn't any wonder that Clint was getting antsy for her to be well enough to dance; they were working on all five Latin dances so that they could compete together in a few months. With Toni new to ballroom dance, they needed all the practice time they could get. When Clint hung up, Toni set the phone down and returned to her lunch.

Her mother walked in a minute later. "I don't like the way that Clint boy works," she said, opening her candy bar. She took a big bite out of it, and chewing, said, "A gentleman should always be there for his lady."

"He had his reasons for not coming, Mom," Toni said and took another bite of sugar-free Jell-O, which was easy on her stomach. At least, they'd said it was sugar free. She'd be pissed if they'd lied about that.

"He's your boyfriend," her mom said with her hands up in surrender. She returned to packing the last of Toni's cosmetics in a bag. "But I'm just telling you that a real man isn't afraid of walking into a hospital room to support the woman he loves."

T he only way Toni avoided moving from the hospital to an in-patient home was by agreeing to go to counseling, both individual and as a group. She went from her hospital room to her old bedroom, which had been converted to a guest room-slash-craft room.

Two days later, she almost didn't go to the first group therapy session. Her mother had to drive Toni there, and waited outside the whole time, neither of which gave Toni much of a chance to ditch the session like she and Carter used to ditch high school drama class once in a while.

The meeting was okay, as far as it went. Toni said little to the ring of women, who all introduced themselves with their name, followed by their eating disorder. She didn't want to be a label. An emotional hour later, when she got back in the car, her mother probed about how it went and what happened. Toni refused to talk about it.

"Sorry, but it's all confidential," she said as she buckled herself in the passenger seat. Her words *were* true; she couldn't violate the other women's privacy by talking about what they'd said. But she *could* talk about what she'd thought and felt. And said, pretending she'd said more than a couple of words.

She just *wouldn't*.

As they drove home, her mother obviously didn't dare pry, apparently satisfying herself by asking, "Are you glad you went?"

Toni shrugged and stared out the window.

Mom tried again. "Are you going back next time?"

"I don't have much of a choice, do I? If I don't go, I'll be locked up with a bunch of crazies in the psych ward."

Her mom sighed. "You still can't see that you have a problem, can you?"

"I *don't* have a problem," Toni said. "It's you and Dad who think I do, so I'm doing this for you."

Her mom was silent for a second. Then, "For us?"

Toni wouldn't look at her mother. "Mostly for Dad. No matter what I do, it's never good enough for him. I've never been good enough. I should have been another son."

"Oh, come on. You're the only child in the family with a pet name. He spoiled you rotten with treats and dresses. All the extra attention drove the boys crazy. I can't count the times they came to me complaining how it wasn't fair that Dad treated you differently just because you're a girl."

"Funny that I don't remember it that way," Toni said, slouching farther into her seat. "He did treat me differently, but not like that. I remember constantly hearing, 'I'm disappointed in you, Toni. But you won't let us down next time, will you?' If I didn't come home with a 4.0, he shook his head and sighed. If I came home two minutes after my curfew, I got a lecture—he expected more of me, even on the same night Brandon came home an hour later than I did. If I used a teaspoon too much peanut butter, I'd hear about it for a week. My whole life, I've either been too stupid or too fat or too thin. Second place in that gymnastics competition when I was ten? Not good enough for him. We're a family of winners, see. Second place isn't a winner. I keep trying, but I'm never good enough. For once I'd like to hear him say, 'Toni, you've made me proud. You're a great daughter.'"

Her mother glanced her direction then faced the road again. She chewed the inside of her cheek as if with worry.

Toni wiped at her cheeks. "And this time I really blew it. If I would have eaten something on Saturday, had more to drink even, I could have avoided this whole thing. And now he's upset because of the hospital bills." Toni hit the door in frustration. "At least I'm not on your medical insurance anymore. I shouldn't have ever let him keep me on it as long as he did."

"I remember why it happened," her mom said quietly.

"I do too, but I should have held out and refused as an adult."

"He was worried about you being on your own. You weren't doing so well financially those first couple of years, you know."

"But I managed." Toni turned to her mother, hoping that she, of all people might understand. "I'm glad that I refused to let him buy me a used car or pay car insurance. Did you know he wanted to pay my utilities, too? He was sure I'd forget and have the water turned off." Toni grunted. She'd always felt the need to be independent. Having her daddy constantly trying to pay her way through life didn't help.

They drove for several minutes in silence, when Toni broke it with, "Do you think I can move back to my apartment soon?"

Her mom smiled through a sigh. "It's been nice to have you home again, sweetie. I know it's been hard for you, especially since Dad's retired and home all the time. I doubt he'll want you to leave anytime soon. But it's really up to your doctor and your therapist."

Even when she had the medical clearance to live alone, she might not leave right away, no matter how much she wanted to. She had two reasons, both of which sucked. She wanted to please her father for once. Leaving while he thought she was sick would give him one more thing to be disappointed about.

And second, her small apartment would feel cavernous and lonely without a connection to Carter. He hadn't tried to contact her since she'd sent him away. Since she'd meant it. But she didn't anymore. She may well have cut off the only person who had always been in her corner.

Chapter 29

A month later, Toni was still going to therapy, but since she wasn't working, she didn't bring in a paycheck. If something didn't change, she'd lose her apartment. For the time being, she pulled money from savings to pay rent and prayed she'd get moved back in sooner than later.

Six weeks after her collapse, she was back to teaching a few afternoon classes a week and practicing with Clint again. They didn't have late dates anymore, because her father had taken on the role of protector. Two nights in a row, he stayed up until she got home. When she walked in, he marched her to the kitchen to watch her eat something, usually a sandwich, and he kept watch while she got ready for bed, so she wouldn't have a chance to throw it up.

He'd effectively turned her back into a child. She often resorted to taking ipecac when her father wasn't looking, so she'd just look ill when it came back up and it wouldn't look intentional.

Clint got a little frustrated with the arrangement, as well. "Come on, stay out tonight. You're an adult." He came up with reason after reason for her stay out, and she agreed with most of them, but never followed through. She didn't have the energy to stand up against her dad. Acquiescence was easier.

Falling to Pieces

Since he refused to come to the Harpers' home for any longer than it took to pick her up at the door, Toni spent many hours at home alone. At least, feeling alone. Her dad was always there, but a hostile environment didn't count as company.

Several times a day, she held her cell phone, her thumb hovering over Carter's number. But her pride wouldn't let her call, no matter how badly she wanted one of their cathartic talks. For one thing, he had a girlfriend to attend to. Neither Carter nor Brooke needed her butting into their lives.

Besides, if Carter had forgiven her for yelling at him, he'd have called her. Eventually he'd realize that, in the light of day, she didn't mean what she'd said. Sometimes she liked one of his Facebook statuses, hoping that would be enough to tell him she did want contact. The ongoing silence hurt more than she could have imagined.

In the mornings, Toni sat on the living room couch, staring out the windows onto the street. She wore baggy sweats most of the time, often with a blanket wrapped around her, even though the house was plenty warm for everyone else. And she thought. A lot.

But too often when Toni leaned against the back of the couch and stared through the windows, her father came in and tried to give her a pep talk. Thing like how simple it was to eat right. How unattractive she was without a "little padding," and how she could make *everyone* around her happy if she'd stop being so selfish and just eat more.

One day Toni's thoughts grew darker and darker, and soon she couldn't see anything beyond her own miserable situation, with no one to turn to who understood. She hated her body; it jiggled all over and was so much bigger than before. She couldn't quite believe the doctors' assurances that it was water weight, that it would go away when her body learned it wouldn't be starved anymore.

Some of it *had* to be fat.

The discoloration and puffiness around her eyes were still there, though—another side effect of throwing up, she'd recently discovered. She worked hard at covering it up most of the time with makeup, but she hated that her eyes—her best feature—looked bad along with the rest of her. Someday she'd be done throwing up, and when that day came, her eyes would look good again. She'd thrown up less than before, and they did look a bit better.

She pulled the blanket around herself and wished for someone to talk to. Not her dad. Not Clint—they didn't ever really *talk*, not like she and Carter once had.

Everything always came back to Carter.

Her eyes blurred, and she sniffed. Her head fell onto her arms, and soon she found herself letting go and sobbing.

Just then, her dad walked in. Toni hadn't heard him come in and wasn't aware of his presence until he put his hand on her shoulder. She jumped. "Oh, it's you," she said, trying to wipe her eyes and keep her voice even, as if he wouldn't realize she'd been crying.

He sat at the edge of the couch and put his arm around his daughter. She didn't move closer. She stayed in the same position and tried to keep her tears at bay. "Come on, dumpling. You don't have it so bad. You've got a great life. Think how much better it will keep getting when you decide to give up this silly habit."

He patted her leg. His words and his touch lit the fuse. Her frustrations came to a head; Toni couldn't stand another minute of it. After years of staying silent, she spoke her mind to her father for the first time. "What do you know about my so-called great life?"

"Oh, dumpling. I know a lot more about you than you give me credit for." He smiled wistfully. She looked away. "Remember, I used to change your diapers."

"I'm hardly the same person. I've changed, if you haven't noticed," she said, motioning up and down her small frame.

"Physically, sure you've changed. You're a full-grown woman now. But inside you haven't changed all that much. You have no idea how much a parent can know about a child without the child ever understanding."

Toni turned to him and narrowed her eyes. "Maybe that's true with some parents. But you don't know me. You've never tried to get to know me beyond the time I was your little tomboy in pigtails. If you did, you'd know how much I've wanted for you to care, how I dreamed of you being proud of something, anything, I did."

His brow furrowed. "What in the world? I've always been proud of you growing up. I came to every recital, every gymnastics meet, every—"

"And never once had one nice thing to say to me. Instead of a pat on the back, I'd get, 'Well, I suppose that'll have to do, but next time you'll do better, won't you?'"

"I knew your potential. It was my job to make sure you'd reach for the stars."

"Oh, that's what you call it," Toni muttered.

He scooted a tad closer. Toni pulled back, and he shook his head. "I tried to support you in everything you did. I don't see—"

"How you made me feel like a failure at every turn?"

His eyebrows drew together. "How could you possibly feel like a failure? Look at your grades and awards and all your other accomplishments. You're absolutely successful."

His words landed hollowly on Toni's ears. Years of actions spoke so much louder. "How could I think so when you compared me to the boys and made me feel that I had to achieve ten times as much as they did to be worth half of what they are to you?"

"I never—"

"Every night I prayed that I'd be good enough." Toni stopped, shocked at the words she'd thought so many times suddenly pouring out. She mustered the courage to go on. "That someday you'd give me a hug and say, 'I'm so proud to have you for a daughter.' But you never did." Tears welled up in her eyes and tumbled down her cheeks. She swiped at them angrily.

Her father didn't say anything for several minutes, and when Toni finally looked at him, he flicked a finger at each eye as if brushing away tears of his own. A stab of guilt hit her. "Dad, I'm sorry. You did the best job as a father you knew how. Compared to most of the kids in the world, I got lucky to have a dad like you. I shouldn't have said anything."

"No, I'm glad you did." His voice sounded husky. He coughed and squeezed his eyes to control his emotions then rubbed hands on his knees. "Didn't know you felt this way. But I'm glad it's out now. I, uh . . ." He stopped to swallow again so he wouldn't cry. "I won't bother you anymore." He lifted a hand as if to pat her leg, but withdrew it, stood, and walked out.

Toni watched him leave. *Call him. Take it back.*

But it wouldn't do any good. The words had been said. Words, that while they were unkind, were *true*. She rubbed at her forehead and stared out the window again, wishing she could call Carter and talk it out how she could both be relieved at saying something yet feel totally guilty about it at the same time.

Chapter 30

Carter sat on his bed, staring at the picture taken with Brooke at the high school dance, which rested on the short bookshelf on the opposite wall. For a reason he couldn't have explained even to himself, he got up and rummaged through his closet for a box of mementos until he found his and Toni's prom picture. To torture himself, he supposed.

He looked from one photo to the other and back again. He compared the women. It didn't matter that Toni was seventeen in the one, while Brooke was ten years older. He saw Toni as she was now: beautiful and striking, with eyes sparkling with life and possibility. He'd put the picture away for years, but seeing it again, he couldn't help but remember what his mother used to say about it—that they looked *right* together.

Then there was Brooke—classy, sophisticated, intelligent, funny. Able to make his stomach do flips in a way only Toni had ever managed to do before. The look she gave him in the picture did it again.

He sighed and lay back on his pillow, raking his fingers through his hair. He and Brooke had been dating for some time now. She'd want to know where he saw the relationship heading, if anywhere; she'd hinted as much a couple of times. They hadn't held a serious conversation about it, but they'd talked about a hypothetical future, about their goals and dreams.

They had another date that evening, but he hadn't decided on which plan to use. First he had to figure out exactly he wanted out of his relationship with Brooke. If he made one decision, he'd go ahead with a romantic dinner at her favorite restaurant to pop the question. If he chose the other route, he'd take her to a choral concert at the university and have a very different talk afterward. He was at a crossroads, and he didn't like it one bit.

He sat up again and leaned forward, his arms resting on his legs, determined to make a choice. It was time to label his feelings for Brooke. They were strong, no doubt about that. Whenever he was with her, what they had seemed like the real thing. He loved how he felt when he was with Brooke; she brought out parts of his personality he hadn't known existed. Time with her was never boring, whether they were raiding yard sales, or he was in her classroom teaching fourth graders about perspective in drawing.

But when he wasn't with Brooke, he wasn't so sure. Shouldn't he feel elated at the thought of her? He felt good when he was *around* her, but what did he feel *toward* her? His gaze slid from the picture with Brooke to the one with Toni. What this whole thing boiled down to was simple.

Am I in love with Brooke? Could he call this feeling love? And if so, was it strong enough to make a marriage? If it wasn't love, could it *become* love? He didn't act like a man in love, did he? Or think or feel like one? This wasn't what the movies or the books made it out to be. On the other hand, maybe his feelings for Toni had kept him from recognizing a more mature kind of love. Here he was teetering between asking Brooke to marry him or telling her that it was over. Either way, he might regret the decision.

And it's all your fault, he thought toward Toni. *If you hadn't kept me on a leash all these years, I'd know how I feel about her.* He didn't want to admit that the leash had been of his own making, that he'd quite willfully latched it around his neck and given Toni the other end. But acknowledging that wouldn't fix anything.

He took one more look at Brooke and smiled. The fact was, she made him want to be a better person. He loved being with her. They had similar goals and interests, and he had a feeling they could work out a pretty good marriage together. Toni had kicked him out of her life.

He let out a big sigh as he made up his mind. He stood and knocked the prom picture face down, leaving only Brooke's smiling image on the shelf. If he didn't do it, someone else would snag her soon. He'd been wallowing in limbo too long.

"I'll do it," he said under his breath, psyching himself up. He grabbed a small velvet box from his nightstand and placed it by the picture.

Chapter 31

Carter canceled the reservation at the restaurant, opting to get the food to go so he could have a candlelight dinner at his apartment. He spent hours getting the details just right and kept watching the clock for when Brooke said she'd be done with a faculty meeting. She had promised to drive over as soon as she could, so Carter raced around the apartment, making sure everything was tidy and perfect.

He'd borrowed his mother's china, silver, and goblets. The food was in fancy dishes, keeping warm in the oven. A single long-stemmed rose stood in the center of the table, and soft romantic music floated through the room.

After Brooke texted to say she was on her way, Carter dished out the food, lit the candle, and went to the bathroom for a final check. He smoothed out a piece of wayward hair then added another dab of cologne.

"This is it," he said.

Sure enough, the doorbell rang as he left the bathroom. He hurried to the door. Brooke stood on the other side, radiant and beautiful as usual.

"Good evening," Carter said, gesturing wide with his arm to welcome her inside. "Welcome to Chez Mackenzie." He took her hand, and Brooke stepped into the apartment. He led her to the kitchen table, where her eyes rested. "Chicken Alfredo?" she asked. "You didn't make this yourself, did you?"

"I dished it out myself from takeout containers."

She laughed as he pulled out her seat, and they proceeded to eat. Instead of having their usual relaxed conversation, Carter kept rehearsing what he would say, how he'd take out the ring, pop the question, and change his life forever.

As the meal wound down, Brooke took a sip from her goblet and looked Carter over. "So what is all this for?" She motioned at the table and the stereo, which kept playing her favorite slow songs. "It's not my birthday. I don't think we've hit any anniversary markers . . ."

"Does a man need an excuse to treat his lady to a romantic evening?" Carter asked, but her felt his cheek flush.

"Oh, you'll never hear me complain about pampering." Brooke leaned over and took Carter's hand across the table. He leaned toward her, and they exchanged a brief but gentle kiss.

Then he stood and held out his hand for hers. "May I have this dance?"

Brooke broke into one of her gorgeous smiles, took his hand, and stood. "It would be my pleasure."

As they walked to the living room, Carter felt for the small box resting in his pocket. They began to move slowly to the music, and Carter didn't even notice that they were dancing in the way he always mocked the students for.

Brooke leaned her head on Carter's shoulder, and after a few minutes of listening to the words of the song, she raised her head. She looked deeply into his eyes and whispered, "I love you, Carter."

Carter opened his mouth to answer, but his voice caught. The words—the correct response—refused to come out. He stopped dancing, and Brooke looked up. "Is something wrong? Should I not have said that? I—"

"No, you're fine."

"Then what's wrong?"

It didn't escape his attention that she didn't ask *if* something was wrong.

"I just realized something," he said.

Brooke's forehead crinkled, and she pulled back. "What?"

Carter released her and went to the stereo, where he turned

the music off. The room suddenly felt too silent. He tugged her over to sit on the couch, where he brushed his thumb across the top of her fingers and wished he didn't have to say what he knew was about to come out. He loved being with Brooke. He loved spending time with her and looking at her and kissing her. But he didn't love *her*. Not enough, anyway. If he couldn't say the words, how could he devote his whole life to her?

"I put this evening together for something special." He pulled the ring box out of his pocket and fingered it.

She nodded. "I figured."

He wished he could just propose; it would be much easier. "I thought I loved you as much as I needed to for us to make a life together. But now I realize that as much as I care for you, it's not enough. It wouldn't be fair to you. As much as I want to be in love with you, I just . . . I'm not. And believe me, I *want* to be." Carter released her hand and ran his fingers through his hair.

Brooke looked up at him, her eyes sparkling with tears. She clasped her hands together. "You know, ever since I met her, I've wondered why you and Toni weren't together."

Carter's head came around at that, but before he could say anything, she shrugged and laughed awkwardly. "When we ran into her after the dance, I noticed that you saw her as more than just a friend. When she was in the hospital, my suspicions grew." She sniffed and looked away, but tried to wear a smile. "I could tell you loved her, but when you said it wasn't anything more than friendship, I believed you. At first, anyway. I sort of hoped it was the truth."

He shook his head. "No. My relationship with Toni has never been anything more than a close friendship. She doesn't see me that way. But this isn't about her. It's about me and you. I can honestly say that you're one of the most incredible women I've ever known. You're beautiful and smart and funny, and you make others love life just by being with you. You're a superhero to your students."

Brooke eyed Carter, and two bright tears trickled down her cheeks. "But?"

He took a deep breath to steel himself. "*But* . . . you deserve someone who can't live without you."

She wiped her eyes and tried keep her composure. "I guess I'll have to do my best to live without you. It's not going to be easy." She noticed the box in Carter's hand and gestured toward it. "That doesn't belong to me. You should probably try putting it on Toni's finger."

With resignation, Carter put the box on the end table. "That won't ever happen."

Brooke looked at the box then back at Carter. "But you want it to, don't you?" she said quietly.

When he saw the pain in Brooke's eyes, Carter found his eyes stinging. He couldn't answer, so he merely nodded.

Chapter 32

T he last week of school, Carter hadn't seen or heard from either Brooke or Toni for days. He went through the motions of class like an automaton. He couldn't find pleasure in anything anymore, even in his art; he'd gone weeks without touching it. The oil portrait of Toni—something he'd sworn would be the last image he'd ever do of her—had been neglected ever since he and Brooke started going out. The cloth he used to cover it had gathered a noticeable layer of dust, as had his paint brushes, sketch pads, and other supplies.

On the last day of school, he handed out report cards and signed students' yearbooks without the usual pleasure from years past. He didn't stop to think that he might miss some of his seniors when they didn't come back in the fall, and he hardly noticed when they walked out the door. Some students signed his yearbook, which was on his desk, but he didn't pay attention to which ones. Eventually the buzz and flow of students stopped, leaving the room quiet.

He stared vacantly out the window, wishing he could call Toni, but knowing she wanted nothing to do with him. At times like this, he regretted his decision about Brooke. If he'd gone ahead with the proposal, he wouldn't have this horrible pit of loneliness in his stomach all the time. They'd be in the middle of wedding preparations by now—engagement pictures, selecting food, getting fitted for a tuxedo.

They would probably have gotten married during the summer break, in July before his pre-school meetings and preparations for classes began for both of them. He caught a glimpse of the cloth-covered oil painting in his office. He might have to get rid of it, he thought as he turned away and sighed.

"Hey, Mr. M, you okay?"

Carter whirled around; Keri stood a few feet away, Sharpie in her hand, probably to sign his yearbook.

"Oh, hi. I didn't hear you come in." He shook off his thoughts and put on the practiced teacher smile that hid his emotions. He reached for her yearbook as she grabbed his from the desk. "Do you have any plans for your summer vacation?" he asked, opening the cover and flipping to a blank spot.

"I've signed up for some university art classes for the summer," she said with a grin.

Carter looked up from the page. "That's great—I'm glad you're going to pursue art; you're so talented. But why not take the summer off after graduation?"

She didn't answer for a moment as she wrote something in his yearbook. She clapped the cover shut and said, "Take a break from art? You've got to be kidding. Once you showed me how to express myself, how to not be afraid of risking, I can't just stop. I feel like I have a million works inside me waiting to come out."

Carter smiled, pleased for the first time in weeks at anything a student said. Keri had made huge strides over the last year. "I hoped you'd keep going."

"I'm majoring in graphic design." She put the book back onto the desk. "There you go. I guess I should head out. I'm supposed to meet some of my friends in the commons to go out for lunch before graduation." She stood to leave but when she reached the door, she stopped and turned around. "Mr. Mackenzie? I just wanted to say thanks. For everything."

"You're welcome," Carter said. "Students like you are why I do this."

With a shy smile, Keri bit her lip, then turned and walked out. Carter slid his yearbook onto his lap and flipped through it. He didn't know most of the faces. No surprise in a large high school, where only a small percentage ever took a class that would land them in his classroom. Some students he recognized vaguely from school dances or from the halls. Others he'd had as freshman or sophomores. He stopped every so often to read a note from a student. Most of the scribbles consisted of things like "Mr. M rocks" and "Have a great summer!"

But then he reached a note almost hidden behind the index in the back—Keri's. He glanced up to where she'd stood a minute ago then back at the page.

Mr. M,

You helped me find the artist inside me. You'll never know how much that changed my life—and all because you challenged me to risk something, to expose what I had inside, and not to be afraid of getting my heart stomped on.

Now that I'm graduating, I want to give something back to you. You said you had never risked anything yourself. Well, here's my gift—a challenge: Go out and risk something. Expose what's inside you. Don't be afraid of getting your heart stomped on. It'll change your life. It changed mine. Thanks again for everything.

Keri

Carter stared at the rounded letters for several minutes. He could think of only one thing that would really constitute a risk for him, and that was something he'd almost tried to do, but hadn't: telling Toni how he felt. Keri was right; doing that would probably change his life, and not for the better. It would probably push Toni out of his life for good. Which was why he wasn't yet willing to take that risk.

She may already be out of your life, he reminded himself. They hadn't spoken in weeks.

He hadn't gone this long without Toni since the college semester he'd spent in Paris. Even then, they'd emailed several times a week. This time they weren't separated by a continent or an ocean, only a few miles and an icy wall of silence—which he'd created by saying something stupid. Carter closed the book with disdain and shoved it away.

As if he could go to Toni as things stood now and say he loved her as more than a friend. Hardly. The idea of telling her without being afraid of getting his heart stomped on would have been laughable if it hadn't been so painful. Images of Toni from years past flashed through his mind, followed by the look on her face when she's lashed out at him in the hospital.

The memories and emotion got the better of him. His eyes burned, and closed them, willing himself not to cry.

Chapter 33

As summer marched on, Toni let the silence continue with Carter; that was easier than reaching across the divide. She kept going to counseling, and although she had yet to move out, her parents no longer sat on her shoulder every minute. She told them that Carter was spending the summer at an artists' retreat to explain why they weren't seeing or hearing about him. A white lie she wished she could believe herself.

She spent more time than ever at the studio, although summer dance camps wouldn't start until July. She choreographed combinations for the camps, planned routines for her fall classes, and practiced regularly with Clint—currently she was learning a *paso doble*, known as the matador's dance where the woman was the cape.

By the mid-June, she'd regained several pounds. She was up to 107, on the low side for what her doctor insisted was a healthy weight at her height. He wanted to see her gain at least another ten. Every pound she gained and maintained felt like something to tell her father about in hopes of gaining his approval, rather than something she was doing for herself.

One afternoon she and Clint practiced their *paso doble* routine again. After running through the dance several times, Toni was fixing her pony tail when Clint eyed her reflection in the wall of mirrors. Her arms paused above her head. "What?"

He shrugged and headed to the sound system to cue the music again. "You used to have such a great body—so little, so feminine. Why are you chubbing up?" He came up from behind and held her close, running his hands down the sides of her hips. She tried not to flinch.

"My little girl," he whispered close to her ear.

Part of her wilted inside, wanted to pull away. Shouldn't Clint be able to see past her body by now? And if not, would she lose him when she continued to put on weight? She stared at her reflection, at her hips, which were still way too wide. Her stomach had never been as flat as she wanted. And she always wore leotards that covered her stomach; she couldn't stand seeing anything jiggle.

When she didn't answer, Clint turned her around and began kissing her. With her back to the mirror, and his lips on hers, all thoughts of her ugly body flew away. After a heart-pounding kiss, he pulled back. "You okay?"

She nodded mutely. "But I'd better go. Promised my mom I'd help her with something." It was a half-truth; Toni had promised to help her mom get ready for the family to come into town for the Fourth of July—which wasn't for another two weeks. Preparations wouldn't start for days yet.

But Toni had to get out of there right away. She forced a smile, gave Clint a peck, and went to get her bag from the corner. She waved goodbye at the door and left, nearly sprinting to her car and hoping Clint wasn't watching her from behind, looking at her fat body, her spreading behind, her jiggling thighs, wishing she were still "little."

She drove home with fingers clenched around the steering wheel, and when she went into the house, she hurried straight to the bathroom, where she weighed herself. One pound up from this morning. It *could* be from all the water she'd had to drink during practice. She stepped off the scale and turned to the mirror to analyze her body. Her hands instinctively went to her hips and then to her stomach as Clint's words returned to her mind. She could feel his hands tracing her hips, could hear his words about how she was "chubbing up."

She pressed her hips, wishing she could shrink them; they'd always be wider than she liked. It wasn't like dieting could change her bone structure. But they didn't have to be quite as big as they were now. She knew *that* from experience.

She eyed the toilet. Clint's words repeated themselves in her head over and over.

Five pounds would do it. She could lose that much and be okay. *Five will be enough to make Clint happy again. It has to be.*

Toni had fully intended to keep it to five pounds—just enough that Clint would find her attractive again. But as soon as she got back into the mind set of dieting, she went into a tailspin. In two weeks, all the weight she'd gained since her hospitalization—and more—fell off. She found herself tracking her calories religiously. She worked out, and when she caved to temptation, purged—often several times a day.

With weeks of counseling behind her, she knew somewhere in the back of her mind that she was in trouble, but she couldn't stop. Night after night, she fell asleep crying. More than once she stared at her phone and willed it to make the quacking noise that was Carter's ring tone. If anyone could help her, if anyone would let her cry on their shoulder, it would have been Carter.

Would have been being the operative phrase. He had to be furious with her. If he'd forgiven her, wouldn't he have checked on her by now? She needed him in her life to ground her, but she'd been cruel to him, and there was all too good a chance that her outburst in the hospital had been the final straw that had broken their friendship's back.

On the Fourth of July, she sat at the table on the deck out back, where the family had congregated for the holiday. They'd been outside for nearly an hour. The grandkids were running around the yard, free from their dinners, and the adults were sitting around enjoying conversation as Toni tried to force herself to finish her dinner. She'd managed to get down a couple of bites of potato salad and a whole serving of green salad without dressing, which pleased her parents, but her dad kept giving her a look that said she'd better eat more.

She couldn't touch the burger or chips he'd put on her plate—not if her life depended on it. As it was, she'd swallowed the salads for one reason: she had a brand-new bottle of ipecac tablets hidden in her closet under a spare set of sheets. Purging had gotten harder lately, and she didn't know why. She relied on ipecac now to get the job done.

Eat a bite of the burger for Dad, she ordered herself *Remember the ipecac.*

She managed *two* bites, and she made a point of chewing obviously and commenting on the delicious burger, so her parents would be sure to notice. "Thanks for dinner, Mom and Dad. I'm just stuffed. Here, let me help clear some plates." She got up and gathered a stack of paper plates from around the table, careful to keep a smile on her face as she worked.

"Be right back," she said cheerily, hoping no one would notice when she really disappeared for a bit longer. And hoping the ipecac wouldn't take long to do its job. No one said a word about her helping beyond the occasional thanks from her brothers and sisters-in-law. Her mother practically beamed after seeing Toni's plate.

Inside, she slipped off her shoes to not make any clicking noises on the wood floor and hurried to her bedroom for the little brown bottle. After a quick check of the hall and kitchen, she locked herself into the bathroom, where she finished off the bottle and made a mental note to buy some more the next day. She opened the cupboard under the sink to throw it away but changed her mind. She'd put the bottle in her pocket to dispose of in the outside trash bin; it would be less likely to be found there.

Knowing that the medicine would take at least ten minutes to work, she opted to return to the porch so she her absence wouldn't be suspicious. If she played things right, her family would assume she'd come down with something. She took her spot on the bench at the table in time for her mother to dish out pie for dessert. Toni tried to be pleasant, but thoughts about

Clint and her hips and Carter and how she was totally lying to her counselor—all of it consumed her.

"Toni, are you all right?" her mother asked as she put a dessert plate with a huge slice of apple pie before her.

"I don't feel well," Toni said. "I've got a horrible headache, and I feel like I'm going to throw up." Better to prepare her family for what was about to happen, so it didn't look intentional. It wasn't lying, because she really didn't feel good. She did have a headache. And she felt faint, too, with a weird pain across her shoulders and into her right arm. Maybe her gall bladder was having trouble; she'd heard that kind of pain could radiate to the shoulder.

"You seem to be getting sick every weekend," her father said with concern. "Maybe we should call your doctor. It could be something serious."

Toni gave him a weak smile. "Oh, I'm fine," she said, waving her dessert fork, which she'd use to cut apart the pie and moved around her plate, so it would look like she'd eaten something. "It's probably just a bug I picked up from the studio." Toni covered her mouth and mumbled, "Oh boy, here it comes." She got up and ran inside.

On her way to the half bath off the kitchen, she heard her father say, "If I didn't know better, I'd think she's having a relapse."

In the bathroom, Toni let the ipecac do its job. Everything came out of her—the potato salad, the burger, her aching sadness. She wiped her mouth and flushed then sat on the toilet lid to wait for her body to stop shaking.

"She's not using laxatives anymore," her mother said from the porch.

Josh spoke up next. "She looks healthier since I saw her last. She must have gained some weight."

"It's probably just a bug like she said," her mother added, clearly pleased that Josh agreed. "She doesn't lock herself in the bathroom anymore, and she's not hiding the fact the she's sick. That should say something. Shouldn't it?"

For a moment, Toni thought that maybe she'd pulled one on the whole family. But then her dad signed heavily.

"Something's not right," he said.

Toni strained to hear more, but the world seemed to shake and tremble. She couldn't focus on anything, and the pain in her shoulder and arm intensified, spreading to her chest. She put one hand to her breastbone and closed her eyes, hoping the sensation would pass.

Instead, on the edge of her consciousness before everything went dark, Toni heard a heavy thud on the bathroom's tile floor and only vaguely registered that she'd collapsed.

Chapter 34

Toni awoke in a hospital bed. Her whole body hurt, but she had no memory of how she'd gotten here—or even of the past day or two. The first face she saw was a male nurse who was checking her vital signs.

"What happened?" she asked groggily, hardly able to keep her eyes open.

"I'll let your mother tell you about it." He turned and motioned to someone beyond Toni's view. "Mrs. Harper, she's awake now." He gave Toni a comforting smile then walked out.

Her mom came into view. Toni reached up and touched a tube going into her nose. She could feel it in her throat, too—a feeding tube. She remembered from last time. "Why am I here? Did I faint again?"

I lost too much weight again. Stupid, stupid. You were supposed to stop at five pounds.

Her mom's eyes sparkled with unshed tears, and her voice caught. "Your heart stopped, sweetie. Dad did CPR until the paramedics arrived."

"What do you mean, my heart stopped?" Toni was a dancer—she was in better shape than some athletes.

"You had a heart attack."

"Dad had the heart attack," Toni said, brow furrowing. She tried to think through the fog, but nothing made sense. Twenty-somethings didn't *have* heart attacks.

"You're lucky to be alive," her mom went on. "Doctor says that heart failure is a relatively common way for people with eating disorders to die."

Her eyes went wide, and a shudder went through her. "Die?" She wasn't *that* sick, not like the girl who looked like a skeleton who'd been on Dr. Phil.

I'm not a freak.

∽

Toni closed her eyes and pretended to sleep so her mother would stop talking; she couldn't bear to see the tears or hear her weepiness in her voice.

And Mom's making this all up. She's trying to scare me into getting better. I just fainted again.

Later that day, though, Dr. Sanders came in to talk. No family was around, and Toni was more alert than before—and trying to understand. He'd tell her the truth.

He shook her hand and sat on the foot of the bed. "It's good to meet you—awake, I mean," he said with a smile.

"It's not so good to be here," Toni replied. She swallowed, hating the tube in her throat. Dr. Sanders might not be stay long, though, so she decided to cut to the chase. "Did I really almost die?"

His smiled softened into a more serious expression. "You went into cardiac arrest. So yes, you could easily have died. Your body was in pretty bad shape. I'm impressed you made it through—you're one lucky woman."

"But I'm not even thirty, and I'm active, and—"

"And you've been taking ipecac."

Toni's mouth shut in surprise. How did he know that? An EMT had probably found the bottle in her pocket. But so what that she'd been taking it?

"Ipecac has something called emetine in it," Dr. Sanders said, clasping his hands and taking on a clinical tone. "Emetine isn't meant to be used regularly. It can build up in your system. Emetine poisoning can lead to permanent heart damage."

Toni didn't want to hear any of this. She turned her head away from him and looked out the window.

"Toni, this is serious." The doctor's voice had returned to its quiet confidence. She closed her eyes, but she was paying attention. "You *should* have died."

She squeezed her eyes tight, as if that would make the reality go away. What if she'd moved back to her apartment and had collapsed there? Or what if she'd collapsed in the car, or at the grocery store, or when she was alone, choreographing at the studio? Or practicing with Clint? She'd bet a lot of money that he wouldn't have known CPR like her dad did.

Her chin lowered. "I didn't know it could hurt me," she said softly. Mentally she added, *I had to do something. I'm sorry, so sorry. But I had to do something.*

"You've been at this for a long time, haven't you?" Dr. Sanders' voice wasn't critical or judgmental like her father's. He sounded like he really wanted to know.

She nodded, but then shook her head. "Not the ipecac part. That's only been the last few weeks. But not eating much. And the binging and purging . . . Yeah. Those have been around for a while."

Dr. Sanders nodded. "Years, am I right?"

Toni nodded, but her brow furrowed. "How could you tell?"

"You've got the bones of a sixty-year-old. Your teeth are eroded in the back from stomach acid. I could go on."

All of that—and more—from dieting? *You know it's not just dieting.* Toni gripped the thin hospital blanket. The room felt so cold, but the coverlet didn't offer much warmth. She took a deep breath and vocalized a fact she hadn't revealed even in therapy. "I threw up for the first time on my second day of college," she said quietly. "It didn't become a big problem until the last year or so. Maybe two. Or three."

The admission felt like the ultimate in failure. At least her parents weren't here to listen to her confessions. She couldn't handle the idea of letting her parents down again. If they knew just how bad things had been, and for how long, it would crush them.

Dr. Sanders patted her leg and stood. "You're here now, and we're I'm going to see that you get the help you need."

"Thanks." It was all Toni could get out.

He moved as if to leave but then turned back. "You have to know, though, that the best doctors and therapists in the world will mean nothing if you don't work your butt off."

She smiled in spite of herself at the term; it seemed so incongruous coming from an MD.

"I'm serious. No specialist can fix this for you. They can show you the path, but you're the one who has to walk it and climb the mountains and face all the scary parts. And there will be lots of scary parts."

Toni almost rolled her eyes and told him thanks but no thanks for the pep talk. But then he added one last bit. "But you know what? I can tell you're strong. The fact that you're still here tells me a whole lot. You won't go down without a fight. You'll make it. In a few years, I expect to see great things happening in your life." He tapped the back of his clipboard in thought then nodded and headed out.

Toni lay back and stared at the ceiling, pondering his words. Amazing that a doctor who'd barely met her could zero in on who she was and what she'd done—and could have such faith in her. She rolled to one side and closed her eyes, trying to relax and let Dr. Sanders' words repeat themselves in her mind. She'd need to keep reminding herself of them.

I'm strong. I'll make it. Great things will happen in my life. I'll climb every mountain.

Chapter 35

The next morning, Toni choked down a few bites of the horrid glop the hospital called oatmeal. She even took a bite from the Jell-O cup, which was nothing but a sugar bomb. She psyched herself up, saying that each bite was another step in showing Dr. Sanders that she would eat, even though every bite was a battle, and more than once, she felt like the meals were her personal Waterloo.

After eating as much breakfast as she could stand, Toni pushed the tray to the side and watched TV as she waited for a nurse to pick it up.

She heard a knock on the door, and, assuming it was the nurse, called, "Come in."

A nurse did enter, but she wasn't one of Toni's. And the nurse was pushing a wheelchair with her dad in it. He wore a matching hospital gown.

Worry washed over her. "Are you all right?"

The nurse wheeled him right up to her bed and set the brake. "I'll be back in a few minutes," she said, and patted him on the shoulder before leaving.

"Thanks, Lisa." When the door closed, her turned to Toni. "Never thought we'd both be wearing these at the same time, did you?" he said, tugging at the top of his hospital gown. "Hate these things. I swear they're see through." He chuckled at his joke, but Toni was in no mood to laugh.

"Dad, seriously, what's wrong?"

"Oh, nothing much," he said, waving her concern away. "Just another heart attack. Happened the morning after you got here. How about that—two heart attacks in the family in one week. That must be a record or something."

Enough with his attempts at levity. "But what about your medication? Weren't they supposed to prevent another one?"

He shrugged. "Looks like this blockage was already there, but they didn't worry about it at the time, because I had so many other part of my heart trying to kill me." Again with the laughter. "Don't worry. This one's not serious; they put in a stent, and I'll be fine. I wouldn't be able to come over if I were as bad off as last time. They didn't need to crack open my chest again or anything."

Toni nodded, still concerned but somewhat pacified for the time being. "No one told me you were here," she said. "I figured you hadn't visited because you were disappointed in me."

"No, no. I asked Mom not to say anything. Figured you had enough to worry about getting better, and I could come see you myself when they let me."

Toni nodded but pursed her lips, trying to think of what to say. The hospital bills must be racking up between her care and her father's. Her bills would hang over her head as another symbol of failure. Her insurance wasn't that great, and her parents would likely end up with the brunt of the bill—or at least insist on paying most of it, even if she did get her life and career back together. She couldn't wait to be able to teach at dance conventions around the country again.

"I'm sorry about all this," she said, waving at her IV, monitors, feeding tube. "This is going to cost a lot. I didn't mean to end up here again. I've been trying hard to fix this, and up until a couple of weeks ago, I was doing really well . . ." Her voice trailed off, and she choked on a sob.

Her dad's eyes grew misty; he reached over and took her hand. "I just want you to be happy and healthy. Don't worry about the bills. It was wrong of me to bring them up last time."

Toni looked at him as if he were a stranger. "But—"

He stroked her hand and shook his head, and for the first time in her life, Toni saw a couple of tears tumbling down her father's rough cheeks. "I've been doing a lot of thinking lately," he said. "About what you said when you came home."

The conversation had been painful for Toni, but she had no idea that her father even remembered it until now.

He blew out heavily to even his breath. "I never meant for you to live your life trying to keep me happy. You were just my special angel, and I wanted everything for you. After three boys, I was so excited to have a little girl. My very own dumpling."

He looked into her eyes, and more tears fell. Her father was crying—actually crying, with tears and everything. Toni's throat tightened with emotion, and she couldn't speak, but he went on. "I was the envy of other fathers. *My* daughter was beautiful, and talented, and accomplished. I remember another dad at a dance recital saying how it looked like you could do anything." He smiled at the memory. "I didn't try to convince him that you were just an eight-year-old, and not Wonder Woman."

He looked at their hands, his rough one holding her weak, pale one. His voice choked. "I never gave much thought to how you must be feeling. I thought that not eating was just you being stubborn. But then I found you in the bathroom, and I thought I'd lost you forever. And I finally remembered what you told me that day on the couch, and I clued in that I'd really hurt you over the years. I never meant to, Toni. Please believe that." Her eyes were pleading and rimmed in red. "But I *did* hurt you. A lot. I know that now. Then I had this second attack, and well, let's just say I think it was a wake-up call from upstairs. It's time for me to set things right. You never know how long the Lord will let you stay. He could have taken me this time, but He didn't. I figure I'm getting another chance. I don't want anything to keep us apart anymore. Life's too short."

He paused and swallowed hard. "I guess what I'm saying is that I am proud to be your dad. I've always been proud to have you for my daughter, and that's aside from any accomplishments. You're amazing and wonderful just because you're you."

Instinctively, Toni reached over and hugged him as she hadn't done since she wore pigtails. She held him tight, and he squeezed her back, as if making up for years of not holding each other.

"Oh, Daddy," Toni whispered through her tears. She couldn't say more, but that was enough.

Eventually they pulled away and found themselves laughing, as if letting off more than two decades' worth of tension. "Thank you, Daddy," she said. "You have no idea how good it feels to hear you say all that."

"You're right; I don't." He reached up and gently wiped some of her tears with his thumb. "But I can imagine how awful it must have been to never have heard it. I never realized that's what I had done." After a moment of silence, he patted her hand. "Now that we're starting out fresh, tell me exactly how I can do to support you. Obviously my methods don't work." He cracked a self-deprecating smile.

"I don't need much," Toni said. "Just to know that you'll love me, no matter what."

"You've got it. I'll say, 'I love you' ten times every day if that'll cure you."

"That's not exactly what I meant." *If a cure for my disorders were only so simple.*

"I know. Tell me, what *would* help? Do you want to talk about anything?"

Toni shook her head in amazement. "I never thought I'd ever hear you say anything like that. I'd love to talk." This person sitting by her was really her father? He seemed like a totally new person. "But let's not talk about my health right now. Between counseling and living in a hospital, the topic's getting a bit stale. It's been a long time since I've had a good talk with a friend."

Her dad's brow furrowed. "You mean Carter? How's he doing, anyway? When does he get back from that art thingy?"

"He's…" Toni sighed and dove into the truth. "He's not at a retreat—never was. I actually haven't seen him since the last time I was in the hospital."

He's probably still dating Brooke anyway.

"But you two have always been inseparable," he insisted. "What happened?"

Her eyes stung, but she didn't want to shed tears about Carter, not now. At least her dad was focusing on that part, not on the fact that she'd lied. "We had a fight, and I basically told him to get out of my life. Haven't heard from him since." Talking about Carter brought up a huge wave of sadness. She'd been riding an emotional roller coaster and doubted she was up to a new round.

"Would talking things out with him help?" her dad asked after a minute.

"After all this time, I doubt he'd want to talk to me. A heart-to-heart probably would be a bad idea when he's engaged." *Or will be. Will I get an announcement?*

"What about that Clint boy?"

"What about him?" Talking about her love life wasn't something Toni wanted to do. What would she tell him, that Clint was a great kisser?

"Can you talk to him about any of this?"

"Oh, no." Toni found herself laughing at the idea.

"Does he support you in some other way? He's probably called or texted a lot while you've been here."

"Sure," Toni lied. She was doing it again. But how could she tell her dad that she hadn't heard from Clint since she had been admitted?

"I never have seen much of him," her dad said. "I'd like to get to know him, especially if the two of you are serious."

Are we serious?

Before Toni had to come up with a response, the door opened, and Lisa the nurse returned. "Time to go," she said. "They'll be thinking you've run away if we don't get you back."

"All right," her father said, then reached over to squeeze Toni's hand one more time. "Let me know what I can do for you. Please?"

Toni smiled and squeezed back. "I will, Daddy. Promise."

Chapter 36

Carter found himself standing outside Toni's hospital room, a bouquet of flowers in one hand. His stomach was twisting and turning, but Mr. Harper only grinned. Carter shook his head and glanced at the door, having second thoughts. He leaned close to whisper. "Are you sure about this? Last time we spoke, she threw me out." Of her last hospital room, no less. They hadn't talked in well over a month.

Mr. Harper nodded, grinning. "I'm more than sure. Let me go in first. I'll let you know when to come in." With that, he pushed the door open and went inside, leaving the door open. He heard Toni talking.

"Dad," she said. "You're—"

"I'm finally discharged. Had to check on my girl now that I can come in here on my own two feet. How are you feeling?"

"Pretty good," Toni said. She sounded tired, but well enough. Carter had to resist the urge to rush in a see her, hug her. "Clint came yesterday. He hates hospitals, so that's saying a lot." Carter's nostrils flared at that. *Stupid, crass, short idiot.*

"He brought me those."

Did she mean flowers? Carter looked at his small offering—three carnations. *Pathetic.*

Toni went on. "He said there were four more, but the hospital wouldn't let him bring those ones in. Some policy about latex."

Ah. Balloons. Good.

Her father spoke next, apparently ignoring all talk of Clint. "Still feel like you want to talk things out with . . . someone?

A friend?" Great stealth, Mr. Harper. Could he have been any less obvious?

"What do you mean?" Toni sounded guarded.

"I said I wanted to do something for you, right? I brought something to cheer you up."

"Dad, *what* did you do?"

"There's a delivery of flowers in the hall that I thought you might like."

Carter took a deep breath, smoothed his hair, and unlocked his knees so he wouldn't pass out.

"I hope I'm not messing things up again, but your mother thought I'd be safe with this."

Mr. Harper leaned around the door and motioned for Carter to enter. *Here goes nothing.* He stepped into the room, flowers first, hoping she wouldn't lob a hospital pillow at him to make him leave.

She didn't. Instead, Toni's hand flew to her mouth. "Carter! What are you doing here?"

Was that good shock or bad shock? Carter cleared his throat as he walked closer to the bed. "Sorry. I, uh, wasn't sure that I should come, but your dad insisted, and . . . well, here's these. I'll—I'll go now." He thrust the flowers onto the foot of her bed and gestured behind him, hooking his thumb in the air.

As he took a step back, Toni quickly grabbed his hand. "Don't go."

He stopped, now facing the door. Was she still angry? Was he insane to be here? Probably. But Mr. Harper grinned at Carter and gave a thumbs-up. Carter turned back around and waved. "Hi."

"Hi." Toni smiled, which gave him a little confidence that she wouldn't throw him out. She pulled the bouquet to her lap and fingered the greenery. An awkward silence settled over the room. Carter couldn't remember having an awkward silence with Toni, ever.

Mr. Harper looked from Carter to Toni and back again. He

jerked his head toward the hall. "I'll just wait out here," he said then quickly made his escape and closed the heavy door.

They watched him leave, Carter glad they could be alone, yet dreading it at the same time.

Toni found her voice first. "It's been a long time," she said. "How have you been?"

He opted for the truth. Carter pulled a chair over and sat on it. "Not so good."

"Oh, no, what happened?"

Aside from my best friend cutting me off? But he couldn't say that. "For starters, Brooke and I split up."

"Oh, I'm so sorry." Toni sounded genuine. Part of Carter appreciated the sympathy; breaking up with Brooke had felt like putting his heart through a trash compactor. But another part of him ached; if Toni wanted him and Brooke to be together, what did that mean for any future he could have with Toni? Because that's where they were standing—on a precipice. "Did Brooke give you a reason, or did she just walk away, like Laura did?"

Carter laughed ruefully. It was no surprise that Toni assumed the breakup had gone that direction. He shook his head. "Actually, *I* broke up with *her.*"

"Oh." Toni clearly hadn't expected that. She let out a breath—of relief? Carter would have given anything to know. "So, what happened?"

Carter picked at some dried paint on his left thumb. "It wasn't right. It wouldn't have been fair to her."

Toni nodded, seemingly in understanding

"I've really missed you this summer," Carter said.

"I've missed you, too," she said. Her eyes welled up with tears. "I'm—I'm so sorry for getting mad and sending you away."

Here it was, the subject hanging in the air between them. "No, it was my fault. I should have kept my mouth shut and not said what I did."

"But every word you said was true; I just wasn't ready to hear it."

Carter moved from the chair to the foot of the bed. "I wanted to help you, and I was terrified you'd die. Afterward, Brooke helped me understand what an ass I'd been—her mother has struggled with eating disorders most of Brooke's life. Once I got it a bit more, I wanted to sit down with you and drum self worth into your head until you understood how much you mean to so many people."

Toni laughed, but it was sharp, like bark of disdain.

Carter brought up his hands in self defense. "I know. Brooke laughed at me too. It's not as simple as repeating affirmations in the mirror every morning, is it?"

"No," Toni said simply.

Carter reached over, and she took his hand. Her touch felt warm and familiar, like he'd finally come home. At the same, something else sparked, something new. Something only he felt, surely.

"I'm doing a little better," Toni said quietly, her thumb gently moving along his index finger. "But not as good as I could be with you around. You have no idea how many times I've wanted to call and talk things out. It's my fault you stayed away. What I wouldn't have given for one of our hours-long talks."

Carter squeezed her hand. "I could have used an ear after breaking up with Brooke." He shook his head. "But that's in the past. I'm finally here now. Maybe we can start over. I'll tell you what I should have said back in April, when I first saw you in one of these beds."

Toni shifted on her pillow into a listening position. "And what would that be?"

"For starters, that so many people care about you, and we want you to be happy. I think that includes God. You're loved not because of your shape or what the scale says, but because of your heart and what you've given to so many people."

Toni lowered her eyes to the peach-colored carnations. "What could I have possibly given to anyone?"

A tear slipped down one cheek. Carter stood and wiped it away with his thumb but didn't take away his hand, instead cradling her face and gazing into her eyes. His eyes tracked to her lips and then back to her eyes. What he wouldn't give to be able to kiss those lips right here, right now. He swallowed and, to break the spell, gave her forehead a quick peck.

He took his spot at the foot of the bed again. "I can't speak for everyone, although I can guess at the joy you've brought your parents. I'm sure you've given a softer side to your brothers—which their wives must be insanely grateful for. And the inspiration you have been to dozens of girls and young women learning poise, confidence and discipline on the dance floor."

Toni bit her lip and seemed to be avoiding his eye.

He pressed on, hoping she'd understand. "As for me, you've made my life what it is today—and that's not exaggeration. You've made me laugh. You've hugged me when I wanted to cry. You've shaken me up when I was intent on having a pity party, and you always believed in my dreams, even when my parents said I'd be poor all my life if I didn't do something besides art and teaching. I'm the man I am today because of you."

"I'm sorry," Toni said, almost under her breath.

Carter threw up his hands in exasperation. "For what?"

"I appreciate what you're trying to say, and I want to believe it all. But look at the facts. I've messed up many more times than I've done things right. I've caused a whole lot more heartache and frustration than anything else. If I've made a huge impact on your life, it can't all be positive, and I'm sorry I've been meddling all these years."

"That's not it at all—"

"I've given you a lot more than smiles. Admit it."

Carter sighed heavily. He wasn't getting through to her. Of course he'd had more than smiles. *She has no idea.* "Fine. I admit it. I've had my share of frustrations with you."

His statement seemed to jolt her. "Excuse me?" She clearly hadn't expected him to agree.

"All right, let's look at them. I've had to watch you throw yourself at a man who doesn't deserve to *speak* to you, let alone date you and touch you and—"

"You don't know Clint." Toni folded her arms and looked away.

"No, but I've heard him talk about you like a piece of meat." When Toni looked back at him, surprised, he went on. "I was backstage when the paramedics carried you away. Clint said some ugly things about you, and it was all I could do not to punch in his face in on the spot." Carter's face turned hot at the memory.

"What—did he say?" Toni asked, but her voice said she wasn't sure whether she really wanted to know.

"The gist was that he was keeping you around because of—let's see I remember all of the points—your dancing, your body, and, oh yes, your amazing ability to turn him on."

Toni dropped her face into her hands. Carter felt ill; he shouldn't have told her. She shook her head and sniffed. "Are you sure it wasn't just locker-room type talk? Acting macho in front of other guys?"

"You'd be okay if it was?" Carter wanted to yell, but he kept his voice controlled. "You are so much more than a body for some scum like him to drool over."

She flinched at that; he guessed he'd hit too close to home.

A nurse came in then to take Toni's vitals, and Carter stood to excuse himself. He gave Toni a hug. "I know you have to get better for yourself, not for anyone else," he said. "But don't forget that in my eyes, you're worth the whole world. Don't listen to anyone like…"

Toni answered with a nod, understanding that he meant Clint. "I'll try. Thanks for coming."

He pressed his lips to her forehead again then headed toward the door, when she called out one last time. "Call me when I get out of here? I'm not sure when that'll be, since once I'm physically stable, I'll be in the psych ward for a while, but…"

Carter smiled, relieved that his speeches today hadn't widened the gap between them.

"Count on it." He headed for the hall, sending Toni a wave as he reached the door.

In the hallway, Carter saw Mr. Harper, who looked like he'd been waiting eagerly for a report. Carter gave him a smile and a thumbs-up. A moment later, he heard Toni talking to her dad.

"Thanks for meddling. This once."

Chapter 37

A few days later, Carter sat on the couch, clicking through movies to stream from Amazon. This had become his typical weekend. No girlfriend. No Toni. And no desire to hang out with his guy friends. Even less desire to work in his studio office at school or ever look at the half-finished painting of Toni again. He wouldn't have to go back to school for faculty meetings for weeks yet.

He found himself searching for *The Philadelphia Story*. Last time he watched it had been probably two years ago. His thumb hovered over the button to confirm the rental, but at the last moment, he couldn't do it. He threw the remote across the room then leaned forward, raking his fingers through his hair. That movie belonged to both him and Toni. He couldn't watch it without her. With also meant he'd probably never see it again.

Carter stood and paced his apartment. Toni's dad had helped bridge the chasm between them, but things weren't exactly back to normal. First things first: Toni needed help, and he wanted to help her. But how? His original efforts had nearly cost him Toni altogether.

Brooke's face flashed into his mind. Carter's pacing came up short, and his head snapped up. Brooke. She'd lived with her mother's eating disorder most of her life. Of all people, Brooke would know what he could do.

Carter pulled out his cell phone and sent her a text. *Do you have a minute? I have a question only you can help with.*

He hit send and immediately regretted it. His words could easily be misunderstood. *Great work, genius.*

He tried to undo the damage by calling her directly, but it went to voice mail. Hearing Brooke's voice—even a short, recorded message—made his heart ache a bit; they'd had some good times. When the message beeped, he hung up. He needed to talk to her face to face before he chickened out altogether. And before Toni was past the point of help.

Carter strode toward the door and headed for the parking lot. But after he got into his car and turned the key, he pulled it back out. What was he thinking? After breaking up with someone who'd thought she might marry Carter, how could he show up and ask how to help the woman his heart really belonged to?

But he didn't have anywhere else to turn. And Brooke would have answers. With a deep breath of resolution, he cranked the key, and the engine hummed to life. Before he could reconsider, he pulled out of the parking lot and drove to Brooke's apartment.

She wasn't there. Carter nearly cursed, but caught himself, and instead returned to the car and tapped the steering wheel anxiously as he decided what to do. School would be starting in a week, so Brooke might be getting her classroom ready. Once again Carter turned the car around, this time so fast that the tires squealed against the pavement. He was determined to get to the elementary school before she left—if she was there at all.

When he pulled into the elementary school parking lot and saw Brooke's blue sedan, he breathed a sigh of relief. He quickly parked and walked into the building and toward her classroom. With about ten feet to go, his step slowed to a crawl, and his heart beat in his throat. What would he say to her? What *could* he say to her?

He peered in the door. Brooke knelt on a counter that almost spanned the far wall. A bulletin board above it was nearly as long, and Brooke was stapling a border around it.

For a brief moment, Carter's heart ached to hold her again. He brushed the feeling aside, knowing that they stemmed from loneliness, not genuine love, and that if he nursed those feelings again, he'd be playing with fire. He'd probably feel better temporarily, but in the end would only hurt Brooke all over again.

She got down from the cupboard and went to a student desk, where she shuffled through a pile of colorful cutouts. She selected what looked like a giant red book, then stepped away to get a better view of the bulletin board. As she pushed a lock of hair behind one ear, her eyes caught Carter's. She stopped mid-stride, and her hand clenched the cutout.

She didn't say anything at first, but her face looked ashen. He didn't know how long it would take her to regain her voice, so he stepped into the classroom and spoke first. "Looks good," he said, nodding toward the barely started bulletin board.

Brooke turned to look over her shoulder and put on an obviously forced a smile. "It's nowhere near finished, but hopefully it'll make the room more welcoming on the first day of class." The lock of hair escaped from behind her ear. She shoved it behind her ear again without looking at Carter.

He stepped further into the room. "You're probably wondering why I'm here."

Brooke let out a strained chuckle. "You could say that." She glanced at Carter, and he winced at the pain in her eyes. He'd hoped that maybe she was already dating someone else by my, even though it had been only a few months. It would have made him feel better.

How could he bring up the reason of his visit—how to approach it delicately? All ideas fled from his mind, so he plunged in. "Toni's in the hospital again."

Brooke's eyes softened. "Oh, that's awful."

"She nearly died this time," he said. "She had a heart attack. It's serious. I don't think anyone realized how serious." Carter swallowed hard and hurried on before the burning in his eyes turned to tears and he wouldn't be able to speak. "I need to help her, but I don't know how."

Brooke stared at the bulletin board for a minute in thought. Finally, she nodded. "Give me a second." She scooped up the remaining colored cutouts and slid them into a wide drawer in the cupboard. Then she headed out the door and down the hallway, Carter following close behind. She led him to the playground and up the grassy hill to the jungle gym, where she stopped at a set of large swings. She took one swing and motioned to the other. "Have a seat."

Carter walked through the soft sand and sat beside her. She was as beautiful as he remembered. Part of him wished he could have loved her. If there hadn't been any Toni in his life, he was sure he would have been picking out wedding cakes with Brooke by now.

Her feet rocked the swing back and forth for a few minutes. She gazed into the cloud-dotted sky. She plunged in without any introduction. "Here's the thing. My mother *still* struggles with her eating disorder, more than forty years into it. Frankly, it's a miracle she's still alive." Brooke sighed and shifted her gaze to the sand. "That's the biggest thing you have to remember with Toni—she's got a lifelong battle ahead of her. She'll *never* be cured."

"Never?" Carter asked, bracing himself on the sand to stop his swing.

Brooke stopped too and shook her head. "She'll have to manage it the way an alcoholic does." She released her swing and went on. "Some people step beyond the grip of the disease and stay on the safe side of the fence, but that takes a lot of strength—and constant vigilance. The longer the battle has been raging before treatment starts, the harder it is to control."

Carter let his swing go again as he thought. How long had Toni been dealing with the disease? Looking back, he'd wager it was years. Not a good sign. "How does your mom stay on the right side of the fence?"

"For years, nothing did. If she'd have been born a few decades later, things might have been better for her. There wasn't much out there about eating disorders when she was fifteen, when the right help might have made the biggest difference. She went in and out of hospitals my entire childhood." She shuddered and gripped the chains tighter.

"That must have been rough."

"You have no idea." Her eyes got a haunted look in them, as if she was remembering how she'd had to grow up too young and take care of things her mom didn't.

Carter almost reached out to touch her as a gesture of comfort but stopped himself. "But things eventually got better." It was as much as question as it was a statement.

"Yeah." Brooke nodded, and a hint of a smile crossed her face. "About the time I went to college, Mom enrolled in a community pottery class. I still don't have the slightest idea what prompted that. Maybe losing one of her babies to the grownup world and trying to fill the void. For whatever reason, she went, and pottery became an obsession. Within a few months, she had her own wheel to throw pots on, and she was trying to convince my father to build a kiln in the backyard, so she could fire her own pots."

Carter didn't interrupt, although he wanted to ask what pottery had to do with eating disorders.

"For a few years there every gift Mom gave to anyone for Christmas or birthdays or weddings—even baby showers—was a vase or pot or plate. I've got quite a collection."

When she paused in her narrative, Carter ventured to ask the glaringly obvious question. "What does pottery have to do with eating disorders?"

"I don't have the faintest idea," Brooke said, shaking her head. "But I do know that focusing on pottery did something to her that nothing else had. It was like she poured her emotions onto her wheel, so she didn't battle them when she walked away. Or maybe pottery helped her break the loop of obsessive thoughts, so she could control them. Or, maybe expressing herself in a new way opened possibilities she didn't know existed. Whatever it was, pottery has been the best thing to happen to her. I can tell if she hasn't had time on her wheel in a while; she's cranky and depressed and starts avoiding food."

"Huh." Carter tried to process the story and apply it to his situation. "Do you think I should find a pottery class for her?"

"No." Brooke laughed warmly. She seemed almost herself now. "You know Toni better than anyone. I'm sure you can find something that will help her the way pottery helped my mom." Her gaze dropped to her lap, and the swing slowed to a stop. "She's pretty special, isn't she?"

He could only manage a nod and a hoarse, "Yeah."

"I hope that someday she realizes what she's got."

Carter couldn't keep the edge out of his voice. "She hasn't 'got' me." He kicked a hole into the sand. "She still has no idea that I . . ." His voice trailed off. Brooke could certainly fill in the details.

Her eyes lifted to his. "Then tell her."

Chapter 38

Carter took the first chance he got to try out an idea Brooke's advice had given him. When Toni was discharged, the hottest days of summer were gone, although crisp autumn air was weeks away. The mountains had a tiny sprinkling of color, which would turn into deep reds, oranges, and yellows over the next two months.

Carter picked up Toni the first Saturday morning she was home and drove her up the canyon. Dr. Sanders had warned her to take things easy, and, of course, she was back in therapy. But her early hours on Saturday morning remained unclaimed.

"So where exactly are we going?" Toni asked as Carter turned off the main canyon road and headed up a winding one.

"You'll see," Carter said, grinning.

They drove for several minutes in silence before Toni spoke up. "I wanted to thank you for coming to see me in the hospital," she said. "Especially that first time with my dad."

Carter glanced at her from the winding road. "To be honest, my visits were as much for me as for you." He blinked away a sudden mistiness in his eyes. "I've missed you."

But Toni persisted. "No, really. I'm grateful. I needed you."

He opened his mouth, but nothing came out. What could he say, that he needed her, but in a different way? A joke? He opted instead to reach out and squeeze her hand. "I'm still here for you."

Toni squeezed back. "I know. And trust me—if I'm going to get through this, I'll be leaning on you a lot over the next while."

As long as you need to.

The dirt road grew bumpy as the car continued to climb. Eventually Carter stopped the car, pulling over on a long, flat area.

Toni looked around. "Wait. Isn't this Make-out Peak?"

"Oh, you've been up here?" Carter gave her a sidelong glance. "Not at night with some young man, I hope." He pretended to be shocked, but instead prayed that she hadn't been here with Clint. Anyone but him.

"Yeah, right." Toni laughed and swatted his arm as she got out of the car.

Carter walked to the edge of lookout and gazed out over the valley, where Toni joined him a moment later. She nudged his side with her elbow. "So I'm guessing you didn't bring me up here to make out." She said it with a smirk, as if kissing Carter was a ridiculous idea.

What would she think if he tried kissing her right here, right now? *She'll probably laugh.*

"Come here." Carter headed back to the car and opened the trunk. He pulled out a large blanket and instructed Toni to spread it out on the flat area a few yards off. He reached back into the trunk and withdrew two large sketch pads—one new, the other old and beaten up, plus two boxes of pencils in the same conditions as the sketch pads. Toni finished with the blanket as Carter closed the trunk.

"All right, what do you have up your sleeve?" Toni asked. She bit her cheek, hands in her back jeans pockets, rocking from her heels to her toes and back again.

"It's not a picnic—no food. Promise."

"Oh. Good." Her voice sounded like the whoosh of a relief. She nodded at the sketch pads. "What are those for?"

"For you." Carter handed over the new pad and pencils. Toni took them and followed Carter's lead as he sat on the blanket.

"I don't understand," she began, looking at the items in her hands as if they were surgical tools as she was asked to do brain surgery.

"I'm going to teach you to draw." Carter said it with satisfaction. If pottery worked for Brooke's mom, drawing could work for Toni. She was already creative, but the dancing world only contributed to her illness. She needed a different creative outlet to funnel her emotions into.

Toni dropped the art supplies on her lap and put her hands up in protest. "No way. You're a pro, and I can't even do stick figures. I'm not going to have you looking over my shoulder and correcting every little detail. No Mr. Mackenzie, thanks." She made a move to stand, so Carter reached for her hands and held them.

"Relax, Miss Harper. I'm not going to lecture or grade your homework."

Toni eyed their hands silently than nodded and sat back.

"I thought you might enjoy doing sketches. It's something I've always found very relaxing. Figured you could use a way to relieve stress. I've heard that knitting is great too, but I can't knit, so you're stuck with pencils." He picked up her case and handed it over, shaking it so the pencil inside rattled.

Toni cautiously took them. "That's all? Promise you won't even look at anything I draw unless I say you can?"

"Promise."

"And you won't laugh when I draw like a six-year-old?"

"This is supposed to be fun. We can come up here and draw nature or the valley, or whatever comes to mind, and just have a good time."

Toni tilted her head as if he'd piqued her interest. "Go on."

"You can watch me for a minute. I'll give you a few pointers to get you going, and then you can sketch any time you want, with or without me."

After a minute of consideration, she nodded. "All right. Teach me."

Carter flipped his well-worn sketch book open and began demonstrating a couple of basic techniques. "Now you try." He purposely snatched her pad and flung it to the opposite side of the blanket, so she'd know she had full sketching privacy.

She smiled at the gesture and crawled over to her pad, where she cracked open her pencil case, selected one from the middle, and began to draw. Carter silently did a sketch too—one of Toni sitting against the backdrop of the morning. He hadn't drawn her in what felt like a very long time.

After twenty minutes or so, Toni looked up. "I'm trying to draw that bush. What are you drawing?" She craned her head as if that would help her see his pad.

"Hey, no fair," Carter protested, pulling his pad closer. "If I can't see your work, you can't see mine."

Toni seemed to consider for a moment but then shrugged and went back to her work. "When I get better."

"Deal."

He watched her intensity as she sketched and erased and sketched again. The sight sent a flutter of excitement into his stomach. If her initial excitement was any indication, maybe Toni would really get into art. And maybe it would help her illness, if only a little. Like Brooke's mom and her pottery.

They spent the following Saturday at the lake with their sketch pads. Toni had filled nearly a third of hers with drawings, many on her own time. As Carter watched Toni immerse herself in her paper and pencil, oblivious to everything around her—including him—he couldn't help but smile with pleasure. He didn't mind being invisible to Toni if it meant getting her thoughts off of food and her figure for even an hour.

School started again, and since Carter and Toni's relationship was nearly what it once had been, he found some interest in teaching and even in making his own art outside of freelance jobs. Toni moved back home, and soon they were texting and emailing most days, but only seeing each other maybe once a week.

Carter saw less of Toni, because she and Clint were practicing extra-long hours for an upcoming competition. Carter had tried to talk her out of competing; she wasn't that strong yet, and her body might not be able to take it. But he refused to turn into a full-on nag, not when Toni called their drawing retreats her *real* therapy sessions.

More and more, she talked out her frustrations with food, her body, her family, and anything else that had built up inside and needed a sounding board. He rarely said much in return beyond encouraging noises, but inside he was grinning and cheering that his plan seemed to be working.

One weekend, they hiked back down a canyon trail from one of Carter's favorite sketching spots. Toni followed as he led the way.

"I'm almost embarrassed to ask this," she said. "But where can I get another pad like this one? I filled up today, and I'll go nuts if I don't have decent paper to draw on. I've tried printer paper." She made a gagging noise.

"Awesome!" Carter said. "I've turned you into a paper snob!"

He drove straight to his apartment, where he pulled two spares from his closet and handed them over. "I usually get mine at the little art store on Main."

Toni hugged the pads to her chest, smiling. "Thanks, Carter. For these, but also for teaching me. And for being here for me. Always." She went onto her toes and kissed his cheek.

Her lips practically burned his skin as she pulled back. Carter wanted to kiss her lips, but as always, forced his emotions down, this time with a cough.

Chapter 39

As Carter headed back to his classroom after lunch, his phone pinged with an incoming text from Toni. *Competition tonight @ the HS, 7PM. No sweat if you can't make it.*

He sighed and put his phone back into his pocket. The competition *had* to be right here at the high school. It was like the universe was mocking him, giving him no excuse to not go—even though he wouldn't. And Toni knew that, too. Her text was a formality. He hadn't make any secret of what he thought of Clint. Knowing that, Toni had hinted that Carter was free to miss the competition to avoid the whole Clint situation, but she's still promised to let him know when and where it would be.

What she didn't know, of course, what how it wasn't just *seeing* Clint that would be a problem for Carter. It would be seeing the jerk do a hot, sultry dance with Toni. *Feelings of brotherly protection,* he thought, trying to convince himself that that was all he felt. Getting rid of his longstanding romantic feelings wasn't working too well, but he still made the effort. Even so, when he thought of the future, of where he hoped to be in ten years, Toni's face insisted on appearing where his wife was supposed to be.

He sat at his desk and went over the day's lesson plan. This early in the year, he did more lecturing than letting students work on their own stuff, especially in the beginner classes. His introductory watercolor class would start in about five minutes.

An older teacher, Mr. Nelson, who had once coached football and now taught driver's ed, leaned in the doorway. "Got a message from an old student of ours—Matt Jenkins?"

Carter thought back. "Didn't he just graduate? I think he was in my class his freshman year."

"That's the one," Nelson said. "He's at Columbia now and wanted Mr. M to know about it." He waved and headed out.

"Thanks," Carter called then went to the row of yearbooks he kept on a shelf in his office to find the face of the boy. He wanted to make sure it was the student he was thinking of. He'd taught hundreds of students, many with the grades and intelligence to get into Columbia. He reached for last year's book and flipped to the senior pictures.

Carter found Matt Jenkins and nodded, remembering the student and his work. The boy had real talent and potential. Carter doubted the boy would ever pursue art for a career, though—probably law or medicine. But it was cool that Matt wanted his former art teacher to know where he'd ended up. It felt good to know that "Mr. M" had made an impact.

Carter flipped the page and glanced over more of the faces briefly, identifying an occasional former student. He nearly shut the book, when his eyes fell on the picture of red-haired Keri Harris grinning at him. He could practically hear her chiding him all over again. "Take a risk, Mr. M. Don't be afraid of getting your heart stomped on."

He closed the book with a snap and glanced at the cloth-covered painting in the corner of the room, something hadn't so much as looked at since he first went out with Brooke. How many months had it been? Snow had still been on the ground last time he'd worked on it, and now autumn knocked at the door.

He couldn't have explained why to anyone, including himself, but when school let out, he picked up his oils and brushes and went straight to the painting. It *needed* to be finished, maybe as a final farewell to old hopes and dreams. He'd sell or give away the painting and move on to other subjects.

As he gathered his supplies, his mind wandered to Toni and tonight's competition. She couldn't really care for Clint like she thought she did, could she? Carter suspected she just craved the attention he gave her, as if it gave her the validation of having a great—read: thin—body.

Even with her eating disorder, he knew firsthand how good it felt for her to be the object of someone's attraction. Someone *she* found attractive. Carter was willing to bet that Clint cared little about Toni beyond her outside wrapper and what he could get out of her to satisfy his hormones. Toni had told Carter about how she kept having to draw a clear line in that regard, one she wouldn't cross with Clint—but he kept trying to push her past that line. Would Toni eventually cave in order to keep him?

Oh, I hope not.

Carter set up his paints and brushes then lifted the cloth and looked at Toni's face. He'd been right, all those months ago when he worked on this piece last; the eyes weren't right. He picked up a brush, added a dab of paint, and with a deep breath, set to work. He deliberately let his mind turn to paths he'd blocked off, letting all the old feelings come rushing out one last time. He pictured what could have happened if he'd told Toni about his feelings and if his fantasy had really come true: he imagined Toni confessing that she loved him back. He imagined their wedding, raising children, watching Toni teach ballet to preschoolers in their basement studio.

And somewhere through every hour he worked, Keri's voice kept coming back with her challenge to take a risk. As Carter shifted his attention to adding highlights to Toni's hair and shadows behind her, Brooke's face broke into his thoughts.

Expose yourself, she'd said. That's basically what he'd told Keri to do.

Being in contact with Toni again had rekindled every spark in Carter's soul. He found that he loved her more than he loved himself. Forget suppressing his feelings; that had never worked, and it never would.

As he worked on the eyelashes and eyebrows, he finally admitted what he'd known all along. He couldn't he couldn't go on living this shell of a life. Something had to change.

Even if it meant risking everything.

Fine, he thought, to get the voice to stop nagging. This weekend, he'd sit Toni down and tell her everything. Maybe he'd give her the completed oil, even though it wouldn't be dry yet. He should have known that this was inevitable. If it had to happen, it may as well be on his terms.

If—when—she didn't feel the same way, so be it. Things would change. Drastically. But at least he'd be out of this horrid limbo. He'd get on with his life, and the voice would stop nagging. Maybe he'd move away, live in Paris doing freelance graphic design for a while. He could freelance anywhere that had an internet connection. He could escape seeing Toni all time.

Then he remembered Toni's plea that she needed him, that she'd missed him as much as he'd missed her. That she loved him.

You don't love me this way.

The sun had set long ago, and darkness had taken over the room. Carter turned on the overhead lights as he made the final touches to the painting. He sat back and looked at the piece as objectively as he could.

Huh. After all this time, I finally got the eyes right.

He signed his name in the bottom right corner. He thought of the many hours he'd spent with this painting, wishing he could be spending those hours with the flesh and blood version, and in the way he wanted to, not as a buddy eating popcorn and talking about her dates with other men.

He set the paintbrush to the side and walked over to the desk in his office, where pulled out a thick file folder and flipped it open. It he was going to walk down memory lane one last time, he may as well go all the way.

This folder contained dozens of drawings of Toni, going back to their high school years, when he sketched her during boring classes. He'd drawn her the way she sat in their algebra class, and when she saw the drawing, she'd laughed at the utterly bored look on her face. He flipped to the next one—here she was laughing in the lunch room. He moved on, reaching pictures from the next years, including many Toni had no idea he'd made.

Sure, she knew he'd done a lot of dance-related freelance work, so in that sense, the fact that he'd drawn her dozens, if not hundreds, of times wasn't a big deal. And she'd seen many of his drawings and painting of her as a model.

But she didn't know this particular file existed, with pictures going back as far as algebra class. He hadn't looked at it in years. He came to a sketch from when they were about two years out of high school, of a Toni in a wedding dress, complete with veil and bouquet—and a pathetic attempt of a self-portrait of Carter at her side. He cringed at that one.

I was such a sentimental idiot. If she ever saw this, she'd think I was a stalker.

He thumbed through pictures until he reached the most recent one, which he'd tucked in only after drawing it a Make-out Peak.

Dropping the last sketch onto his desk, he scanned the pictures, which now lay haphazard all over the surface. In some, the hair and clothing styles gave away which year they were taken. In others, though, Toni had her ballet bun in, and she wore dance clothes—often a black leotard with pink tights and which dated the pictures.

More than once, the feelings that had prompted a drawing returned as he looked at it. Other times, he remembered how he'd been trying his hand at new techniques—charcoal, an experiment with light, a mosaic. Though many were portraits, not all showed Toni up close. Many showed her dancing at a distance. Another had her walking through a field or sitting on a couch, curled up with a book and her puppy at her feet. Even though she'd never owned a puppy.

The oldest ones, from high school, sometimes had him in them. Those ones were all full of the hopeless romantic in him. The two of them held hands as they watched a sunset. Toni leaned in to kiss his cheek. They stood on a bridge, gazing into each other's eyes.

I'm pathetic. Was *pathetic.*

Carter didn't analyze his work or bother thinking about how his skill had improved over the years. All he saw was the young woman he'd always loved. He should have gone on a long run tonight, followed by an hour with his weights. That would manage his emotions better than looking at the past.

He set a final sketch to the side then stared at the array of pictures around him, set off by the colorful oil to the side.

Tonight he'd indulged in his feelings for Toni more than he ever had; he'd let them surge close to the surface for hours. But this experience—this attempt at looking at the past, at their relationship and his feelings over time—made him do something he'd never tried.

He went into the classroom and found a notebook then trudged back to his office and began writing what he wished he could have said to Toni at some point in the past. Maybe the day they both graduated from college. Tonight, his art had been cathartic in one way, but he still needed something else to express himself, if nothing else than to sort out his thoughts and know what to say when he took Keri's challenge and spoke the words to Toni face to face. He couldn't go unprepared and blubber like a schoolboy.

He wrote several pages by hand, pouring out his feelings for her, recounting their years of friendship, many of the times he'd yearned to say, "I love you," how hard it was to see her kissing Clint that day in the rain, the heartache when she sent him away in the hospital. The joy that she'd returned to his life. The sadness that it all had to end, but that it was better for them both this way.

Five and a half pages later, he read over his words, surprised at the passion he'd allowed to flow from the pen. He pushed the notebook away and ran his fingers through his hair.

He couldn't tell her any of this. It would only torture her.

Sorry, Keri. I can't do it. I can't.

Feeling unsettled, Carter stood and stretched his back. He had to get up, walk around, and eat something. He hadn't stopped painting for dinner, and lunch had been who knew how many hours ago. Maybe a little food would settle his emotions, too.

He went down the long hallway and down the stairs to the candy machines, where he got himself a Snickers and a Dr. Pepper. The Snickers not because he liked them, but because they had a little protein in the nuts, and he needed protein to think straight. The Dr. Pepper because he was going to fall asleep at the wheel going home if he didn't get some caffeine into his system.

As he chewed a bite from the candy bar and swigged from the can, he paced in the dimness of downstairs school hall. This wasn't working; he needed air. He'd left his building keys in the classroom, but what were the chances of someone breaking in and vandalizing the place at this hour? He found a fist-sized rock, which he used to prop the door open. Then he went out into the night and paced the parking lot, breathing in the cool night air like an elixir.

Not until he headed back from the parking lot did he look down at the main campus and see the big windows of the auditorium at the side of the courtyard. Two memories slapped him in the face: the time he and Brooke had run into Toni, and the last time he'd been in the auditorium, when Toni had collapsed.

He pictured Clint and Toni dancing together at the competition, this time doing all five of their Latin dances. Was the competition over yet? He had no idea how long they went, as this was her first ballroom one.

He pictured Clint's so-called "chemistry" oozing all over Toni as they danced. Keri's voice returned to his mind, but he shook his head, dreading this weekend.

What Toni felt for Clint was powerful, but he was convinced it didn't go beyond physical attraction, and that if she felt a shred of real love for Carter, he'd have a chance.

He also knew that by telling Toni his feelings, he'd almost certainly shatter one of the most important things in his life. He'd never have the future he'd dreamed of if he told her. He'd never have it anyway. He may as well set her free. For a brief moment, he wanted to be with Brooke again, if only to have the security that her feelings brought. But it wouldn't be right to be with her, knowing their relationship would never go anywhere. Because of him.

The craziness of the situation struck him hard. He never expected to be sitting on both sides of a fence at the same time, yet here he was, yearning for one woman who might never love him, while rejecting another who did.

Carter finished off the soda then crumpled the can and tossed it into a wastebasket before heading back to the art building. He felt much more clearheaded. He trotted up the stairs and went back to his classroom. He'd put away the sketches of Toni and the notebook and go home. On second thought, he'd shred the notebook, destroy all evidence of his moment of insanity. Shred all of the old pictures, too.

But when Carter walked into the classroom and headed to his office in the corner. One step inside, and he froze. Toni stood on the other side of the room, hair slicked into a tight bun, bright performing makeup on her face, and fake eyelashes making her eyes look huge. The competition must have ended.

Carter's eyes strayed to hers—Toni held several drawings in her hands.

"Oh, Carter," she said, flushed and misty eyed. "I had no idea."

A knot the size of an orange formed in his throat. He couldn't speak. What was Toni thinking? She wasn't supposed to find out this way. He couldn't move, even from the doorway.

"I came to tell you that we took second place," Toni said as if breaking the silence would bridge the huge chasm suddenly between them. "I tried calling your cell, but when you didn't answer, I thought maybe you were working with your headphones on and didn't hear it ring." She paused awkwardly. "I wish you could have seen it."

Carter nodded mutely then mustered the guts to speak despite his constricted throat. "Me, too." With two words out, he managed to get the use of his limbs again. He walked over to the drawings scattered over his desk in a much messier condition than he'd left them in. How many had she seen? How long had she been in here? How long had he been outside?

He snatched the notebook, hoping Toni at least hadn't read that, but then he looked at her. She glanced at the notebook and then away, her cheeks flushing. He quickly began putting the drawings back into their folder.

"I didn't expect you to come here tonight," he said. *Obviously*.

"These are all so beautiful," Toni said, gesturing at what drawings remained on the table as he scooped them up. "Why didn't you ever tell me about them?"

Carter looked up, his hands full of sketches. The one on top had Toni as a bride, him as a groom. He closed his eyes against the burning sensation threatening to build behind them then shoved the picture into the folder, out of sight. "I didn't know how you'd react."

"To portraits as beautiful as these?" Toni said, looking at one of the drawings of her dancing before surrendering it.

"You know that's not what I mean," Carter said dully, tucking the final paper into the folder then shoving the folder into the drawer.

"Yeah," she answered softly.

With the last of the drawings put away, Carter shoved his hands in his pockets nervously and kept his gaze on the floor. "I was planning to tell you. I took all this out tonight for the first time in . . ." He shook his head. "I didn't expect you to find out like this." He tried to laugh, but it came out wrong.

He'd have given anything to undo this night and never tell her after all, just keep it inside forever. The risk wasn't worth it, no matter what Keri said. He couldn't get himself to even look at Toni for fear of what he'd see in her eyes. But something had to be said, if nothing but to acknowledge the enormous elephant in the room.

"Listen, it's been so long. I couldn't keep it inside anymore. I was going to tell you this weekend." He took a deep breath and plunged in. "What it boils down to is this." He raised his eyes to hers. "I love you, Toni."

"I love you too—"

"No." Carter cut her off abruptly. She wasn't getting it—or didn't want to. "I'm *in love* with you. Always have been. Ever since algebra." His face and neck burned. His chest constricted, and his heart physically hurt.

"I had no idea," she repeated.

He had to keep going, get it all out now, like ripping off a bandage. "No matter how many years have gone by, nothing has changed, except that my feelings have grown stronger." Toni had taken her eyes off him. Now it was her turn to shift her weight and stare at the floor. For the first time, he didn't care that she was uncomfortable. He'd lived his entire adult life feeling uncomfortable—for her sake.

"You wondered why I had to break up with Brooke—I was in love with the idea of someone loving me. But I found out that's not enough." An awkward silence ensued, when Carter pinched the bridge of his nose and tried to gather his thoughts and find a way to end this torment. "Just—just tell me what you're thinking. If there's even the smallest chance of your ever loving me back. That's all I need to know—yes or no?"

"Of course I love you, Carter."

A wave of hope wanted to surge into through his body, but he could hear a *but* coming.

"You've been my best friend forever, so I can't help but love you . . . in a way."

The glimmer of hope crashed into a pit somewhere in Carter's middle. "'In a way,'" he repeated said with a cynical laugh. "Figures."

Toni stepped forward and tried to take his arm. He couldn't stand the idea of being touched by her, not now, when it would be nothing but pity. He pulled his arm away and stepped toward the door, hoping she didn't catch the water in his eyes.

She followed. "What do you want me to say? Do you want me to lie? Say I've been passionately in love with you since I could drive?"

With his back to her, Carter looked at the ceiling, willing away the tears threatening to fall. He almost never cried. He ordered himself to stop. He almost managed it, until Toni reached up and touched his shoulder.

"I'm so sorry," she said. "If I'd only known . . ." Her voice trailed off, leaving an awkward silence.

Carter reached for her hand and turned around, holding it in his. Toni choked back a sob of her own, likely at the tortured expression he wore. "If you had known, what?" A single bright tear finally escaped and fell down one cheek.

Their eyes locked, and after a moment of silence, Toni shook her head helplessly. "I don't know."

"Exactly. We probably wouldn't have been best friends this long." He looked at their hands and rubbed his paint-stained thumb against her pearly white skin. "That's probably over."

Toni's eyed widened with horror. "What are you talking about? We'll always be friends. I can't live without you—being apart for those weeks about killed me. You should know that."

Carter did his best to smile through blurry vision. "Oh, you'll manage fine without me. You'll find a great guy to marry and create that life you've always dreamed of."

"But we can still be friends then."

A pained chuckle escaped Carter. "No husband in his right mind wants his hot wife spending late nights talking with her best friend, who happens to be a man who's crazy about her." He reached over with his thumb and wiped a tear from her eye, wishing she could feel what he felt, knowing that this small gesture could be the last time he ever touched her.

She felt something very different than he did, and he knew exactly what it was, because he felt the same way about Brooke—and it wasn't enough.

"Besides," he said with a light shrug. "You won't miss me then when you find the guy you fall madly in love with."

Toni pulled her hand away and threw both arms around his neck. "I may not feel the same way about you, but I still need you. I'll always need you as a friend, and you need me, too, don't you?"

Carter tried not to inhale too deeply to smell her perfume. Her embrace alone was sending his entire frame into overdrive. He pulled back. "I'm not sure 'just friends' can ever be enough for me. Not anymore."

Toni shook her head emphatically. "No. Don't say that." Tears streaked down her face. "Please don't. I can forget I saw anything in here, and we can go back to exactly the way things have always been. Just don't—"

He put a finger over her lips and shook his head. "Just don't what? Don't change anything? Things have changed, Toni. You know that as well as I do."

She spoke fast, words tumbling out of her mouth. "No, things will be the same. We'll go on walks, and talk on the phone, and—"

"And you'll tell me your innermost dreams about your latest boyfriend?" Carter shook his head. "I don't think so."

"Is that the way you want it?" she asked desperately.

"That's the way it is," Carter said, aware somewhere in the back of him mind that they were quoting *The Philadelphia Story*. He suddenly hated that movie. Maybe he'd go home and watch *Die Hard* instead.

Toni looked at Carter for a minute before nodding. "I suppose you're right," she said. "Some things will change. But don't lock me out. Not all the way. I need you."

"I can't promise anything, but I'll try," Carter said. But the words felt hollow. How could he keep up a friendly veneer when they both knew something deeper lived just below the surface?

Chapter 40

Over the next few weeks, everything felt strained between Toni and Carter, but she wasn't about to let her best friend disappear on her, no matter how hard he tried.

Toni made a special effort to call Carter and spend time with him, although he brushed off at least as many potential evenings together as he accepted. At first Clint balked at losing evenings with her, but Toni assured him it would be temporary. She wanted to show Carter that even after what she'd seen in his classroom, she could still be his best friend. She wouldn't give Carter up for Clint.

Her plans for time with Carter always seemed perfect beforehand, but whenever they came face to face, things became awkward. She couldn't get the words from his notebook out of her mind, and he knew it.

But who knew Carter could be so passionate? How did he have an entire side she didn't know about? *Because he's kept it hidden from you, ever since algebra.*

When she scored tickets to the university football game, Toni immediately called Carter to see if he wanted to go. "The tickets are practically in the nosebleed section, but—"

"I don't think so," Carter interjected.

Toni was taken aback. "They're the only tickets I could get. I didn't think the seats would make that big a difference."

"That's not what I meant." He sighed. "Listen, Toni, I appreciate what you've been doing lately, but all of these little outings are hard for both of us."

Fear gripped Toni's heart. "I can't let our friendship to die. I'm still the same old Toni."

Silence for several moments, then, "Listen. Why don't you take Clint to the game? Don't feel guilty about me. I'll spend the afternoon at a museum or something."

Toni couldn't help but think of all the times she and Carter had gone to museums or art lectures. "You really don't want to go?"

"I really don't want to go," he repeated. "But I appreciate what you're trying to do."

"Well, all—right," Toni said slowly, unconvinced.

"I'll call you next week. I just need a breather."

He probably also wanted to have the ball in his court, to be the one in charge of making the next contact. *Message received.*

"I'll talk to you then," she said, and hung up.

She stared at her phone, replaying Carter's words, hearing his depressed tone in her mind. He'd made it pretty clear that she would have to wait for his call. She supposed had been pestering him. But she was desperate to keep their friendship alive.

What would her life look like if Carter wasn't in it? She refused to find out.

On Saturday, Toni took Clint to the game, even though he wasn't much of a football fan, and on the few occasions he cheered, it was always for the away team. Worse, he made snide remarks every so often, always aimed at Carter.

As the second half began, he said, "Bet Carter would paint that lady's shirt. But he'd do a great job capturing the essence of the loud flowers."

"Stop it," Toni said. "You don't need to be jealous of him. The more you snark about him, the worse it makes you look, not him."

"Oh, come on," Clint said. He took a big bite from his hot dog and spoke around it. "You'd rather be here with Carter. Go ahead and admit that you have two boyfriends. What is this, reverse polygamy?"

"Clint . . ." Toni said between her teeth.

"Bet he's getting more lip than I have lately. Must be a good kisser. Tell me about his technique. Maybe I could learn something. Or is he getting more action all around than I am? Do you put out for him?"

"You make me sick." Toni stormed out, refusing to hear any more of the vileness coming out of his mouth.

"Hey, where are you going?" Clint called after her. He jumped up and followed, but by the time he reached her, Toni had made it most of the way down the bleacher stairs. He gripped her arm, hard, and whirled her around. "I said, where do you think you're going?"

"Anywhere but here. I won't sit around listening to you badmouth me and my best friend for another second."

Clint dragged her toward the stadium tunnel. "Quiet!"

Toni ripped her arm away and talked even louder. *Let the crowd see this.*

"I'm sorry if you're too immature to grasp my *friendship* with Carter, or if you're jealous of the time I spend with him. That's your problem. If this . . ." She struggled for an accurate word. "This *thing* we have were actually going anywhere, if we were getting serious or talking marriage or doing something more than making out half the time, I might consider my relationship with Carter inappropriate, and maybe I'd see less of him. But as things are, you an immature, hormonal jerk."

"Would you stop it?" Clint said, looking at a group of students who stared as they passed. "People are staring."

"I don't care if the entire world stares at us," Toni said then walked away. This time Clint didn't follow.

Toni walked blindly to her car and drove up a hill near the stadium, tears streaming down her face. What had she just done? Who was she to chew out Clint? She, who was ugly, fat, and pathetic, while Clint was one of the most attractive and talented men in the world? What made her so special that she deserved anything better?

She drove around the city, deep in thought, not even remembering that Clint had no way home without her. She didn't know where she was going. Her first thought had been to try

Carter's apartment, but a block away, she turned around. She couldn't tell him about what Clint had said about him—that would be cruel.

Besides, I'm supposed to wait for him to contact me first.

Suddenly she found herself face to face with a cathedral. It had gorgeous spires and stained-glass windows. She glanced at her sketch pad, which she'd tossed into the backseat and covered with a jacket in hopes that Clint wouldn't notice it. She looked back at the cathedral.

A few minutes of sketching would calm her down, she decided, and that building was a great thing to try her hand at. She parked her car on the street then walked over to a small, grassy hill across from the church. Bright shafts of afternoon sun sparkled on the windows. She wondered if the church was open, so she could see the magnificent reds and blues and yellows shining through the interior. She took a deep, cleansing breath. If she hoped to find peace anywhere in the city, this was a decent place to start.

Even though I'm not Catholic—or particularly religious.

She opened the book and began sketching the walls, the windows, the spires, the arched doorway. As she did, her mind began to wander, as it often did when she sat down with her pencil and paper. She tried to think of other famous religious buildings she could try her hand at and came up with Krishna temple, a Mormon temple, a Greek Orthodox church, and a handful of others.

As she drew in some shading, she thought of how beautiful the structure was, and how it was built by people trying to commune with God—a holy place. As she added details of trees and grass, she remembered reading about a church that had been bombed in the South at the height of the Civil Rights movement. Of a Mormon temple that had been burned and then flattened by a tornado. Of Kristallnacht, when a community of Jews lost their synagogue to angry Nazis.

She found her eyes watering. How could anyone do such things to buildings built for God, whatever the beliefs? Such buildings were precious and beautiful and deserved to be preserved and cared for.

The thoughts of the burning synagogue and bombed church somehow made her particularly sad, with their innocent victims who'd wanted nothing but to commune with Diety. A deep sadness filled her at the idea of tearing down someone else's temple. A tear tumbled onto her paper. She brushed it off quickly, but before she could resume her work, her eyes grew too blurry to draw. She laid the pad on her lap and gazed at the sacred structure before her. The sun had shifted slightly, making different parts of the stained glass stand out.

A scripture came to her mind as if someone were reading it to her.

Know ye not that your body is the temple of the Holy Ghost which is in you, which ye had of God, and ye are not your own?

There was surely a more modern translation, but her parents' old Bible was the King James. As a little girl, Toni had pulled the leather-bound volume off the shelf and flipped pages, reading the lyrical language, stopping at a few parts one of her parents had marked with a red pencil.

As far as she could remember, this wasn't one of the spots they'd marked. But she had a vague memory of a Sunday school children's class when she was maybe ten years old where the teacher had read it. The image it had evoked was beautiful, and Toni imagined what it would mean for the Holy Spirit to be *in* you, and for your body to be a sacred place.

Like a voice from the past, the words struck her like a thunder bolt.

She thought of how she'd treated her body, starving it of basic nutrients, throwing up and ripping her esophagus, rotting her teeth, and more. Ending up addicted to the thrill she got from such fake control—because she could see now, in this moment, the sense of freedom and order she got from her eating disorders were nothing more than an elaborate mirage.

Know ye not that your body is the temple of the Holy Ghost . . .

Ever since she'd started therapy, Toni had tried to love herself more, to accept her body more, to do all the things the experts said to do. But it was still centered on her—what she felt and thought and did. Through it all, she'd never considered that maybe her body wasn't hers to mess with and destroy. The idea seemed to stand before her in broad daylight, so bright that her mind almost needed to shield itself: her body didn't belong to her. It was a gift from God, and she had no business desecrating it.

This is what they meant in therapy by "surrendering to a higher power." She got it now.

Shaking, Toni stood and wiped her cheeks, and although tears kept falling, to her surprise, as she walked back to her car, they gradually turned into tears of joy. Suddenly, she knew that she'd found the tool she'd need to defeat each battle with anorexia and bulimia coming at her in the future—and there would be many. No getting away from that.

But the answer wasn't in looking inward. It was in looking outward. Maybe she'd have to start going to church again.

She got into her car and set the sketchbook onto the passenger seat. She'd found something that would give her the strength she so desperately needed when the monsters came out and whispered in her ear.

No more trying to stay strong for her dad, for Carter, or even for herself. That hadn't worked. But maybe she could be strong because God had trusted her with a temple.

Chapter 41

That night Toni had a restful, happy night in her apartment. She put on an old pair of sweats and watched two classics over a bowl of unbuttered popcorn—none of which she purged. She was tempted to call Carter to tell him of her new breakthrough but knew better.

Her mind turned back to Clint's comments. To her surprise, she didn't fume over them. She almost laughed. If Clint had hoped to make Carter look bad, his plan had backfired miserably. He could have earned a lot of points by praising her best friend instead. Several moments from the last few months came back to mind, things she'd brushed off or explained away at the time.

Now she realized how frequent those moments had been, and that Clint never actually apologized for anything, never tried to understand what her feelings had been, or why she'd been hurt. Just to get over it already.

He and I are a bad match, through and through. Surely Carter had known a long time ago. Why hadn't he said anything? *Same reason he's never told me to break up with a guy.*

She'd missed so many signs with both Clint and Carter; the realization blew her mind. How had she missed it all?

The doorbell rang, and Toni grudgingly got off the couch, even though she'd hardly paid attention to the show. She looked through the peephole and let out a light wince—Clint. Even though she wanted to break it off with him, she was painfully aware of her shabby sweats and that her makeup had pretty much worn off. Even though he would soon be part of her past, she fluffed her bangs a bit to get rid of their stringy look before opening the door.

"Didn't expect to see you," she said.

"I can tell." Clint looked her up and down with a laugh. Toni gave his joke nothing but a blank look for a response—his "jokes" weren't funny, and she wouldn't write them off as trivial. No more. He coughed and drew his right hand from behind his back, revealing a bouquet of three roses. "I got these for you. To make up for earlier."

Toni didn't take them. Instead, she folded her arms and stared him down.

"Um, can I come in?" Clint asked.

"You can talk out here for a minute." Toni said, leaning against the doorjamb to block the walk. May as well officially end it right now, while she still had her nerve and felt nothing for him but pity and disdain.

Clint held out the roses again. "Am I forgiven?"

She ignored them. "You're not even sorry, are you?" He'd offered her flowers and a joke, but no actual apology. "You still believe everything you said, and you aren't sorry for any of it. You just wish you would have kept your thoughts to yourself so that you hadn't gotten into trouble."

He held out his arms. "Oh, hey now. You know how much you mean to me, babe." He reached for the side of her face in the familiar move that always came before his most passionate kisses. In horror, Toni watched herself not moving away.

Turn your head. Don't let him kiss you. But before she knew it, his lips were on hers, and she was kissing him back. It didn't feel as good as it used to, but for the moment, she felt drawn into his spell.

Her phone went off with a duck quack, meaning someone on her favorites list was calling. *Carter?* The sound dissolved the moment and brought Toni back to her senses. *Shoot. What did I do?* She hurried to the coffee table and answered her cell. "Hello?" Her voice was breathy, and she hated herself for it.

"Toni?" came a hardly audible squeak.

"Mom, is that you?"

"I'm at the hospital."

A knot gripped Toni's throat, and all thoughts of Clint vanished. "What happened? Did Dad have another heart attack? Is he all right?"

"It's not a heart attack," her mom said, clearly trying to keep her voice steady. "Dad was in a horrible accident on the freeway. He died on impact."

Toni's hand flew to her mouth, and she shook her head. "But Dad can't be dead," she whispered, as if saying the words would make them true.

"I know, sweetie," her mother said. "I know."

Toni got a few more details, and she promised to get there as soon as possible. She hung up and instinctively began looking for her purse. She was almost surprised to see Clint still standing at the door. "I'm sorry. I have to go. My father's been in a bad accident."

Clint nodded. "Guess this isn't the time for these anymore, is it?" he said, looking at the flowers. He leaned into her apartment and tossed them onto a speaker. "Call you later." And he walked off before she could tell him to go to hell.

She hadn't gotten to the point of breaking up with him, and he thought they were still a couple. But he'd just left? He didn't so much as offer comfort, a ride, a hug—anything.

She shook herself back to the moment and somehow found her purse after a five-minute hunt, even though it sat in plain sight on the floor by the couch. She slipped on a pair of ballet flats and headed toward the door, so distracted that she almost didn't look at the man walking toward her.

"Toni, what's wrong?" At the sound of Carter's voice, she stopped short. He took her arm and looked at her closely. "What is it?

On impulse, she collapsed into his arms. "How did you know?"

Carter held her tight and rubbed her back. "I don't know anything. Just had a feeling you needed me. I saw Clint driving off. Did you two have a fight?"

Toni shook her head. "My mom called from the hospital."

Carter took her by the shoulders and gently pulled her back

so he could look into her eyes. "Another heart attack? Is he going to be all right?"

She shook her head several times. "No. A car accident." Toni choked on her voice. "He's gone, Carter. He's gone." She fell back into Carter's arms and sobbed into his shirt.

He wrapped his arms around her again. "Come on," he finally said. "I'll take you there. You can't drive like this." With his arm around her, he gently led her to his car.

Chapter 42

Somehow Toni made it through the next couple of days by having Carter at her side. He took a few days off work to be with her as she helped her mom with funeral preparations. He was the one who gently reminded her to take a nap when her eyes turned red from fatigue. Who made sure she drank water and didn't go too long without eating something, even something little. Who ran errands for Toni and her mom when they realized they were out of bread or gas or computer paper.

On Sunday as she and her mother tried to write up the obituary, Carter quietly handed her a water bottle and a small bowl of grapes then went back to the kitchen and did some dishes. Toni had hardly thought about food at all since the night of the accident; if Carter hadn't made sure she ate something, she probably would have slipped right back into anorexic behaviors.

She popped one grape into her mouth then put her fingers back on the keyboard to type the words her mother was dictating. One bite, and the grape burst with sweetness in her mouth. So good. The urge to hole up, to binge and purge, washed over her again. It *would* relieve stress in the short term; she knew that from lots of experience.

"I need to go lie down for a bit," her mother said.

"But we aren't even half done with the obituary." Toni pointed at the screen.

"I need a break." Her mother patted her shoulder and stood then shuffled her way to the master bedroom.

Toni sat there, painfully aware of her own stress and anxiety building up. Her eyes strayed to the paper on the desk listing things that needed to be done for the funeral. They kept adding to it, and the list was already huge. So much to do in such a short period.

I could do more if I calm down. I could calm down if I purge.

True, but she didn't do that anymore. She wasn't that person anymore. After swallowing the grape, she deliberately ate one more, slowly. She reached into her purse, which was hanging on her chair, and felt for a folded piece of sketch paper. After pulling it out, she opened it and looked at the cathedral again.

My body is a cathedral. I will take care of it.

The words had become a mantra to get her through many hours of wanting to release the stress and pain of her father's death by binging and purging or by not eating at all.

With Carter in the kitchen cleaning and her mother lying down, Toni pulled a miniature sketch pad from her purse—something Carter had given her, of course. She curled up onto the couch and drew, pouring her emotions and stress onto the paper, waiting for the purge craving to go away.

This time she drew an imaginary building. She adorned it with a turret and balcony and a wide staircase out front. One of these days she'd need to learn how to draw people. She could do a decent flower or tree or other inanimate objects, but people and animals still eluded her. If she continued to use drawing as a way to manage her cravings, she'd end up becoming a total pro drawing just about anything, she imagined.

I hope it doesn't take that long. But it probably would. She now knew enough from what her therapists had said to realize that this would be a condition she'd have to battle every hour of every day for the rest of her life. She couldn't think too far ahead like that; the battle was exhausting, and the idea of it never ending could be enough to make her give up. But at the moment, she'd use drawing and thinking of her body as God's creation as two solid coping mechanisms.

They weren't cures.

She drew for almost a full hour, until she noticed her brother Kevin's car pulling into the driveway. The other brothers would be here with their wives soon too. The worst of the craving had passed. With Kevin and his wife here, she'd find it easier to stay distracted, so she set the sketchbook aside to help carry in luggage just as the phone rang.

Carter emerged from the kitchen holding the phone. "Caller ID says it's the funeral home."

"Thanks." Toni took the phone from him and answered as she headed for her mom's room, so she'd be aware of any plans. She answered the phone.

"Is this Patricia Harper?"

"This is her daughter. I'll go get her for you."

The master bedroom door was ajar, so Toni knocked on it with one knuckle. "Mom?"

Her mother was just getting up. She smoothed out her hair and dabbed at her eyes as if checking her makeup before taking the phone and mouthing her thanks. Toni stayed close by as her mother talked to the director and hung up a minute later.

"If we want to say goodbye in person, we need to go over right now."

Toni had braced herself for the possibility of seeing her father's mangled body on Tuesday morning before the "viewing," a total misnomer, as the casket would be closed because of the damage done to the body in the accident.

"Why now?"

"They're preparing the body for burial. With a closed casket, I guess they want it done early." She shook her head wearily. "I don't know. They just said to come over."

Kevin had barely arrived, but moments after hugs and greetings, they were back in their car and headed for the funeral home. The other boys were almost in town, so she called each of them and said to head straight to the mortuary.

All the family members—plus Carter, whom Toni insisted on coming—arrived within half an hour of each other. They waited in a dim hallway until the director entered and greeted them with handshakes and whispers.

He turned to Toni's mother. "How about I bring you back first?"

"That would be wonderful, thank you."

Toni watched her mother follow the director down the hall. They hadn't been able to see his body at the hospital. Just how bad was it? Was his face injured? Unrecognizable?

She sat on a padded bench with Carter and grabbed his hand. He squeezed back affectionately, which helped her calm down.

"You sure you want to see him?" Carter whispered. "It may be better to remember him as he was."

Toni shook her head. "No. I can do this. I want to see him."

Kevin took his turn. He wasn't in there long; he came out pale-faced and shaky. He sank onto the nearest bench and dropped his head into his hands, trembling all over.

"Never mind. I can't do it," Toni said, pulling Carter to his feet. "Mom, I'll see you guys back at the house."

Without further explanation, she left the funeral home with Carter. As he drove back to her parents' house, she sat in the passenger seat in silence, kicking herself for being such a wimp. Carter parked out front, unlatched his seatbelt, and turned to her. "Let's walk around the block."

Toni assented with a nod and got out. One minute into the walk, she was glad she'd gone. She didn't want to go back into the house yet, not when her father should still be alive, making one of his fruit and vegetable smoothies and teasing her about getting married and giving him grandchildren.

Her mind went in circles. She walked with her arms folded tightly across her chest, as if the act would give her some comfort or sense of security.

Carter eyed her for some time before he ventured to speak. "Want to talk about it?"

Her lower lip quivered, but she tamped down the emotion. "I wanted to say goodbye to him, but I chickened out. I *needed* to say good-bye, to let him know that everything's all right now, that I don't blame him anymore. He died not knowing that I'm going to be okay with this disorder."

Carter paused in his step and put an arm around her, and Toni drew closer to put her head on his shoulder. "You don't need to see his body to say goodbye."

"It's not that."

"You need closure," he said. Toni nodded and put her head on his shoulder again. "Maybe you can find your own way of saying goodbye, something fitting for your relationship, and then you can tell him everything you want to. That would probably mean more to him wherever he is now anyway, more than standing over his shell would."

Toni smiled up at Carter, the first smile she'd felt on her face in days. "You're right. I'll do it."

They finished their walk and then Carter dropped her off at the house. "Call if you need anything."

She nodded. "See you at the funeral?"

"Definitely."

She gave him one more big hug then went inside, grateful beyond words that Carter was still here, still in her life. What would she have done if he'd backed off completely like he'd said he would?

What will happen after the funeral?

Toni brushed off that thought. She had to focus on one thing at a time. She went into the storage room in the basement and rummaged through boxes from her childhood. After thumbing through old journals and school papers, souvenirs from vacations to Yellowstone and Disneyland, she found her second-place medal from a gymnastics event. *Perfect.* Not first place, but second—it was a classic symbol of their relationship and how she needed gold to win his approval, she but didn't always get it.

She tucked the medal into her purse, put the boxes away, and left her mother and brothers at the house. Before pulling out to drive to her apartment, she texted Carter.

I figured out how to say goodbye.

At six the next morning, Toni left her apartment with the medal into her jacket pocket. She drove to the spot where her father had first taught her how to fish. She wanted something connected to one of her happiest memories about him, untarnished by expectations and disappointments.

Toni parked then walked down the steep embankment to the edge of the rushing river. She took the medal out of her pocket, put it around her neck, and closed her eyes. She thought back to the gymnastics meet she got the medal. She was ten again, only in her mind, her father was in his late sixties, not his forties as he had been at the meet. His hair was nearly silver instead of black.

This time, the ceremony played out differently. She watched tears fall down his cheeks. She pictured him racing up to her, lifting her off her feet, and twirling her in the air, yelling, "Second place! Amazing!"

The entire scene played out, rewriting the past. When he put her down again, he leaned down, fingered the medal then gave her another big hug. "I'm so proud of you, dumpling," he said. "And I always will be, even if you never win anything again. I love you so much."

Ten-year-old Toni jumped into his arms and placed a kiss on his rough cheek. "I love you too, Daddy."

Standing on the riverbank, adult Toni choked on a sob. A few raindrops landed on her. She lifted her face heavenward, eyes still closed, and felt the rain running down her cheeks and mingling with her tears. Toni glanced around to make sure no one was around. With a deep breath, she removed the medal and, with all her might, flung it downstream.

"I love you, Daddy," she whispered as the red, white, and blue ribbon with its silver circle was engulfed in white foam and green waves. "Everything's all right now. Don't feel bad. In my mind, it happened the way we both wished it would have. Don't need to worry about me. I'll be fine. I'll be around for a lot of years, and not as a bag of bones."

She watched the river carry the medal away. She stayed there for several minutes even after it had been carried well out of sight. Cool raindrops wetted her hair and jacket as she turned back toward the embankment. She felt light, as if a burden had been lifted from her and she could stand straight again. When a shaft of sunlight suddenly broke through the clouds, Toni looked up and smiled, as if it was a sign that her father had heard and accepted her farewell.

As she walked away, she knew how silly the whole performance could have looked to an outsider.

But it was exactly what I needed.

Chapter 43

Toni took the entire week off work for the funeral, and Jill, another teacher at the studio, took over her classes. When she returned to work the following Monday, Toni felt as if she were entering a world she had left behind long ago. She had undergone so much in those days that if age were measured in emotion, she would have aged at least ten years that week.

As she came through the studio doors, Allen left his office to express his condolences—for the tenth time. He'd come to both the viewing and the funeral, sent flowers, and offered to let Toni take up to a month off work, which she declined. All totally un-Allen-like.

"How are you doing?" Allen asked from his office doorway.

"I'm fine, thanks," Toni called over her shoulder and headed toward the big studio.

"Is there anything—"

Toni turned and smiled at him. "The best thing for me right now is to get back to as normal a life as I can, as quickly as possible."

"Sure." Allen shrugged lightly. "But let me know how I can help."

"You've been wonderful, and I really appreciate it." Toni came over and gave Allen a light hug, something neither of them had ever done before. "Thanks again."

Toni got to her classroom with almost fifteen spare minutes, enough time to get her music ready and make sure she remembered the routine she had been teaching before she left. She put on her jazz shoes, found the music for her first class, and started marking the routine. Halfway through, the door opened. Toni turned to welcome her first student, instead, she saw Clint. He closed the door behind him.

"Hi," he said.

Toni hadn't even thought about Clint since he had left her apartment the day of her father's accident. He seemed to belong to a world she'd left behind. "What's up?" she asked, turning back to the mirror. Odd that she hadn't missed him during such a hard time.

But no, even weirder was the fact she hadn't seen him at all. Surely her boyfriend could have found out the times of the viewing and funeral, if not by calling her, then simply checking a newspaper.

"What have you been doing all week?" she asked, hoping her comment would open a door for him to explain himself.

Clint walked to the center of the floor. "I've been doing a lot of thinking." He reached forward as if to get a kiss hello, but Toni moved out of the way to warm up. It was a small act of defiance, but it sent a surge of victory go through her. She'd never been able to resist Clint's touch before.

"Thinking about what?" she asked casually as she began a new stretch.

He produced a heart-shaped box of chocolates, but Toni paid no attention to it. She mentally rolled her eyes at the idea of giving someone with an eating disorder a pound of chocolates. *Brilliant move.*

"I've missed you," he said, still holding the box out.

Toni straightened and looked right at him. "Oh, please. You may as well say what you mean. You don't miss me, you miss making out. I'm nothing more to you than a pair of lips."

"You're more to me than that," Clint interjected.

"Oh, right. You also like my body, as long as I don't gain any weight. Face it—you don't have enough of a heart to care about anything beyond getting a turn-on."

Clint looked stunned as he put his hands up in surrender. "Hey, I just wanted to talk things out, but if you don't want to, I'll just come back another time."

Toni almost laughed. "You've got to be kidding. *You* want to *talk*? As if we could do much of anything but exchange a few kisses in the time before my class—something completely inappropriate at work, I might add."

Clint's jaw hung slack. Toni had never spoken like this to him, and they both knew it. "Now if you don't mind," she said, finding that it liberating to speak her mind, "I have a class to teach." A few students had already come in, and they continued trickling in as Clint headed toward the door.

As he reached it, he turned back. "I'm not sure I understand," he said. "What does this mean for us? Will I see you Friday?"

Toni hardly thought about what she did next; she just did it. She went to her dance bag, where she quickly found her now well-worn Latin heels. "Here," she said, dangling them in front of his face. "Take these. We aren't a couple anymore, in any sense of the word." She pressed the shoes into his chest, and when he took them, she turned on her heels and gathered her students together to begin class.

Clint looked dumbfounded—he probably wasn't used to being the dumpee—and silently walked out, closing the door behind him. For once, a gift hadn't smoothed a girl's ruffled feathers.

It's time he learned that.

Toni felt so good about getting rid of that albatross called Clint off from around her neck that all three of her classes flew by. Her teaching had never gone better, and she couldn't remember having enjoyed it so much. How long she had gone through life half numb, except for the intensity that Clint's touch—and purging—gave her?

As her last class ended, she looked at her body in the mirror and noticed that her hips had gotten a bit rounder again.

Huh. It took me three hours to notice that. She remembered Clint's hands running over her hips and saying how she shouldn't be "chubbing up." Instead of feeling anger toward him, she felt pity.

Clint must really dislike himself to focus on women so much.
All he did was try to gain power over them, and determine
how they felt about themselves, so that he always had the upper
hand. Poor guy had no idea what it felt like to like himself.

Until recently, she hadn't either. Not until she had realized
her value as a divine creation. Her students were gone, but Toni
felt too energized to leave just yet. She drank from her water
bottle then cued some music to improvise to.

As she turned and leaped and stretched, she thought over the
past several months and realized just how twisted her
relationship with Clint had been, and for how long. She'd wanted
more from him, but how could she justify that when she was
such a wreck herself? How could she think she deserved
someone who treated her right, when she was already such a
failure?

Now she knew better. She was better off, and happier, alone
than with a jerk who tore her down. The realizations about
Clint's true colors had been gradual in coming, and she couldn't
have pointed to a day on the calendar to mark when they began.
But she did know that it started with her first hospital
stay—when she had realized she wanted more—and culminated
somewhere after she found out that Carter had loved her for
years.

If Carter thought she was attractive, other men could, too,
right? Good men, not like Clint?

As she danced, she watched her reflection and saw a new
person, one she really liked, hips notwithstanding. She almost
laughed aloud at sense of freedom, which made her want to fly.

Soon the receptionist and nearly everyone else in the studio
had left, leaving the building in almost complete darkness. Allen
left last, after popping his head into the studio. Toni had to
assure him that she was fine and would lock up in a few minutes.

"You sure you're all right?" he asked.

Toni grinned. "I'm doing great," she said. "Better each day."

"You're looking good," he said. "Your cheeks have a healthy
color to them again. Glad to see it." Allen waved and headed out.

Toni turned to look at her cheeks specifically. Allen was
right, and the color wasn't just because the room was warm and

she'd been dancing. The outside door clicked shut, leaving her alone in the building.

Toni went to the sound system and searched her phone for music she hadn't danced to in a while. She found a playlist of some of her favorite songs. She cranked up the volume until she could feel the heavy bass of the music in her bones and let herself loose.

She hadn't danced this big, this freely, since the day Clint had walked in on her to ask for money for the vending machine. Joy sent a liberating thrill through her, something she'd gone far too long without.

After three songs, she dropped to the floor and stared at the ceiling, breathing heavily but loving the slightly weak feeling that followed a burst of adrenaline. As the song ended and a slow one began, she closed her eyes and let herself be carried away by the melody, one she'd always loved.

The song was of a woman searching for her one true love, only to realize years later that she never did have to search; her true love had been in her life the entire time. She'd known the lyrics before, but today they pierced her to the center. She jumped to her feet and turned off the music. She unplugged her phone and, with shaky a hand, put it in her dance bag.

I don't feel that way about Carter, she kept reminding herself. *This song is not about me.* She hurriedly put on her sweats and sneakers as if she were late for something, but really to keep herself from thinking about the song, which insisted on playing in her mind again and again.

Carter Mackenzie? No.

Even so, the chorus would not leave her mind, and the words were now accompanied by images of Carter's drawings of her—of them.

The very idea of being romantic with Carter was ludicrous, right?

She sat on the studio floor, facing the mirror, and watched her hands keep trembling. *What is my problem?*

Sure, she knew Carter better than anyone, and cared for him. She hadn't realized how good looking he was without glasses until he switched to contact lenses. But that didn't mean he was the one she was destined for. Even if Clint had turned out to be less than desirable, she did know one thing: after experiencing such a powerful physical response to a man, she couldn't settle for platonic. That went against every romantic ideal she'd ever known.

Toni picked up her dance bag and headed out the door. The night air felt colder than it was as it hit her body, which was still warm and lightly beaded with sweat. She shivered and headed toward her car, when a man emerged from the shadowy parking lot. She jumped in surprise then laughed with relief when she realized it was Carter. Fright turned to confusion as the song kept playing in her head.

Your search can end too . . . He's right in front of you.

"What are you doing here?" she asked, trying to hush the song.

"This is the first day back to work since the funeral. Just wanted to make sure you were doing all right."

"I'm doing better than I thought I would be." Toni glanced over her shoulder at the darkened studio. "My classes ended almost half an hour ago. How did you know I'd be here?"

"I've been here for a while."

Toni blushed. "Then I guess you saw me in there making a fool out of myself." She wouldn't have dreamed of dancing alone if she had known anyone had been watching through the big windows.

"It was beautiful. I've never seen anything like it." He grinned. "I knew I was missing out on something by never seeing you in your element."

Toni glanced over her shoulder at the building. "I don't know about it being my 'element' anymore." She began fiddling with her keys as they walked to her car.

"You aren't going to stop dancing, are you?" Carter asked. "That would be worse than a tragedy. Don't you dare."

Toni laughed. "No, I'll dance until I'm too old to stand up. I meant the studio." She leaned against the driver-side door of her car. "It may be time to move on to a new job."

Carter leaned against his own car, parked next to hers. "I don't follow."

"The studio is where I met Clint, where we spent dozens of hours together, where . . ." She almost said, *When he first kissed me* but stopped herself. She couldn't share those things with Carter anymore. Had she known his feelings before, she never would have dumped her boyfriend problems on him. "Just about every inch of the place reeks with memories of him."

"So you and Clint are . . . "

Toni put her hand up as if making an announcement. "Totally over," she said knowing Carter would be pleased. "I even returned the shoes he gave me. We're history."

"That's great," Carter said. "I mean, breakups are hard, but he didn't deserve you."

"Darn right," Toni said, cracking a smile at hearing herself admit that she was worth more. "Besides, he has no taste in food or old movies. He hadn't even heard of *The Philadelphia Story*."

Carter gave a mock snort of disgust. "How can a man like that live with himself?"

Toni laughed and tugged on Carter's shirt. "Come on. Let's go get some nachos. I promise to eat a sensible amount and *not* sneak off to the restroom afterward."

"And I won't notice either way."

Toni reached up and gave Carter a big hug. "You have no idea how much I've needed you lately. I couldn't have gotten through my dad's death without you."

"Yes, you could have," Carter said. "You're strong."

Toni shook her head as she pulled back. "No. I've gotten stronger lately, but you've helped me to get where I am. You made me believe in myself. You're the one who gave me a way to express my feelings and thoughts on paper. And thanks to that, I'm going to be okay. A few weeks ago, I didn't think I had any right to expect more from a man than Clint was giving me. Or taking from me. All of that is thanks to you."

Carter hung his head as if hiding his face in the darkness. He sniffed. "That's what friends do, right?"

Chapter 44

The next morning, Toni went over to her mom's. Together they tried to pick out a headstone and decide on the style and what to write on it. They narrowed it down to three possible stones and images. Her mom wanted to have a couple of days before making a final decision.

Toni got up from the table. "I'm going to head out in a few. Do you need me to grab some groceries or run any other errands?"

Her mom got up from the table, moved to the living room couch, and beckoned Toni over. "No errands today, but thanks. I want to talk."

"O-kay," Toni said. She sat by her mom, wondering what in the world they were going to talk about.

Not my disorder. Please.

Her mother didn't speak right away, but the serious look on her face told Toni that whatever was on her mother's mind was important to her. "I've been thinking a lot about you lately. About you and that Clint boy, and about you and Carter."

"Mom," Toni said, afraid of where this was headed. "I broke up with Clint. And things with Carter are kind of complicated."

"There are lots of things you don't know about me, Toni," her mom said as if she hadn't heard a word Toni had said. She clasped her hands and put them on her knee. "For starters, I wasn't in love with your father when I married him."

Toni felt kicked in the gut, as if all her childhood illusions about her family suddenly had come crashing down in pieces around her. All the stories about her father being so smitten with her mother at first sight took on a new significance. "You never loved Dad?" Why tell her daughter this right after his funeral?

Her mother smiled wanly. "I didn't say that." She gazed longingly at the wedding picture handing on the wall above the piano. "I loved your father dearly. After forty years of marriage, I loved him more than I could have thought possible on our wedding day. A part of my heart died with him." She dabbed at the corners of her eyes and put on a brave smile.

Toni's eyebrows furrowed. "I don't understand . . ."

Her mother patted her hand. "When your father proposed, I cared for him, very much. I did love him, but I wasn't *in love* with him. You know what I mean, don't you?"

Toni nodded miserably. She did know, all too well. "So why on earth did you marry him?"

"I knew we'd be happy together. I knew we could make a good life with each other. He was a dear friend, and I couldn't live without him. I took a gamble that the other kind of love—the passionate kind most of the world calls love—would come later."

Toni's attention was piqued now. "And?"

"And it came. The more years we spent together, the more fulfilling our intimate relationship became. All in all, we had more passion than most young couples ever have." She giggled lightly. "I remember one time when you kids were still little. Your father came home from a business trip, and when he walked in the door he had this look in his eye. He said one word, and I knew what he meant. See, we had this nickname for—"

"That's enough, please." Toni put a hand up to stop her mother from saying more. "I don't want to know that kind of stuff about you and Dad."

Her mom just laughed. "My point is that a strong, existing love without the spark can make one of the best foundations you'll ever find. It's much less of a gamble marrying someone you know and trust, than to commit to someone who can tie your stomach into knots but who turns out to be a bum."

Toni looked at her parents' wedding picture with new eyes. She breathed out hard. "So you think I should throw myself at Carter."

"I just don't want you to overlook something that may make you truly happy. If Carter isn't the one, fine. But don't dismiss the idea before you've really given it a chance, because I'm pretty sure you never have, and I'm just as sure that he's head over heels in love with you."

Was Toni the only person to not know how Carter really felt? How blind had she been? She took a deep breath. "Okay. I'll give it some thought."

Chapter 45

With life slowly returning to normal after the funeral, Toni feared that Carter would finally walk out of her life completely; she was pretty sure he'd stuck around because she needed him during a crisis. When he texted asking if she'd get his mail and newspapers and water his plants while he took some art students on a trip, she breathed a huge sigh of relief.

An hour later, he showed up at her door to hand over his key. She wanted to invite him in, but her mother's words sent Toni's insides squirming, and she couldn't think straight.

"I'll be leaving Thursday morning, and I'll be back Monday afternoon," Carter said. "The plants need watering on Thursday, and again on Monday, but I'll be home late on Monday night, so if you can't do it then, that's fine. I can do it when I get home. Just leave the key on the table."

"I'll be going out of town myself on Monday," Toni said, trying to sound casual.

"Where?"

"I'm chaperoning the studio's youth company tour. I'll be back that Saturday."

Toni hadn't been assigned to the tour at first, but she'd begged Allen to let her go—even mentioning the fact that he'd asked if he could help. And getting away would help. She needed space to think about Carter, about the idea of a platonic marriage with Carter with the hopes it would turn into something else.

Recently, Carter's touch sent a tingle up her arm, and his texts made her heart beat more quickly. But was any of that because things had changed? Or was it simply because her mother had planted an idea in her head?

Then again, it could all be an anxiety response—sweats, heart palpitations? Yep.

She took the key, suddenly aware of his touch and wondering why it felt different now. "If I can't make it on Monday before we head out, I'll leave the keys when I come for your newspaper on Sunday," she told him. "Who still gets the Sunday paper anyway, though?"

They stood on opposite sides of her threshold for several moments. Toni couldn't help but wonder what it would be like to kiss Carter—purely as a scientific experiment. It wasn't like she wanted to.

He took a step back and put his hands into his back pockets. "I'd better go. Have to pack and stuff."

"Yeah. See you went I get back."

I hope.

∾

Toni watered Carter's plants and got his mail and newspaper faithfully while he was gone. She also missed him, but had he been around, she wouldn't have known what to say or do around him—not since talking with her mother.

The final tour plans changed, so Toni wouldn't be leaving until Monday night, so on Sunday, she didn't leave the key behind on the table after all. She went over on Monday afternoon to water the plants one final time.

On the way over, her mother's words still tumbled around in her head. Of course, typical daily life wasn't filled with romance at every turn. It hardly consisted of nothing but roses and chocolates—more like scrubbing toilets and making dinners and paying bills. She had to agree that a friend whom she already loved would make a far better husband than someone like Clint, even if he couldn't stir her physically.

Chemistry alone doesn't make a marriage, she kept reminding herself. She and Clint certainly had chemistry, and look how well that had turned out.

Carter would make such a good husband. She knew him almost better than she knew herself—she bet she knew him better than many brides know their grooms on their wedding day.

She tried to envision a platonic future for herself, but Toni simply couldn't imagine raising a family with someone she had never felt passion for. You couldn't count the fleeting moment of attraction when she'd run into Carter and Brooke by the auditorium, or the fleeting moment of excitement she'd felt outside the studio when he'd waited for her. Or when he's handed her his key, and her hand had tingled.

Okay, it's been more than once or twice. Still doesn't count.

She'd just about convinced herself she could never be Carter's wife, but the teen company tour would give her the chance to sort it out once and for all. She'd make a decision and tell him where they stood when she got back.

Toni parked on the street in front of his building. As she went up to his apartment, she kept thinking about what a platonic marriage would mean. She could still have the basic essentials of her dream—children, a house, a dance studio—but could she live without ever feeling that rush of passion that Clint had given her with a single wink?

She slipped the key in and went inside. Mechanically, she grabbed the watering pot from above the fridge and filled it up then went from the two plants hanging in the kitchen to the ficus tree in the corner of the front room. As she straightened, she heard a door open somewhere inside the apartment. At the thought of an intruder, fear gripped her stomach, and she froze.

"Hey, who's there?" a voice called. Then, "Toni!"

At the sound of Carter's voice, Toni relaxed.

Carter stood by the bathroom door, having obviously come straight from the shower. His hair, wet and disheveled, had been pushed back. He wore no glasses—nothing, for that matter but a bright blue towel around his waist.

She yelped. "Whoa!" she cried, her hand flying to her mouth. Her surprise at finding him home early was nothing compared to her shock at seeing Carter as a man—his defined chest and stomach, cut biceps, the works. Had he always been that ripped?

"Whoa," she said again, this time quieter, and for a different reason—the same reason she said it when looking at Colin Firth. As much as she wanted to keep looking at his body, she turned away, embarrassment—and something stronger—racing through her.

Oh, wow, he's hot.

She couldn't handle looking at Carter like that, even though every detail was burned in her mind. Her face had to be flaming red. The picture of his body would not leave her mind; she had an unruly desire to run her hands up his chest, muss up his hair, and kiss him soundly.

This is Carter! she screamed inside.

"I, uh, I thought you weren't coming home until tonight," she stammered, looking at the carpet.

"I didn't know either. My plans changed last minute." he said. "I figured you'd be out of town by now."

"I don't leave until five," she said, examining the leaves of the ficus but still blushing to the tips of her ears. Whoa. Carter was all man, and a fine one at that. Drops of shower water had trickled down his pecs to his abs.

This is Carter.

The guy who'd seen her pop zits and cut toe nails. *And* the guy who loved her more than life.

Stop it! But the thoughts kept coming, one after the other, sending warm ripples through her and her heart hammering against her rib cage. The song from that night in the studio came back to her mind, and with it the idea that her search was over. But instead of feeling any clarity, only felt confusion.

"I'll, uh, go get decent," Carter said, and backed into the bathroom.

When the door clicked, Toni breathed a sigh of relief and collapsed on the couch. Her hands trembled, and she gripped them together to keep them still. She eyed the keys in her hand and then the kitchen table and considered just calling out to Carter that she was leaving before making a quick escape but couldn't get herself to move from the couch.

It's a fluke, she whispered. *I was just thinking about how Carter could never make me feel anything physical, so of course the minute I see him, he affects me that way.*

Carter came out just a few minutes later, this time wearing perfectly fitting jeans and a dark shirt she'd never seen. He rubbed a towel in his hair and tossed it onto a chair. She could hardly take her eyes off him and thanked the heavens that he'd put on his glasses, because he looked even better without them, and that would only serve to mess with her head right now.

"Sorry about that. At least I had my towel on, right?"

"Right," Toni said, trying to laugh along, but knowing she sounded like a recording.

Carter's face clouded. "Are you all right? Did something else happen with Clint?"

"No," Toni rushed in. "He's still history." She paused awkwardly and strained to come up with something to say—something she couldn't remember ever having to do around Carter. "I've gained two more pounds. That's good news."

He eyed her and shook his head. "I know you. There's something up behind those gorgeous eyes of yours."

"My what?" Ever since boys lost their cooties, she'd wanted someone to think she was pretty aside from her body.

Carter's the first.

"Come on," he said. "I can tell by your eyes that something's bothering you."

"That's not what you said."

"What did I say?" Carter looked at the ceiling as he thought. "I said that something's behind your gorgeous eyes. Haven't I mentioned them before? They're your best feature, but they drove me nuts in my drawings. I never could capture them. I think I came close in the oil, though."

Toni looked around awkwardly, trying to keep herself from trembling. Not so long ago, her life had made sense, but everything had turned upside down.

"Toni, what is it?"

She stood and headed toward the door. "Nothing. It's—no, it's nothing. No one's ever said my eyes were pretty before."

Carter stood and blocked her path to the door. He reached forward and brushed some hair away from one eye. "You have beautiful eyes."

Toni swallowed hard and looked away. The tingling suddenly erupted into a flame that seemed to consume her body, and she couldn't think straight. She wanted him to touch her again, but at the same time, his touch only confused her more.

"You should probably know that your mother called me the other day."

That brought Toni around. "Oh, no." She needed to sit for this one. She pulled out a kitchen chair and sank onto it.

Carter did the same. Their knees almost touched but didn't. She couldn't decide whether she wanted them to. She totally did and totally didn't at the same time.

"She told me about a talk she had with you."

Toni's head hit her hand. "Tell me she spared you the details."

"Pretty sure I heard most of it."

Toni groaned. "I'm sorry she put you through that. I had no idea."

Carter tried to laugh, but it sounded off. "I didn't realize she knew how I felt."

"She's more observant than I am, apparently," Toni said quietly.

"Anyway . . ." He cleared his throat and went on. "She thinks I'd have a chance with you now."

Toni froze; Carter rolled his eyes. "Come on. You should know me better than that."

She managed to crack a smile. "This keeps getting more and more awkward, doesn't it?"

"You have to know one thing."

Toni could tell he was trying to keep his emotions at bay.

"I don't know if you've thought about what your mother said—and I don't want you to tell me right now, either."

Toni closed her mouth and nodded.

"I want you to know what *I* think about what she told you." Carter sighed to even out his breath then took her hand; a pleasant jolt went up her arm and sent her heart racing. "I agree with your mom about friendship being the foundation for a good marriage. But I *don't* want you to come to me saying you've had a change of heart because we're *compatible*. I don't want . . . a *compatible* relationship. That's not enough for me, and I know it's not enough for you, either. I'd rather see you marry some other guy and know you'll be happy with him."

Carter took off his glasses and rubbed between his eyes. He looked so good without them. The same thrill went through her again, and Toni had a temptation to grab his other hand so he couldn't put them back on. But at the same time, she crushed the thought.

I'm not attracted to him, she chided herself. *I'm not.* Why was she suddenly feeling like this? Her mind was playing tricks on her. She couldn't wait to be away for a week, so she could clear her head.

But Carter wasn't done. "There have been times, brief moments, that I've suspected you feel something for me . . . in that way. If you do, even a little, I'm willing to wait to see if anything comes of it. But if not . . ." His voice trailed off. He swallowed and went on as if he'd gathered his courage. "I know it would be hard for both of us, but if we . . . if *this* is all our relationship will ever be, we have to stop seeing each other completely."

Toni's eyes widened. The idea of not having Carter in her life sent a wave of horror through her. She couldn't handle a lifetime apart from him, especially now that they were together again, after she had stupidly sent him away for trying to help. She was making such progress with her health—because of him. Toni shook her head emphatically. "You can't mean—"

He held up a hand and kept talking. "I can't do this anymore. It's too hard."

Toni nodded mutely, knowing there was nothing she could say to change how he felt, yet wanting to scream at the thought of losing her best friend. But he was right; this wasn't fair to him. She'd had the better end of the deal for thirteen years.

"So now what?" she mustered.

"You tell me."

Toni stood and paced to the other side of the room,

conflicting emotions clashing inside her. "You can't expect me to say anything and risk having you walk out of my life forever." She put her hand to her forehead, trying to calm her thoughts.

"Did I imagine those moments?"

She didn't have to ask which moments he was referring to. "I don't know how I feel about anything anymore. The only thing I do know is that I can't bear the thought of never seeing you again."

Carter rose and put his arms around her. The butterflies went crazy in her stomach but being in his arms simply felt *right*. "You'll be fine no matter what happens," he said. "You're a fighter. You'd have managed fine without me. And I'm sure you'll find some Prince Charming out there waiting for you to walk into his life."

Eyes watering, Toni shook her head. "You don't understand. I can't go out of town knowing you won't be here for me when I get back."

"Then go on your trip. We'll talk when you get back."

Toni's throat constricted, and her eyes burned, so all she could manage was a nod. She headed straight for the door and didn't stop until she collapsed in her car and burst into sobs. She wished she'd never found his pictures of her, or that damn notebook. If she hadn't, none of this would have happened, and things would be going as they had been.

Including the fact that Carter would still be silent and miserable. That wasn't fair.

Her breath evened out, and after wiping at her face, Toni realized she still had Carter's spare key. She sat back and looked at the key, then back at his building.

I can't go back up there, she thought. *Not until I can tell him where I stand. I'll return it when I get back.*

She wondered briefly if returning the key would be the last time she'd ever see him. She shoved his key into her purse and drove away.

Chapter 46

Toni promised herself that she'd use the time away to think about Carter and their future. Instead, she spent the first two days avoiding all thoughts of him. She threw herself into the teen company's activities, managing rehearsals and last-minute problems, coordinating travel plans and concerts. During the professional workshops she took herself, she focused hard and didn't let her mind stray beyond her technique and what the instructor was saying.

On the third night, after making sure all the company members were accounted for and their lights were out, Toni retired to her motel room, which she shared with Jill.

Toni stretched out on the bed, her exhausted muscles complaining from an extra hard day's work. "My legs are killing me," Toni said. When Jill didn't respond, she looked over. "Jill?"

Jill glanced up from her laptop. "Hmm? Oh, sorry. I'm writing to my fiancé. What did you say?"

Toni waved her off. "Nothing. Go back to your love letter."

Jill closed her laptop. "Who said it was a love letter?"

Toni sat up. "Well, what else is it? It's to your fiancé, isn't it? The man you're desperately in love with?"

"Well, sure," Jill said. "But I have a lot more to say than gushy stuff. Although, yeah, there's some of that."

Toni rolled her eyes. "What, you've been apart three days? Why don't you just text or call?"

Jill shook her head. "Apparently you and I haven't talked in a while." Jill sat on the bed opposite Toni and tucked her feet underneath herself. "Mike's been in Japan for the last five months. He's hoping to get transferred back soon, but until then we keep in touch with email. With the time difference, calling and texting don't work as well. It happens, but only once a week or so."

"You're engaged to a man you go *months* without seeing? How?"

"How what?"

"How can you be sure that the spark is still there when he's not around?"

Now it was Jill's turn to roll her eyes. She swung her legs off the bottom of the bed and opened her laptop again. "A real relationship is based on more than hormones."

Toni wouldn't let Jill off so easily. All of the thoughts she'd suppressed so far this week about Carter resurfaced like a beach ball she'd tried to keep under water. One on top of the other, they demanded answers. "How did you know you should marry him?"

A warm smiled spread over Jill's face. "It was pretty gradual. I didn't get one of those lightning bolt moment you hear about. I would have like a thunderbolt from Zeus saying, 'Yes, he's the one.' But about a month before he proposed, I just knew he had what I wanted. It was right. Mike's the best thing that ever happened to me. He knows me better than anyone else." A tender smile spread her lips. "I guess what it came down to is that I can't picture my life without him."

Toni envied Jill's calm, peaceful assurance. She didn't look like many of the ditzy engaged people she'd known over the years who couldn't think of anything beyond making out. Those people reminded her too much of what she looked like with Clint, and that wasn't what she wanted in a marriage. But she didn't want the platonic other extreme, either. "Were you friends first, or romantic first?"

Jill had to think about that one. "Both sides developed at the same time, I guess." Toni nodded in thought and didn't say anything else for a minute. "Why, do you have someone you're getting serious with?" When Toni blushed, Jill jumped on it. "Do you think he'll propose soon?"

Toni's mind called up the image of Carter's face as he told her it would have to be over if things didn't change. "No, he won't," she said. "That is, unless I give him a reason to."

Jill once again abandoned her email. She curled up next to Toni on the other bed, her eyes eager for Toni to dish. "Do I know him? It's not Clint, is it?"

"Clint? Absolutely not."

"Then who? Tell me all about him."

Toni had learned over the years that talking out problems helped her to think through them. This was one problem that definitely needed thinking through, and she couldn't exactly use Carter as a sounding board on this one. Jill would do nicely. "His name is Carter Mackenzie, and we've been best friends since before I could date."

"Ooh, I like it already," Jill said eagerly.

Toni gave the *Readers Digest* version of what had happened since she walked into his classroom and saw his pictures. She ended the story with, "But lately, I can't help but think that . . ." Toni's voice trailed off, and she didn't know herself what she wanted to say next.

"Thinking you do want something more?"

Toni shrugged in frustration. "Maybe. On one hand, we have something special, a lot like what you described with Mike. We've known each other for so long that I can't picture my life without him, but I went thirteen years before feeling any attraction for him."

Jill waved her hands. "Wait. Back up. Did you say went? As in past tense? That you *have* felt attraction to him?"

The image of Carter with his towel popped into her head, along with the thrill the sight had sent through her. She remembered other times when she'd had smaller moments of feeling the same butterflies and excitement.

"All right, fine. I've some moments of attraction. But it's weird to think that way about Carter. He's closer to me than a brother."

Jill's smile spread to a huge grin. "He's *not* like a brother. *Closer* than a brother could very well be boyfriend material."

Toni blinked at the realization. "He's not like a brother. He's more than that. But when I get home we're going to talk, and that may be the last time I ever see him."

"But you can't picture your life without him," Jill confirmed.

"Not in the least."

"And he's the best thing that ever happened to you."

"Easily."

Jill kept firing off questions. "Is he good looking?"

"Oh, yes."

The memory of his wet hair, with droplets falling onto his chest, sent a flutter through her. The definition of his abs. The loose towel held up by nothing but his hand below his waist. Toni trembled slightly at the thought, but for once, she didn't fight it. Her cheeks flushed as she let herself enjoy the image of Carter in a towel. Even his contacts made him more attractive.

"He's *hot*. But I haven't been attracted him."

"Until now." Jill laughed. "I can totally see it in your eyes. You're so gone on him. You're blushing bright red. You're so totally attracted to him. Deal with it."

Jill leaned back on her hands. She screwed her eyes onto Toni's face. "All right, picture this. In ten years, you come home from a tour with the dance company. The front door opens, and your two little kids run out to meet you. Who's behind them—who do you want to give a proper hello to? And I don't mean a handshake."

Toni couldn't say anything for several minutes. She swallowed hard, and when she spoke, it was almost a whisper. "I'm really in love with him, aren't I?"

Jill grinned. "I'd say so. You've got the glow. I'd recognize it anywhere. You're in love." She grabbed a pillow and put it on her lap. "Tell me more about him."

And Toni did, willingly. She talked about prom, about their nacho parties, about *The Philadelphia Story*, about Carter holding her up through years of hurts and pains, all the while never dreaming he loved her. She talked about their inside jokes, the cartoons he drew during art lectures. How much he'd helped her through her eating disorder and her father's death, and even giving her the strength to walk away from Clint's influence.

As she talked about Carter, Toni couldn't remember ever feeling so light or happy at the thought of anyone. Sure, all her past boyfriends—Andrew, Paul, Keith, and most recently Clint—had sent her into senseless raptures of a kind, but none had given her this sweet, excited, peaceful feeling.

And this feeling had nothing of the intense uncertainty she had come to expect from "romance." That's why it hadn't occurred to her to label it *love*; it didn't feel like anything she had felt before, or what she expected it to feel like. Yet the more she and Jill talked, the more Toni felt as if she could practically float to the ceiling if she wanted to out of her love for Carter.

She hadn't realized until this moment that loving someone, really loving someone, didn't need to be melodramatic and overwhelming or knee-buckling intense to be real. It didn't have to be confusing or frustrating or anything negative at all. The flames of passion she'd experienced with past boyfriends had burned out as fast as they had sparked into being.

This feeling for Carter was completely different; it simmered and smoldered, warming every inch of her being, and it couldn't be easily quenched, if ever. She knew that now.

Toni hardly slept that night. She wanted to call or text Carter, but knew that wouldn't be wise, not yet. She needed time and space, and what would she say? Nothing that she wouldn't rather say to his face.

She spent the last days of the trip aching to get home—and into Carter's arms. The company's performances no longer held any interest for her. Fortunately, they had no more workshops, because she wouldn't have gotten anything out of them; she would have just gone through the motions. Saturday night after their arrival at the studio, she climbed into her car with the temptation to drive straight to Carter's apartment to tell him.

But tell him what, she thought. *And how?* A fear suddenly gripped her chest as she remembered what Carter had said before she left. What if he didn't believe her when she said she really did love him the way he wanted her to, that she wanted to be with him always, and not just because they were compatible?

Chapter 47

Toni didn't go home. Before her nerve ran out, she drove straight to Carter's apartment. But by the time she stood in front of his door, her heart beat so fast she could hear it in her head. She had seen his car in the parking lot, so she knew he was home.

She raised her hand to knock then stopped and grabbed her hand to stop it from trembling. She was so nervous, her hands had turned white, and she couldn't get herself to knock on the door or ring the doorbell. The idea of Carter opening the door and each of them standing opposite each other in awkward silence was more than she could bear.

As she stood there trying to decide what to do, she glanced at her purse and remembered the spare key. That would solve it; she'd open the door. She was the one about to make the move to change their lives forever. She may as well take this first step too.

Toni fumbled through her purse, hands still shaking and refusing to cooperate, but eventually she found the key. With a deep breath, she managed to slip the key into the lock and turn the knob. She gulped, realizing that Carter had probably heard the door open, and now that the first step had been taken, she couldn't go back.

She opened the door a crack and peered inside, but before she opened the door any more, she stopped. The television was on, and her favorite scene of *The Philadelphia Story* had just started.

She didn't see Carter, but she could hear the hot air popcorn popper running, so he had to be in the kitchen. She slipped into the front room and sat on the couch, still nervous but incapable of not enjoying Jimmy Stewart and Katharine Hepburn in the swimming pool scene. Toni tucked her feet beneath herself and smiled. If only every story could end so neatly packaged as this one did, every character with the right person.

Closing her eyes, she whispered a prayer to know how to tell Carter, then opened them suddenly when he came around the corner. "Toni!" He practically yelled her name in surprise, and popcorn flew in all directions. "I didn't hear you come in," he said, fumbling on the floor to clean up the mess, which had landed in front of the TV.

Toni joined him on the floor. "I still have your key," she explained, as they scrambled together to pick up stray popcorn. "I think that's all of it," she said a minute later, taking hold of the bowl the same time Carter did. They stopped and locked eyes then sat back down on the carpet. Toni didn't fight the excited flutter in her stomach, but all her nervousness came back, and she couldn't speak.

Carter spoke for her. "I guess you've come back for that talk."

She nodded and pointed to the television. "It's been a long time since I've seen this scene."

"Me, too," Carter said. "Had to watch it again today. Didn't know if I'd ever want to watch it again." He certainly had no problem alluding to the subject. And he was the one expecting to be rejected. "So, do you know yet?"

She didn't have to ask about what. She nodded again, wishing she could blurt it all out and say, "I love you, Carter Mackenzie, and I always have, I just didn't recognize it because I'm a blind idiot."

He watched her struggle. He nodded glumly and turned his attention back to the television. "Okay, I get it. You don't need to say anything. Don't feel bad. Why don't you stay for the rest of the movie, and then—"

Carter never finished his sentence, because Toni had finally managed to find a way to give him the message. In one fast motion, she reached across the popcorn bowl, pulled him close, and planted a long, hard kiss on his mouth. Carter's eyes popped open for a second, but then closed again as their kiss deepened.

This is what it feels like to kiss Carter. Fireworks went off inside Toni.

He hadn't exactly pulled away from her kiss, but even so, she finally leaned back with a sheepish look on her face.

Carter eyed her. "Does that mean . . . you . . . we . . . Are you *sure?*"

A grin spread across Toni's face, and she nodded, biting her bottom lip as a happiness she'd never known filled her from the top of her head down to her toes.

"I don't understand," Carter said. "I thought—"

"I thought so, too." Toni put a finger over his mouth to stop him and scooted close. Now that she'd taken that first step, she could speak, and oh, how she needed to. "I didn't see it. I kept waiting for this massive flame to come over me."

Carter pulled back slightly. "Then you're still just feeling friendship?" His face and voice sounded dulled.

"No! Didn't you notice how flustered I got when I saw you in that towel last week?" Toni raised her eyes and laughed with embarrassment. "I thought I was about to die if I couldn't get the picture of your body out of my mind. I've pretty much been turned on since Monday."

Carter answered slowly, still a bit suspicious. "So to be clear... this *isn't* because you don't want to lose me as a friend?"

Toni reached around his neck and pulled him close. She leaned her forehead against his. He seemed to shudder slightly at her nearness. "Listen and listen good, Carter Mackenzie. I am in love with you. And I always will be."

Apparently daring to believe in his dream now, Carter eagerly pushed the popcorn bowl aside and drew Toni close. He traced her jaw line with one finger as if amazed at a long sought-after treasure he'd just been given.

Slowly, he drew her face to his and gave her the most incredible kiss she'd ever experienced. Forget fireworks; nuclear bombs exploded inside her as his lips moved against hers, filling a decade-old hunger in them both. Her entire body felt alive, every sense heightened. His hands ran up and down her arms, making shivers go through her. He kissed her neck and then her hairline, and her mouth again, where she poured her soul into his.

They finally pulled apart, both breathless. Toni could hardly speak as she whispered, "Golly."

Lost Without You
A Harvest Valley Romance

CHAPTER ONE

So what are you saying?" Christopher asked, eyes darting from the road to Brooke and back again. His hands gripped the steering wheel a bit tighter.

Brooke eyed the climbing speedometer and lowered her voice. Christopher had always been a safe driver; she'd never seen the needle go so much as five miles above the speed limit with him. "I guess I'm saying that you're not the one for me."

"I see." Christopher's voice was quiet. His jaw tensed, and his eyes practically bored holes through the windshield. Brooke couldn't help but stare at the look in his eyes, as if some other personality had taken possession of him. She hardly recognized the man sitting beside her.

They were in the middle of the canyon for an evening drive, and there wasn't a good place to turn around. Christopher kept driving, deeper into the canyon and not slowing down, even at the tight curves. Brooke's fingers gripped the edges of her seat. They made it all the way to Junction City before turning around and racing through the canyon the other direction. Christopher didn't say another word the entire time; neither did Brooke. There was no point in discussing the matter or causing bigger wounds. They both knew it was over.

They'd dated for only three months, but Brooke had thought Christopher might be the one. That is, until he started acting moody and possessive over the past couple of weeks. Then he began hinting that she needed to change for his mother to approve of the match. The changes seemed benign at first. His mother preferred to be addressed as *Mrs. Morris*. She hated hearing her son referred to as *Chris* in her presence. But when Mrs. Morris began suggesting changes in Brooke's hair and clothing—and Christopher insisted Brooke comply—she realized she'd gotten more than she'd bargained for. This was a case of the umbilical cord never getting cut.

Breakups were never easy or fun, so she'd expected Christopher to be hurt. She *hadn't* counted on him reacting by swerving between lanes, barely missing a collision with a truck when he decided to pass a Jeep already going ten miles over the speed limit. "Could you slow down a bit?

Christopher glanced over and pressed harder on the pedal, the dark look in his eyes now accompanied by a thin smile. A knot formed in Brooke's stomach as she mentally calculated how much longer the drive home would be.

After he dropped her off, they'd probably never see each other again. She'd miss him, in a way. Not the Christopher of the last two weeks—the one she'd talked to at the ice cream parlor until their pistachio ice cream puddled and their fries were hard. Two and a half great months with him . . . gone. This new side of Christopher destroyed everything. She couldn't have one side without the other, so tonight she said goodbye to both.

As they crossed the light by Will's Pit Stop, the car sputtered, grew strangely quiet, and then gradually slowed to a stop.

"We're out of gas," Christopher said tonelessly as the car rolled to a stop—the first words spoken in the last half hour.

With a *wham*, they jerked forward violently to the sound of crushed metal. After a moment of stunned silence, they whipped around to see what was left of the red sports car that had just rear-ended them. The front had caved in, making a mockery of what had been an elegant vehicle. The air bag had deployed, and as the driver got out, he coughed at the bag's fumes. Christopher and Brooke both jumped out and ran to the rear to assess the damage. The back bumper had a good-sized dent, and a lot of paint had been scraped off, but otherwise Christopher's car seemed fine, especially in comparison to the other one.

"I guess you got lucky," Brooke said.

"Yeah—*lucky*," Christopher said sullenly.

The other driver, no more than seventeen, let out a few colorful words and kicked the front tire. "Dad's gonna kill me," he said, pulling at his hair. "He's gonna kill me. And all because some idiot didn't speed up at the light like he was supposed to!"

"Hey, I saw the light," Christopher snapped. "I just ran out of gas."

The young man turned on him. "In that case, I guess you're not an idiot. You're a total moron."

Christopher threw a few nasty and colorful descriptions back at the driver as he took his cell phone off its clip and called the police. Brooke returned to the car, wishing she could hide. The two cars blocked the intersection, with dozens of others piling up and people staring at them. All because Christopher had been too upset to notice he was running low on gas. She fished her cell out of her purse, hoping to call someone for a ride, only to realize that the battery was dead.

I should probably stick around to make a witness statement, she decided. It was either that or leave the scene, walk to the gas station, and hope she could both use their phone and get hold of someone to pick her up—while risking for of Christopher's ire.

Might as well stick around. Civic duty and all.

The police arrived, probably only a few minutes later, although to Brooke it felt like an eternity. She tried to stay in the background as the officer took care of the formalities of paperwork and clearing the accident, but as she sat in the car, he called out to her through the open passenger window.

"Miss? Could you come over here? I need you to fill out a witness statement too."

At least he called me "Miss," she thought. With her thirtieth birthday just a few months away, she was getting all-too used to being called *ma'am*.

She got out, closed the gap, and took the papers from his hand without a word, but as she turned away, he flashed her a smile. Brooke hated herself for noticing the dimple in his left cheek and the name on his tag, G. Stevens.

Not tonight.

She had just broken up with Christopher; this was *not* the time to be thinking about or noticing other men. Brooke laid the papers against the back of the car and began filling them out.

"Your car looks drivable," Officer Stevens said to Christopher.

"Yeah, but I ran out of gas. I'll have to hike back to the gas station to get some," Christopher said, the tips of his ears finally turning red from something other than anger.

Eventually a tow truck arrived for the sports car. The paperwork had been completed, their car was pulled over onto the gravelly shoulder, and traffic had nearly returned to normal. All that remained was for Christopher to return with the gas.

"I'll stay with you until your boyfriend gets back," Officer Stevens said.

"Oh, he's not my boyfriend," Brooke said quickly, then flushed, cheeks hot. "I mean, not anymore. We just broke up. Tonight. Right before the accident. I mean…" She managed to stop herself from speaking by biting her lips together.

Why did I say that? I sound like a silly high school girl.

Here she had just broken up with one man, only to make a perfect stranger aware of it. As if this police officer was planning to ask her out. Hardly. And as if she wanted him to. He was probably married anyway, although she hadn't noticed whether he wore a ring. But he was far too good-looking *not* to be married. Except for the extra short hair. He'd look better if he grew it out a bit. But cops often had short hair. She wondered if it was to make them look more intimidating or something.

"Thanks for the concern," Brooke said, looking down to avoid seeing the dimple again. "But I think he'll be back any minute. I'll be fine."

"Just the same, I'll stick around for a minute or two. Until he gets back." He glanced toward the gas station and added with a trace of disappointment, "Looks like he's on his way now."

"Thanks again," Brooke said, dreading the ride home with Christopher. "It looks like crises are following me tonight. We can hope this is the last you'll see of me."

"Oh, I wouldn't mind seeing you again," he said, then quickly stood to his full height as if he hadn't meant to say that. "And here he is." At that instant Christopher came up behind the car. Brooke was an inch away from asking Officer Stevens for a ride, but her courage failed. She still had a lingering hope of ending the evening on a less sour note with Christopher. Surely she could find the kernel of the guy she thought she knew before saying goodbye.

It took him only a moment to transfer the red container's contents into the gas tank. Soon they were on their way. Christopher didn't say a word as he drove, changing lanes with abandon, cutting off cars, the engine straining before each gear shift. Without turning her head, Brooke watched him; his eyes looked like those of a stranger, as if something had snapped inside him. She tried to remember better times, but his cold glare made it impossible. He turned left at a light and narrowly missed getting broadsided by an oncoming car. Brooke gripped the armrest and hoped they'd make it home without another—more serious—accident for the evening.

They arrived at Brooke's townhome complex without anything more hazardous than a few honks and curses from other drivers. Christopher stopped in front. He stared through the windshield—then looked at her expectantly. He'd never opened the car door for her before, but he'd always gotten out with her and walked her to the door. Not today.

"I'm—I'm sorry it had to end this way," Brooke said. "I really am."

She reached over to hug him goodbye, but Christopher pushed her away with one swift motion. "Get out."

Falling to Pieces

She fell against the door, her arm smacking against the handle with blunt force. She stared at him without a word, too stunned to move. Christopher's eyes burned with anger. She fought back her tears. Who *was* this man?

"Goodbye, *Brooke*." He said her name like a dirty word.

Her wits returned enough for her to grab her purse and open the door as she tried to ignore the throbbing on her arm. Before she could step out, he grabbed her left arm. She turned to face him, hoping for a kind word—maybe an apology.

"I want the bracelet back."

Stunned into silence, she removed his only gift and dropped it in his hand before getting out. He barely waited for her to close the door before hitting the gas pedal and racing off, tires squealing as he pulled out of the parking lot and onto the road. Brooke hugged herself for warmth, even though the evening wasn't cold.

She turned and walked to her door, with a confusing mixture of relief, sadness, and anger swirling around her. She went inside with another emotion—feeling very, very alone.

∽

Christopher drove home, where his mother would be waiting for him. He knew something wasn't right with him; the feelings surging through his body, the thoughts filling his mind, felt like something trying to take control over his body. He'd felt this way before, but not in years. He was younger then, less mature. This time, he'd handle it on his own.

He pulled into the driveway and killed the car but didn't go in yet. Mother couldn't see him like this; he had to calm down first or she'd ask whether he'd taken his meds.

Rather, my poison. I'm fine—I don't need any meds.

He hadn't needed them for nearly two years, but he'd taken them faithfully despite the side effects until March, nearly two months ago. He blamed his extra twenty pounds and receding hairline on those pills. Not to mention the headaches and nausea.

And tossing and turning every night, unable to sleep. Poison—that's what those chemicals were. Brooke deserved a man without love handles or a shiny scalp. So he went off them.

Still gripping the steering wheel, a surge of emotion shot through Christopher again. He looked over at the passenger seat and stroked the spot where Brooke had sat minutes before. He wanted nothing but her. He *needed* her. What went wrong? Everything was perfect until she pulled that surprise out of nowhere tonight. Back and forth his hand went, stroking the seat. No matter. He'd win her back. The two of them would be together, in this life or the next. No matter what it took.

He tried to even out his breathing, so Mother wouldn't ask any questions. Even if she didn't shove the pills down his throat, she might trick him into taking them inside food or, worse, drag him to see Dr. Hamilton again. He couldn't risk that. So he leaned against the headrest and closed his eyes, breathing deeply while running his fingers across Brooke's seat.

After a few minutes he adjusted the rearview mirror to peer into his eyes. He blinked, searching his expression for anything Mother could find amiss. With one final breath, he got out, closed the car door, and headed up the porch. He glanced at his watch. Mother would be watching one of those news magazine shows. If he came in with a smile and gave her a kiss on the cheek, she might not ask why he was home early.

Christopher reached for the doorknob then gave one final glance at the passenger seat. Brooke would be his—he'd see to that. As he opened the front door, he couldn't help but smile.

About the Author

Annette Lyon is *USA Today* bestseller, a Whitney Award winner, an eight-time Best of State medal recipient for her fiction. She is the author of many novels, a cookbook, and a grammar guide as well as over a hundred magazine articles. She's one of the three founders—and the original editor of—the Timeless Romance Anthology series, and she's a co-author of The Newport Ladies Book Club series. She's worked for Eschler Editing and Precision Editing Group and is a cum laude graduate from BYU with a degree in English. When she's not writing, editing, knitting, or eating chocolate, she can be found mothering and avoiding the spots on the kitchen floor. Annette is represented by Heather Karpas at ICM Partners.

www.ingramcontent.com/pod-product-compliance
Lightning Source LLC
Chambersburg PA
CBHW071728190726
48292CB00003B/663